T0285301

PRO BONO

PRO BONO

Thomas Perry

THE MYSTERIOUS PRESS
NEW YORK

PRO BONO

Mysterious Press
An Imprint of Penzler Publishers
58 Warren Street
New York, N.Y. 10007

Copyright © 2025 by Thomas Perry

First Mysterious Press edition

Interior design by Maria Fernandez

Library of Congress Control Number: 2024945212

ISBN: 9781613166161
eBook ISBN: 9781613166178

10 9 8 7 6 5 4 3 2 1

Printed in the United States of America
Distributed by W. W. Norton & Company

For Jo

PRO BONO

1

AUGUST 2007

McKinley Lawrence Stone was the name he had given himself in the court papers he'd filed three years ago. When the change had been certified he held a party for himself with a few cronies using the last of the money he had left from his time as Steven Wallace. He called it his Launch Party. He had played with variations on the new name, and the one he felt most comfortable with was Mack Stone. The name Mack Stone would mark him as an unpretentious man, and the McKinley had a subtle scent of historical priority and maybe even inherited wealth, with the possibility of some education that he would be far too modest to mention. The party guests included several of his favorite people—Dickie O'Connell, who ran a card game and could deal any hand he wanted each player to have, a pair of women friends named Tracy and Faith, who operated an escort service offering housewives supplementing their incomes, and Ike Potter, a thriving dealer in mail-order pharmaceuticals who had often filled orders for him. It was a memorable party for sure. He was remembering it three years later.

He was thinking about it because at the moment he was at about the same point in the cycle where he'd been at that time, only better. He was driving a beautiful new black BMW 7 series sedan with a load of optional features. Inside the trunk was a leather carrying case that held new socks, underwear, casual shirts, and pants, and a portfolio of stock and bond accounts bought with money that had recently been the property of Linda Warren, but were now in his own permanent name, the one he'd been given at birth. He had never divulged this name to anyone since his family had moved to a new town when he was eight and they'd all made up new names.

He was already far north of Los Angeles, heading east across Nevada. Professionals like him knew enough not to head for Las Vegas. It was the first place the hunters looked. It was exactly the tempting distance from Los Angeles or Santa Barbara or San Diego to make a stupid person think he had left the police and his victims far behind and could relax. Vegas was nowhere near far enough. It was a bright, sunny, sparkling trap.

He had spent the day settled back in the scientifically designed, ergonomically perfect, expertly crafted leather seat while he looked out the window at the jagged, rocky, skillet-hot hellscape of the southern part of Nevada. Now he was enjoying the smooth, silent ride watching the mirages pool ahead on the highway, then dissolve as he approached. The afternoon sun seemed to be throwing its light ahead of him on the future. He had swung north, taken Route 50, and was in northeastern Nevada and moving fast but still barely above the speed limit on the two-lane highway.

A vehicle was coming up fast behind him. He stared at the mirror. He saw it was a gray passenger car with only the driver in it. He had a certain envy, because if he hadn't been driving with three or four million dollars on paper that he didn't want to be asked any questions about, he'd be going the same speed.

Mack kept his speed exactly as it was—not fast enough to prompt a cop to wonder why so fast, or slow enough to wonder why so slow. He'd had the throttle on cruise control for nearly two hours. He watched the other car approach in the mirror, holding himself back. He didn't want to start racing some idiot, when winning meant nothing, and a tiny mistake could be fatal. He had heard that the only ambulance service in the empty parts of Nevada was manned by convicts from the prisons. He'd heard other people say that wasn't true, but he had decided he'd better believe it anyway to keep himself cautious. Right now, he had everything he had ever wanted—almost too much money, a good car, freedom, and his next woman writing him long, passionate emails every day, with pictures intended to make him choose her house as his next address.

He kept his eyes on the road for a few minutes, but the other car kept coming, and whenever he looked, the car was closer. It wasn't just on the straight, level stretches. No matter what the road looked like, the car was gaining on him. After a few more minutes, the car was nosing its grille up to his back bumper, like a race car drafting to defeat the wind. The yellow light on his left mirror began to blink to indicate the car was going to pass. Why didn't it?

Mack couldn't stand it anymore. He couldn't see the other driver very well, but he was slight, probably young. Mack very gently touched his foot to the brake pedal, just to make the brake lights glow and maybe shave a mile an hour off the speed to remind this kid what he was doing. The kid wasn't the only one whose life was in his hands when he was driving.

The gray car slid forward and bumped the rear of the BMW, jolting Mack's seat so the back of his head tipped hard against the headrest. The bump didn't hurt, but it shocked and addled him for a second until his eyes found the horizon again. He was instantly angry. He hadn't carried a gun in years. He had stopped because a couple women he'd been with had gotten so enraged when they learned about the money that if they'd found the gun, they might have used it. Right now, he regretted selling the gun.

He decided to force the driver to pass. As he was letting his speed decrease, the gray car began dropping back slightly. *Damn right*, he thought. *You'd better.* He kept going at the reduced speed for a few seconds, searching ahead for a place where they could both pull onto a flat shoulder and have a frank discussion. Then a jolt made him look up into the rearview mirror. The gray car had slowed to build an empty space between it and the BMW, but then the driver stepped hard on the gas pedal, shot forward, and hit Mack's car again.

Stone's BMW received the force with a bang, punched forward by the gray car. His eyes opened wide and he uttered a cry, and when he heard his own voice, he realized he sounded terrified. This kid was some kind of road rage case, out of control. He was trying to hurt Mack, maybe kill them both. Mack wondered if he could have done something to set this kid off without knowing it, maybe cut him off way back on the highway. He stepped on the gas pedal and pressed hard to get some distance from the threat.

The broken stripes on the road flashed under his car now, coming toward him like tracer bullets. As he glanced in the mirror again, he saw the kid was right behind. He knew the car he was driving was an incredible machine, capable of much more than the hundred he was going now—certainly faster than the gray car. But he had been driving on this road for over half an hour, long enough to have a feel for it. He could drive faster, but he doubted he could take a severe curve at these speeds without spinning out. There had also been heavy rains all over the west this winter, and plenty of curvy mountain roads had been undermined or blocked by mudslides. What if—

The car behind him edged up close to nudge him again, but he would not allow that. He pressed the pedal harder, and as he did, the gray car was left behind. Mack was still accelerating when the BMW's right front wheel hit a pothole and dropped to the right, bounced up, then launched itself a foot into the air, off the road, landed in a drainage ditch, and slammed into a tree.

◆

Andy Minkeagan sat in the bus next to his friend Alvin Copes. It was a bright, clear, show-off day to be out traveling, and he supposed that someday one of them would remind the other what this was like after weeks of smoke and sweat-soaked masks. Alvin was good to sit with. They had known each other for years, so there wasn't a lot of tiresome talk—just the easy, natural kind that made the mile after mile of road pleasant and restful.

They had been on the fire line in California for three weeks fighting the Prickleback Fire, a big one made worse by the weather, with temperatures in the hundred-and-five-plus range, and winds that would blow one way for a while and then reverse, like something big turning back because there was something alive back behind it that it had forgotten to eat. Sometimes the something seemed to be you.

Everyone on the bus was a model prisoner from Ely State. That was why they all got to spend the past twenty-one days on vacation on a fire line in California fighting fifty-foot flames with shovels on terrain so vertical and tough that the only way out was on the feet that had brought them there. The pay was ten dollars a day.

Minkeagan and Copes both had eventful criminal records with enough terms like "grand," "aggravated," "armed," and "conspiracy" to have kept them in Ely for a long time, but neither had ever been convicted of homicide despite some experience with it, so they had been eligible to fight fires. Neither of them was lazy either, so they'd both taken other courses besides Firefighting Basic Training One and Two. Copes was Black and Minkeagan was white, and they'd spent some time vouching for each other with men of their races when they'd taken their first course, Automotive Technology, together, and they had found it a comfortable way to take other courses.

They had taken Commercial Driver's License and Heavy Equipment Operator. These had been easy to agree on because they were practical, even though Copes and Minkeagan never expected to be out of prison young enough to get jobs. They felt lucky to have programs at all, because Ely was the designated maximum security prison. They took Arborist because it was an opportunity for outdoor exercise, and it was peaceful. They took Culinary because it was a rare chance to taste something besides prison food.

"Copes!" came the voice from the front. "Your turn at the wheel."

Taking a shift driving the bus was one of the privileges of having a commercial driver's license, but at times it was a drawback too. The driving could be hard, and it carried a lot of responsibility. Minkeagan stepped into the aisle to let Copes out of the window seat and make his way to the front as Stapleton, the current driver, slowed the bus and pulled off onto a gravel patch.

When Stapleton got up, Copes sat down in the driver's seat, picked up the clipboard on the dash, and put his initials beside his name on the driver list. He strapped himself in, looked at the mirrors, signaled, shifted, and made the bus growl up onto the pavement of Route 50 and begin to gain speed.

Copes was pleased to see that there were no cars coming up behind, because the bus was climbing on this stretch. Driving a bus going home to Ely was complex. The average altitude around Ely was 6,788 feet, but within fifty miles the up-down variation was over 4,000 feet. It took time to bring the bus up through the gears to build up speed, and he didn't want to tempt some fool to risk swinging into the oncoming lane to get around the bus and slamming into a driver coming the opposite way.

As though to prove his point, a sporty gray sedan shot around the next curve toward him so fast that the wind from it rocked the bus a little. Copes had stared right into the face of the gray car's driver, and he had looked very young and very—what? Not scared. It used to be that a kid who was barely surviving doing something stupid would at least show some appreciation for the fact that his ass was still on the planet in defiance of the odds. These days they didn't seem to feel that.

Copes blew out a breath and then took one back in and kept going, paying acute attention to the road ahead. It would have been a real joke on him to survive eight years in maximum security and fighting fires and then have some idiot turn his car into a torpedo and punch it through the front of the bus and into his lap.

Two miles on, the bus came to the spot where a new BMW had gone off the narrow shoulder into the ditch and hit a tree. Copes didn't have to tell anybody. The wreck was in plain sight through the bus windows, and Copes slowed the bus down and pulled past a big pothole and a broken-off chunk of road, past the car, and everybody got a look while he eased the bus onto the shoulder.

The car was gouged along both sides, the front wheels were pigeon-toed inward, and the grille was wrapped around a tree so far that the headlights were looking at each other. The driver's-side airbag was still inflated so it didn't seem as though the driver could have gotten out. Copes pulled a few feet farther uphill so there wouldn't be any gas trickling under the bus if there was a leak from the BMW, and opened both doors. "Okay, let's see what we can do," he called.

Minkeagan took a chemical fire extinguisher and others took shovels and ran out the two doors toward the wrecked car. Copes engaged the hand brake of the bus, but he didn't turn off the engine, in case they needed to transport the driver.

By the time Minkeagan arrived, the men had stabbed the air bag to deflate it, and two of them were pulling the driver out of his seat. They laid him out on the ground. Minkeagan leaned in and turned off the BMW's engine.

"Is he alive?" Copes asked.

"Nope."

"Are you sure?"

The man who had made the declaration smiled and looked into Copes's eyes. He was Holloway, and Copes and the others knew he was the one the newspapers had called "the Night Dispatcher" even though the authorities didn't. He'd seen plenty of dead men and knew how to make them that way.

Minkeagan said, "All this blood. Is that from the windshield or did somebody light him up?"

"Broken neck and head trauma," Holloway said, "but I don't think it matters. Dead is dead."

Minkeagan was moving to the back of the car, and Copes noticed he had taken the keys with him. Copes said to the others, "You're right. Let's get back on the bus, and we'll call the cops at the first stop. I guess that'll be the diner with the red roof."

The others had lost interest when they'd learned the man was past saving, and they were tired, so they shuffled toward the bus. Minkeagan lingered. He used the key fob to open the car's trunk and saw the leather case. He lowered the trunk lid a few inches to verify that the others were facing the bus and not him, then leaned in and opened the case. He saw the stack of cash, saw the manila envelope full of account reports with the names of banks and finance corporations. He left the cash, took the envelope, and slipped it up under his shirt and down behind his belt, closed the case, and then locked the trunk. He handed Copes the keys.

Copes knew better than to have the conversation now, so he joined Minkeagan and they trotted to board the bus with the last of the others. He got into the driver's seat, waited for Minkeagan and the rest of the stragglers to sit, called out, "Everybody set and seated?" and then began to drive.

Minkeagan sat near the front, a few feet from Copes. He couldn't talk, couldn't tell him what he thought he had. He could keep it under his shirt for now, but very soon he would have to make a decision about where to hide it next. The ideal place would be somewhere inside the bus, but there was no part of the bus that didn't get seen by somebody fairly regularly. The inner lining of one of the seats would be good, but the seats were getting pretty worn from normal use, and all the fire crew travel last year had accelerated that. This summer was likely to bring as many fires as last. A place like the cargo bay under the bus might have some spaces that could be opened and then closed, but it was full of fire gear right now. Time felt as though it was speeding up. When the bus got back to Ely, the guards would search everybody right away for contraband before they were brought to their cells.

Minkeagan didn't get a chance to talk to Copes until they stopped at the restaurant and the others all got out to loiter around the parking lot and wait for the police. As soon as they were twenty feet from the nearest prisoner Minkeagan said, "It's a bunch of stock, bond, and bank accounts.

All the ones I saw were in the name Daniel Webster Rickenger. There's some ID in that name too, some of it old, like his birth certificate. If we work this right in the next fifteen minutes, we're rich. Once the cops get here the chance is gone."

"I'll go talk to the manager and look around," Copes said. He walked toward the front door, studying the building as he went. He made it as far as the front entrance before a man in a necktie, a man with a cook's white coat, and a waiter came out to head him off.

"How can we help you?" the man with the necktie said.

Copes said, "We're a fire crew from Ely, just heading back after three weeks in California. We found a man who had been in a single-car accident two point three miles west on Fifty. The man is deceased. We stopped to ask you if you would please call the police and tell them, or let me use your phone to call them myself."

The man with the necktie said, "Just you?"

"Yes, sir," Copes said. "I'm driving the bus, so I feel like it's part of the job."

"Everybody else stays outside?"

"That's right."

"Come in."

The man held the door open for Copes to enter, and followed him in, "You can use the phone over here by the lectern. It's for taking reservations." He guided him over to the lectern, which was empty now, the person replaced by a sign that said, "Please seat yourself."

Copes dialed 911 and listened to the female operator's greeting, "911, what is the location of your emergency?"

Copes told her as precisely as he could, gave his name and the group he was a part of, and said he would hold the bus and wait for the police to arrive and give them the keys to the wrecked car. He said he would hand over the phone to the manager of the restaurant and did. When the man had verified that Copes was real and hung up, Copes thanked him for the use of the phone and walked to the front door and went out to the parking lot again.

He was scanning for Minkeagan, saw him leaning on the side of the building, and approached him already talking. "There's a hood with a ventilator running on the wall above the stove. I think they clean the fan from inside, and the vent is on the roof." He kept walking while he was talking, drawing Minkeagan with him. They reached a spot near the back of the building where the roof sloped down to a height of about ten feet. He squatted and knitted his fingers to give Minkeagan a stirrup.

Minkeagan didn't talk, just stepped onto his cupped hands and stretched his arms above his head while Copes lifted. He caught the edge of the roof and pulled himself upward while Copes kept pushing. In a few seconds Minkeagan was up. He bent low and walked as quietly as possible up the red roof. He had no trouble finding the vent because he could hear the hum of the fan. The rectangular sheet metal shaft rose above the roof about a foot and a half and turned sideways. Its mouth was a metal flap on a hinge. The flap was wavering outward an inch or two to emit a smoky, meaty smell from the grill. Minkeagan moved close to it, opened the flap and looked. Inside the shaft about a foot and a half down there was a screen, probably to keep any animals from using it as a way to get into the kitchen. He took the envelope out of his belt, slid it into the shaft so the bottom edge rested on the screen and the envelope was curled close to the inner side, so it might not be seen even if somebody removed the flap. It was a fairly tight fit without blocking the vent. He looked under the flap again, then took a step back. The vent was high enough to keep the mouth above the snow level, and the opening and flap faced southeast. There wasn't going to be a better place.

Minkeagan hurried down to the edge of the roof, lay down, and lowered himself. When his legs reached the edge and draped downward he felt Copes wrap his arms around them and lower him to the ground. They walked past the front corner of the restaurant and saw that the other prisoners had gathered around the bus again. They joined the group and participated in the general complaining about how long it was taking for the cops to come, how long the drive from California had been, and the predictions of screwups to come. The police would try to blame the driver's death on them, and treat everything they said like it was a lie just because. They would keep the bus waiting here long enough so they'd miss dinner at Ely.

A few minutes later two police cars and an ambulance pulled into the parking lot, and Copes went to meet them. One set of partners was a pair of large men, and the other car held a man and a woman. Copes gave the car keys to the first cop who approached him, and then told all the cops at once where the man and his car were. The male and female cops and the ambulance drove toward the accident scene, while the two men stayed behind and interviewed Copes and Minkeagan for the police report. After some conversation on their car radio, one of the cops told Copes and Minkeagan the bus could return to the prison.

By then, most of the fire crew were back inside in their seats, so the loading didn't take long. Copes got in, looked at the clock, and saw his shift was over. He looked at the roster on the clipboard and called, "Daly! It's your turn to drive." He and Minkeagan went back to sitting together near the rear of the bus as it pulled back up out of the lot onto the highway.

The next day during exercise period while they lifted weights Minkeagan described to Copes every detail he could remember seeing in the packet of financial papers. They were finally far enough from other prisoners to speak freely about the accounts, and about how, in reality, they were already rich. The money would stay where it was safe. In fact, it would grow. As soon as either of them could get out of Ely, he would go back to the restaurant, climb up on the roof, and retrieve the envelope. Within a few days he would become Daniel Webster Rickenger and make his way to Los Angeles to convert their wealth from investments into spendable cash. He would put half in a special account for the one who was still here in Ely. A life sentence was not an easy thing, but it seldom meant a man's full life. Now that they knew what the future held for them, the years ahead were going to fly.

2

When Charlie Warren was fifteen, he was on his school's swimming team. The culmination of the season was a sectional meet in Santa Barbara at the University of California's big pool complex, where six schools competed over a three-day period during winter break. They stayed in the University's vacated dormitories, ate at the student union, and competed during the day, with each event run in several heats.

On the third and final day, Charlie swam his best event, the 200-yard Individual Medley. He touched the wall a body length ahead of the others and then, panting heavily, grinned up at his friends and coaches and savored their shouts and hand clapping for a moment. As he was getting out of the pool he glanced at the bleachers and saw his mother waving at him.

He'd had no idea that his mother would be at the sectional meet. Since his father had died when he was eleven, she'd continued to attend athletic events as a parental duty, usually only home meets or games, but here she was. She hurried to the bottom row of the bleachers, trotted up as soon as he had his towel around him, and hugged him. Then she pulled back and said, "Charlie, this is Mack Stone. We knew today would be the finals, so we figured we'd drive up and surprise you. Mack, this big guy is my baby."

Mack had a suntanned face and aviator glasses, and an expensive haircut slightly too long to be showing gray on the sides. Was he about Linda's age, or had they both just slipped into the vagueness of middle age, not young but playing young, like actors? He was mainly shocked that his widowed mother was here with a man. Mack Stone held out his hand, smiled, and said, "Congratulations, Charlie. That was a terrific effort."

There was a condescending upward tilt to Mack's head so he could look down his nose and give a fake smile. Charlie said, "Thank you."

Linda said, "I guess the meet must be about over. Maybe you can sneak off with us and go to dinner before we start the drive home. I'll tell the coach so he doesn't wonder where you are."

"I've still got the relays," Charlie said. "You go ahead. I've really got to ride home on the bus with everybody else." He glanced over his shoulder. "In fact, the coach is giving me the eye right now. I'll see you at home tonight." He brought himself to look at Mack Stone. "Nice to meet you, Mack. Thank you both for coming."

When the school's bus dropped Charlie off at home a bit after midnight that Sunday night, a strange not-new Mercedes was in the driveway. He went inside the house and there were only a couple lights burning, one in the foyer and the other on the stairs. In the morning when he woke up, Mack Stone was in the kitchen and Charlie's mother Linda was cooking breakfast for him.

After that, his mother spent much of her time going places with Mack Stone. Charlie came from school to an empty house many days, and on the other days it was worse, because they were both there. The period when Linda was the clear hostess and Mack was a guest didn't last very long. Soon she stopped referring to her bedroom as "my room" and called it theirs.

Mack didn't appear to do anything the way Charlie's father had. He never seemed to go anywhere, or talk about friends or acquaintances. When Charlie asked his mother, "What does Mack do?" She said, "What do you mean?" He said, "For a living." She said, "He's in business."

Charlie tried out that idea for a couple days, but couldn't find any substance in it. He tried to google Mack's name, but there were millions of Stones. He noticed Mack had a laptop computer, and would spend time tapping away at it, but when Charlie would get close enough to look at the screen, it was usually on some catalog or advertisement. Whenever Mack referred to anything on the screen, it was "I found a really great deal on a hotel in Cabo," or "You'd look great in this dress."

Finally, Charlie asked him directly what he did for a living.

Mack said, "Why do you ask?"

"I just wondered. You never seem to go anywhere, unless it's with my mother. Do you work when I'm at school or something?"

"I'm an investor," Mack said. "My money goes out and works for me. I sometimes direct it from one place to another, or use the profits and dividends to invest in new companies. But most of the time a smart investor picks something good and sticks with it."

Things remained this way until Charlie's freshman year ended, and then his mother announced a surprise. She'd decided he was going to attend a summer program at a school in northern California. She gave him a glossy, colorful booklet describing what the place offered. It seemed to value the skills that would have been good for an aspiring knight—horsemanship, archery, martial arts, and literature. There were also tennis, golf, swimming, and kayaking. The place was coeducational, and the photographs included roughly equal numbers of male and female students. Charlie decided that since his mother had already made up her mind, his smartest move would be to agree to it, and since he was going to agree, to do so without visible reluctance or audible complaint.

He went for six weeks in July and August, and they were the best six weeks of his life so far. Being with contemporaries of both sexes in a place where the only real adult supervision consisted of coaching and ended with dinner was like a dream. His only regret at the end of the program was having to leave.

He flew into Los Angeles on August 16, when the temperature was 108. He stepped out of the baggage claim door, waited for forty minutes, and then watched Mack's Mercedes pull up to the white curb and saw him and his mother both smiling. The air conditioning was blowing through their hair in a frigid breeze.

At dinner on the 19th, Linda announced to Charlie that she had hired a very special and well-known consultant in educational futures, who was coming the next day to present to him a proposal for his. "Her name is Camilla Barton. Mack, tell him what you think of Camilla."

Mack replied, "Charlie, a guy like you needs an Ivy League school, and getting people into those schools is a whole study in itself. I asked some friends who have hired her for their kids. She knows how to do the trick—what works now and what doesn't anymore. She also has connections and relationships, and that's the ingredient you can't fake."

Charlie had a strong feeling that this was some kind of scheme to keep him out of their lives a bit longer, but he didn't want to start an argument without knowing what he was objecting to. He had been skeptical about his mother's idea of sending him up north for the summer, but the summer had been much better than she knew or would ever have allowed. He would wait a day and see.

Camilla Barton turned out to be a middle-aged woman with very short dark hair and a briefcase. She wore a lot of jewelry—a necklace and bracelets made of large chunks of transparent plastic with wisps of gold leaf embedded in them.

She said, "I've studied your records, and talked to your counselor and your academic advisor, Charlie. The smartest move that someone like you could make, and one that could change your life, is to transfer to the right prep school now, before it's too late. The school that I consider your best bet is old, and it's known to admissions offices everywhere. It's in New Hampshire."

Miss Barton left him with a collection of brochures for eastern prep schools. The one she had recommended most highly was the Thorsen Academy. He looked up the school online and learned it was 2,960 miles from Los Angeles. His mother was trying to do her best for him, but she was also at least acquiescing to Mack's plan to move him out of the way of their relationship.

There seemed to Charlie to be no point in resisting their effort to push him out. In two years, he'd be applying to colleges no matter where he was, and he'd probably never live at his mother's house again for longer than a school vacation.

Charlie went off to the new school, made friends easily, and discovered that the place deserved its academic reputation. For a Southern California teenager, the New Hampshire fall was a beautiful curiosity. A bit later the iron-gray skies, rain, cold winds, and then later deep-drifted snow seemed unnecessarily harsh, but by then he'd learned that the strategy for enduring dissatisfaction was to work harder.

When Charlie flew home for winter break, his mother and Mack Stone met him in the front entrance of the house and told him they had decided to get married. When he came home again for summer break, there was the wedding. His mother had told him months earlier that Mack wanted him to be his best man, but Charlie had replied that he wouldn't. After a lull, she had written him a letter formally asking him, as her only close living male relative, to walk her down the aisle. He had written back, "Down the aisle of what?"

She called him and said they had rented a wedding venue named Ocean Ranch Celebration Gardens for the ceremony and invited three hundred guests. She said, "I know you disapprove. I know you will dread it. But please do this for me because I need you to."

He did as she asked. The scene of the wedding was lush, a parklike expanse above the ocean with a pavilion shaded by tall eucalyptus trees. He noticed that just about every one of his mother's friends and her supposedly extinct male relatives was there, together with spouses and children, including some surviving Warrens. She wore a light blue gown that looked elegant on her long, thin body and her slightly graying hair was styled the way it had been when he was a child. Everyone seemed to have a good time at the wedding. Early the next morning she and her new husband Mack Stone flew off to their European honeymoon. Before they returned ten days later, he had left for New Hampshire, where he'd enrolled in a late summer session.

When Charlie returned at the end of that year, Mack and Linda were living about the same, but he could see that there was tension. The first time Mack was out and he was alone with his mother he said, "You and Mack aren't getting along the way you were when I left. Did something happen, or what?"

She said, "It's nothing, really. It's just that some of Mack's invest-ments haven't been doing so well this year. And you know how I can be—worried and anxious when there's really no need to be. You prob-ably remember how your father used to be. He could tell you the bank balance without looking at the checkbook, how much was coming in or going out. I didn't realize how comforting that was for me. Things are different now. Mack isn't like a man who works in an office and operates a firm. Investing is different. And he has the personality for it."

"What's that?"

"You know. Optimistic and confident. If I say we shouldn't buy something, he tells me I'm being silly, timid for no reason. 'The markets go down, but they always go up again.'"

Charlie began to ask her more questions when she was alone. Even with her vague answers, he came to realize that Mack had been living for two years like a very expensive pet. He had a beautiful new BMW. It had been bought only in his name because he said that made it easier for him to bargain for the best price, insure it, and take it in to be serviced. He also had a new wardrobe and a lot of stories about the wonderful places they had visited in the past year.

It settled on Charlie that his parents had not been very good at survival. His father had achieved himself to death and died of a heart attack unselfish but early. His mother had judged her second man by assuming he was just like her first, but on no evidence. Over the summer the strain on the marriage became impossible for Linda to hide. Around the Fourth of July, Charlie heard her ask Mack if he knew why the June deposits from the investment accounts hadn't turned up. He said "They have. I used them for the kid's June 30th tuition payment."

Charlie knew there was no June tuition payment. Tuition was charged at the beginning of fall semester and at the beginning of spring semester. Schools didn't defer billing until the end of an academic year in June. That night, when Mack and Linda were out to dinner, Charlie looked around in his mother's office that Mack seemed to have taken over. He checked the file drawers where his mother had always kept the account statements from her banks and investment companies and was able to trace a decline in the balances, which seemed to have accelerated over the school year. His mother's bank statements showed large checks written to credit card companies, and her long-term accounts had numerous cash withdrawals.

The most disturbing to him were the investment statements. This seemed to have been a good year for stocks. Each of the accounts had some increase in value each of the nine months while he'd been away, a couple of them large, but a decrease in balance. On the first day of each month for years, there had been a transfer of the same sum of money from the stock funds to the joint bank account. But last year, beginning in September, sometime before the fifteenth of each month, there had been an additional withdrawal of an irregular sum that seemed roughly proportional to the recorded increase in stock value. If the value went up five percent, the withdrawal was about that much. Mack had been tapping the accounts, but trying to make it less glaring by timing it. Charlie noticed that Mack was an optimist. Four times he had overestimated the rise in prices, twice drastically.

Each time Linda and Mack were out together, he looked deeper, searching for signs of where the money had gone. Charlie needed to wait for a day when Mack was out without Linda before he could show her what he had discovered. She sat at the desk and stared down at the figures as he pointed them out, then went back month by month and showed her the same phenomena. Charlie watched her closely, and it was only about ten minutes before she began to cry. He pulled the paper she'd been looking at away from her. "Don't get the statement wet," he said. "We've got to keep him from knowing."

"I don't want to keep him from knowing," she said. "I can't believe he's been doing this to us. The minute he gets back here I'm going to be in his face."

"If you do that, he'll know that you caught him," Charlie said. "As long as he doesn't know, maybe there's something you can still do."

"What? Send him to jail? Sue him? He's my husband."

"I don't know," Charlie said. "I'm not married to him, and I'm not even legally an adult, so nobody will listen to me. If somebody does something, it's got to be you."

"But what can I do about it now?"

"Something. Get on the phone and cancel anything they'll let you cancel—his credit cards, his permission to sign things at your banks and brokers. Withdraw anything you can and transfer it to a new account. Change every password. If there's any card you can't cancel, report it missing, maybe stolen, so they have to freeze it and send you a new one. You must have an accountant you had before he came along. Call him and tell him what's going on. How long is Mack going to be gone?"

"He said he'd be back around six. He has a haircut appointment, some kind of business meeting, and then he was going to shop for clothes."

"It's not even ten now. That gives us some time. Pick out the accounts that are worth the most and try to save those first. I'll try to find the right phone numbers and dial them so you can just talk."

They both worked frantically. There were papers that would have to be signed in person, accounts she couldn't deny Mack access to, things that couldn't be done until the next day when Mr. So-and-So could approve them, or couldn't be done by phone, or needed both her signature and Mack's. If Mack's access to an account couldn't be canceled, she would withdraw funds and have the checks mailed. If she couldn't withdraw everything from an account, she withdrew what she could and moved on. After the most obvious things had been done, or at least attempted, Linda called the attorney she and Charlie's father Matt Warren had hired to write a will leaving their money to Charlie, and then more recently, to change her will so Mack was included. Linda told her what had happened and said she needed a new will and a divorce.

A couple hours later, the lawyer called back. She and a colleague had been working on securing large assets, and he had discovered that McKinley Stone had approached a real estate agent within the past week and tried to arrange a sale of what he called "the family house." The title search had revealed that the house had been placed in a living trust in Matt and Linda's names with Charlie as the only contingent beneficiary sixteen years ago. Mack had no right to sell it. She would try to find out more and let Linda know what she learned. She also said, "Meanwhile, get out of that house before he comes back. When these guys get found out, they aren't ever pleasant, and sometimes they're violent."

Mother and son packed suitcases. They agreed to each drive one of the cars to keep them both out of Mack's hands. They would meet at a hotel in Santa Barbara and keep working on preventing Mack from finishing the job of stealing the money Linda and her first husband had put away for them. Linda would drive the Jaguar, and that would leave the Toyota Charlie had driven whenever he'd been home from school.

Charlie carried his mother's luggage to her car and saw her off. As he was about to leave, he realized that he should bring some more of the financial papers with him. He went back into the house and selected the monthly statements from Linda's account drawer that were the clearest evidence of what Mack Stone had been doing, put them in his bag, and then, as he was opening the back door, heard the whisper of the BMW's tires on the paving stones of the driveway.

The BMW stopped on the driveway, blocking Charlie's car in. The only thing he could do was retreat into the kitchen, unlock the back door, then slip into the pantry and wait. He heard Mack come in the front door talking loudly on his cell phone. He said, "Well, I'm home now, and I can prove this is just a misunderstanding. My wife will explain to you that I have a perfect right to move any of our assets from one place to another any time I please." There was a pause while the other person said something, and then Mack said, "Then first she can explain that they are joint assets." There was a pause. "Linda!" The next time his voice came from the staircase. "Linda!" The third time, the voice was faint because it was coming from the second floor. "Linda!" Charlie could hear strain and frustration in it. Charlie slipped out the back door with his suitcase, carried it across the front of the house and the next three to the nearest corner, and took out his phone.

His friend Kyle Sung lived a couple blocks away, so he called him. He said, "Look, I've got to go out of town for a few days, and my car is blocked in the driveway. It will be clear in a couple hours, but I'm in a big hurry. Could I borrow your car for the trip and leave you the keys to mine?"

"Sure," Kyle said. "I don't need to drive anywhere tonight. I'll pick you up in a minute."

"Great. Can you make it at the corner by Nora Hartz's house?"

"Sure."

Kyle's car was much better than the one Charlie had been using. It was a practically new Audi and had a big engine, but it was sleek and had a dark gray color that made it look understated and expensive. Charlie left the house and walked down the street past Nora Hartz's house carrying his suitcase. When he got near the corner Kyle was already in sight. As soon as Kyle pulled over and popped the trunk, Charlie put his suitcase in and got into the passenger seat. As Kyle drove back to his house he said, "You feel like telling me what's going on?"

Charlie said, "It's basically my mother breaking up with the asshole she married. I've got to stay out of his way for now, and he just pulled his car into the driveway and accidentally blocked my car in."

"Wow. That's bad timing. You think he'll give me a hard time when I come to get your car?"

"I think he'll be gone in a couple hours. If he isn't gone yet, he'll be all smiles, pretending to be a great guy. Thanks for this."

"No problem."

When they reached Kyle's house, Kyle got out and left the motor running. "Good luck with all of it, man."

"Thanks," Charlie said. "I owe you a big favor." He handed Kyle the keys to the Toyota.

Charlie got into the driver's seat and pulled away very smoothly, not going too fast so Kyle wouldn't worry. He thought about heading for the 101 freeway to Santa Barbara, but then he decided that there was no reason now to be in such a hurry. If Mack was gone already, he could return Kyle's car and go back to the plan. He was driving a car that Mack wouldn't recognize, so he could just drive past and look for the BMW.

As he reached his street, he saw that the BMW was still in the driveway, but immediately saw Mack stepping out of the front door. He slowed down and watched. Mack slammed the front door, hurried to his car, got in, and pulled away fast.

As soon as Mack turned the corner, Charlie parked Kyle's car, ran to the house, and went inside the back door to the kitchen. Everything looked the same. Charlie was about to go back outside, but then he sensed something was off. The air was wrong. It smelled different. Had Mack left the oven on, or something? He checked the dials and burners, then touched the oven door, checked the air fryer and microwave, and walked toward the front of the house. Suddenly there was the screech of the fire alarm. It was coming from upstairs. He ran back to the kitchen, grabbed the fire extinguisher off its rack on the wall, and sprinted to the stairway and up to the second floor. His mother's bedroom was filling with smoke. Charlie saw that the flames were just taking hold, flickering up the curtains. Mack must have lit sone papers in the trash can and pushed it under them.

Charlie sprayed the curtains and the trash can, and the fire went out in seconds. He turned on the air conditioning fan and threw open the French doors onto the balcony, and in a moment the terrible noise of the alarm died out. He closed and locked the French doors, pivoted, and ran down the stairs. His eyes seemed to be seeing things through a red film in front of him. Mack had tried to burn the house down on his way out. As soon as Charlie had seen the fire, the rage had gripped his chest. He dashed out the front door to the street, already reaching into his pocket for the keys to Kyle's car. He was not going to Santa Barbara anymore.

He threw himself into the driver's seat, started the engine, and had the car in motion before his seat belt buckle clicked. He knew the intersection where Mack Stone would be stopped. It always took sitting through the long traffic signal, sometimes twice, before a car could get through onto Sunset in the late afternoon. Mack's car wasn't stuck at the signal so Charlie didn't wait for the light to change. He just veered left, shot straight through, and kept adding more speed. In another second or two he was weaving in and out of traffic, knowing that he would be able to see the BMW before long. He was not used to driving this car, but he was quickly building a feel for its controls. The car was small, but it had a powerful engine and was the right weapon for what he was determined to do.

It was three days before he spoke to his mother again. When he reached her hotel, she demanded to know where he had been and what he'd been doing. He told her he'd needed to be alone to think. She never asked him again, maybe because within another day or two, the authorities had notified her about her husband's death, and she knew a reason not to.

3
MAY 2021

Vesper Ellis climbed up on the step stool to reach the deep blue glasses in the cupboard. They had been nested inside one another on the top shelf since the last time she'd used them, which had been over a year ago, and she needed to wash them all again before she could add them to the tray.

She inspected them as she took them down, two in each hand, set them on the counter, and reached up for the next four. The color was gorgeous, a perfect sapphire, the eyes of the angels in Renaissance paintings she'd seen, a pigment which she'd read had been made by grinding up lapis lazuli.

It almost made Vesper feel guilty for hating the glasses. It did not seem to her to be wise to serve anybody anything outdoors in a vessel that wasn't fully transparent. As a child she had been given lemonade in a deep green glass, and when she took a sip, the hornet that had flown into it for some of the sugary drink had stung her lip to make its escape.

One of the adults present that day made the predictable remark that pretty girls' lips were sometimes described as "bee-stung." She wished him dead for over an hour, and then determined to forget he existed, which was as close to obliteration as she could achieve.

Vesper arranged the blue glasses on paper doilies on a tray of their own, but kept them all upside down. It would have been unthinkable not to have enough glasses for the garden party, and all the clear tumblers and stemware and highball glasses had been placed on the dining tables and the bar according to their natural purposes.

Vesper felt slightly dizzy for a second as she stepped off the stool. This was George's fault, and she mentally placed it on his side of the balance sheet. He always seemed to have his most desperate desire for her at inconvenient times—often so late at night that she didn't get back to sleep before the alarm went off. This time it had been at dawn, when he was fully aware that she was preparing to entertain three dozen people at midday and had to get started.

All her emotions about the day were strong—first rage at his selfishness and uncaring attitude about the effort she'd been expending for days and the importance, not just to his business standing, but to her reputation too, damn it, for getting social events right. And then there was the warm feeling of being adored and desired by her husband, a sensation that started out faint and not at all fair compensation for her annoyance, but grew as the closeness and touch continued, until it made the negative feelings start to seem foolish and distant and then overwhelmed them completely. The feelings were vivid, but then once again they ended with her having to rouse herself from a state of profound relaxation to start performing tiresome chores in rapid succession to make this day happen.

She had once very tentatively and obliquely asked her mother about George's timing, or really, alluded to it, just putting it in front of her in case she knew something that Vesper should know. Her mother, whose name was Iolanthe, a crime of a name perpetrated on her at birth that she had also visited upon her daughter when she called her Vesper, said, "He's going to feel that way about somebody. If he's worth keeping, you should do your best to make sure it's you. You're lucky you're so beautiful that what happens is up to you. You're both in your twenties, young enough to find ways to make both of you happy."

This morning Vesper had just given George a final kiss before she climbed into the bath, and now she was fresh, subtly perfumed, powdered, and made-up. She was all efficiency and motion.

There was pride too. Vesper could have spent a lot of money putting on these events for their friends and George's colleagues. There were caterers in the Valley who were very good, even excellent. They brought their own dishes and linens and tables and chairs and five or ten staff to deploy them and to park the guests' cars. She still believed there were advantages to doing things the way her mother and grandmother had done them. People didn't pay magicians because they wanted rabbits removed from hats. They wanted the pleasure of seeing rabbits appear from the hats so smoothly that it seemed natural and inevitable. She stepped onto the back porch and looked at her preparations. Yes, she had done it again—rabbits.

Everything was right, tastefully chosen and arranged. The tables were set, the food was cooking, the bar was overstocked with liquor bottles with famous labels, wine of four kinds to pair with the entrees beside the correct glasses ready to be filled.

In a moment the first guests were arriving. Vesper greeted five or six couples with hugs and then swooped away to the kitchen to pick up a platter the timer at the back of her brain told her was ready and return with it. When she was back, there were enough other women who were looking for a chance to help, and a couple men too. The next trays and platters were brought out behind her and she simply had to say, "That goes over there," and point.

Couples were coming into the backyard steadily now—people didn't want to be fashionably late at noon. George appeared at the bar making sure everybody was coaxed into having a glass of liquid to hold, and when the stream of people produced its own pourers to relieve him, he went around greeting guests he had missed and chatting with each of them. Vesper had assumed he would become the social George, and here he was, as expected, another part of the magic she was performing. When he wanted to, he could be magnificent—the warm friend who looked you right in the eye and asked about you as though he had been looking forward to seeing you all week. He remembered your kids' names and wanted to introduce you to this other friend who had the same interest you did.

She walked toward the kitchen because she had to keep things moving. She had not forgotten any of the timers she had set—the oven, the sense of how long things should simmer on the stove, how long other things should cool in the refrigerator. On the way toward the house, she glanced at the levels of people's drinks and how many of the hors d'oeuvres were gone and adjusted her sense of when the next trays should materialize.

Because the number of guests at this afternoon party was near the limit of the house's capacity, Vesper allowed four of her friends to deputize themselves to help in the kitchen and in the serving. This time when Vesper went out the kitchen door, she was bringing main dishes, and she was one of five carrying large trays. As soon as the trays were placed at the ends of the long tables, the five were on their way back into the kitchen for the next load, an array of side dishes.

This was the part where coordination and timing were at their most crucial, and Vesper kept the machine moving steadily. At one point, as she was coming out to the kitchen steps with two large bowls, George held the door for her and said quietly in her ear, "This is great, Ves. Everybody loves everything," then kissed her cheek as she passed.

Her hands were full, so she couldn't brush off the damp spot from his kiss, and she felt it for a few seconds before the sensation faded and was replaced by impressions about how her arrangements were working and decisions about what she would do next.

After the two-and-a-half-hour lunch, alcoholic drinks reappeared. The afternoon was hot and the drinking seemed to gain popularity more strongly than Vesper considered ideal, so she and her friend Tiffany Shaw deployed the tray of fresh iced tea and lemonade pitchers and glasses and called them to the attention of the guests at each table. Soft drinks had been in bowls of ice in visible places all afternoon, but an hour later she gauged that she needed to do some more adjusting. Alcohol had the advantage that it impaired judgement enough to make more alcohol seem like a good idea.

Vesper was aware that bringing out coffee was like playing the Last Dance music, but she judged that the coffee hour had been reached. She filled and plugged in the big coffee maker and Tiffany came out carrying the tray of cups and saucers. Others delivered plates of cookies and light dessert items. Soon the competition between liquid refreshments turned, the sun had sunk west of the rooftop, and the air was cooling.

Almost an hour later, people began bringing plates, glasses, and silverware into the kitchen, and many of them took this opportunity to thank their hostess and then follow the driveway out toward their cars parked along the street.

Vesper had begun a phased clean-up hours earlier, as soon as the entrees had been served, and the trays that had carried out food and drinks had returned with plates and glasses. By now most of the items from the early parts of the party had been through the dishwasher and put back in the cupboards.

During this part of the day, while the sun sank further, Vesper had to begin circulating again, mainly to oversee the reloading of the last trays that were headed for the kitchen, but also to get thanked, hugged, and bid goodbye. She made sure she was smiley and relaxed about all of this as though it had happened by itself, while frequently giving credit to her deputies by name. As the afternoon light began to fade and evening approached, she wondered where George was. She supposed that he was walking guests to their cars and saying goodbye. George was like that, a host who paid personal attention to each guest. She still had so many things to occupy her that she had to set thoughts about him aside for the moment. They'd tell each other everything later.

When the work was almost all done, Vesper was finally alone. She sat on one of the tall stools along the breakfast counter and looked at the spotless kitchen. With a lot of help from her friends, she had managed it again. She looked up at the clock. It was eight fifty. The lunch party had lasted over six hours, and the final cleanup almost three.

What the hell had happened to George? Every time she had seen him, he had been circulating, laughing at somebody's witticisms, introducing people to each other, serving them something, or handing them a glass. They had exchanged a few waves, a brief touch or a word a few times. But now he had been gone for almost three hours. She started thinking of reasons why she shouldn't be irritated at him. She had a few to choose from, so she picked the one with an element of self-interest.

She didn't want to have done this huge undertaking and then end the long day with an argument. She deserved praise and gratitude, and she would get them if she didn't start a fight. George was sometimes a dope, but he was appreciative. There was also a bit of uncertainty in her mind about where he was and why. Maybe he was driving someone home who'd drunk too much to drive safely. He was that kind of guy too, and he would be thoughtful enough to have done it quietly to avoid embarrassing the inebriated couple.

While she was waiting and her curiosity was in danger of becoming worry, the last load in the dishwasher finished, so she opened it and put everything away. He still wasn't home. She switched on the outdoor lights and went out into the backyard to see if she could find anything that hadn't been picked up, wiped off, stacked, or straightened. This kept her physically occupied for a few minutes, but she kept her cell phone in her hand in case George called her to pick him up.

She was back inside and called his cell number, but when the call went to voicemail, she felt her heart pumping in her chest and wondered if this was the moment when everything went bad. In spite of the fact that she'd been on her feet for most of the day, she couldn't sit still. She began to pace back and forth in the living room. She called her friend Tiffany Shaw to ask if she'd happened to see George near the end of the party. Was he talking with anybody in particular? Heading in one direction or another? She called two more friends, but none of them described seeing him doing anything Vesper hadn't seen or assumed. Then she saw headlights appear at the end of the driveway, and her pulse began to slow. He must have driven the couple home and then waited for a taxi or Uber instead of calling her to pick him up, because he'd known she'd be worn out.

She stared out the front window without trying to pretend she wasn't. It wouldn't hurt for George to know how much she loved him and worried about him. She saw a man in silhouette getting out of the car in the space behind the glare of the headlights, but it didn't look like George from here, and the Uber didn't back out and leave. The driver got out too, and the car's lights went off. The driver was short. She was a woman.

Could that man be George? No. They were probably a pair of guests who had left something. People were always leaving their phones somewhere, and that was one of the few things nobody could bear to be without until the next day. The two converged at the front of their dark car and headed up the front steps. Vesper turned on the porch light and saw the night-colored uniforms and the gleam of the badges, and she knew that they'd come to tell her this part of her life was over.

4

JULY 2024

The client arrived in the reception area of the Charles Warren & Associates law office carrying a two-handled basket-woven bag full of dark blue file folders. She looked down at the woman behind the reception desk and saw that the name plate on the surface said Martha Wilkes. Martha Wilkes's hair was buzz-cut around the sides, a bit longer at the top, and she wore a dark blue sport coat with a brooch that looked a bit like a flower with a yellow gemstone in the center. She scanned the appointment calendar in front of her and said, "Mrs. Ellis?"

"Yes."

"Please take a seat." The way to the chairs was blocked by a large black Labrador retriever lying on his side on the carpet. Martha saw the problem and said, "Alan, please. Over here."

The dog got up, walked to the other side of the desk, and lay down again. The woman at the reception desk said, "I just have to be sure we've got all your contact information and so on." She typed the name on her computer, scrolled down the screen, and said, "It's all here." She dialed a single number on her desk phone, and said, "Mrs. Ellis is here," then stood and said, "Come with me." They started toward the door across the room.

The door swung open and Charles Warren came out. He smiled and said, "Hello, I'm Charlie Warren."

She set down the bag of files and held out her right hand. "I'm Vesper Ellis."

He shook her hand, picked up her bag, and said, "Come on in." When she entered, he closed his office door, walked across the room to where his desk was, and gestured at the pair of armchairs facing him while he got over his surprise. Her name had made him imagine someone older and not so eye-catching. She had long hair with a slight wave, and she wore a blue dress that showed a hint of a slim but shapely figure. Her face was strikingly beautiful. He was determined not to let himself be distracted by her appearance or even let her suspect that he had noticed. A woman like her would probably be sick of the male gaze.

She sat.

Warren looked at the empty chair beside her and said, "Will anybody else be joining us?"

"No," she said. "My husband died about three years ago, so it's just me."

"I'm sorry," he said.

"Don't be," she said. "I'm not happy about it, but it's been a while."

He set the bag of files on the empty chair beside her and went to sit behind his desk. "What brings you here today?"

"Tiffany Greene recommended you. You probably remember her as Tiffany Shaw."

"Both. I represented her in the divorce, and our office also handled the name restoration, so I know. Nice person." They both waited for a couple seconds, and then he said, "I can't say anything more about a former client than that."

"Oh," she said. "I was waiting for more. I should have realized there would be rules. Tiffany said you're a CPA besides being a lawyer?"

"Yes. Is that the kind of legal issue you have?"

"It might be. I've noticed that some investment accounts have been getting smaller when I think they should have been growing."

"What sorts of investments are we talking about—businesses, property?"

"Stocks, bonds, mutual funds, and the money-market funds from dividends. The only real estate I have at the moment is my house. My husband George handled our investments. We met when we were both twenty-four. He was ambitious and hardworking. He'd sold cars for a while, and then real estate, then managed a small shipping company. He always saved, and he invested. He already owned the condominium where he lived and some empty land in Santa Barbara County that he rented out to a farmer who was growing garbanzo beans and things on it. I was working as the IT department for a medical clinic, and we put away most of my salary too."

"What happened after your husband died?" Charlie said. "Did you keep up the investments?"

"Yes. I had the payroll system programmed so that kept happening automatically. By then my little company did IT for five medical partnerships. George's salary had been most of our income, but I didn't need much to live on, and we had life insurance, so I left the investments alone."

"When did you notice something odd was going on?"

"Not until just about three days ago. After he died, all I tried to do was just keep his system from falling apart. He always stuck with paper copies of monthly reports. He put them in folders and stored the folders in file drawers in order. I kept doing it. At tax time the companies sent

1099 forms, and I gave them to the tax accountant with everything else, signed the 1040 and 540 forms, wrote checks, put them in the mail, and forgot about the long-term investments except to stick the reports in the file drawers once a month. I sold my business about a year and a half after George died. I still didn't bother to pay attention to those accounts because the sale produced enough so I didn't have to for a while longer."

"What changed?"

"Nothing, really. My birthday was coming up, and one day I just happened to get curious about how much money had accumulated, so I took a look."

"And what was the matter?"

"The numbers seemed smaller than I had expected, so I began to read the actual reports. I saw some withdrawals." She lifted the big bag of financial papers and set it on Charlie's desk. "I'd like you to take a look."

"You hadn't made them?"

"No. So I called and asked who had requested them. They said George did. As I told you, I lost George three years ago."

Charlie eyed the bag. "I'll see what I can find out, and then I'll call you."

"Okay, then," she said. "I guess that's all we can do until you've taken a look." She stood, so he did too. "I'll be waiting to hear from you. I gave my numbers, email address, and so on to your assistant."

"Thank you," he said. "I promise I won't take long. I'll start looking right after my last appointment today."

"Good. Then I'll talk to you soon."

He walked her to the door.

When he'd closed it, he turned to his assistant, Martha Wilkes. "When have we got the next person coming?"

"You're free for an hour and a half."

"Thanks," Warren said. "I'll be in there. I want to take a quick look at the stuff she brought."

"I hope you're not putting her ahead of your other clients just because she's the best looking," Martha said.

"By that logic I should be looking at her, and not a bunch of papers."

"You're such a good lawyer, Charlie." Martha went back to the reception desk, and Charlie went into his office.

He picked out the six most recent folders and opened the one from the first of this month, examined each of the reports, then set that folder aside and went on to the one for the previous month, and then made some notes on the legal pad at the corner of the big desk. He had already detected two irregularities.

He looked at the top of each report. All the accounts were in the names George W. and Vesper R. Ellis. She had apparently not notified the financial corporations when George died. There was no blame to attach to Vesper Ellis. Once George had died, she was the only living signatory on any of these accounts. Removing the name of her deceased husband would hardly have seemed urgent to her, and making the changes to all the accounts, deeds, credit cards, insurance policies, ownership papers, car registrations, and things after a death was a lot of work. For Vesper Ellis these stagnant accounts must have been easy to let slip. She had still been working and running a business, and that meant spending her days off doing laundry, grocery shopping, and other chores. By the time she'd sold her business she'd probably forgotten about removing his name. She'd mentioned she had an accountant do her taxes, but for at least the year of George's death he'd had income to be taxed, and maybe the accountant hadn't been told about the death, or he'd had an assistant do the forms who knew nothing about her.

As he noted discrepancies and irregularities, he was also writing down the questions he would need to ask Vesper Ellis about various specific entries, and also about the general picture he was getting. He kept getting the feeling that he was looking at his mother's papers seventeen years ago. Vesper Ellis was a lot like his mother. His mother had been married to Matt Warren, the kind of man who had done his best to make sure she was safe and secure, and after he was gone, she had still relied on the provisions he'd made for her. What he couldn't do was make sure that after he was dead, she would only run into people who could be trusted.

Charlie fought the feeling of dread that was coming on about the Ellis accounts, and kept his mind on the work. More questions. Had she notified the IRS that George was dead, or had her accountant just kept filing joint returns after the first one? How about the Social Security Administration and the Franchise Tax Board?

It occurred to him that maybe maintaining the joint investment accounts was part of a swindle too. Vesper could very well have notified somebody who had decided to keep the dead husband listed as co-owner, and had been using his signature power. Vesper had not withdrawn or transferred money, but she'd neglected to look for other activity. In at least some corporations, it might be possible to have any notices sent to "George" at another address from Vesper's.

Warren made notes of all these thoughts and the questions they raised. He brought the big bag closer and looked down into the folders to see if he could spot any notes attached to the reports or paper clips on the folders. People often kept slips of paper that included or alluded to valuable evidence without realizing that was what it was.

Warren went back to looking at the monthly reports, and reminded himself to use his notepad whenever he saw a surprising number so he could check it later. Often the surest sign that something was wrong was when the numbers were too good. Another was when investment results were summarized as upward curves or increasing percentages. Many people hated numbers. They preferred summaries, and predators loved summaries.

He wasn't sure of the exact moment when he had begun to think of these minutiae as evidence, but it had been early on. He straightened the pile of file folders he'd looked at, massaged his desktop computer to life, and looked up Vesper Ellis's telephone numbers. He jotted them on his yellow legal pad, picked up his office phone, and dialed. The phone rang ten times and then offered to let him leave a message after the tone. He said, "Mrs. Ellis, this is Charles Warren. I'd like to talk with you as soon as possible." He recited the office number, which he knew she had already, and then added his cell phone. He dialed her cell phone, which also went to voice mail, and left the same message.

He went on studying the monthly reports for Vesper Ellis's accounts. The number of puzzling entries grew, and his list of questions grew too. He had to interrupt his work to meet with the attorney of a building contractor he had sued on behalf of a client whose house had been partially demolished and never remodeled. The contractor's attorney, after issuing threats that Charlie received impassively, finally settled for full costs plus damages to save the contractor's license. When he had walked the attorney out the door, he asked Martha, "Has Vesper Ellis called?"

"No. I'll let you know as soon as she does." At five, she came into his office and said, "I'm going to take Alan home unless you need me."

Warren said, "No, thanks. I'll be staying a little while, so please lock the door on the way out. I think Mrs. Ellis's problems are at least as serious as she thinks they are, so if she returns my call tomorrow, I'll need to know it right away."

"Sure thing," Martha said. "Good night, Charlie."

"Night, Martha."

Warren devoted two more hours to the Ellis matter and then realized he had begun to think of it as a "case." He supposed that had occurred when his own notes had grown copious enough to deserve their own file folder. He called Mrs. Ellis's cell number again. This time he added, "Please return my call as promptly as possible, I'm leaving the office now, but you can still reach me on my cell phone at—" and he recited the number again and the number of his house phone and hung up. He was now too tired and hungry to trust himself not to miss any entries he needed to notice. He locked the Ellis monthly report folders in the office safe, looked up the phone number of Bernardine, one of his favorite restaurants, and ordered a dinner to take out, and walked to the elevators with only his notes on the legal pad in his briefcase.

He drove to Bernardine, gave his car to the parking attendant, went inside, and waited at the bar for the waiter to finish packing his food.

Charlie was a steady customer, familiar to the bartender and the waitresses. He usually came with a date, was respectful to everyone, and tipped well, so Bernardine and a few other good restaurants always took special care of him. He had ordered a dinner of salmon, spinach, and a baked potato, and when it arrived, he took it, left a large tip to preserve his welcome for his next visit, and went outside to reclaim his car.

In his mind he was still compiling his notes and questions about Vesper Ellis's investments. He had not planned to keep at it late, but when he'd started this afternoon, he'd seen things that made him think that the bad behavior was still happening. The thought had made him feel some of the panicky urgency he'd felt in high school when he'd seen what was happening to his mother.

Con men and women were sociopaths, every one of them like Mack Stone. They had no sense that the people they were robbing were anything but prey. Other people had no rights, their feelings and thoughts and hurts weren't worth noticing unless emotions made them more vulnerable. In his legal career he had never seen even one of them who stopped stealing from a victim voluntarily before their victim was left with nothing. There was no such thing as a con man who decided to leave his victim enough to survive. They stopped when there was no more that they could take.

He was determined to work quickly to save what Vesper Ellis still had. The thought made him take his phone out of his pocket and look for a missed call, but there hadn't been one. He probably had found enough irregularities in the files to establish a reason to freeze the assets, but he wouldn't do that yet without her knowledge and consent. His power of attorney was hours old, and hadn't been established with any financial corporation, so there would be delays and maybe even inquiries to the culprits from their superiors that would tip them off.

While Warren was waiting for the attendant to bring the car to the curb, he noticed a Range Rover idling in the right lane. It seemed to be waiting its turn to pull ahead and have an attendant come and park it. The odd thing was that there wasn't a car in front of it. There wasn't a rule that a car had to pull forward as far as it could, but it was the normal thing to do. Warren stepped back two steps so he could see past the head-lights, and saw there were two men in the front seats of the Range Rover.

A moment later the attendant drove Warren's car to the curb and stood holding the driver's door open, so Warren walked up, handed him the money, got in, and as he fastened his seat belt, looked in his rearview mirrors, trying to be certain the other car wasn't about to move forward just as he pulled out. The Range Rover was immobile, and it was blocking other cars from coming along in the right lane, so Warren took the opportunity and pulled out and away from Bernardine.

The Range Rover pulled forward, but the driver didn't swing close to the curb and turn it over to the parking attendant. Instead, the car sped up and followed Warren's. It looked as though the two men had been waiting for him. Were they cops? For half his life he had been having that thought, but there was no rationality to it anymore. If anything was going to happen, it would have been seventeen years ago. That was over. If the police had wanted to talk to him about a client, he wasn't hard to find. He spent most of his days in an office with his name on the door. If they had suspected him of something and wanted to do surveillance on him in a plain car, then presumably they would have stayed back and preserved the distance between them.

He thought about driving back to his office to pick up a few of the reports Mrs. Ellis had brought in. He turned to the right and drove a block, then realized it had been an unrealistic idea. He had his legal pad in his briefcase in the trunk with several pages of dates and amounts of transactions, names of people responsible for accounts, and related questions and thoughts. He still hadn't had dinner, and he had enough information on his computer to keep him busy all night. At the office tomorrow he could get help with some of the time-consuming tracing. He pulled into a driveway, backed out, and saw that the Range Rover from Bernardine was a block away, coming toward him.

They had followed him from the restaurant, and gone around the block when he had. They were up to something. Robbery? He drove toward them as though he had no memory of seeing them earlier. He knew he had to decide quickly. He could try to lose them, or at least get so far ahead that he had time to use his remote control to open the iron bars that blocked his building's underground garage, get inside, close the barrier, and then disappear into the elevator or up the stairs. His dilemma was that they had made a mistake, and he couldn't be sure they would ever make another. He decided he had to use this chance to get behind their car and take a picture of its license plate.

If they had been waiting to pull a follow-home robbery on somebody just because they had enough money to pick up dinner at Bernardine, they had not been very clever about it. Their tactics seemed more like an attempt to intimidate him than to surprise him. He was in the profession of fighting clients' battles, and he was good at it, so there had to be a growing number of former opponents who hated him for old cases he'd won. If any of them had reached the point of hiring people to do something about it, this might be his only chance to find out who they were before they did it.

He turned right again, drove at high speed for two blocks, and pulled over at the curb near the corner, where he could see the cars going by on Wilshire Boulevard toward his condominium building, turned off his lights, but left his engine running. If they were trying to come after him, they would have realized by now that he had eluded them. They would have no logical choice but to double back onto the Boulevard and try to catch up with him before he reached home.

Warren watched and waited for the black Range Rover to go past. Black was a common car color in Los Angeles. The Range Rover had tinted side windows, and a lot of cars had those too. Every time a black car sped across his field of vision from right to left, he jumped a little, ready to go after it, but it was always the wrong black car. Minutes went by, but he still didn't see the Range Rover. He became more and more primed. He told himself that each second when he didn't see it brought the time closer when he would see it. His eyes were focused on the cars speeding past, almost afraid to blink for fear of missing it. He took out his phone and pressed the camera symbol so it would be ready. And then he realized that too much time had passed.

He put his phone into his coat pocket and reached for the headlight switch. His hand didn't reach it, because in that moment, a metal implement swung against the passenger side window and smashed the glass. Warren's head spun toward the noise and he saw the white hand, the black sleeve, the tire iron, and fragments of glass spraying onto the empty seat and his lap. The man's other hand reached in through the jagged gap, feeling for the door handle.

Warren stomped on the gas pedal and his car shot forward. The man with his arm in the door didn't get his arm out of the broken window in time, and was jerked forward with the car. Warren hit the brake again after ten feet and the man was hurled forward against the door frame and then slid out. Warren pulled forward and stopped again, his eyes on his rearview mirror. In the red glow of his own brake lights, he saw the man curled up on the pavement near the curb clutching his arm, and beyond him about a hundred feet was the Range Rover. He couldn't see the second man.

Warren hesitated. He couldn't make himself forget that using a car as a weapon for self-defense was legal, but using it once the threat was over was not. He pulled farther ahead, made a right turn onto the Boulevard, and accelerated. It occurred to him that he was still in the same situation. This was his chance to take a picture of the car's license plate.

Right now, both men were out of their vehicle, and one of them was hurt, so it would take thirty seconds or so for them to get back into their seats and drive off. He made a quick right turn and drove hard. He took his phone out of his coat pocket and engaged its camera again, made the second right turn, and raced toward the third. When he got to the corner he slowed, made the final turn, steadied the phone on the top of the steering wheel, and accelerated again, taking pictures in rapid succession. He moved the phone to his left hand while he switched on the high-beam headlights and kept taking pictures.

The second man was helping his injured companion into the passenger seat when the bright light caught them. The man let go of his friend and reached into his coat. His hand came back out with something black in it.

Warren hit the brakes, dropped his phone, spun the steering wheel, and shifted into reverse. The car swung around, he shifted to drive, and headed away, accelerating as much he could, and ducking low to present a smaller target. He heard a "pop-pop-pop" behind him. He turned right at the first cross street, turned again toward his condominium, and sped away. He drove aggressively, moving in and out past the slower cars, stretching the yellow lights to gain the extra block without stopping. He had needed to drop his phone to evade the two men, and now he knew he shouldn't pull over and stop to find it on the floor, so he made his bet on getting to the garage fast.

◆

The injured man said to his companion, "Let's get the hell out of here now. This was a bad idea."

"It was your idea," the driver said. He put the car in gear and pulled out onto the street to the right, away from where Warren was going.

"I'm suffering for it now," the injured man said. "I felt like his car was going to tear my arm off. But I was stupid. I knew who the guy was, and I should have remembered that was still going to be who he is, instead of thinking he was going to be somebody different. We weren't going to scare him. All we did was piss him off. Unless you hit him and he's bleeding out right now."

"I'm pretty sure he's not hit. We blew our chance to take him by surprise on the first try, but nothing else has changed, and nothing else gives him an edge."

◆

When Warren reached his building, he pressed the remote control to raise the steel bars of the garage gate, pulled in, and watched the gate close. He found his phone on the car floor, got out and called 911, and told the operator what had happened. He paced as he described to her precisely how he had injured one of the men, gave her an accurate description of the black Range Rover, and read out the license number from one of the photographs that was brightly lit by his high-beam headlights. As he was talking, his eyes strayed to the back of his car and he noticed three bullet holes punched into his trunk, so he mentioned that too.

She said that a police car was on the way to the side street where the encounter had turned violent, and told him to hold on. After about two minutes she gave him the unsurprising news that the Range Rover wasn't there anymore, but added that another police unit was on the way to his building and would be there shortly.

Warren was waiting when the police car arrived at his building. As soon as he saw the black-and-white pull up and stop, he pressed the remote control to open the garage and walked out to meet the two officers who got out to speak to him.

"Mr. Warren?"

"Yes," said Warren.

"Are you injured?"

"No."

"Good. Is your car in there?"

"It's that one right there."

They followed him to it, looked at the broken window and the bullet holes, and one of them took out a flashlight and leaned to look into the car while the other looked at the photographs Warren had taken. He carried Warren's phone to the patrol car, spoke on the car radio for a couple exchanges, read the license number into the microphone, and then came back. He handed Warren's phone back to him and said, "I sent the pictures to the station."

The other cop, who had been examining Warren's car said, "Do you mind if we take a look in your trunk?"

"Not at all." He pressed his key fob and popped it open. As the two officers used their flashlights to search for spent bullets or fragments or holes in the front walls of the trunk, Warren noticed something.

"My briefcase is gone."

"It was in the trunk?"

"Yes. I stopped at Bernardine on the way home from work. I left the car with the parking attendant, picked up a take-out dinner. I don't know who took the briefcase."

One cop added a note to his notebook and asked, "Was there anything valuable in it?'

"Not monetarily valuable, but important. I had a legal pad in there with a few hours of notes I had been making about a client's financial records in a case."

"So you lost your work, and the value of your briefcase?"

"Yes, but that's not as important as the information in the notes. Somebody now has quite a bit of confidential information about the client's investments, savings, retirement accounts, and so on. If they know what they stole and how it can be used, it could be a serious loss."

"Can you define 'serious loss' for me?"

"Sophisticated criminals could probably steal a lot of my client's money."

"Do you think the guys who shot at you knew you had the notes?"

Warren said, "I don't know. The briefcase had to have been taken while the car was parked and I was waiting for my order to be put together. If they took it, I have no idea whether they opened it, or looked at the notes, or understood them. If the briefcase was what they were after, and they already had it, why follow me at all, let alone chase me all over the place?"

"So, no." the cop said.

"It seemed as though what they wanted was to do me some kind of harm. Since I'd never seen them before, they must have been hired to do it. One of them smashed this window with a tire iron to get to me, and the other one shot at me when I was driving away."

The cop was writing furiously to preserve all he could of this. During this pause, the older cop came back. "They identified the Range Rover. It's been reported stolen from an owner in Pasadena. He's an anesthesiologist, no record, and he's seventy-two years old."

"I guess going for the pictures was a waste of effort," Warren said.

"We'll probably find the car abandoned in a day or two. If we don't, it will mean it got to a chop shop, here or in Mexico. A detective will be in touch with you tomorrow. Sorry about the damage to your car, too. Don't get it repaired until the detective gets a look."

◆

The next morning Warren woke feeling irritated and uneasy. He had no idea why the two men had followed him and tried to do him harm. He kept thinking about his practice and each of his recent cases, searching for a reason why someone would be willing to commit a string of felonies to get back at him. Most of the clients and opponents in his cases were civil litigants, none of them criminal cases. This brought him back to the one current case that might be an exception—Vesper Ellis. The thought added to his irritation. By now, Vesper Ellis should have listened to at least one of the recordings her lawyer had left on her phones asking her to return his call as soon as possible. Why had she not done it?

5

W arren called his insurance agent, who gave him the number to call to have a rental car delivered to his building so he could get to work. At the moment Warren & Associates consisted of Charlie, Martha Wilkes, and Martha's dog, Alan. Occasionally Martha would recruit her wife Sonya, who had worked as a paralegal, to help out on demanding cases.

Warren & Associates took on a variety of clients and cases. Warren did a large business in divorces, child custody, and estate planning, which tended to bring him the sort of clients who could and would pay his fees. A few times a year he had sued insurance companies when their treatment of their clients or others was particularly outrageous or defended clients from meritless and predatory lawsuits from business rivals. He shied away from criminal defense, only agreeing to step in for a current client on a temporary basis—getting the defendant bail, and sometimes attending their indictments while referring them to the best specialists.

This morning he came in and stopped at Martha's desk. "Good morning," he said. "I assume that Vesper Ellis hasn't returned my call?"

"No, she hasn't."

"Anything else that's urgent?"

"Not yet," she said. "You know that whenever I say that, the phone rings."

"True, so let me quickly fill you in on my evening."

"Okay."

"I worked on the Vesper Ellis thing until nine or so, and then stopped at Bernardine to pick up a take-out dinner." Then he told her about being followed, attacked, shot at, and having his briefcase stolen.

She said, "God, Charlie. Do you know why?"

"No."

"Do you need a rental car or anything?"

"Got one, thanks."

The telephone on her desk rang, and she said, "Law Offices," then, "One moment please," and then pushed *Hold* and said, "Sergeant McHargue?"

He took the receiver and said, "Hello, Sergeant. This is Charles Warren."

"Yes, sir." The voice seemed to belong to someone large. "I wondered when you can be free to meet me at your home."

"I'm at my office right now, but I can be there in fifteen to twenty minutes, depending on traffic."

"I'll see you there."

He hung up and handed the phone to Martha. "I've got to meet him at my place. Then I'll get back here and see if we can get through to Mrs. Ellis. They're probably robbing her right now."

"You know, after having your briefcase stolen last night, do you think it might be smart to scan the papers Mrs. Ellis brought in? That way we can do what we need to with them, and still have them locked in the safe."

"I think it's a great idea." He put his sport coat back on. "See you later."

Martha said, "I'll get the papers scanned while you're out. If you need to see the first ones, they should be up before you get finished with the cops."

It took Warren twenty minutes to reach his building, and the man who was probably Detective McHargue was there waiting for him. McHargue was about six foot two and broad-shouldered, and he was wearing a coat and tie, which nobody in LA but cops and lawyers did. He had a face that Warren thought of as reassuring—not quite smiling, but not unfriendly. He was at an unmarked car talking to a pair of men in dark blue coverall suits like a forensic team. Warren parked on the street and approached.

McHargue said, "Mr. Warren, I'm Detective McHargue. These officers and I would like to start by taking a look at your car."

"Right over here," Warren said.

As they walked toward the entrance to the garage, McHargue said, "We've read the report, so we know what to look for. One thing is that the person who took your briefcase might have left a print or two on your car."

Warren pressed his remote control and the iron gate rose to admit them. "That sounds good. I should mention that when I went to dinner I gave the car to a valet parking attendant, so his prints will be on the car too."

"Do you mind if we take the car to the station so they can have a closer look at everything?"

"That's fine," Warren said. "I've got a rental car."

"I figured you wouldn't mind. The flatbed is on its way. Can you give these officers the key? Don't forget to hold on to your other keys."

"Thanks," Warren said. He handed McHargue the car fob, and McHargue handed it to one of the men in overalls. The two examined the car closely from hood to trunk. McHargue walked all around the car and used his phone to take a few photographs—the trunk, the broken window, the interior where the glass had sprayed.

As they finished, the flatbed tow truck arrived and backed up the short, wide driveway. One of the two cops guided the driver with hand gestures, and the other drove the car out. While Warren and McHargue looked on, the men loaded the car onto the flatbed and drove off.

McHargue returned his attention to Warren. "It looks like three shots hit your trunk. Is that what you heard?"

"I think I heard a fourth, but I was accelerating to get out of there, and taking a turn. If there was a fourth shot it must have missed."

"Do you happen to own any firearms?"

Warren said, "No. It's not that I object to them, but I work long days, and I own my firm, so I don't have a lot of time to do things like go to a firing range. A gun would just be another thing I spent money on that I never used, like my skis and scuba gear, and I'd have to lock it up."

"It doesn't matter, really. But I was thinking, if you wanted to shoot a driver who was speeding away from you, then you'd want to aim for a window. This guy aimed too low. There's not one shot through the back window."

"Maybe he was just trying to scare me off so I couldn't get a good picture. I got a few, but the officer last night said the car was stolen."

"Yes," McHargue said. "Do you have anything going on in your firm or your life right now that might explain any of this?"

Warren shrugged. "I've been wondering about that. Nothing in my personal life. No married women or anything."

"How about legal cases?"

"I don't think so. I had a meeting with the other attorney in a case yesterday afternoon, and he agreed to settle for what we had demanded instead of fighting it in court. I'm sure he wasn't happy, but this is what civil lawyers do. Sometimes a client is in the wrong and the job is just to make sure the settlement he pays is fair. The lawyer gets paid for his work, and his client will pay for the damages, and tomorrow morning the alarm clock goes off and we go on to the next client's problem."

"Any of those opposing clients who might want to scare you off?"

"Not that I know of. There is something odd. Yesterday afternoon, a new client came to me with a collection of financial statements because she suspects some of her money might have been diverted. After she left, I spent a few hours reading through the monthly reports, and I think she's probably right. I left the office late, and on the way home I stopped to pick up a take-home dinner at Bernardine, planning to do some more work on her case. I had all my notes in my briefcase. When the parking attendant brought my car, that was when all the following and chasing and the attack happened."

"About your briefcase that was stolen, anything else in it besides the notes?"

"Nothing. I don't usually carry anything home with me except things that I need to work on that night."

McHargue was nodding. At first he said nothing, and then, "How long have you been in practice?"

"Seven years."

"Has anything like this happened before?"

"No."

"If anything about that case—or anything else—starts to look like it might be the cause of what happened—give me a call."

"Sure will," Warren said.

"For the moment we'll be looking at other incidents to see if there's been anything similar lately that we can connect with it, or see if the lab turns anything up."

McHargue got into his unmarked car and drove off. Warren watched him for a few seconds. He had no hope that the two men would be found. He had already reconciled himself to the loss of his briefcase and notes. It was time to chase down Vesper Ellis so he could get to work on her problem.

6

Warren walked into the office and looked at Martha, who was at the reception desk. Alan was beside her desk in his Sphinx position. She said, "Mrs. Ellis hasn't called. I would have let you know."

"I figured you would, but I had to check."

"Her monthly portfolio summaries are all scanned, so they're available, and the originals are back in the safe."

"Thanks, Martha."

He called Mrs. Ellis's number again. She didn't answer, but the phone invited him to leave a message. He changed his tone slightly. "This is Charles Warren. Please call me, either at my office number, which is—" and he recited the number, and then added, "or my cell phone," and then recited that number too. "If you use the cell number you can reach me at any time of the day or night. It's very important that you do. This is not a matter that will wait. It's urgent that I speak with you about your case."

He hung up, turned to his computer, and typed in Tiffany Greene's name. In a second, he was looking at the file for her divorce. He found her cell phone number and dialed it. He listened to a few rings and got another recorded speech and a chance to leave a message. He said, "Hi,

Tiffany. I wanted to thank you for referring Vesper Ellis to me. I also wondered if you have another number for her, or know anything about where I might be able to reach her. I've tried both the numbers she gave to my assistant, Martha, with no luck." Then he gave his office phone number, which she certainly had already, and his cell number, and hung up.

He turned to his computer and began scrolling through the column of emails in case he had missed one from Vesper Ellis. He hadn't gotten very far before the phone on his desk rang. He snatched up the receiver and said, "Yes?"

Martha said, "Can you talk to Tiffany Greene on line one?"

"Sure. Thanks." He heard the switch take place and said, "Tiffany?"

"Hi, Charlie. Got your message. When I heard your voice, I thought maybe you had found me more money my ex made disappear during the divorce. Did you?"

"No such luck," he said. "I've been trying to reach Vesper Ellis, and it occurred to me that if she asked for your advice on a legal problem, she might be close enough to you to tell you if she was leaving town or something."

"We're close, but I'm afraid this time we're both out of luck. I haven't talked to her for a few days."

"Do you know anybody else who might have seen her in the past twenty-four hours?"

"She's always been somebody with a lot of friends, even before George died. She's a great hostess, one of those women who knows how to make it look effortless. I could go look up some phone numbers and explain who they belong to and all that, but it'll be quicker if I'm the one who calls. I'll let you know what I find out."

"Thanks, Tiffany."

"Bye."

He hung up the phone and went out to Martha's desk.

"You're good at sizing up clients. Did she strike you as somebody who would ask a lawyer to look over some suspicious financial records and then not return his phone calls, even after he left messages that it was urgent?"

"In other words, an idiot? No. She seemed to be serious and decisive, maybe more so because she had lost track of a few things that her husband used to handle before he died, and now she was taking charge."

"That's the way she struck me too."

He went back into his office and spent the time while he was waiting for Tiffany Greene to call going through more pages of monthly reports, this time on the computer screen. He collected the rest of the names, titles, and phone numbers of the advisors who had controlled Vesper Ellis's accounts, put them into a note file, and typed in as much of the contents of his lost notepad as he could bring back from memory.

Warren couldn't help being reminded of what had happened to his mother's money after his father died. When there was an accumulation of money in a widow's accounts, it shouldn't surprise him if somebody had noticed it and started devising strategies for taking it. He made a note to find out from Tiffany Greene whether Vesper Ellis had acquired a particularly enthusiastic and tenacious boyfriend over the past year or so.

He looked for more transfers of funds authorized by George Ellis, and he knew that he was also building a list of possible defendants in future prosecutions. The companies were some of the largest and, seemingly, most solid financial corporations in the country. If the men and women they had placed in charge of Vesper Ellis's accounts had taken part in swindling her money, they would be eager to fix it before it came to the attention of the authorities.

He also spot-checked a few of the prices presented in the monthly reports against the records of the company whose stock it was to see if the numbers matched.

Warren saw one of the buttons on his phone light up and thought, "Vesper Ellis," but it was Martha saying, "Detective Sergeant McHargue on line two."

When Warren heard the transfer he said, "Hello, Sergeant."

McHargue said, "Hello. I called because we found the Land Rover the two men used. It was abandoned at the curb of a street off the 405 freeway in Inglewood. The forensics people are going over it to raise a print or find any blood, since you might have left the one guy with some scratches, but I'm not optimistic. The inside of the car smells like ammonia, and you can see where a lot of the surfaces were wiped down, so if we find anything it just got missed in the cleanup."

"I guess I was prepared for that kind of news."

"Your car, on the contrary, has too many prints—yours, the valet parking guy's, three smaller ones that are probably women, since the hairs in the car are all long, and about three men that have been sent in to see if they match anybody with a record."

"Am I free to take my car to the dealer to get it repaired at this point?"

"I'm afraid so. You can have the repair shop pick it up any time. If your insurance company needs a copy of the police report, let me know where to send it."

"Thank you."

They both hung up. Warren looked at his computer screen with the columns of stock names and symbols and numbers. This didn't seem to him to be the priority anymore. It was time to start concentrating on finding Vesper Ellis.

7

Warren called Tiffany Greene's number. When she answered, he said, "I'm sorry to bother you again, but what have you learned so far? Has anybody seen her or talked to her?"

"Not for the past couple days. After I told her to go see you, she told a couple other friends she had an appointment she was going to, but nobody I've talked to seems to have heard from her how it went, or really, anything. I mean, we're not teenage girls who are on the phone with one another all day long, so nobody thought much about it. I told everybody I talked to that we're trying to get in touch with her."

He said, "Has she been dating anybody lately? Anybody she might go on a trip with?"

"There's nobody she liked very much, and I doubt that anybody like that turned up in the hours between your office visit and eight o'clock or so, when I called her."

"What about her family? Where do they live?"

"She's from somewhere in the east. She went to Bryn Mawr. That's in Pennsylvania, but I think she was brought up in Ohio. Same difference, I guess. She was very close to her mother, at least growing up. She's

always quoting her, and she did say some sharp and funny things, but I
don't know if she's even alive now. Vesper had a sister, too, but she died
for sure. An especially bad form of breast cancer that swept her away in
a few months."

"Are you the kind of friends who have keys to each other's houses?"

"We used to be years ago. She and George lived a couple blocks from
Bill and me, so it made sense. If I locked myself out, I could just walk
over there and get my key, or she would drive over with it. But after you
got me the house in the divorce and I had the pleasure of kicking Bill
out, I sold it and bought this place, which is miles away. When I moved,
I gave her key back."

"Is there anybody else who might have that kind of relationship
with her?"

"Not that I know of," she said. "And none of our old mutual friends
lives that close to her now, so it would probably be somebody new."

"Well, thanks," he said. "Please don't forget to let me know if you
hear anything."

"Sure," she said. "You sound worried about her."

"Just trying to save myself a lot of extra work later," he said. "My
motives are selfish, I assure you."

After the call ended, he thought about what he'd learned and what
he'd said. He judged that his tone had been sufficiently even and unemo-
tional at the end to calm Tiffany down and prevent her from telling her
friends something might have happened to Vesper Ellis. He continued
to be surprised at how often his profession required him to lie.

He dialed the phone again, listened to the ring signal, then heard a
voice say, "Major Crimes, Sergeant McHargue."

He said, "Hello, Sergeant. This is Charles Warren again. Do you
remember that when you asked me whether there was anything

in my business that might be connected with the attack the other night, I mentioned I had a client who noticed money disappearing from investment accounts? I've been trying to reach her since that afternoon. She hasn't answered any calls. I just got off a call with the close friend of hers who referred her to me. She's called everybody they know in common, and nobody else has seen her or been able to reach her either."

"Were they expecting to?"

"There wasn't a specific event, but I'm told this isn't normal for her. Normally she would have told that friend what had happened at her meeting with me, for instance. She didn't. Others had been trying to reach her too. I wondered if you could have an officer drive by her house and do a welfare check. I could meet him there."

"Do you have a reason to think somebody did something to her?"

"I think it's a possibility. I've been finding more evidence that someone has been diverting funds from her accounts. The fact that someone came after me within three hours of our meeting makes me think somebody may have been watching her."

"I'll ask for a check. Can you give me her address?"

Warren read the address on his computer screen.

"Got it."

"Thank you, Sergeant. I'd like to be there when the officer does the check. How soon do you think that will be?"

"I'd say you should start heading over there now."

"Thank you again."

In a moment he was walking across the outer office, putting on his sport coat. "I'm heading over to Vesper Ellis's house to see if she's there. I may not be back, so when you leave, make sure everything that can be locked or turned off is."

The house was in Encino, a two-story white colonial-style building with black door and shutters, two chimneys, large oak trees, manicured lawn, and a rose garden. It looked as though it had been picked up and moved from Connecticut. There was a walkway made of cobblestones leading from the driveway to the front steps.

Warren had just parked at the curb when the police car arrived. The officer who got out and walked to the front door was a short woman with dark hair in a tight bun. She pushed the doorbell, and as Warren got out of his car, he could hear the chime sounding inside. He walked to the foot of the driveway and said, "Hi, officer. I'm Charles Warren, Mrs. Ellis's attorney. I'm the one who asked for a welfare check. She doesn't seem to be responding."

"Not so far," she said, "but I just got here." She pushed the doorbell again.

"Do you mind if I hang around while you do the check?"

"Suit yourself," she said.

She rang the doorbell again, they heard the chime and waited for about ten seconds, and then she knocked on the door loudly and they both listened, but there was no sound of footsteps. She knocked again, this time more loudly, with no response, and then she rang again. Next she stepped to the front window and looked in. "I can see the alarm panel, and the green light is on, so it isn't armed." She tried the doorknob, but it was locked.

Warren leaned so he could see into the window over her head, but he sensed that he had made her feel uncomfortable, so he stepped back about five feet, and half turned away.

The cop said nothing, but began to walk along the front of the house. When she came to the next window, she leaned close and peered inside, her hands framing her eyes, then moved on to the next one and did the same. Warren was relieved, because her moves made it seem natural to lag one window behind and maintain his distance. He noticed that before she moved each time she looked down to stare at the ground for footprints or other evidence of problems.

Every angle he had seen of the living room and foyer looked neat and orderly—nothing out of place, no shade variations between parts of floors that could indicate wetness or staining, no places on walls that looked as though anything had been wiped or smudged.

When the cop reached the back steps of the house she went up to the door, rang the back doorbell once, waited, and then rang it again, knocked once, knocked harder, tried to turn the doorknob, but failed. She looked in the glass on the upper part of the door, but Warren was pretty sure that she couldn't see much, maybe a part of the kitchen floor and a view of the rest of the room veiled by the gauzy curtain. When she came down, she continued her circuit of the house, and appeared to be giving every inch of the property the same intense scrutiny. She walked to the upper end of the driveway and looked in the row of windows at the top of the garage door. "No car," she said, returned to the place where she had left off, and continued the rest of the way around to the front of the house.

As she walked past him, Warren pretended to take a picture of the house's front porch, but timed it to take her nameplate, because he expected she would leave now and he might need to know that later. The plate said, "N. Porter."

She surprised him by continuing across the front lawn to the house to the right of Vesper Ellis's. She rang the doorbell and took a step back. A moment later an elderly man came to the door. He was tall and slim, with a slightly bent spine. Officer Porter said, "Good afternoon, sir. I'm here doing a welfare check on your neighbor, Mrs. Ellis."

"Vesper?" the man said. "Has something happened to her?"

"It's just that some friends of hers haven't been able to reach her. Do you know when you last saw her?"

"I saw her rolling one of her empty trash bins up the driveway. You know the noise that makes. Trash pickup is Tuesday on this block, so it had to be Tuesday. I glanced out the window because you do that even though you recognize the sound and know what it must be. Or it could have been Wednesday, because sometimes if you come home after a long day at work and having dinner out and don't feel like doing it you put it off until the next morning."

"Yes, sir. And have you heard or seen anything from her house since then? Like music, or voices or a door slamming?"

"No. She's a quiet neighbor. She and her husband used to do a lot of entertaining, but that ended when he died."

"Thank you," she said, took a notebook out of her pocket, asked for his name, wrote it down, then crossed the street and rang that doorbell and repeated nearly the same conversation with the younger woman who answered that door. Next she went to the house to the left of Vesper Ellis's house, but nobody answered that doorbell or the knocking. She looked at the Ellis house again, this time staying as far from the siding as possible, and craned her neck to stare up at the windows. She walked the whole perimeter, stopping every few feet to look down at the ground and along the fences, then up at the next second-floor window.

When they reached the street again Officer Porter said, "I'm sorry. That's about as far as we can go. No response, no car in the garage, nothing broken or obviously tampered with, no scrapes like a door was jimmied, no broken windows, no tracks or paint chips or anything near the windows, not even any scrapes on the fences as though somebody had climbed over. The neighbors haven't seen or heard anything. Mrs. Ellis is an adult, so if she wanted to leave, she had every right."

Warren said, "I know. We have to assume that's what happened. But I have a bad feeling about this."

The cop looked around her as though to be sure nobody was going to hear. "So do I. But the world has gotten sick of cops who had an unsupported suspicion and acted on it. We've got nothing to hang it on."

"I know. But she came to me with evidence that some of her investment accounts are being drained. It's pretty unusual for a client to come to me with good reason to believe she's being robbed, and then disappear and stop answering her phone, even when her closest friends call her. And meanwhile I had two men follow me on my way home and shoot at me. It's unusual to have people shoot at me."

"I'm sure it is," Officer Porter said. "You've got a detective assigned to your case, right?"

"Yes. Sergeant McHargue."

"Must be another station. You can ask him to apply for a warrant and take a look inside. You know that, right?"

"Sure. I may give that a try, but I don't think I've got anything that a judge would call probable cause. About all I can do right now is report her missing."

"I think that's the right thing to do. But don't call the Missing Persons Unit. Go in person to the West Valley Station at 19020 Vanowen. It will help that they can see you're not a lunatic or a creep."

"You're sure they'll see that?"

"Reasonably sure." She didn't smile. They could hear a call coming in over her car's radio. "Sorry we didn't find anything here. I've got to go take one of these calls." She got into her patrol car, pulled away from the curb, and drove off.

Warren watched her car turn and disappear, and then went back along the side of the house. One of the reasons he had tagged along on her search was so the neighbors would see him with her, a uniformed cop. Given unconscious sexism, people had probably assumed the man in the suit was the female uniformed patrol officer's superior.

The welfare check had not settled anything in his mind. Even though Mrs. Ellis's car was gone, that didn't mean she'd taken it. She had seemed eager for his phone call, but she wasn't answering her phones. Her house was locked, but the alarm wasn't turned on. At least that observation gave him something he could use. He cut across the back lawn to the trunk of a big tree beside the roof over the back porch, jumped to grasp the lowest branch, pulled himself up, reached for the branch above him, pulled himself up onto it, crawled a few feet on the limb to get above the roof, and stepped down onto the shingled surface. He stood and walked toward the place where the porch's roof met the side of the house.

Some people in Los Angeles cooled their houses before the summer got too hot by opening upper windows. Sometimes when they closed the windows later, they could be lackadaisical about fastening the latches. Why worry? Nobody on the ground could see whether an upper window latch was open.

He reached the first set of windows. There were screens on them, so it was possible they were sometimes opened. He came close to the first one and saw the latch was locked. He moved to the second one, and that was locked too. He went to each window and leaned close with his eyes shaded and studied the inside of the house, half expecting to see the body of Vesper Ellis on the floor or on one of the beds. He saw nothing but expertly made beds and floors that shone with polishing. He paused. Maybe this was a foolish idea. Vesper Ellis had not seemed to be a person who would leave an unlocked window in her house.

The fourth window was different. When he looked closely, he could see that the latch was turned in the opposite direction from the others. He could hardly believe it. He reached into his pocket, took out his pocketknife, and opened the blade. He inserted it into the narrow space between the screen and the sill and pried the aluminum frame of the screen up very slightly, pried the hook out of the eye with the blade, pulled the bottom of the screen outward, slid it out of the guides that held the sides near the top, and set it down. Then he pushed the glass window upward with his thumbs until he could fit his fingers under it and slide the sash all the way up. He climbed in, slid the screen back into its guides, and hooked it in place, then closed the window.

Warren listened. He was aware that he had just committed the crime of breaking and entering, and that was enough to get him disbarred and possibly jailed, but he didn't want to devote any time to thinking about that now.

He took a step deeper into the room. He knew that this was Vesper Ellis's bedroom. The room was larger than the other bedrooms he'd seen from outside, and the bed was a California King rather than a double. The bed was made, with fresh sheets and the blanket pulled tight. There was no way to be sure if it had been done by Mrs. Ellis or by someone else to make it look as though all was well, but it was clear that she had not slept here the night after the bed had been made. He looked in the slightly open sliding door of the closet, and saw nothing but women's clothes. None of them was the dress she'd worn to his office.

Warren moved on. He made his way from room to hall to room through the house. The most important thing he was looking for was any indication that Vesper Ellis might have been injured or killed or had left her house under somebody else's power. He touched nothing, and he kept looking down to be sure he wasn't about to step on any spot that might contain evidence. Before entering each room, he studied it from the doorway, first to be sure there was not a security camera. There seldom was one on the upper floor of a residence, but he didn't want to be wrong and get recorded. He looked for anything that seemed to be out of place, any sign that a rug had been removed, or a spot on the floor that might have been cleaned with too much care.

The ground floor was perfect—too perfect. It was not strange that the spare bedrooms upstairs were perfectly clean, neat, and looking untouched. It wasn't surprising that a woman like Vesper Ellis kept her own bedroom impeccable. The ground floor was not different, and it should have been. It had nothing out of place. The living room had no magazines or books on a table, no signs that it had been inhabited. There were a couple very good vases, but no flowers in them. He looked inside the mouths of both and could tell that in the past there had been water for plants that had left rings. It seemed to him that if a criminal wanted to mask the fact that the woman who lived here was gone, it would have been a good idea to remove any flowers, which would have wilted in a couple days.

The dining room looked as though it hadn't ever been used, but that didn't mean much. A young widow might not arrange formal dinners very often—might even have given it up when her husband died. He was eager to keep going to reach the kitchen. Almost anything on her counters or in her cupboards might tell him more than he knew now. What he was almost certain to learn something from was her refrigerator. Most of the food packages would have labels with dates on them, and if anything was out of character or out of place, he might spot it.

As he walked toward the doorway to the kitchen, he passed a tall wooden sideboard. He looked more closely as he walked by, and saw the slim silvery profile of a cell phone. It was lying on the top of one of the small glass-fronted cabinets that supported the big mirror of the sideboard, nearly six feet above the floor.

Warren's gut tightened. Nobody, and especially no woman, would knowingly go anywhere for two days or more and leave her phone on top of a sideboard. He turned toward the window across the dining room. Why hadn't he or Officer Porter seen the phone through the window? They had both looked, and both had suspected there was something strange going on.

He looked at the top of the sideboard again. The light had changed since they'd walked around the house. As the afternoon sun had sunk lower, its rays had shone more directly in the window and through the thin white curtains. The phone was almost fully in a ray of bright light now. He looked at his watch and noted the time. It was five eighteen exactly.

Warren turned, walked to the staircase, and climbed back up to the second floor. He went into the master bedroom, climbed out the window, walked along the roof to the overhanging limb of the big tree, lowered himself to hang by his arms, and dropped to the ground.

He walked around the outside of the house and looked into the dining room window to be sure. Then he took out his phone and called Sergeant McHargue.

When McHargue answered, Warren said, "Hello, Sergeant. This is Charles Warren. I think that Officer Porter and I missed something when we were doing the walk-around at Vesper Ellis's house. I'm at the dining room window, and I see something on top of the big sideboard that might be a cell phone. I don't know if it's hers or not, but if it is—"

"I get it. I've got the address," McHargue said. "I'll be there as soon as I can."

8

Detective Sergeant McHargue arrived at the house in about twenty minutes. He pulled up at the curb behind Warren's car and walked toward the driveway. As Warren joined him, he said, "What made you look in the windows a second time?"

Warren said, "I've never had a paying client with a legitimate need for my help drop out of sight before, and I've never gotten shot at. She was eager to get my call, but then she didn't answer any calls. Her doors were locked, but the alarm wasn't armed. Officer Porter, who did the welfare check, was thorough, but I just didn't feel satisfied, so I took another look."

"You didn't go inside or anything, right?"

"I'm a lawyer."

"Not exactly an answer."

He had to lie. "The answer is no."

They reached the dining room window, and Warren said, "There's a big piece of furniture along the wall on the other side of the dining table. There's a metallic object on the top left side of it. When I looked the second time the sun was low and shining straight inside, and I could see a reflection. I think it's a cell phone."

McHargue stepped up, shaded his eyes and looked in. He stepped to the left side, then the right. "There's no sun shining on it now."

"I know, but there was at 5:18 P.M."

McHargue turned to look at him for a second. Then he walked back down the driveway to his unmarked car and came back with a large black flashlight and a black object that looked like a small suitcase. He stepped in front of the window again, set the case on the pavement, and stepped up on it. He pushed the lens of the flashlight against the glass and switched on the light. The dining room was lit up with a glare that made Warren squint.

After a few seconds McHargue switched the light off and stepped down. "Bad news." He picked up the case he'd been standing on.

"Wait," Warren said. "I'm sure I saw the phone, and—"

"Yeah, me too," McHargue said. "That's what I meant by bad news. People who take off voluntarily seldom leave their phones behind. I'm going to request a warrant to search the house, and to have the tech people take a look at what's in the phone. I'll also get a search going for her car. I'll be in touch."

"Thanks," Warren said. He resisted the impulse to say anything else. He watched McHargue get into his car and drive off fast. Police departments were big and ponderous machines, but he could tell McHargue was determined to get the machine moving, and that was all Warren could hope for.

When he arrived at the office, business hours were over, and the parking levels were nearly empty. He parked in a visitor's space on the level above the Warren & Associates spaces, hoping that if criminals were watching for him, they wouldn't identify the rental car. He took the elevator up to his office's floor and found that Martha was still at her desk.

"Hi," he said. "Why are you still here?"

"Or you could say, 'Martha, once again, you're employee of the month. You stayed fifteen whole minutes to help me freeze Vesper Ellis's accounts.'"

"You anticipated that I was going to freeze her accounts?"

"She still hasn't called back. What else can you do? So I've gotten a start on it. I copied some of the letters you used during the Bagler divorce, and some others from *Rice v. Scorton.* Where there was an overlap, I copied both, so you'd have a choice. I haven't dug up the requests for court orders. I figured it was too soon for that."

"That's terrific, Martha. Thank you. Take Alan home, and you and Sophia and have a nice evening."

"We will," she said. "The letters to all the banks and financial corporations to freeze the accounts are in the Vesper Ellis file." She took her purse out of the deep drawer of her desk and went to the door, with the dog following her. "Don't stay too late. Tired people get stupid."

"I won't. Goodbye."

He walked into his office and went to work. The letters in the file were his first priority. As he read each one and found it free of errors and appropriate to this case, he would print it and leave it in the tray while he went on to the next. Each demanded that a company freeze all its Vesper Ellis accounts immediately, not make any trades in equity accounts or transfers of funds, even from one of her accounts to another. He demanded that no records concerning the accounts be in any way altered or made unavailable. Any previous agreement to allow anyone else access to her funds, records, history, or business affairs was hereby revoked. Any dividends, interest, or other income should be left in the accounts to await her personal decision regarding its disposition. Any deviation or delay would be met with legal action.

He was identified in the documents as Vesper Ellis's attorney. These companies did not need to know how recently that had become true. He was hoping that the companies' legal departments would decide to ask for proof of his status as soon as tomorrow morning. When they received photocopies of the hiring documents she had signed and saw the date, they would realize that he had been hired to solve a specific problem, and that the problem was the kind a client would characterize as an emergency. To them, that would mean she thought waiting would cause her financial harm. That, in turn, might cause their company financial harm too.

Legal departments in large companies tended to exist outside the normal chain of command. Lawyers were in charge of nothing but their own offices. All they did most of the time was give advice, but the people they gave advice to were at the top—CEOs, CFOs, the board of directors. If they were any good, they would spend tomorrow morning looking very closely at the accounts of Vesper Ellis. As soon as they did, some of them would see what Warren had seen. Somebody in at least two of these companies was stealing.

He was aware that there were demands in these documents that were open to dispute, and he couldn't imagine that he wouldn't at some point be having those disputes. He wasn't going to give that much thought for now. The purpose of what he was doing was to shorten the process of isolating and identifying the person or people who had been meddling with Vesper Ellis's accounts.

He could not be sure that the thefts had anything to do with the disappearance of Mrs. Ellis, but he knew they were the problem he'd been hired to fix, and stopping them was something he knew how to do. He was worried about her. Missing woman cases that had already gone more than forty-eight hours before anybody started searching had a dismal, heartbreaking history. The only way to operate under these circumstances was to assume that she hadn't driven off for a week at a spa or something, but that something had happened to her. He could only act on the unproven theory that her absence might have some connection with the thefts from her accounts.

He had to abandon his career-long practice of thoroughly investigating every question and collecting all the facts before he acted. This time he had to try to freeze the legal and financial landscape of Vesper Ellis's life exactly as it was right now. He turned back to his computer and began converting each of his letters into emails and sending them to the companies. As soon as he had finished, he went through the pile of printed letters, signed them, printed the envelopes, and got them ready to go out in the morning.

He called the messenger service that his firm used for serving subpoenas and other legal documents, and made arrangements for an early pickup and delivery of the letters.

He had to make up for lost time. He began working on the papers that would be necessary to obtain a court order to force the companies to accede to his demands. A court order might not be necessary for all the companies, but the ones for which it was necessary were most likely to be the ones that had some wrongdoing to conceal. He was going to find out.

His cell phone startled him. He answered, "Charles Warren."

"This is Douglas McHargue. The judge granted the warrant, and we're going over there now. I'd like to have somebody to serve with the warrant. Are you able to accept it?"

"I'm on my way," Warren said.

When Warren got out of his car at the Ellis house, he saw Officer Porter, the cop who had performed the welfare check in the early afternoon. She was leaning against the hood of her patrol car, and she came forward when she saw him. She said, "I hear you found something I missed."

"I missed it too."

"But then you remembered you could see through walls."

"I didn't need to. All that happened was that the sun got lower in late afternoon, which it does every day, and a strong beam of sunlight went in through the dining room window and lit up the top of that big sideboard."

She didn't take her eyes off him. "I know you think this could be life and death, but I hope you didn't find the phone another way."

"I'm far too selfish to do anything that would get me sent to jail and disbarred."

"Do you think I would arrest you for taking a personal risk to save a client's life?"

"Yes," he said. "I'm pretty sure you would."

"You're right. But I would admire your courage and compassion while I was putting the cuffs on you."

"That would have been comforting," he said. "But of course, that's not the case."

At that moment McHargue walked up to Warren and handed him the folded warrant. "As her attorney, you get this."

"Thank you, Detective." He opened it and looked to be sure it was perfect. Then he folded it and slipped it into the inner pocket of his jacket. Sometime soon he was going to have the responsibility of telling Vesper Ellis what had been done and why. He hoped he would, anyway.

McHargue, Porter, and two male uniformed cops went around to the rear door of the house. One of the cops produced a ring of keys, selected one and tried it on the lock, bent over and looked closely at the doorknob, selected another and tried it, then withdrew that one too. The third key opened the lock and he pushed the door inward, then stepped off the small porch while his partner went back around to the driveway and disappeared.

A minute later four crime scene people arrived, put on coveralls, covered their shoes with plastic booties, and pulled on gloves and head coverings, then stepped inside through the kitchen doorway. Through the open door, Warren saw flashlight beams sweeping the room, then disappearing as they went into the next room.

Warren waited. After only a couple minutes one of the crime scene people came out carrying the cell phone in a plastic evidence bag.

McHargue saw it and turned to Warren. "There's the phone, as the warrant specified. You might as well go. You'll hear from me."

9

He'd been sure that he'd needed to get Vesper Ellis's case into the hands of the police. He had to leave them alone now and trust that they'd do their jobs. There were still some things he could do that they wouldn't.

He drove to his condominium, opened his computer, and went to work. Vesper Ellis was clearly the victim of some embezzling. It was difficult to imagine how anyone could have drained her accounts without someone inside the corporation doing the work. The most likely person would be the one the company was paying to maintain and control her portfolio.

He began with Patrick Ollonsun. He was listed as the advisor for her account at Great Oceana Monetary Fund, the account from which withdrawals had been made at the request of George Ellis after his death.

Warren found a page called *About Us* on the Great Oceana website. Ollonsun's profile said he had graduated from Boston University nineteen years ago, which made him about forty-one years old. He had worked at two other well-known financial corporations before Great Oceana.

Warren collected all the incidentals—office address, phone numbers, home address on Mulholland Drive, posed picture, names of other people tagged in candid photographs. He went back to the Great Oceana site and identified a couple of those people. He went to their personal sites and found small bits of additional information—pictures of people in front of houses and cars, some labeled.

Vesper Ellis had told Warren that her husband had been the one who had selected and watched over their investments. Was it possible that Ollonsun didn't know that George had died? Since Vesper hadn't bothered to remove George's name from the account, Ollonsun might not have known he was dead right away, but George had now been dead for three years.

When Warren had exhausted the information in easily available sources, he moved on to the other advisor who was listed for an account with discrepancies, Ronald Talbert at Founding Fathers Vested. As he collected the same sorts of information about Talbert that he had for Ollonsun, he felt increasingly impatient.

Time was passing while he stared at a screen. He had no idea where Vesper Ellis was, or what that time was feeling like to her. She could be alone and afraid, locked in some basement, or undergoing some brutality to force her to sign permissions for her robbery, knowing that the robbers would have little choice but to kill her afterward. She could be dead already, and if she was alive, all Charlie's legal maneuvering might be too late.

He had to do things that had a chance of shortening the process of finding her. He called Tiffany Greene's number.

She said, "Charlie?"

"Hi, Tiffany," he said. "I'm sorry to bother you, but I had a question. Can you tell me what kind of car Vesper Ellis drives? Anything will help—new or old, big or small, color."

"She has a new white Mercedes C-300. It's a hybrid."

"Thanks, Tiffany," he said. "I really appreciate all your help."

"Have you found her car?"

"For now, I'm just trying to find out everything I can, and see if I can get in touch with her. When I do, I promise I'll tell her how concerned and helpful you've been. Thank you."

He went through his closet and his dresser, selected a black KN95 mask, a black baseball cap, black leather gloves, and a black hooded sweatshirt. He looked in a drawer in his closet island and retrieved a half dozen AirTag transponders from among his travel gear. Then he took the battery out of his phone and went out.

Patrick Ollonsun's house was in a gated development along Mulholland Drive. Warren had been inside the gate a few times to meet with clients who were in the midst of divorces or other legal issues. In each case he had used the excuse that he'd needed to have the client sign papers, but he had actually wanted to get a look at something in the house. He hadn't wanted a client lying about something like damage done during a fight, or the environment a custodial parent was maintaining for the children. The houses were all large and two-story, with attached garages, pools and pool houses, and hot tubs. Each was on one to two acres of land.

Whenever he had entered before, a client had called to tell the guards manning the gate he'd been invited. He didn't think that without the call the guards would let him in, and he didn't want to be on the photographic record of who had been admitted to the complex this evening. The false excuses for a visit he could think of didn't seem likely to work—that he was the attorney of one of the residents and was hand-delivering some papers he'd been working on, or that a client lived here but was in Europe and had asked him to pick up the mail and pay the bills. He couldn't think of anything that a guard would hear and simply open the gate for him without calling for verification of permission. He was going to have to sneak in.

He turned off the road onto the flat surface of a scenic overlook that provided a panoramic view of the San Fernando Valley. He locked his cell phone in the glove compartment and walked to the boundary of the complex, climbed the wall, and dropped to the ground inside. He hid in some nearby bushes for a few minutes until he was sure he hadn't triggered a silent alarm, and then walked toward Patrick Ollonsun's address. As he walked, he was reminded that these people not only had a lot of living space, they also seemed to have more cars than anybody needed. There were all multiple-car garages, and there was also, near the end of each driveway, a parking lot for visitors. Most had cars parked there.

It took him about ten minutes to walk to Patrick Ollonsun's house. There were lights on in windows all over the house, and other lights along the eaves. He made a slight detour to see the back of the house, where there were three cars, but none of them was Mrs. Ellis's white Mercedes C-300. He kept going past the lot to the rear of the property and found a dark, shadowed area by the pool house where he could crouch and study the place.

He'd known that the chance of Vesper Ellis's car being here was extremely unlikely, even if Ollonsun had something to do with her dis-appearance. Warren also knew that the car his two attackers had used had already been recovered by the police. He wasn't sure that he would recognize the men if he saw them again, but the house was certainly illuminated enough to make a sighting possible. The swimming pool was not lighted tonight, nor the pool house, so he was able to watch from where he was, and he stayed.

He watched the lighted windows, and every few minutes he would see somebody walk across a room. The first was a middle-aged woman, and his heart sped up for a half second, until she turned to the side and he saw the hair she wore pulled tight behind her head was blond. Vesper Ellis's hair was dark. The woman was also alone, something kidnappers could never allow. The next person he saw was a young girl with long blond hair, a T-shirt, and commercially shredded jeans. If their husband and father was a criminal, he certainly hadn't brought that part of his work home with him. It didn't make him seem innocent. All it did was strengthen the possibility that he was paying somebody to do the ugly stuff—somebody like the two men who had gone after Charlie Warren.

Warren went to the parking area behind the house to examine the cars. There was one that looked to him like the sort of car a financial services guy would drive to work. It was a black BMW 5 series that had been polished so well that it reflected a streetlamp about five hundred feet away. Warren reached in his pocket for one of the AirTags he'd bought about six months ago to keep track of his luggage on a trip to Europe. He lay on his back and wriggled under the side of the car near the back seat, reached up, and attached the AirTag to a brake line.

The second car was a red Lamborghini, not a car to use if a person wanted not to be noticed while he was doing something criminal, but he attached a second AirTag to it anyway. The third car was a staid white Prius. He attached one under that car too.

Warren went behind the pool house to climb the perimeter wall. He made it back to the outer fence of the complex in the same ten minutes the walk to the house had taken. He looked and listened until he was sure no car was coming and then scaled the tall fence and dropped to the outer side. He got into the rental car and drove.

He waited until he had descended to the flats and was miles away on Ventura Boulevard before he pulled over, replaced the battery of his phone, and looked at the screen. Detective McHargue had not called, and it was a few minutes past midnight. It meant that the cops had not opened some closet or looked under a bed and found Vesper Ellis's body. He had now abandoned the hope that she was somewhere pleasant, simply putting off returning his calls.

He took the battery out again and drove. He knew that the silence didn't mean that the police hadn't found anything at all. It didn't even mean they were still searching. He was aware that from here on they would only contact him if they thought he could contribute something they wanted. He was no longer going to be somebody they thought about much, and he didn't want to be. He wanted them to concentrate on Vesper Ellis. She had now been missing for about seventy-two hours.

He drove toward the address where Ronald Talbert, the advisor for Mrs. Ellis's Founding Fathers account, lived. When he found it, he was not surprised that the house was large. What surprised him was that this house, like the last one, was still lit at this hour. The Los Angeles finance people he'd known were usually in their offices by 9:30 A.M. Eastern time, when the New York markets opened. That was 6:30 A.M. Pacific time, and that meant that they had to be up and on the move by around 5:00 A.M. Pacific. That was less than five hours from now. He kept going until he was past the next curve and saw that there was a side street to the right, so he turned there and parked.

He moved to the sidewalk and walked to the edge of the property. The lights meant that someone in the house was probably awake. He hoped it also meant the alarm system hadn't yet been activated for the night. He stepped on the edge of the grass by a wall that had beside it a row of identical twelve-foot trees of the new variety that seemed to grow a foot a month and walked up the sloping lawn, then cut to the driveway. He moved slowly, staying close to the side of the house, ducking under each window he passed, up to the garage. He stayed at the corner of the garage and only leaned out an inch or two to look at the windows. He saw that the upper floor windows of the house were dark. As he looked in a side window on the first floor he could see through a rounded arch a large living room and, on the distant wall, a television screen, which he estimated at seven feet wide, displaying human shapes clothed in some fabric that resembled burlap running and jumping and twirling while swinging swords at each other.

This didn't necessarily mean everybody in the family was at home. Daddy might be driving Vesper Ellis's body to the desert tonight. Warren stepped in front of the garage door and looked in the row of small windows along the top. There were two nearly identical-looking black SUVs inside. There was no white Mercedes C-300. He also saw that there was a human-size door on the right side of the garage. He had guessed that if people were still awake, the alarm system for the house had not yet been engaged. The garage was not attached to the house, but that didn't mean it was on a separate circuit. Would anybody turn on the alarm for the garage but leave the rest of the alarm system off? He decided to take a chance that they hadn't. He went to the side door, tried the knob, and found it wouldn't turn.

Vesper Ellis's time could be running out, and this could be a way to find her before that happened. He looked at the ground near the door for a place where a key could be hidden—a fake, hollow stone sold for that purpose, a brick, or single real stone to hide the key under. He didn't find anything of the sort. He took out his wallet and began removing cards from it. He tried to push a credit card into the crack between the door and the jamb beside the knob, but the door was too tightly fitted.

He tried his library card. It fit, but it was too worn, and simply curled at the end when it reached the plunger. No card worked. He put his wallet away. He saw the row of trash bins near the back of the garage.

He decided the blue recycling bin would be the best place to start. He opened the top and tried to see what was inside. He found a tuna can that had been opened, but the lid was still attached by a very small bit of uncut metal. He took off his KN95 face mask, cradled the can's top in it, gripped the mask so it protected his hand from the sharp metal top, and inserted the top into the space beside the doorknob. He slid it up and down a bit, and then pushed, keeping his grip tight so it didn't slip. The can top went in, bent just enough to slide along the beveled plunger, and moved it out of the way. He leaned on the door and it swung inward.

He went inside. The only light in the garage came from the door he'd just opened and the row of small windows along the top of the garage door. He knelt beside the first car, reached up under it and attached an AirTag to a wire bundle under the hood, then attached one to the other car, and stood up. He didn't want to spend another minute at the Talbert house. He had been forcing himself to stay, each moment feeling increasingly risky and dangerous, and now he had done all he could expect to do. He stepped to the side door, went out, and closed it behind him. He left the can in the bin, moved past the house, and made the turn to cross the lawn. In a moment he was beside the wall lined with trees. As he started down the sloping lawn, the light in the house went dark. Someone would be arming the alarm system right now.

10

Warren sat at his kitchen table with his phone and pressed the *Find* icon to search for the AirTags he had attached to the five cars this evening. When he'd bought them for the trip to Paris six months ago he had named them C 1–3 for his bags and R 1–3 for his girlfriend's in his phone. As he looked at the displays on his screen, he remembered that the technology communicated with him using any iPhone within thirty feet of the tag. That would probably be fine in the daytime or when the driver was in the car, but right now the tags weren't transmitting.

Morning began when the phone rang. He grasped it, looked at the screen, and then answered, "Charles Warren."

"This is Doug McHargue. We found Mrs. Ellis's car at the airport."

"A white C-300 hybrid?"

"That's the one."

"Have you figured out who drove it there yet?"

"No. We have people going through the surveillance footage from the lot's cameras to see. Other people are looking through the recordings from the airport terminals and checking with the airlines in case she left it in the lot and got on a plane. They're also dusting the car for prints and swabbing for DNA. They'll put a rush on anything that makes it to the lab, but that's not magic. It takes time."

Warren said, "I don't think she drove it there. Do you?"

McHargue paused. "People do weird things all the time, cars get stolen, and people are harmed. I'll wait for which it was."

"I've been working on Mrs. Ellis's financial reports, and so far, I've found two local men I think have something to worry about in an audit."

"Can you send me an email with the two names and the simple version of what you know?"

"I'll do it right now."

"Thanks. I'll talk to you later." Warren showered and dressed, then sent the information. He gave Detective Sergeant McHargue the two men's names, home addresses, and the positions they held at the two companies. He attached to Patrick Ollonsun's section two pages of Vesper Ellis's reports from different months recording sales of stock shares and cash withdrawals that had been requested by the late George Ellis within the last year.

The attachments to Ronald Talbert's page showed sweeps of dividend and interest income that had produced cash. The cash had then been labeled as used for investments, but there were no new shares of anything, either then or on the next months' reports.

When he had breakfast earlier, he had checked his phone to track his AirTags. It was early, but two of the cars had already moved. One of Talbert's black SUVs carrying R1 had moved to one of the financial buildings in Century City, and one that was Ollonsun's C1 was on Olympic Boulevard. They were the two trackers he had identified as Patrick Ollonsun's and Ronald Talbert's personal cars.

Now, Warren opened the file again to see if any of the other cars had moved. One of the cars from the home of the Ollonsuns had gone southwest, looking as though it was headed for Malibu. He remembered looking in the windows from the dark shadow beside the pool house and seeing the daughter. He slightly revised his image of the Ollonsun family's day so it made sense to him. The father had driven the expected vehicle, the black BMW, to his office in Century City very early in the morning. It fit with his image as a vice president of a big investment company. The Lamborghini had seemed to Warren to be what the wife might drive to the Beverly Hills Hotel for lunch at the Polo Lounge or something like that; this AirTag showed the vehicle was heading for the ocean. He rechecked the identifying codes and verified that the car heading for the ocean was the white Prius. That had to be the daughter going to the beach.

The two black SUVs he'd bugged at the Talbert house were both out now. One of them was still at the investment company office in Century City and the other was just pulling up to park at the UCLA hospital in Westwood.

It was all pretty routine and normal, and told him nothing. He stood up to leave for the office when his cell phone rang. He looked at his screen and touched the green oval. "Warren."

"Hello. This is Vesper Ellis. I'm returning your calls."

Warren hesitated, and then realized he'd been holding his breath. "We've been thinking you—"

She interrupted. "I apologize. I haven't been able to call. I want you to hold off working on my embezzlement problem for the moment. I think it's only for a week or so."

She sounded unnatural. Maybe she was just scared, but Warren had to be sure it was really Vesper Ellis. All he could think of was, "What's your mother's maiden name?"

"Iolanthe Burness. Iolanthe, like the nymph. It means violet flower in Greek. All the women in my family were given special names."

"Are you in danger?"

"I'm alive and unhurt."

"If you're still in Los Angles say please."

"Please listen to what I've got to say."

The call went dead. He said, "Mrs. Ellis?" but he knew he was talking to nobody. He'd gone too far, and the kidnapper had been listening to her side of the call. But then he thought this was the moment when he had to verify the call. In a minute he would be calling the police, and they would need to know if it was Mrs. Ellis, or some other woman impersonating her because she was dead.

Warren set his cell phone down, plugged it into its charger, and used the house phone to call Tiffany Greene.

"Hello?" she said.

"Hi, Tiffany. This is Charlie Warren. I'm just checking again to see if you've heard from Vesper Ellis."

"No," she said. "I can't imagine what she's thinking. A simple phone call could save a lot of trouble."

"I know," he said. "I'm going to have to be able to get some more information from these companies directly. While I've got you, do you happen to know what her mother's maiden name was?"

"Why do you need that?"

"You know what she hired me for, right?"

"Yes. She thinks a couple of her financial advisors are robbing her."

"Right. I have the account numbers, but sometimes they ask for something that's not on paper. Usually that's the mother's maiden name."

"Her mother had a weird name too. Some kind of a family thing so when they were kids the other kids wouldn't give them some common nickname, and as adults people would remember them," Tiffany said.

"Let me think for a second. It began with an 'I.' Iolanthe. Vesper's maiden name was Rowan. Her mother's maiden name I don't think I ever heard."

"Well, thanks. That should help." Warren said. "We'll talk soon."

She hadn't had the whole name, but it was close enough to indicate that the caller really had been Vesper Ellis. He also knew that he had been too aggressive when Mrs. Ellis had called, and the kidnapper had detected the attempt to subvert his plan. Warren didn't move from his chair or set down the phone as he waited for her next call. It should come right away. This time he would not ask questions, just listen.

Warren waited, but the minutes passed and the call didn't come. Ten minutes seemed like a long time. When thirty minutes came, then an hour, he felt as though he had taken a blow to the center of his chest. It was hard to expand his lungs to take in enough air.

Had he just listened to her frightened voice and then confidently thrown away her only chance to live through this? The kidnappers clearly did not intend to get fooled by an ad-libbed code that told him her location. As time went by, he was increasingly aware that he hadn't told the police about her call. He had done what he was supposed to do so far, but maybe getting the police involved had been exactly the wrong thing to do. Things weren't supposed to work like this.

Every expert had always said that the families or friends of kidnap victims needed to turn their cases over to the police instantly. The police would know what worked, and they probably would call in the FBI, because kidnapping was also a federal offense. But here he was. He'd called the police right away, before he'd even known there had been a kidnapping, and after that he'd gone to great effort and risk to get the police interested in Mrs. Ellis's disappearance. Now that didn't seem to have been the right thing to do. What should he do next?

He had a feeling that he should wait for Mrs. Ellis or the kidnapper to call back. He waited nearly two and a half hours, and the call didn't come. He realized that as long as he had his cell phone he didn't have to wait in his condominium. He had been preparing to go to work when Vesper Ellis had called. He picked up his cell phone and went out the door.

Warren drove toward his office, and as he drove, he thought about crimes against the weak. He remembered the way he'd felt when he had seen the true extent and nature of Mack Stone's feelings toward his mother. Stone had devised ways to use her while also taking all her past and future savings so they could never be duplicated or recovered. He'd seen her as a resource to be fully exploited, like livestock. When the real estate broker had told Mack Stone her house wasn't something he could steal from her, Stone's impulse was not to just leave, but to punish her by burning the house down on his way out.

Now Warren couldn't help feeling the same rage about this kidnapping. People who did this captured a living person who had feelings and converted that person into money. The abductors threatened to kill that person unless they were given a certain sum of money, and even after they received the money, lots of them killed the victim anyway because it was easier and safer than letting them go. As he drove, his anger grew until he forced himself to calm down. He needed time to think.

He pulled into the underground lot, parked his rental car in a visitor space, got out, and was suddenly between two men in their fifties or possibly sixties. One of them was Black and the other white. They were both unusually fit, with slim bodies. They both wore dark, conservative suits and neckties in muted colors. Both men produced identical black identification wallets with their pictures, the words Special Agent, a gold badge, and FBI printed on them. As they held the identification up so he could see it, he also saw that they had shoulder holsters with pistols under their coats.

The Black agent said, "Mr. Warren?"

He said, "Yes."

"Special Agent Stamford and Special Agent Foltz. We would appreciate it if you could spare some time this morning for an interview about the disappearance of Mrs. Vesper Ellis."

"Of course," Warren said. "I'd be happy to tell you everything I know."

"The Bureau has set up a command-and-control post not far from the victim's neighborhood, where we're monitoring communications and doing our preliminary interviews. We'll take you over there and then drop you back here afterward."

They led him to a large sedan with little chrome or decoration, and he sat in the back seat. He looked at his watch. His call from Vesper Ellis had been hours ago. He was aware that he had better find an excuse for his silence about it.

Agent Stamford drove the car onto the 405 freeway and over the hill to the San Fernando Valley, then along a series of residential streets under big trees—sweet gum, Aleppo pine, camphor, magnolia—and Warren sensed he was getting closer to Vesper Ellis's house. Agent Stamford turned into the driveway of an unremarkable single-family house in Sherman Oaks. There was a red brick facade and white clapboards around, with an attached garage. Stamford opened the garage with a remote control, pulled all the way in, and lowered the door behind them.

The garage was practically empty. There were no tools, and no stored supplies on the shelves. He tried to get out of the car, but the door had been automatically locked, a safety feature to keep passengers in their places. Stamford touched a button on the driver's side, Warren's door clicked, and he let himself out. He was standing by a big sign on two sharpened stakes. He was pretty sure it must say *For Sale*, but it was facing the wall. He supposed the FBI must make arrangements with real estate companies to lease houses when they needed them on a temporary basis. He thought about asking, but these two didn't seem likely to want to engage in small talk about bureau procedures.

Foltz led the way, unlocked and opened the side door into the house, went through a mud room with empty coat hooks and into the kitchen. Warren could tell somebody had remodeled the kitchen and replaced the appliances and cabinets. When they reached the marble island in the middle, Stamford said, "Stop here."

Warren stopped.

Stamford said, "I'm afraid we're not allowed to let you enter a command post without being searched. Please put both hands flat on the counter."

Warren complied.

"This won't take long. Are you carrying anything that might compromise physical or electronic security of this building?"

"No."

Stamford reached into Warren's jacket pocket and extracted his cell phone.

"Is it necessary to take my phone?"

"It's not just a phone," Stamford said. "It's also a high-capacity recording device, a camera, a global positioning system, and a radio that can archive unlimited quantities of information in the Cloud."

Stamford said, "I need to pat you down and check your other pockets. You're not carrying a firearm or other weapon, correct?"

"Correct."

"Are you carrying anything that might injure my hands?"

"I've got a pocketknife in my right pants pocket, but it's closed."

Foltz removed Warren's car keys, wallet, and pocketknife and put them with the phone on the marble surface of the island. Stamford said, "They'll be here when you leave. When you do, I have to caution you not to turn on the phone again until you're back in your office."

The two guided him into the living room. "Have a seat on the couch."

Warren didn't like it much because the couch put him in a lower position than the two straight-backed chairs where they sat. The couch was soft and yielding, so he knew he couldn't get up easily.

Agent Stamford said, "Vesper Ellis is a client of yours, right?"

"Yes. She was referred to my firm by a friend of hers I had represented a few years ago. She believes someone is stealing money from some investment accounts of hers."

"Any other connection? Do you have a personal relationship, or are you dating her or anything?"

"Absolutely not. I never met her until a few days ago. As I said, she was—"

"We've cleared that up," Stamford said. "What we need to talk about is you."

"Sorry?" Warren said. "Me?" He felt a chill up his spine. Did they think he was the one who had kidnapped her? Did they know about her call?

"We have some information that we'd like to discuss with you," Agent Stamford said.

Agent Foltz said, "We'll start with what we know about you. In the summer when you were seventeen years old, your mother, Linda Warren Stone, was robbed by her second husband, who specialized in marrying rich women and walking off with their money. McKinley Stone was just what he was calling himself this time. On August 14, the day he realized he'd got as much money as he was going to get, he drove off in the BMW he'd bought with your mother's credit card. You followed him in a borrowed car to Route 50 in Nevada. Then you drove him off the road into a crash that killed him."

Warren was good at controlling his facial expressions to conceal what he was thinking or feeling, but this was like a sudden drop in the room's air supply.

"There was an article about you in the *Los Angeles Times* when you got your law degree and started practicing. Do you remember that?"

"That article didn't say or imply I ever drove anyone off a road."

"It said your widowed mother had been robbed by a con man, and that the culprit had died in a one-car crash, and that you were hoping to start a law practice that stood up for victims," Foltz said. "Just a coincidence?"

Agent Stamford said, "I want you to think back to the moments right after you ran McKinley Stone off the road into the ditch. You turned around and headed west, back toward California. You were going fast, so you had to swing a little wide on a curve. There was a big passenger bus coming the other way. You kept your head and didn't let the centrifugal force slam you into the front of the bus. Instead, you accelerated coming out of the turn and shot out of there, just missing the bus."

"I can't believe I'm listening to this stuff."

Agent Stamford said, "You don't have to deny anything or work out a plea or tell us anything. It's a free chance for you to learn what we know. While you were heading for the front of that bus, you may have noticed that the bus driver behind that big windshield was a Black man. A handsome Black man."

Warren's eyes widened.

"I think he gets it," Foltz said. He smiled, leaned forward toward Warren, studying him, and then spoke in a raspy whisper. "You're right, we're not FBI agents, dumbass."

11

C harlie Warren was silent. He had remembered the bus from the first moment when fake agent Stamford had mentioned it. The bus had been a regular feature of his dreams for the past seventeen years—half his life.

He crafted a slight smile and said, "Why drag me here? What do you want?"

Stamford said, "That morning I was driving a busload of fire-fighters who had been fighting a wildfire in California to the state prison at Ely. When you were coming at me, I saw your face. My friend here was also on the bus, and he saw you too. For the first few years it was hard for us to find out who you were. We did learn your mother's name.

"We were in prison, so we couldn't do much on our own. But there was a guy there who had gotten really good at preparing appeals cases for other inmates. He had been a lawyer somewhere before he killed his wife and her boyfriend, and he kept busy by researching these cases and filing them. We asked him if he had a way to do research on people on the outside. It turned out he did, because he had to locate witnesses, solicit their testimony, and so on."

Foltz said, "We had your mother's name. He found her and pulled all the public records about her—the deed to the house she owned, her two marriage licenses, your father's will, car registrations. And your name. We read the story about you in the *LA Times* online. You were twenty-six then, but you looked about the same, so we knew it was you. We had long sentences, and time can answer a lot of questions."

Warren said, "How did you know my mother's name, and why did you bother?"

Foltz said, "It started a few minutes after you went past us. Our bus was headed east, and we went right by the wrecked BMW. We stopped and backed up. The car's engine was still hot, and the driver was stuck in the wreck with the air bag holding him there. We dragged him out, but he was dead. The other guys all got back in the bus, but I hung back. I turned the engine off and used the keys to see what was in the trunk. There was a fancy leather bag with clothes and a little cash money, but the big thing was a manila envelope. I opened it, and it was full of papers, the kind that companies used to report on investment accounts. The current accounts were all in a man's name, but there were some withdrawal receipts that were from bank accounts in the names Linda Warren Stone and McKinley Stone, all cash. Stone wasn't the name of the man that was on all the big investment stuff. That was all I had time to read, because the bus was filling up and we all knew we had to get to a phone and call the police before they came across us. I left everything except the envelope. That I shoved down the front of my pants and covered with my shirt. When I got the chance and could talk to my friend here, I told him what I had."

Stamford said, "I stopped the bus at a restaurant and called the state police and told them who we were and that we'd found the wreck. We hid the envelope in a vent on the roof of the place."

"On the roof?"

Foltz said, "Yeah. So it would be safe."

"Years later I got out of prison, went back, and retrieved the papers. The envelope was greasy and sooty, but the papers inside were just fine. I waited for him to get out so we could do what we'd been planning for over fifteen years."

"What was that?"

"Get the money," Foltz said. "It was all in the name that wasn't McKinley Stone. The envelope had his real identification—license, birth certificate, social security card, all the stuff people collect. The picture was McKinley Stone. We hired a guy to do a version of them that had a few old pictures of me on them."

"Of course, it didn't work," Warren said. "It was subject to escheatment by the state."

"That's the word. Too much time had passed. All the banked money got confiscated by the states where the banks were, because they hadn't heard from the owner for so long."

"Legally it's not confiscated," said Warren, "just held. It also isn't your money, and never was. And by the way, it would be pretty unlikely that a man who never touched any of his accounts in seventeen years isn't dead, no matter whose picture is on his ID."

"So we thought of you," said Stamford. "What Stone took was your mother's money."

"That's right," Warren said.

"And we figured that since he had married her, he probably thought he could take the money without a legal problem, but then he ran out on her without getting a divorce. Since he died right after that, she's his legal heir. Right, Your Honor?"

"That's right," Warren said. "Even if he hadn't stolen it from her, whatever he had when he died goes to her in the absence of a will. That's how it works in California law."

"So now you know," said Stamford.

"Right," Warren said. "So now, I suppose you're going to tell me why I should help you take my mother's money."

Stamford said, "The short answer is that this guy was really smart. We figured out from the papers in his car that he must have converted every withdrawal from her accounts into cash, converted that into bank accounts, and then used those to invest in new accounts with new companies. No single company handled both a withdrawal and a new investment. No match there. The amount withdrawn never matched the next purchase. They never happened within months of each other, so that didn't match.

"The biggest thing is that the owner's name didn't match. McKinley Stone was an alias. At the end of the process, a man with a different name, social security number, license, and birth certificate, all of them real, opened a new account and invested some money. Nobody who looked for it found it. The reason is that nobody had the name. We have the name, and we have the papers."

Warren starred at the two men. "So, what do you want?"

"We've been researching you, following your life for years. You've grown into a successful lawyer who is known for finding hidden stashes of money for clients. We also personally saw you as a teenager right after you killed the man who conned and robbed your mother. We know you've got a pair of balls on you. You're somebody we want to be in business with."

Foltz said, "We give you the information necessary to go get your mother's money—the name, the identification, and all the papers. You and she get half the money. We get half. Simple."

"What? No threats or anything? Fifty-fifty is unheard of for thieves. 'Hands up. Give me half your money.' That just doesn't seem to happen much."

"What?" Foltz said. "You want to haggle?"

"Actually, I have no interest. Offering half means you intend to kill my mother and me and take it all."

"You must realize that we're not even asking you to do anything illegal. But if you're not on our side, we also can't just take you back to your office and let you go."

"The answer is still no," he said.

"Get up. We want to show you something."

They pulled the guns out of their shoulder holsters. Then each took one of Warren's arms and pulled him to his feet. Foltz led the way to the short hallway and stopped at a door, then knocked loudly, unlocked the door, knocked again, and called, "Coming in."

He pushed the door open. It was a bedroom with a single twin bed and plywood nailed over the windows. The light was turned on and there was a door to an attached bathroom. A woman came out of the bathroom carrying a hairbrush.

Warren said, "Mrs. Ellis. Are you hurt?"

She saw Warren and said, "Oh my God. You too?"

"Okay, you've seen her. Come on." Foltz pushed Warren toward the door.

Warren said to her, "Don't be afraid." He looked at the others. "Give me a couple minutes to talk to her alone." Stamford and Foltz went out, closed and relocked the door.

Warren whispered to her, "Go in the bathroom and lie in the tub with the door locked."

He stepped to the door and waited while she went into the bathroom. When she was inside, he stood just to the side of the door to the hallway. He called, "All right."

The door swung open and Foltz had one hand occupied with pulling the key out of the lock. Warren pivoted around the door, got his forearm under Foltz's chin and squeezed his neck in a chokehold, then swung him around so Foltz was between him and Stamford.

Stamford danced from side to side with his pistol, but Warren kept Foltz between them. Stamford was angry. "How did you let him do that?" Foltz's head was dragged back so he couldn't speak or look down. Warren tightened his grip.

Warren said, "Toss the gun or I break his neck."

Warren used the moment of distraction to snatch the gun out of Foltz's shoulder holster and pointed it in Stamford's direction. Stamford saw nothing he did was going to be in time to keep at least one of the two from being shot, so he dropped the gun.

Warren said, "Step away from it."

Stamford did, then said, "Now what?"

"Sit on the couch." As Stamford did, Warren pushed Foltz onto the couch with him. He aimed Foltz's pistol at them as he squatted to pick up Stamford's pistol.

Warren stood and held both pistols pointed downward. "I don't plan on killing you, which I've been tempted to do for a few minutes."

"What's stopping you?" Foltz said.

"After I thought about your pitch, I got curious. My mother and I could have used that money that my father had saved—for my college and law school, and a lot of other things. We both had to start all over again. She spent the first few years working two jobs and another on weekends. I've been working ever since. A lot of times I've wondered who Mack Stone really was. I would like to find out for her. There's also you. I know you've been planning to have that money for a long, long time. I also know you wouldn't be bothering me or my innocent client if you didn't need this. It's what keeps you going. So here's how this is going to work."

"Wait a minute," Foltz said. "Who put you in charge?"

"You did," Warren said. "I listened to you. Now you listen to me. After that, you get to talk again. I want Vesper Ellis. You're giving her to me, and you will give your word never to go near her again. In return, I'll do my best to keep you out of jail for taking her. You will stop saying I killed Mack Stone. I did, but we aren't going to get anywhere by incriminating each other. Agreed?'

Stamford said, "All right." Foltz was silent until Warren lifted the muzzle of one pistol about an inch. Then he said, "Agreed."

"When the time comes, you will give me all the papers and other information you have, including whatever you dug up on me and my family. If I persuade any state governments to give the money back or prevail in the court cases with the ones who resist, I will give you a fair cut."

"Who's to say what that is?" Stamford asked.

"The person most qualified to determine that is me," Warren said. "Not only am I trained in the law, but I'll be the one doing all the work, and the money is my mother's." He paused. "But I concede that the money would never have been found without your past dishonest efforts, and I'll be mindful of that. I give my word that you will receive part of the money. We'll call it a finder's fee or consulting fee or something like that. We'll report it to the IRS and you'll pay taxes on it. In fact, I'll have my firm do your taxes and file them. As of this afternoon you will not do anything that's against the law. You'll clean this house of all prints, remove the plywood, repair any other damage, and leave the property the way you found it. I advise you to do it fast, so the owner doesn't show up with the police."

"The owner is a bank," Foltz said. "We could probably stay here for years before they ever send anybody to look at it. When prices hit the right level, they sell them in bunches to other companies."

"Do it anyway," Warren said. "I noticed you did a great job of cleaning Vesper Ellis's house. The police didn't find any prints or even DNA. This time don't forget any phones."

"All right," Stamford said.

"One more thing," Warren said. "Foltz was the woman the LA criminal court building is named after. Stamford is the nice town in Connecticut you drive through right after you leave New York. What are your real names?"

"Alvin Copes," said the former Agent Stamford.

"Andrew Minkeagan," said the former Agent Foltz.

"Don't call me. Write down a phone number you never used to call me and I'll call you from a new, clean phone and give you that number. Clear?"

"Clear."

"Then let's go set Mrs. Ellis free."

12

Warren called out, "Mrs. Ellis? It's Charlie Warren again."

"Come in."

Warren said, "Get your stuff. I'm taking you home."

She immediately got her purse, threw into it whatever she had taken out during the past two days, and followed him across the living room and into the kitchen, where he reloaded his pockets with his belongings. He called an Uber and said, "Good timing. He'll be here in a minute. Come on."

They could see the car by the time they had walked down the driveway. They got in and the female driver said, "Fifty-six nine eight nine Wilshire?"

"That's right," he said.

The driver took them over Laurel Canyon to Crescent Heights to Wilshire and then to Warren's office, where they got into his rented car and drove out of the underground garage. He said, "I'm taking you to your house. We can talk on the way."

"What happened?" Vesper Ellis said. "How did you get them to let us out? Are the police coming?"

"It turns out this isn't what I was afraid it was," he said.

"What is it?" she said.

"You were not their intended victim. They only took you in case they needed leverage to negotiate with me."

"Are you saying they're not criminals?"

"No, they're criminals, all right. They served long sentences in a high-security prison. They were watching my office the day when you came to see me. When they saw you, they thought they'd found something to hold over me. You were attractive, well-dressed, and about my age, so they figured you might even be more than a client."

"Isn't that what kidnappers do? They abduct somebody that someone else will pay a ransom for?"

"This time there were no ransom demands, no death threats, or any of the things that people have nightmares about. It was a bad decision made by people who aren't very sophisticated."

"You sound like you're their lawyer."

"I'm your lawyer. I've just made an agreement with them that includes your immediate release and a permanent prohibition on any future contact with you."

"What did you get in return?"

"You, for starters. Also, they actually did have a business proposal for me. It would not begin until after your case is completed."

"What do you mean?"

"Your problem with your investment portfolio takes precedence over everything else. I've been trying to bring you up to date on it since the evening after you brought me the monthly reports. I've found the discrepancies you mentioned and a few more. I've started by freezing your banking and investment accounts so no more money disappears. I think the financial advisors assigned to two of your accounts have been embezzling. If you want to continue with my services, I'll take your case pro bono."

"Why?"

"Why what?"

"Why any of it? And why help me for free?"

"Because it's the right thing to do. I was the cause of your frightening experience—unknowingly, but still. One obvious move would be to withdraw from your case, but as I said, I've made progress and I think the best thing I can do for you isn't to abandon you. I've used my status as your attorney to freeze your investment accounts, and notified the two companies you'd been robbed. Next, we see what the companies want to do."

"I get that," she said. "Why help those two who grabbed me?"

"Partly because that was their price for you, and, secondarily, because they actually do have something to offer me. They have important information pertaining to my family that nobody else in the world has, including me."

"To keep them out of jail you'll need my silence, right?"

"Worse. I need to persuade the police that there was no kidnapping."

"You want me to lie." She studied him. "I think you should tell me why. You have to tell me more about what this information is."

"That's fair," he said. "About twenty years ago my mother, who was a widow, got married to a con man. He was calling himself McKinley Stone. Right away he started to siphon off money from the investments she and my father had made. He used all kinds of methods—taking cash advances on her credit cards, withdrawing money from stock portfolios, setting up monthly draws from accounts in her name into a joint checking account, borrowing money, and forging her signature. His last act was to set fire to the house and take off in the new BMW he'd bought with my mother's money."

"Wow," she said.

"He drove hard and made it to northern Nevada before he ran off Route 50 into a ditch and was killed."

"It sounds as though he deserved it."

"Maybe," Warren said. "The first people on the scene were a busload of prisoners who were returning to Nevada after fighting a big fire in California. They stopped and went to the wreck to see if the driver was alive, but he wasn't. One of them found an envelope full of receipts for withdrawals, deposits, and investments, and the dead man's identification."

"This isn't making me want to take a huge risk to keep them out of jail."

"My mother and her lawyers could never trace what McKinley Stone had done with her money. They learned McKinley Stone was an alias, but not the name he had used to deposit my mother's money. They never knew that name. But inside the envelope the convicts found were the man's real birth certificate, social security card, driver's license, and passport. The pictures were the face of McKinley Stone."

"So my kidnappers told you they have everything you need to get back the money he stole from your mother."

Warren nodded his head. "I believe they do."

"You're doing this for your mother?"

"It seems to be the last chance for me to fix this for her."

"The story is hard to believe. How do you know it's true?"

"They have to come up with the papers before I do anything. Either they have them or they don't."

She stared at him for a long moment, and then spoke. "When my husband died a few years ago, it destroyed me. I arranged his funeral, got through it, and then collapsed. I cried continuously for days, and some days I couldn't get out of bed but never really slept for more than a few minutes at a time. I went to the doctor, and he prescribed a sleep medicine and an antidepressant. I took them both and had a bad reaction."

"What kind of reaction?"

"I got in our car without really being awake. I was dreaming. I drove, and what had really happened got mixed up in the dream. He had been driving a couple home who'd had too much to drink, and I was waiting for his call to go pick him up. I think I thought I was driving to find him. I disappeared for two days—basically until the medicine wore off. They put me in the psych center at UCLA for observation. It was apparently just a drug interaction."

"Is this documented?"

"It's in my medical record at my doctor's office, and I'm sure UCLA must keep their own records, and my insurance company certainly wouldn't forget what it cost. The thing is, I still have the pills in their original bottles."

"You do?" he said. "Why?"

"There wasn't anything wrong with them that I know of if you don't take them together. I kept them in case I needed one or the other sometime." She looked at him. "But it means I can tell the police I made the same mistake when I got upset and depressed all over again after I found out the money George set aside for our future was being stolen. I blanked out and drove off."

"As I was listening, I realized how crazy this idea is. I'm sorry for putting you in this spot."

"I want to do it."

"Why?"

"I guess because I got to feel a little bit of what your mom went through, and I don't want to stand in the way of your getting everything back for her." She paused. "Maybe because you didn't just shrug it off when I was abducted. Or maybe because you said you still want to help me with my problem."

"If that drug interaction happened to you again today and you made it home, what would be the first thing you'd do?"

"I don't know," she said. "Yes, I do. I would call my friend Tiffany, because I know she's got to be worried sick. I had told her I'd call and let her know how the meeting with you went. That was three or four days ago."

"Okay. But first we'll have to do something else."

13

C harles Warren drove Vesper Ellis to the beach at the foot of State
Street in Santa Barbara and left her there. She took off her shoes
and walked along the beach toward Montecito, lay down on the sand,
got some of it in her clothes, and then walked back to the foot of State
Street and then to the train station about two blocks away. She bought
a ticket and took the approximately ninety-mile train ride from there
to the train station near the Burbank airport, and then took a taxi from
there to her house in Encino. When she got home, she left the sandy
clothes in the laundry basket and took a shower, dressed in comfortable
clothes, and used her house telephone to call Tiffany Greene. After that,
she called Charles Warren's cell phone. What she said was in the script
that Warren had written.

He answered, "Charles Warren."

"Mr. Warren, this is Vesper Ellis. I just checked my messages and
found your calls."

"Mrs. Ellis? I've been going crazy waiting for you to call. Are you all
right?"

"Well, yes. I think so, but I seem to have lost a couple of days."

"Lost them? What do you mean?"

"I woke up this morning lying on the beach in Santa Barbara. I didn't know where I was at first, but I got up and I walked a little, and found myself in sight of the harbor, and recognized it. I don't know how I got there. I still had my purse, wallet, and keys—thank God—but I must have lost my cell phone somewhere. I looked for my car, but I never found that either. I remembered the train station was just a block or two up from the beach. My husband and I used to take the train from LA once in a while and rent bikes. I took the train home."

"The kidnappers left you in Santa Barbara?"

"What kidnappers?"

"When you disappeared and nobody could reach you, we were sure you had been abducted."

"I don't know anything about that."

"I'm not really getting this. I had a completely different impression. Is it possible that someone gave you something? Put something in your drink?"

"I'm starting to think I know what happened," she said. "Since I noticed problems with my investments, I've been very upset and anxious. I couldn't sleep, and had to take some pills. The day I went to your office I took an antidepressant. That night I took another sleeping pill. I'm thinking I may have had an interaction between the medications. I had one right after my husband died, but I didn't think I'd taken enough of the sleeping pills to cause that again."

"Where are you now?"

"I'm at home."

"Stay there. I've got to call the police detective who's been running the search for you. And don't take any more medicine of any kind."

Warren ended the call. She had deviated from the script only a couple times, but what she'd said sounded genuine. He called Detective McHargue's number.

"Sergeant McHargue."

"Sergeant, this is Charles Warren," he said. "I've just had a call from Vesper Ellis. She's home, and she insists she was never kidnapped. She's been non compos mentis for days, apparently because of a prescription drug interaction. She took sleeping pills for multiple nights and then an antidepressant and woke up two days later on a beach in Santa Barbara. She made her way home by taking the train."

"Mr. Warren, I have an emergency call on another line. I'll call you back as soon as I can." McHargue hung up.

It was over an hour before McHargue called back. He said, "When you called, there was an officer heading for my door with the recording of Mrs. Ellis's call with you. I listened to it and so did two other detectives, including my captain."

"What did you think?"

"So far we all think it was a lot better than getting a ransom demand and then having to go see a body, which is how I was afraid this one might go." He paused. "We've got some officers on the way to her house to bring her in for an interview."

"I guess I jumped to the wrong conclusions after she disappeared, and my mind fitted everything else I learned into that story, so it's my fault."

McHargue said, "But you weren't wrong that something was off. You picked that up right away, and you were right to call."

"Right now, I'm embarrassed, but I'm mostly relieved that I was wrong. And there's a lot more to be relieved about. She was lucky nothing happened to her while she was wandering around in that state and ending up unconscious on a beach at night. Anything could have happened."

"True," McHargue said.

"Well, I guess I'll see you in a few minutes."

"You're coming to the station?"

"I'm the only lawyer she has, so it's my job."

Warren left for police headquarters as soon as the call ended. This was supposed to be an unthreatening police interview of a woman who had been assumed to be a crime victim, but had just revealed she wasn't. The cops were aware she was probably in a vulnerable mental and emotional state. But he knew that, because of the deception, this interview could easily turn into something else.

When he arrived at police headquarters, Vesper Ellis was already there. He was directed to an interview room where Detective McHargue was sitting with her.

McHargue looked up when he came in, and said, "Ah, Mr. Warren. Do we proceed or do we call it off?"

Warren said, "What do you think, Mrs. Ellis? Are you physically and mentally up to answering questions about your experience?"

"I'm okay," she said.

McHargue said, "Good. You've told Mr. Warren you don't remember any kidnappers. Does that mean that you weren't kidnapped, or you just don't know?"

She hesitated. "I don't remember anything about kidnappers. There are some other things I also don't remember—how I got from one place to another, why I wanted to, what happened to my car and my phone."

"When you dropped out of sight, police did a welfare check at your home, and your cell phone was seen through your dining room window. Since nobody who knew you thought that it was normal for you to leave without it, a search warrant was obtained and served to your attorney.

Your car had been found at the Los Angeles airport, so it was towed and searched for evidence of foul play."

"I'm so sorry to put everybody to so much trouble, and waste your time." To Warren, she seemed genuinely sorry.

Only a couple times did he advise his client that she didn't have to answer questions. Once was when McHargue asked her to explain the effect of the prescription drugs. This was the bit of information he and she most wanted on the record, and she looked good answering it. She said that she thought she must have had a bad drug interaction, because she'd had one years before with the same two prescriptions for antidepressants and sleeping pills. It had happened right after her husband died. She said she had been anxious and unable to sleep again last week when she'd discovered money had been disappearing from her investment accounts. The discovery had brought back some of the depression of losing her husband. The money that they'd saved and invested together felt like one of the last vestiges of him. She had been careful not to take as much medicine as she had years ago, but the reaction felt about the same.

McHargue said, "I know you must have thought you'd driven to Santa Barbara, but you couldn't have. Do you remember the trip now?"

"No."

"How did you get back?"

"I took the train."

"Do you remember the number, or the time, or anything?"

She lifted her purse from the floor and set it on the table in front of her. "I don't, really, but it should be on the ticket." She rummaged around in the purse for a few seconds. "Yes. Here it is." She held the ticket up and said, "It says—"

McHargue reached out. "Mind if I have a look?"

She handed it to him. He examined it and said, "Do you need it for anything?"

"I don't think so," she said. He put it into his notebook like a bookmark.

"And how about the two medicines you took?" he said. "Do you remember their names?"

"I always pronounce the names wrong, but you can read them off the bottles." She dug into the purse again and brought out two pill bottles, one of them clear brown plastic with a white childproof top and the other opaque white with a blue childproof top. Both had the same doctor's name and the same prescription date three years ago.

He examined them, read the labels out loud, made some notes on his notebook, and then used his phone to take a picture of each label, and unscrewed the tops to look inside, then handed them back. He looked at her and then at Warren. He watched Warren as he said, "Would you be willing to take a blood test?"

Warren said, "That isn't something you have to do."

"I suppose not, but shouldn't I? In case there's something wrong with the pills?" She looked at McHargue. Where do I go for that?"

"There's a phlebotomist on call for alcohol and drug tests. He'd come to you." He looked at Warren.

Warren said, "Mrs. Ellis isn't exhibiting any symptoms now, and it's been at least twenty-four hours. The drugs are probably out of her system." He said, "Mrs. Ellis, it's up to you."

"Let's do it," she said.

All three got up. Warren and Mrs. Ellis followed McHargue out and a female police officer went with her to have the test. Warren and McHargue went back to sit in the hard plastic chairs by the table, which was empty except for her purse. Warren was more aware than ever that the cameras high in the corners of the room were still running, recording nothing but a lawyer and a cop sitting in uncomfortable chairs.

About fifteen minutes later Vesper Ellis was returned to the interview room. Warren could see she wasn't irritated, scared, or sick, but she was clearly getting tired, and that was not a condition he wanted her in during a police interview. He said, "Detective McHargue, if you don't have any more questions for Mrs. Ellis that need to be answered tonight, I'd like to take her home."

McHargue said, "I think that's probably a good idea. Thank you for your cooperation, Mrs. Ellis." He stood and walked to the door to hold it open for them to leave.

They left the building and walked to the visitors' lot, and then got into his rental car. He started the engine and she looked in his direction. He held his index finger over his lips and immediately said, "You did a very good job of letting the police department know what really happened. I was a little worried that you might not feel well enough after your ordeal, but it was fine."

At first, she looked at him as though she thought he might be deranged, but then she seemed to realize he was talking to an unseen microphone that might not exist. He went on, "I know some of the details are still vague, and that there are periods that you don't remember well. But I've read that sometimes memories return and can sharpen and come into focus over time. If anything like that happens, you should let me or Detective McHargue know right away. Even if it's a small detail."

"I will," she said.

After a few minutes on the Hollywood Freeway he said, "I'm hungry. You must be too."

"Starving. You know what I'd really like? A hamburger."

They took the Ventura Boulevard exit and pulled into the driveway of In-N-Out and drove away with a big bag of food.

He drove her to her house, walked her inside, and went through the house to be sure it was still empty and safe. Then they went outside onto the patio and sat at one of the long tables to eat their hamburgers. He said, "Are you all right?"

"I'm tired," she said. "I figured they'd want to test my blood, so I took a quarter pill of each kind. It should be just enough for traces to show up."

"Are you sure that was a good idea?"

"I'm pretty sure it wasn't, but it's done. I assume what you were saying was because you were afraid your car was bugged?"

"Right. Sometimes when there's a kidnapping, they bug the phone that they think will get the ransom call. I don't think they bugged my rented car or your house, but they clearly bugged my cell phone. When they believe they're trying to save somebody's life, and they've got a bunch of warrants for searches and electronic surveillance, they might have bugged anything."

"Isn't what we say to each other under attorney-client privilege?"

"Yes. All it means is that it can't be used to prosecute you. But at this time, I think what they really want must be to be sure what's going on. That's what we want too. If they understand that you're not in danger, and you're not doing anything illegal or unethical, they'll leave us alone until we need them."

"Good. I'm exhausted, with everything that happened and the interview and the medicine. The food was great, but now things are catching up with me. I just hope I can calm down enough to sleep."

"If you'd like, I can stay until you wake up in the morning and you're sure the medicine is all out of your system."

"That's sweet of you, but—"

"It's the least I can do, after what you've done in the past day or so to clear things up."

She said, "You know, I think I'll take you up on that. There's a guest room upstairs near mine."

"I know," he said. "I was here when they searched your house."

"Come on, then."

As they were climbing the stairs to the bedrooms, she said, "The bed in the one on the right has the best mattress."

After she was settled in the master bedroom he made the rounds of the house, checked every lock, and studied the street and nearby yards for activity. Then he set his phone's alarm to wake him three times during the night so he could check again. He had not forgotten that Copes and Minkeagan had not stopped being professional criminals.

He didn't hear Vesper Ellis moving around until seven A.M. He got up, showered, dressed, and went downstairs. She had made him a breakfast of eggs Benedict that could have come from the restaurant of a good hotel and served it on a set of dishes in a modern pattern. He said, "This is wonderful, and it wasn't necessary."

Vesper Ellis shrugged. "I heard the shower and figured you'd be hungry. I used to entertain a lot, so my head is full of recipes I hardly ever use anymore. It was kind of fun to cook something nice again."

"It's great. Thank you. I hope you'll cater my disbarment party."

"It depends on how many friends you have. I don't want any big jobs."

◆

After breakfast he helped clean up and put the pans and dishes in the dishwasher, stripped the sheets off the bed in the guest room, then said,

"Quick question. Do you ever meet with the advisors who handle your accounts?"

"No. My husband did at least a couple times, but those accounts were started a few years ago, so I'm not even sure the advisors are still the same people. I've never seen any reason to ask for a meeting. They would call me about once a year and suggest it, but I sensed a sales pitch, and I was still busy running a small business and trying to hold on to my sanity."

"Not surprising," he said. "I'm going now. I'll be in touch, probably with other questions. If a day goes by when I don't call you, then call me. I want to be sure you're okay. And call me right away if any of those investment companies contact you." Then he added, "If you see either of the two kidnappers, even from a distance, call even faster."

"I will," she said.

"When you do, don't forget that both of our phones still might be tapped."

On his way to his condo building, he called his car dealer to have his bullet-damaged car towed to their shop for repairs. Next, he drove to the car rental agency to trade in his rental car, because his new associates Copes and Minkeagan had seen it. He replaced it with a black Honda. The car didn't look fancy, and it wasn't large, but it had good acceleration and maneuverability, and tinted side windows. He hated driving with tinted windows, but he liked not being easy to recognize. He stopped at an electronics store on the way to work and bought four burner phones with cash.

He was still at the office before ten. The first thing he did when he arrived was to check on the cars he had tracked with AirTags. The two cars that usually went to work at financial firms were parked where they usually were during business hours. The Lamborghini that was usually parked behind Patrick Ollonsun's house was on the road. At this moment it was moving along Route 1, heading north along the coast past Malibu.

The tags he had installed on the cars had been a sensible move when he had still thought one of these men had arranged to have their client kidnapped. It made less sense now that he believed they were nonviolent white-collar criminals engaged in long-term, gradual embezzling.

As he closed the laptop, he heard Martha's key slide into the lock and then turn. He remained seated behind his desk rather than startling her by standing up. Martha entered the office with Alan the dog, saw Warren, and said, "Good morning, Charlie. You're here! I was planning to get in touch with the police to find out where you were being held so we could consider bailing you out."

"Consider?"

"I might have had to save up. It could have taken weeks. I'd still have to get my hair done, get manicures, clothes, and so on. It all contributes to the tone of the office."

"I get it. I just didn't have anything to report until after hours. Next time I'll call and wake you up. If I do, answer the phone, because I really might need bail."

She stopped and stared at him. "You're serious. What's going on?"

"As of right now, Vesper Ellis is alive and free. There were no kidnappers. I just misunderstood, jumped to that conclusion, and involved the police. She still has the theft problem. Have we heard from the financial companies that hold her accounts yet?"

"Three have frozen her accounts and written to tell you so. Two have answered to say they can't do that without confirmation from Vesper Ellis that it's what she wants."

"Founding Fathers Vested and Great Oceana Monetary?"

"Correct."

"Thank you, Martha. When I get around to it, I'll ask Vesper to give them a call, or maybe even bring her to their headquarters."

"I thought you'd be in more of a hurry."

"I think that they've already placed a hold on any transactions. They know from my letter that they've got a problem, and therefore liability, and the obvious way to keep it from getting worse is to freeze Vesper Ellis's accounts. They might have strategic reasons not to let me know they did what I asked, but I'm betting they did it."

"Okay. I'm glad you didn't lose our new client. Congratulations." She went to the reception desk in the outer office, patted Alan's head, and started paying attention to her computer.

Warren closed his office door, then unwrapped, assembled, and charged all four of the burner phones. He picked one and dialed the number of Copes's phone. He was still afraid that Minkeagan's call might have been picked up on a tap, but Copes hadn't called him.

When Copes answered, Warren said, "I'm calling from a burner phone, and I've got two for you and your friend. Where do I go to get them to you?"

"You don't have to. We're less than a mile from your office. We'll drop by and get them now."

"Call me when you drive into the lot. Park near the elevator and wait. I'll be there soon," Warren said. He ended the call and went back to work.

When the next call came, he went down the hall to the elevator and pressed the down button. He arrived at the B level, and when the door slid open, Copes and Minkeagan stepped inside. He held the Close Door button, handed each of them a phone and charger, and said, "Use it to call me or each other. Nobody else. I set them to automatically dial. You're One, you're Two, I'm Three."

"What about the guns you took?" Minkeagan said.

"You agreed you won't break any more laws. It's illegal for you to possess firearms in this state, and they wouldn't help us claim the money."

Minkeagen's eyes seemed to turn icy, but Copes said quietly, "Let it go." But then Copes looked at Warren. "For now."

Warren pressed the button for six, and the elevator began to rise. "Throw away the phones you've been using." When it stopped, he pushed the B button and got out. "I'll call you when I'm ready to see the papers." The door closed again and the elevator containing the two men headed back down.

Martha looked up as he entered, and said, "Now are you going to tell me what's going on?"

"I'm going to try. I've told you the important part, which is that Vesper Ellis is alive and well. The main carryover problem is that I dragged the police in right away and persuaded them that it was a kidnapping. Now, among other things, I'm trying to keep the police on our side after I wasted their time and tested their trust and strained my credibility."

"That's all you're going to tell me?"

"If you know specifics, your legal situation will be drastically worse than it is now. Women's prisons are better than men's, but still no place that you want to be. I wouldn't be your friend if I were to drag you deeper into this."

"What gave you the idea you're my friend? I'm an employee."

"The employee thing is not a good defense. But let's move on to today's issues. We need to get back to work on Vesper Ellis's problems. What I think we need to do is get the paperwork ready to file the lawsuits against Great Oceana and Founding Fathers. We can fill in everything but the date. I'll write the body of each suit today. I'll include the specific withdrawals and transfers approved by her husband after he was dead, and the misstatements of values and prices and so on that I flagged in the monthly reports from both companies."

"What can I do?" she said.

"Look for anything in the reports that I missed. Remember the statute of limitations. There's no point in digging up any felony more than three years old, or misdemeanor more than one year old. We've already got enough to prove this wasn't some normal set of mistakes or a couple faulty procedures. It's a pattern of theft, but I don't want to miss any dramatic examples."

"Right. What about the other companies?"

"We've narrowed the problem down to two of the five companies, so we can just put the other three sets of reports in the safe and return them to her later." He paused. "Am I forgetting anything?"

"Not that I know of, except that as soon as you file suits against two big firms, there will be plenty of work to keep us busy."

"Right. So let's do as much as we can in advance. Conference adjourned."

By the end of the business day, the two lawsuits had taken something like their final form. Warren inserted statements in several appropriate places that the list of acts included in the suit was not exhaustive, and that it was the responsibility of the fiduciary entity to produce timely and accurate accounting for all investments.

When this stage was reached, it was already past working hours, and Martha had left. He was just preparing to follow when he heard the ring of the phone on Martha's desk. He looked at his phone and pressed the lighted button. "Charles Warren and associates," he said.

A woman's voice said, "I'm calling from Great Oceana Monetary Fund. Mr. Foshin, Vice President for Legal Matters, would like to meet with Mr. Warren." Warren prepared himself to enter the unreal back-and-forth that often happened with these calls.

"This is Charles Warren. When would Mr. Foshin like to meet?"

"If possible, sometime tomorrow, or if that's too soon, the next day."

"I have an opening at ten."

"Oh, I'm afraid ten is already taken for a meeting."

"That's too bad."

"This is something that was arranged long before he received your correspondence. There are twenty attorneys attending, and some of them are flying in from our offices in London, New York, Chicago, Hong Kong, Bangkok."

Warren had known how big Great Oceana was before he'd ever heard of Vesper Ellis. The fact that the woman was trying to use this intimidation tactic made him realize he had struck a nerve. Warren said, "Okay. Why don't you give me some times when Mr. Foshin can come to our office?"

She was taken aback. "I . . ." She paused. "Let me look." She went silent again as though she were looking at a schedule. "That meeting is expected to keep him busy until one, and he's got to make a plane at four, meaning his driver will have to pick him up here at two, the way the airport has been." She was about to make the case for Warren going to their giant offices, where they would have a chance to surround and overwhelm him with a mob of lawyers.

"Well, okay then," Warren said. "I guess maybe we'll have better luck another day, possibly after the lawsuit has been filed and the Great Oceana legal staff has had a chance to go over it. He might prefer that."

"I'm not able to comment about substantive legal matters. Let me just check with him. Do you mind being on hold while I do that?"

"You can call me back. I won't be leaving the office for ten minutes or so." He hung up. It wouldn't be ten minutes. He estimated five. It was three. "Hello?" he said.

"Mr. Warren?"

"Yes."

"Mr. Foshin asked me to convey his sincere apologies for the incon-venience, and to ask you if you would please come to the Great Oceana Monetary Offices at one tomorrow. That would be a full hour before he has to leave."

Warren was tempted to say he was too busy to do it, but he had made his point. There was no question that Foshin had either been listening to the call or a recording of it. He also had calculated that this was not the stage in the process when he should enrage the opposing attorney. "I can arrange to make it," he said. "You can tell him I'll see him at one."

Things had gone as he had planned. A complaint sent in from a client about her account would usually be stuck in the office of her financial advisor, probably forever. A letter from her lawyer who made no secret that he was preparing a lawsuit had kicked the matter straight to Legal.

He used his desk computer to let Martha know that he had a one o'clock appointment at Great Oceana's offices, saved the drafts of the two lawsuits, and put on his coat, then placed the burner phone he had programmed as Number 3 into his pocket, locked the office, and took the elevator down to the level where he had parked the rented black Honda. He began to anticipate the traps that could be laid for him—to make it appear that he was offering a chance for the company to buy his assurance that this case was not going to the police, or that his pur-pose was extortion. As he drove toward his condominium building, his phone rang.

"Hello?" He was wondering which it was: Detective McHargue, one of the two old convicts, or the lady from Great Oceana calling his cell phone just to let him notice that the giant conglomerate could get the number.

"Charlie, this is Vesper." Somehow the level of familiarity seemed to have ticked up, he thought. She had the right. She'd spent hours lying for him to the worst possible audience, police detectives. She said, "Where are you?"

"In the car, driving home."

"Would you mind stopping at my house? I think I need to talk to you."

She had remembered that his phone had been tapped, and so had hers, and neither had been told that the taps were gone yet.

"I'll be right over."

"Thanks."

When he arrived in her neighborhood, Warren took a slight detour to circle two blocks away from the Ellis house. At each corner he stopped and looked up the street to see if there was anything odd going on. He hoped that Copes and Minkeagan had not broken their agreement to stay away from her.

He had thought they would be smart enough to keep their word, but hadn't forgotten they were criminals. He had looked up their trial records in the Nevada criminal justice system. Minkeagan had been convicted of a string of armed robberies, which was bad, but Warren had noticed that the prosecutors had thrown in a lot of things that were incidental to those crimes—car thefts, firearm infractions, assaults, and so on. It had the look of a law enforcement system that was pretty sure the things he hadn't been caught at were serious enough, so they'd wanted to keep him locked up forever. Copes had been the leader of a crew that had been captured in a warehouse he'd owned that was full of loot from hijackings and burglaries, including two in which a person had been killed. They hadn't been able to prove he had been involved in any of the acts of violence, but he'd still gotten a long sentence.

He thought about Vesper. She was unusual, a person who'd had money disappear from her accounts at big financial institutions and gone to a lawyer about it instead of first wasting a year going through the Byzantine procedures for "disputed statements" while time ticked toward the statute of limitations deadline, when her rights would disappear. By now, not only the institutional hierarchies of two companies, but the people they paid to keep things like this from happening, knew she'd caught them.

He moved in a block closer and only made it to the first stop at Vesper Ellis's street. There was a man sitting in a sedan on the opposite side of the street from her house, where he could face away from it and watch it in his rearview mirror. Near the other end of the block was another man in a car parked on the same side of the street as the Ellis house, also able to watch the house in his mirrors.

Were these cops doing surveillance on Vesper? Were they private detectives working for one of the financial companies he had threatened to sue in her name? He'd hired detectives for suits himself a few times.

To these thoughts were added the question of whether the phone call from the Vice President at Great Oceana had been a genuine attempt to head off trouble by a having a frank and open discussion with a possible plaintiff's attorney right away. It might have been simply a ploy to be sure that they were tying up her attorney so they could get her to accept a low settlement.

He kept going around the block, parked, and then looked at his phone. The sun was nearly down. He had worked late, and he'd stayed even later for the idiotic phone call from Great Oceana. Driving into the Valley had taken time. The weather app said that sunset tonight was 8:11. It would be dark soon. He sent a text message to Vesper, "Slight delay. I'll be at your back door in fifteen minutes."

Warren waited until the sky was dark, and then walked around the corner to the side wall of her yard, where he could not be seen from the street in front of her house, walked across the back lawn to her door, and knocked. She opened the door immediately, he stepped in beside her, and she closed the door and slipped the dead bolt.

"Hi," he said. "Have you noticed the two guys in cars at the ends of the block?"

"That was what I wanted to talk about, but I didn't think it was smart to do it on our phones. Who do you think they are?"

"I guess the most likely theory is that they're police officers. If they're not, my next guess is that they're private security people hired by Great Oceana Monetary Fund."

"Why?"

"I got a call an hour ago from a woman arranging a meeting with me for her boss, the head of their legal division. It might mean they're checking you out in preparation for a lawsuit, or leverage tactics."

"What are those?"

"To make you an offer that just amounts to giving you back your own money immediately in return for signing a nondisclosure agreement, a promise never to sue them, and so on. But you have to sign right away or they'll be forced to file countersuits and bad-mouth you to the credit bureaus, and on and on."

"Would the company really do that?"

"Threaten you? If they thought it would work, sure. Would they go through with whatever they threatened? Almost certainly not. They have too much to lose if they got caught at it and it hit the news organizations or the SEC or the FBI. I assure you, I would do everything in my power to make sure all of them would hear all about it. But those two men could be anybody."

"What should I do?"

"What I recommend is that you pack a bag, leave some lights and a television on timers, and activate your alarm system as you go out the back door with me. We'll sneak through your neighbor's yard to my car, and you can spend the night at my place."

"Is that necessary?"

"I don't know," he said. "If they've come to do you harm, yes. If not, it's just a brief change of scene. It's pretty peaceful. I don't live in a fraternity house or above a bar. It's a three-bedroom condo on the second floor of a very secure building."

"Can you give me a few minutes? I have to make some decisions about what to take."

"Of course."

Vesper disappeared up the stairs and Warren went to the front window and moved the curtain a quarter inch to look at the street. The two cars were still there. As he looked at the one near the right corner, another car pulled up behind that one, and as it did, the newcomer's headlights illuminated the reflective license plate for a moment before the driver turned them off. The car that had been parked turned on its lights and pulled away.

Warren looked to the left corner. As he'd expected, he heard another engine sound and he caught the sight of another car arriving and the one he'd been watching pulling away.

A minute later he watched Vesper coming down the stairs with the strap of a leather bag on her shoulder. "What were you doing?"

He said, "Watching the changing of the guard. The two who were here when I arrived were just relieved by two others."

"You never stop, do you?"

"If you think somebody's watching you, it's always a good idea to watch them too. I don't think these people are police."

She set down the bag, went to the living room, and plugged a timer into the wall outlet, set the on and off times, plugged the television into it, and used the remote control to turn it on to a 24-hour cable news station. She set the living room lamp timer to remain on for the evening and switch off ten minutes after the television at 12:40 A.M. and turn on at 6:10 P.M.

He stepped toward the stairs, but she said, "I already set the bedroom and bathroom ones."

"Then you're ready to go?"

"Yes."

He picked up her bag, walked to the back door, and waited. She punched in the code on the alarm control panel to arm the system, they stepped out, and she locked the back door with a key. They walked into the darkest part of her backyard, in the shadows under the tall oak trees, and stopped at the back wall.

Warren squatted and held his hands at knee-level with the fingers laced. She stepped into his hands, straightened her leg as he stood, and pushed down with her arms to help lift herself up onto the top. She sat on the wall, swung her legs to the other side, and then turned her body and lowered herself to the neighbor's lawn.

Warren set her overnight bag on the top of the wall and she took it. He hoisted himself to the top of the wall, went over, and joined her. He took her bag and they walked quietly along the side of the neighbor's house to the front lawn. His car was fifty yards up the street where the neighbor wouldn't see it. They walked there and got in. "You're so good at that," she said.

"Maybe if I don't succeed in getting your money back, we'll give burglary a try," he said. They hurried down the street to his rental car, got in, and drove off. After he had gone a few blocks, checking his mirrors every few seconds, he said, "Are you hungry?"

"Sort of. Nothing urgent."

"Have you been to Honfleur?"

"The French town?"

"The restaurant."

"No," she said. "And I really don't feel in the mood for spending two hours in a fancy restaurant. I feel like hiding."

"That's the plan. But stopping there on our way to my place takes about the same time as it does for them to pack a take-out order."

"That sounds better."

He put his phone on speaker so he could drive while they ordered. When they reached the restaurant, he left the car running while he hurried inside and came back with a large brown bag. He put it on the floor behind his seat and drove on. It took a much shorter time to reach his building. He pulled into the gated lot, and they were inside his condominium in another minute.

He set the bag on the kitchen counter, and Vesper Ellis stepped closer to it. "I've been smelling this in the car and it was making me hungry."

"The food has been fine when I've been there." He washed his hands at the sink and began to bring out silverware and plates and glasses.

"That's comforting. You have a pretty pleasant lifestyle."

"If you knew the truth, you'd feel sorry for me. Being a lawyer is spending your days in an office writing that horrible legalese that everybody else complains about and then driving home to spend your evenings finishing the work you couldn't during the day. The rest of the time you argue or plan to argue."

She stepped in and began to help him bring plates, silverware, and glasses to the table. They worked smoothly and easily together, so in a few minutes the dining room table was set and they were opening the bag to serve the dinner they'd brought.

She said, "This is such an odd contrast. The past few days are some of the most frightening in my life. Realizing I've been robbed, then being kidnapped, then saved, then being interrogated by the police, and now having suspicious men watching my house."

"I know it's been bad," he said. "But all you need to do now is to be safe and not be available to people who might wish you harm. I've frozen all your investment accounts, so nothing is being stolen right now. By tomorrow afternoon we should have a better idea of how the Great Oceana Corporation intends to handle the situation they're in. If it's satisfactory, we'll get it in writing and concentrate on Founding Fathers."

"You make it sound so clear and simple," she said.

"It usually is if you can prove you're the victim of a crime," he said. "That's the advantage of living in a country governed by laws."

"No argument there," she said. "But what I learned in this is that while we're waiting for that process to take effect, anything can happen, and a lot did. There wasn't anything I could do about it."

"I know that's a terrible feeling," he said, "but we'll just stay alert, try to bring the law to bear as fast as we can, and hold on."

They finished their dinner and cleared the table. He picked up her overnight bag and led her into a hallway and past a row of doors. "This is the main bathroom. There's also a private one off each of the bedrooms. These two doors on the right are the two guest suites. You can pick the one with a color you like or that has the best bed or feng shui or view or whatever. This door on the other side is my office, and beyond it is my room."

"You choose."

He went to the second room, opened the door, and turned on the light.

"This one looks great." She reached for her bag, but he stepped forward with it and set it on the bed. "But I'm curious. Why did you pick this room?"

"Somebody looking for you would go to the closest bedroom first, and this way we might hear him go in. And this room is closer to my room, so I'd be able to help you if I had to. There are towels and the usual sorts of toiletries and things in the bathroom, if you forgot anything. I'll be working at the kitchen table for a while, so don't hesitate if you want a snack or anything."

"Thanks," she said. "It's been a tiring few days. I think I'll take a bath and try out the mattress."

"Okay. Sleep tight." He went to the table where his laptop was lying, took off his sport coat, and hung it on one of the chairs with the shoulders fitted over the chair's back.

Vesper turned and went back to the bedroom suite he had chosen for her and closed the door. She sat on the bed and let her mind work its way through the few days since the moment when she had opened her car door near Charles Warren's office and the two old kidnappers had pushed her in and then climbed in after her. There had been days of contemplating her death in the boarded-up room where she was being held. Then the door had swung open and the person she saw standing there was Charlie Warren.

From that moment on, the terrifying predicament she had been in had changed into something entirely unexpected and surreal. Within hours, she had been drawn into inventing, presenting, and providing evidence for a giant lie to the police. It felt like a dream. Not only was everybody else acting on motives that were brand new, but she was doing things to help them that she had never believed she would do.

She had read that people in very stressful situations were sometimes prone to mental states that seemed to outsiders like temporary insanity—identifying with their captors, even joining them, or having complete changes in their personalities. She felt sorry for them. They'd seen their normal protections to be mere assumptions that they wouldn't be harmed, not actual barriers to harm. A small voice deep in their brains suddenly grew loud. "This isn't working, really never worked, and wasn't real. I've got to do something else."

Vesper's shock seemed to shake loose some things she had become attached to. She had been mourning her husband George for too long. On the afternoon when Charlie Warren had come to free her, a lot of facts had suddenly become visible to her, and one of them was the realization that she was thirty-six without ever having been thirty-three, thirty-four, or thirty-five. This was a lot to take in at once.

She began to unpack, taking each article of clothing out and hanging it up in the closet so it wouldn't wrinkle, taking toiletries into the bathroom and arranging them in their usual order on the counter, taking her shoes out and setting them on the floor, socks and stockings and underwear in the top two drawers of the dresser. She reached into the bag for sleepwear to lay out on the bed to put on after her bath, a pair of charcoal gray flannel pajama pants and a blue pullover football shirt.

14

Charlie heard the sound of bath water running in Vesper Ellis's suite, so he knew he was alone. He had not paid much attention to the movements of Patrick Ollonsun and Ronald Talbert since he had learned that they weren't the ones who had kidnapped Vesper. He took out his phone to track the AirTags he had attached to their cars. He began with Talbert's two black SUVs. He saw that one of them was in the garage on Valley Vista. The other was somewhere else.

It was on Mulholland Drive. The car was in the gated enclave where Patrick Ollonsun lived. He switched to the Ollonsun cars.

There they were—the small white Prius, the Lamborghini, the black sedan, all parked in the area behind the house. And right beside them was the black SUV that belonged to Ronald Talbert. Warren could hardly believe it. Several days ago, he had been trying to track two people he suspected of committing crimes against Vesper Ellis, but he had never given a minute's thought to the idea that he would ever find them in the same place on a Monday night. Ollonsun worked for Great Oceana Monetary and Talbert worked for Founding Fathers Vested. They were competitors. Ollonsun was a few years older and seemed to be richer than Talbert. All they had in common was working in financial services.

He had read their official biographies posted on their companies' websites and on LinkedIn. They had never worked in jobs at the same company. They had never gone to the same school or college or grown up in the same city. What the hell were they doing together? Was it to make some kind of joint response to Warren's meeting with the legal staff of Great Oceana tomorrow?

Warren stood up and went down the hall toward the bedrooms. He went into his room and began to change. He took off his business clothes and put on black jeans, a blue hoodie, a black baseball cap with no logo, and running shoes. He put a black KN95 face mask into his pocket, and then took another one in case the elastic snapped, and put black gloves in the pockets of his hoodie. He went to the door of Vesper Ellis's room and knocked.

He heard Vesper's voice. "Hello?"

"Vesper, I'm sorry, but I've got to go out for a while. You're perfectly safe here, but if anything happens, call me and I'll answer and come right away. And there's always nine-one-one."

"Wait," she said. "Come in and talk to me for a second."

"Okay to come in now?"

"Yes."

She was in the doorway of her bathroom with a towel around her and half hiding behind the door. "What happened?"

"I just learned that the two advisors from different companies who have been ripping you off are together right now at the home of one of them. I've got to go there and see if I can figure out what they're doing."

"Come back and tell me. I'll be up."

He went out and closed her door, and she heard his heavy footsteps hurrying down the hall, and then silence.

Warren was driving out of the building's garage, looking for any cars that might be on his block doing surveillance on him. This was a street with high-rent apartments and high-priced condominiums. There were more parking spaces than cars left out at night, so they would have been easy to spot now that he'd seen the strategy at Vesper's house. There were none.

He drove toward Mulholland without using a driving-directions app. He had taken the battery out of his regular phone, and kept the burner phone off to keep the GPS function dead. He had driven to Ollonsun's house the night he had planted the AirTags, so he was sure he knew the best way there. It bothered him that he'd told Vesper she could call him, and had now disabled his phones, but he just had to hope she didn't need him in a hurry.

When he reached the viewpoint lot surrounded by boulders where he had parked on his last visit, he maneuvered his rental car to a spot near the crest on the outer edge of the lot, where the headlights of cars passing on Mulholland Drive wouldn't sweep across it on the curve and light it up. It was only a little after nine o'clock, too early for the police to get curious about it if they noticed it. He got out and began to jog, as a self-explanatory reason to be here on foot, and ran directly to the spot along the chain-link fence where he'd climbed in before. He put on his mask and gloves and climbed. He was more sure-footed this time than the first time and didn't pause. As soon as he was on the ground, he headed for the Ollonsun house. He took quick strides along the sidewalk until he could see the house coming up, and then looked in every direction to be sure nobody was in sight or coming toward him in a car, then veered to his right and faded into the shadowy area in the broad spaces between the big houses that sat far back on acre-size lots.

He went to the backyard of the Ollonsun house. It was not anything like what he had been expecting. This was not the dark, tightly closed spot he had visited the first time. The outdoor lights at the rear of house were on, and a long picnic table was beneath them. He could see a large stainless steel propane stove was open, he could smell a smoke-and-meat aroma, and he could see the remains of a feast on the table—dishes and bowls, crumpled napkins, empty glasses and bottles.

The pool's underwater lights glowed and the gentle swells on its surface threw a dappled light on the trunks of the trees along the back fence. There were four kids around the table laughing and talking—a boy about ten with very short light hair, and three girls. All four were wearing T-shirts, shorts, and flip-flops. The girls all had their long, wet hair combed out into strings. One was the old-enough-to-drive teenaged girl with blond hair he'd seen on his last visit. There was another, younger girl with dark hair, and a still-younger girl with similar features. It was clear that the swimming part of the day was over, and so was the dinner.

As Warren watched, adults appeared from the kitchen doorway. A man he recognized from the Great Oceana website as Patrick Ollonsun, forty-one with a golf tan and a receding hairline, came first, and then there was a man who looked a bit younger with longer, thicker hair. He was looking down as he descended the steps, so Warren wasn't positive at first, but when the man reached the bottom, he looked up, and Warren was sure he was Ronald Talbert. They came out to the table and began to pick up plates and collect the trash into a black trash bag. After a little cajoling from the men, the four kids got up and started to help clear the table. He heard Ollonsun call out, "Zelda, help the younger kids with the dishes." The older girl went to the top of the steps, leaned down, and said something to the younger kids, and they formed a chain, passing bowls and glasses from one to the other until they reached her in the doorway.

Warren hadn't been prepared for this display of domestic harmony and happiness, and it made him uncomfortable to think that he had already sent to the men's employers the evidence that could end their careers, and maybe send them to prison.

He watched the single file line of Talbert and Ollonsun children climb the steps with the last of the bowls and disappear into the kitchen. He saw that Patrick Ollonsun had not headed into the kitchen. He was bent over tying the top of the black trash bag. In a moment he would be heading toward the back corner of the yard, to the enclosure that held the refuse cans and Charlie Warren.

Warren ducked around to the back of the pool house and pressed his back against the wall. He heard Ollonsun coming. There was a slight rhythmic sound of cans clinking together as he walked. Then there was the top of the plastic trash can opening and then falling down to clap into place, and the sound of Ollonsun walking back to the house.

Warren ventured to the far side of the pool house and crouched in the shadows. He watched the kitchen door swing open again, and saw the blond woman he'd seen on his first visit come out onto the steps carrying a tray that held a bottle and four glasses. He assumed she was Ollonsun's wife and the mother of the blond teenager.

The door opened again and another adult woman came out carrying a transparent bucket, glass or plastic he couldn't tell, full of ice cubes. She had blond hair, nearly the same style and color as the first woman's. He studied her face, the shape and movement of her body as she went down the steps.

Warren moved to the back wall. He had to use the time while the four adults were concentrating on negotiating the back steps and choosing seats at the conversation pit to hoist himself up and over. Then he headed along the border wall separating Ollonsun's yard and the neighbor's yard to the street. He jogged to Mulholland, climbed the chain-link fence, and jogged up the road to the small lot overlooking the city where he had left his rental car.

He drove to his condominium building, watching for any indication that he might be followed, then drove around the block to make sure, and pulled into the garage and left the car in his space. He hurried up the steps into the lobby, up the stairway to his condominium, and went in. He saw Vesper dressed in gray pajama pants and a blue shirt, with her feet curled under her. He had forgotten she'd said she would wait up for him. She stood and followed him at a distance while he tossed his baseball cap and hoodie on a chair and went toward his computer on the kitchen table.

He said, "They're sisters."

"Who are sisters?"

"I'm pretty sure they are, anyway. The wives of Patrick Ollonsun and Ronald Talbert." He opened his laptop and began typing. He had tried the social media sites at the start of this case and found nothing personal about those two. Their stuff was all business, mostly ads for their companies.

Vesper said, "I found some herb tea in your cupboard. It's pretty good."

He seemed to be pulled back from a distance. "Yeah, somebody left it."

"Can I pour you some? It says it won't keep us awake, and there's still hot water in the kettle."

"Uh, sure. Thanks." His attention went back to the computer.

Vesper heated the kettle some more while she found him a cup and saucer. She poured the tea, then watched him working, staring at the screen and clicking on things.

Warren googled the name Zelda Ollonsun. There she was, at the beach, then outside a high school that had a lot of eucalyptus trees and a big athletic field, then at some other house with friends of both sexes. Those were tagged with the names of the kids, which meant nothing to Warren.

There were summer vacation pictures. Zelda was standing with the ten-year-old boy and her father in some European city with narrow cobbled streets. There was a second picture with her mother, and he could see the distinctive inlaid stone wall pattern of the cathedral in Florence. The next one was on a mountain trail, with other mountains as a backdrop for her and her mother and the other blond woman he had seen tonight and the boy—the four blond people. It was tagged "Me, Mom, Aunt Fran, and Cousin Geoff." He found a close-up of the two women sitting on a bench by a river. He turned his laptop around on the table and said, "Look at this."

Vesper stepped closer and leaned down to look at the screen. "Those are the wives? They're pretty."

He leaned in and looked at the picture again, as though to evaluate her statement. "I'll grant them that. The point I was interested in is the family connection. It might explain why two men in different companies have been ripping off the same client." He went back to the four-shot.

"Oh no. Kids? Both couples have kids?"

"And there are two more. I saw them when I was sneaking around the Ollonsun house tonight."

"I can't help feeling bad for them."

"It's not in our power to send anybody to prison. At most we'll be filing civil suits against the companies. It's hard to say what any criminal prosecutors might do, if there are any."

"It was gutsy of you to go out there to find out all this tonight. Thank you, Charlie." She leaned close and hugged him.

He was surprised, but he remained still while the hug lasted. Then he stood, went to the counter, and took the tea she had made. "Thanks for this—"

"I'm sorry," she said. "I didn't mean to freak you out just now."

"You didn't. I'm sorry if I gave you that impression. It's just that attorneys aren't supposed to step across certain lines with clients. I know you weren't thinking about that, but I'm the one who has the ethical responsibility, according to the bar association."

"Well, I was going to go to bed over an hour ago, so I'll do that now and let you get back to work." She turned and walked into the hall toward her room. He watched her fade into the dark end of the hall and close the door behind her. He couldn't tell her the part that mattered, which was that her hug had felt better to him than it was supposed to.

15

P atrick Ollonsun held up his crystal whisky glass and looked at the patio light through the amber single-malt scotch. He loved the glow, the strong natural scent that seemed to strengthen in the still summer air as he swirled it around in the glass, the solid feel of the glass itself, the thick bottom adding weight in his hand. "Cheers." He took a sip and savored the liquor flowing along the top of his tongue, just enough of it to warm it and then stream into his throat. He leaned back in his Adirondack chair and cradled the glass on the top of his slight middle-aged belly.

"Cheers," Ronald Talbert said. He took a sip of his scotch, and then set the glass on the low circular table between them. He lifted his head and turned to look over his shoulder at the kitchen window. Francesca and Christina were doing something at the kitchen counter, their blond heads just visible through the window. They were having an animated conversation, talking and then turning toward each other and laughing.

"Don't worry about them," Ollonsun said. "If we don't stop them, they'll talk all night. Chris is always saying they don't get together enough anymore. Time changes everything. When the kids were all little, it was easier to herd them around together."

"Yeah," Talbert said. "I keep thinking about how old my kids might be before I see them again if I go to prison. It keeps me awake at night."

"A better use of your brain power would be to help figure out how to keep us out of prison. I've taken a few precautions already, but as this goes on, we might need to do more."

"What do we have to do?"

"We've got to start with the assumption that no matter what, people are going to be taking a very close look at both of us. If you have anything at all in your past that won't look good, you have to fix it."

"I never did anything that was illegal until I met you," Talbert said. "Don't look at me like that. It's the truth."

"I don't doubt it, Ron. I trust what you say. I just think that at this point the blaming stuff doesn't help. We've got to pull together and defend ourselves and each other from this threat. I acknowledge that I was the one who got you involved in this. What I'm doing now is trying to help get you out of it."

"At the time you told me you already had ways to make sure we wouldn't get caught."

"I remember. It was about a year or two after you married Francesca. You took me aside at a birthday party and said you were scared she was going to dump you because you weren't making enough money. I said that marrying a Welbrower sister was a commitment to come up with what it costs to stay married to one. I told you all about how I stayed on the good side of Christina, helped you learn the tricks, how to step over the land mines."

"That's exactly what I was talking about," Talbert said.

"That was how long ago? Let's see. I think that was Zelda's fourth? No, third birthday. Zelda is now seventeen. So the methods I taught you worked without a hitch for fourteen years. You're still married to Fran—happily, right? People go out of their way to congratulate anybody who's been married for twenty years like they ran a marathon on their elbows, and you're only about four or five years from there. And this is the first time there was anything worth worrying about."

"I appreciate that," Talbert said. "And Fran hasn't been the spoiled princess she was when I met her. She's been a great partner." He took a too-large gulp of his scotch, and it made the soothing liquid turn fiery. He winced as though he'd swallowed medicine.

Ollonsun took a sip of his scotch. "Every time before, if a client thought there was something wrong with his account, he would call me, I would promise to take a look, and I'd transfer funds to make it right that day. I said it was the damned new computer program that hadn't been tested sufficiently, or a digit in the fifteen-digit account number had been misread by the electronic reader—whatever fit best. If, instead of contacting his account advisor—me—the client called customer service and a case number was assigned and it got shifted to the fraud pipeline, I would fix the discrepancy as though I'd already caught the mistake by myself. I taught you all of this, and I'm sure you did it."

"Of course I did," Talbert said. "A number of times."

"And it worked, right? It's like picking pockets. If the guy feels your hand or notices he doesn't feel his wallet, you release it, back off, and pretend you bumped him by accident. But usually, he doesn't notice. You get away with it. Most of the time, investing is money somebody puts away in a retirement or long-term account and looks at once a year. If the total is a little higher than last year, he doesn't even read past the first pages, never looks at individual stocks and bonds. He puts it in a drawer and goes back to whatever he does for a living."

"I know," Talbert said.

"On the one occasion when I couldn't smother the problem with bullshit and manipulation, I used my get out of jail free card."

"What is it?"

"Years ago, when I hadn't been in the business very long, I had a sort of combination mentor and role model. He was the one originally assigned to show me around, give me an orientation, get me used to the computer equipment on the big common floor. He was a couple years older than I was, maybe three. I not only learned from him, I admired him. He was obviously the most promising young guy in the company, the one the bosses expected to do great things over time. I studied him. I watched how he did everything and imitated him. After a while it went so far that I was almost spying on him. He didn't seem to mind. Maybe there was some ego involved. It's easier to be a savior if you have disciples.

"I learned a lot. One of the things I learned was that he was skimming money from clients—a lot of them. He was also selling company secrets to three other companies—things about our corporate clients that they could use to make trades. While he was showing me how to do things, he had demonstrated on his computer, and while I was looking over his shoulder, I memorized his passwords. I collected evidence of everything he did. One day I went into his little office and told him what I knew and gave him the evidence. I said I'd done it as a warning, a favor to him because he had been such a friend to me, and that I hadn't kept any copies of it."

Ollonsun smiled. "We never mentioned it again. As I expected, he was promoted out of our section soon afterward. Over the years he was promoted regularly. He moved upward in the building, floor to floor, like a fire. And on each promotion he got, I would smile and think about how much more valuable the evidence I had kept had become. He's a brilliant man, too smart to think for a second that I hadn't kept copies of everything. When I finally got in trouble a few years ago I never even called him. He immediately and quietly got me out of it, and never spoke to me about it. He's been promoted twice more since then. He's a member of the board of directors of Great Oceana now, part of his regular job as president of the European Division."

Talbert said, "That's fine for you. It does nothing at all for me. He doesn't have any influence at Founding Fathers."

"It depends how I use him. If we can't come up with enough money to cover the fake trades we invented in Vesper Ellis's accounts, I can mention the problem to him, and I know the money will come. If things came to the very worst, and you and I were about to be indicted on federal securities charges, we could go to the prosecutors together and say we want to cooperate. We can make a deal to give them my mentor. That's the way they do federal prosecutions. The first one to walk in their door gets to testify as a friendly witness, maybe does ninety days, and then goes home. I'd hate to sacrifice him, but if we need to, I will. And there are also a few other things I've got in the works, so don't start getting panicky."

This time when Talbert took a sip of his scotch, his hand was steady. "What sorts of other things?"

"I'm keeping track of developments. I hired some guys to start paying attention to Vesper Ellis, and to report to me regularly."

"For what?"

"I want to know everything I can about her, her lawyer, and anybody else she drags into this, where they're going, who they see, and so on."

"What if they see these guys? Won't that just make them scared and turn this into a police thing?"

"Trust me. It will be nuanced, based on what Vesper Ellis and Charles Warren do. If they realize that attention is being turned away from us and onto them, they may be intimidated and back off. If they overreact and turn hostile, we might be able to make her seem hysterical and him opportunistic and unethical. I hired reliable, serious men. They can judge the exact level of force that's necessary. Best of all, they're capable of operating at any level that's called for."

"Wait. 'Force that's necessary'? Are we talking about violence?"

"Not necessarily. It depends on them, Ron. If somebody is bent on destroying our family, what are we supposed to do?" He pointed at the lighted windows in the kitchen. "We're talking about people making us lose those two women in there, seizing our money so our four kids won't ever go to good colleges, and getting us locked in prisons until we're old or dead. Maybe even charging our wives with crimes too. Wouldn't you be willing to do what's necessary to prevent that?"

"I'm mainly concerned about 'what's necessary.' What does that mean?"

"For the moment, very little. You can help me come up with the money to pay the men I hired. Beyond that, make sure your record is clean."

"It's clean."

"There's no time when you had a fight in a bar? There's no woman who could pop out of the past to say you had sex with her at some business conference when you and Fran weren't getting along? Nothing?"

"No."

"Okay. Then relax and let the pros do their jobs."

Zelda opened the back door and walked down to the table where the two men sat drinking and talking. She said, "Uncle Ron? Aunt Fran asked me to let you know your kids are getting sleepy."

Talbert stood, his eyes still on Ollonsun. "Thanks, Zelda. I guess we'd better get them home. Thanks for the great barbecue and everything, Pat." He began to follow the girl up the slight incline toward the back steps.

Ollonsun snatched up the bottle and recorked it, then swallowed the last bit of scotch in his glass. "Our pleasure," he said, and made his way up after them and went inside. He looked down on the backyard of his little estate and wondered what his new employees were doing right then at Vesper Ellis's house.

◆

In the darkened guest bedroom of Charlie Warren's condominium, Vesper Ellis looked at the glowing screen of her phone, struggling with the fine print of the California Bar Association's Rules of Professional Conduct. She was glad she had chosen the larger screen model. She turned her phone horizontal so she could make the print bigger, and read one paragraph at a time. Rule 1.8.10 (a):

"A lawyer shall not engage in sexual relations with a current client who is not the lawyer's spouse or registered domestic partner, unless a consensual sexual relationship existed between them when the lawyer-client relationship commenced."

That seemed only too clear, but also lent itself to easy lying. Paragraph (b) was a definition of "sexual relations," which, not surprisingly, was pretty much the definition she had always assumed the world agreed on. She moved quickly to paragraph (c):

"If a person other than the client alleges a violation of the rule, no Notice of Disciplinary Charges may be filed by the State Bar against a lawyer under this rule until the State Bar has attempted to obtain the client's statement regarding, and has considered, whether the client would be unduly burdened by further investigation or a charge."

Vesper turned her phone vertical again, scrolled down her emails, saw nothing she wanted to answer right now, turned off the phone, lay back, and closed her eyes.

16

t seven thirty A.M., Warren wrote a note:

"Dear Vesper, I'm going to the office to do a little work and get ready for my meeting. Please keep the door locked and the curtains closed for now. There's food in the refrigerator and you can call me anytime."

He set it on the kitchen counter beside the coffee.

He was out the door and headed downstairs for his rental car before it occurred to him that he should have reminded her that both of their phones could still be tapped, and she should use the burner, but he was pretty sure she wasn't the sort of person who would forget that. He went to the edge of the garage opening to see whether the two surveillance cars had moved from Vesper's block to his, but he didn't see any parked cars with drivers in them this time, so he went to the rental car, drove out to the street, and then went around the block to be sure he hadn't missed anything before he turned toward the office.

Warren couldn't help thinking about Vesper Ellis as he drove.

He had felt he was being normal and professional to maintain his distance from her. He still had a clear picture in his mind of Vesper with the big bath towel wrapped around her when she'd peeked out of the bathroom door to talk to him, and then the feel of her hug two hours later. He'd felt that as a client she was trusting him to stifle any thoughts that led in that direction. Now he felt he'd offended her by stepping away. It had all been clumsy and bad. Reevaluating the mess also forced him to picture her again, to remember the sound of her voice, to feel the hug again. Pushing her out of his mind gave him a foretaste of the feeling of loss.

Approaching the office building helped sweep the topic away for the moment. He parked in one of the visitors' spots on the floor below his reserved space, went upstairs, and opened the office. He went over the two lawsuits again, signed the final copies, and put them in Martha's inbox. Then he went back to his own office and began to read through the backlog of paper and computer messages that had accumulated over the past two days.

He looked particularly for any communication from Founding Fathers Vested, the company that hadn't yet responded to his complaint. He was curious about why they hadn't responded quickly to head off the possible scandal. There was nothing yet.

He was expecting something from the office of Mr. Foshin, Great Oceana Monetary's vice president for legal affairs, too, but what he was expecting was delay. So far there was nothing from Great Oceana, but the timing they would probably prefer was just before the one o'clock meeting, to inflict the most inconvenience on him.

He moved on through the routine business. It was interesting to see how steady the demand was for wills, divorces, contracts, minor lawsuits, and the like. He had already told Martha to warn these potential clients that he was fully committed at the moment, but that he had recommendations of several other excellent firms who specialized in those matters.

When Martha and her dog Alan arrived at the office, she said, "Good morning, Charlie. Need anything for your meeting today at Great Oceana?"

"Thanks, but I think I've got everything I can use. I'm expecting Mr. Foshin to either get sick or be running late so I'll only have five minutes or so before he leaves to catch his plane. Every delay he can cause helps them."

At twelve fifteen, Warren began to gather the papers he would take with him to the meeting. Then he remembered that his professional-looking briefcase had been stolen, so he took the backpack that he some-times used as a carry-on for flights and began to pack it. He included two years of monthly reports from Great Oceana on Vesper Ellis's account with plastic clips on the most damning pages, copies of the letters he had sent the Great Oceana Monetary offices so far, and a copy of the lawsuit he was ready to file. He didn't plan to show all those papers to Mr. Foshin, but if he changed his mind, he'd have them.

The attorneys for a major company should be good enough to recognize when they had no defense and be inspired to start talking seriously about settling. He put on the lightweight sport coat he had selected. Martha nodded her approval. Then he picked up the MacBook Pro that had been left charging on a shelf and slid it into the big pocket at the back of the pack.

He put on the pack to test the weight, decided it was tolerable, and left the office. He rode the elevator down to the level where he had parked the rented Honda. He set the pack on the floor in front of the passenger seat, got in, and drove up to the exit from the garage. When he approached, he saw that the wooden barrier arm was down across the threshold. He craned his neck to see if an attendant was around to raise it, then got out of the car to see if he could do it himself, leaving the motor running and the driver's door open.

He didn't let the lowered barrier unnerve him, but he didn't want some malfunction like this to make him late. He stepped forward to examine the place where the arm connected to the machine. Some of them he'd seen were bolted, and others had some simple mechanism to disconnect. He reached the arm and looked down at it, when he heard a voice behind him say, "Hold on, Mr. Warren." He felt relieved—help had come—but the relief lasted only a second before a strong hand grabbed his arm and jerked him backward.

Warren shrugged his right shoulder to free his arm and pivoted to the left to face the man. He pushed the driver's door into him, knocking him backward, then charged into him and pushed him down onto his back, pivoted into the driver's seat, slammed the door, and accelerated through the opening, snapping the wooden arm and sending it spinning into the street.

Warren glanced in the rearview mirror and saw a plain white van slide forward along the curb behind him and across the lot exit. Warren turned to the right and accelerated into traffic, and by the time he could look in his mirrors again he was too late to see where the van had gone.

He drove along Wilshire to La Cienega, turned south, and kept checking the mirrors for the white van. It was only a few blocks to West Olympic, but the way contained a continuous row of restaurants and stores, and pedestrians walking to and from them, and there were traffic lights and congested stretches. He made it to Olympic, and he knew the Great Oceana office building was only a few blocks from that corner. He had just had at least two men try to keep him from leaving his office for the meeting by stopping his car. They were sure to be looking for it now.

When he passed a public parking lot, he pulled the black Honda in, selected a parking space next to a tall SUV, where it would be hard to spot from the busy Boulevard, took off his sport coat, folded it into his backpack, got out, and put the backpack on. He took a ticket from the attendant, and began to walk along Olympic at a brisk pace. He tried to make himself part of the steady stream of people on the sidewalk, and not stand out. He had changed his appearance a bit by taking off the sport coat.

He didn't look back up the street over his shoulder, which could get him noticed. He looked at the street ahead to watch for the van to pass him, and he kept wondering who those men could be. When men had been watching the Ellis house, he hadn't seen a van, and he had been too far away to get a look at their faces, but he suspected that these two were connected with that group.

As he walked, he heard, faintly at first, a single set of footsteps coming up the sidewalk, shoes hitting the pavement some distance behind him. He thought it might be time to look back, but at first decided to resist the impulse. If the van was about to pass by along Olympic, then both men would see his face. And even if they were far behind, nothing helped a pursuer spot a person better than having him look to see if he was being chased. But then the footsteps grew louder, and soon he heard a man's panting breaths. He began to turn. As he did, a hand grasped the strap of his backpack and jerked him back.

Warren spun and freed an arm from his pack, and when the arm came around, he hooked it into the man's jaw. This was the same man who had grabbed him at his office building. The blow rocked the man sideways and made him raise his hands to his face. Warren ran at him, pushing the backpack against his chest. The man retreated backward, but after three steps his feet weren't moving fast enough, and he fell over backward onto the sidewalk. Warren saw the man start to get up, and realized his right hand was reaching into his jacket.

Warren turned and began to run. After three steps he had his arms through the straps of the backpack again, shrugged it up onto his back, and ran harder. He accomplished only about fifteen more steps before he felt an impact pound his back and hammer him ahead a step.

It was only then that he realized he had heard a shot. He needed to run a few quicker steps to recover his balance and avoid falling forward, and as he did, he understood what had just happened, and his alarm goaded him to a sprint. The man had freed his pistol from his coat and shot Warren in the back. As Warren ran, he wondered if he was one of those shooting victims who was dying but didn't know it at first because he was in shock.

It didn't matter what was enabling Warren to run. He was glad he could do it. He heard two more shots, but he didn't feel anything. He reached the next corner on a green light and dashed across the street, and as he did, he saw the WALK sign begin to flash. He glanced behind him, and he could see the man with the gun was up and running after him, but now he was almost a whole block behind. Warren judged that the light would turn red before the shooter reached the corner, but he could also see that his decision to look back seemed to have made the man speed up.

He was beginning to think more clearly now. He was sure that what must have happened was that the man's first shot had hit his backpack, and the assortment of stuff in it had diminished the bullet's energy enough so it hadn't reached his back. It would have pierced the backpack's fabric, then hit the laptop, and if it had gone all the way through the metal case, the screen, the circuitry, the keyboard, and the other metal side, it would have needed to pierce at least two reams of paper to get to his folded sport coat and then the inner side of the pack.

As he reached Tillis Avenue, which seemed to be the final cross-street before the Great Oceana office on Olympic, time sped up. The white van arrived at the same intersection, Olympic and Tillis, less than a second later. Warren's momentum had already carried him out into the street, and he saw the driver spot him and glance ahead up Olympic to see if he had time to make the left turn to hit Warren as he tried to run across the open pavement. The driver decided to chance it, and swung to the left toward Warren. There was the loud blare of a car horn and the squeal of brakes as the driver of a car coming toward the van on Olympic tried to stop to avoid hitting it.

The front of the white van appeared to expand as it roared onto Tillis Street toward him. He took two steps and dove, landed on a dusty patch of weeds and grass, and struggled to his feet as the white van streaked past behind him. He saw the shooter was in the passenger seat, and guessed the van's driver would try to stop and let the shooter out.

He ran hard for the length of the block toward the Great Oceana building until his hand grasped the door handle on the right side of the double glass doors and tugged the left door open. As soon as he was inside, he felt the relief of the air conditioning. He kept going deeper into the lobby toward the row of elevators. While he waited for the elevator, he slapped his sleeves and pant legs to get rid of the dust from his dive.

Warren was breathing hard and sweating. He realized that the next thing to do was to call the police. He glanced at his watch. Parking his rental car had cost him time, and it hadn't protected him. His meeting was in eight minutes. If he called the police, those eight minutes, and maybe eighty more, would be spent explaining hundreds of details that would only waste time. The elevator door opened and he stepped inside, then pressed the button for the seventh floor, the highest number on the panel. He was alone in the elevator, so he used the gauzy reflection in the stainless steel doors to see while he brushed off the rest of the dust, pulled his coat out of the pack, gave it a shake, slipped it on, and straightened his collar.

When the elevator opened on the seventh floor and he stepped out he saw a circular console with three men in dark suits looking at computer screens. The one nearest to him said, "Yes, sir. How can we help you?"

"I'm Charles Warren and I have a one o'clock meeting with Mr. Foshin at Great Oceana Monetary."

The man studied his computer screen. "Yes, sir."

He pushed forward a clipboard with a form clipped to it and a pen. "Please print your name here, sign beside it, and over here put Mr. Foshin's name." Warren followed the instructions and slid the board back to the man.

"Take this elevator to the twentieth floor." The man pointed, and Warren stepped into it and let it take him up. He could feel the speed of it tugging his innards downward, but appreciated being spared stopping repeatedly to let people on and off. He barely had time to check his watch, which said 12:58.

He stepped off the elevator and found a woman in a dark blue suit standing with her hands folded in front of her. "Mr. Warren?"

"Yes, ma'am."

"I'm Hannah Soames, one of the deputy vice presidents for legal affairs. I'm afraid Mr. Foshin has been delayed. He asked me to let you know, and see if you would mind meeting with him another time—as a professional courtesy."

Warren said, "Oh, gee. I'm sorry. My coming over here to talk with him today before filing the lawsuit and holding the press conference was all the professional courtesy my schedule allows. So that's that, I guess." He reached into the backpack and felt his way around pieces of broken glass or plastic and a jagged curved shape like a splash pushed up from the side of the murdered laptop. He felt the sheaf of paper of the right thickness and tugged it out. He glanced at it and could see the bullet had penetrated the back of it, but she couldn't. He held it out to her and said, "Here's the lawsuit. So I guess I may see you in court."

She held her hand up in a panicky gesture as though the packet of paper was a snake. "Wait. Please." She produced a cell phone from a pocket he hadn't noticed, and backed away about twelve feet, pressed a spot on the screen, and began talking quietly. A moment later she was back. "He's going to wrap up now and join us in the conference room." She began to walk, and Warren assumed he was supposed to follow. He had detected nothing that indicated she knew he had been attacked. She had been deceptive, but it was the level of deception that many people in business visited daily, lying to help her boss evade him, not enabling his murder.

She opened the door of a big glass-enclosed conference room dominated by a table that he estimated to be eight feet wide and over thirty long, with a dozen chairs on each side. At the far end was a television screen that filled the whole wall. As he entered, he watched himself and Hannah Soames on it. He assumed that their entrance was being recorded, and that someone was simultaneously watching the feed. The outer wall was a row of large windows that overlooked the Hollywood Hills.

She took a few steps along the waist-high cabinets below the glass inner wall. "Can I offer you something to drink?"

"If you have water I'd love it," he said. She opened one of the cabinet doors and he saw that it was a refrigerator. She brought out two plastic bottles of water and a couple paper cups from a cupboard, set one on the table at a chair three down from the head, and then the other at the same level directly across from it. He sat down at his bottle, opened it, and took a drink. She sat down and opened hers, but it looked as though she was only imitating him. She didn't drink it.

They sat there in silence, waiting. He looked at her as long as it seemed a sane person would, then checked his image in the television screen, ran his hand through his hair, and rearranged his shirt so the row of buttons ran straight from his Adam's apple to his belt buckle. After his long run in the afternoon sun the heavily air-conditioned room felt very pleasant.

He lifted his backpack from the floor to the seat beside him, took out a pile of papers, and organized them. He used the opportunity to open his pack wide enough to verify that the thin laptop had a fatal through-and-through wound. He was tempted to take the pack to the wastebasket by the cabinet and dump the remains into it, but he resisted. He had been in a few trials in which experts had removed hard drives, reinstalled them in the same model computer, and read them.

"There you are!" a man's voice said. A man who had to be Donald Foshin appeared in the doorway. He was thin, about fifty-five or sixty with an expensive haircut that made the most of his thinning hair. He wore a dark blue suit, possibly the whitest shirt Warren had seen in years, and a good gray tie that was exactly the current fashion. He stepped up to Warren and shook his hand. "Mr. Warren, I apologize for rushing like this. Please, sit back down," and he sat down himself in the chair at the head of the table. The door opened again and three, no, five, no, seven men and women in serious business suits streamed in and seated themselves around the table.

Warren inhaled to begin, but Foshin said, "We've been troubled by the material you sent us about Mrs. Ellis's account with us. Of course we're going to do our best to repay her losses."

"Yes, Mr. Foshin, but—"

"And yes, we are aware that we should come to an agreement about damages in addition to undoing the harm."

Warren said, "Then we agree in principle about the main points. I appreciate your—"

Foshin looked at his watch and then instantly back into Warren's eyes. "Yes. I'm sure you do. I regret that there's more to this. Great Oceana was founded on the fortune of the Pacific trader McGuane Parmonikoff in 1872, and has grown to a size and complexity that he could never have imagined, in spite of his travels."

Warren sensed a trainload of pretense and intimidation was just chugging into the station.

"Size is great," Foshin said, "but in a situation like this, being bigger means that for a thief, there are many more victims to rob, and many more transactions to provide cover." He sighed. "Polter?"

"Yes, sir." This was a man about forty. He opened a file folder on the table in front of him and passed a stack of papers from it around the table. When it got to Warren, he took one, set it in front of him, and passed the stack to the place beside him, which was unoccupied.

Polter began to read it aloud. "This is a supplement dated October twelfth to the current Summary Prospectus, Statutory Prospectus, and Statement of Additional Information for all Great Oceana Monetary account holders, Investment Services clients, Mutual Funds, Retirement Funds, their employees, heirs and beneficiaries, creditors and other interested parties. Please read and retain it for future reference.

"Effective immediately, Patrick Ollonsun no longer serves as a Financial Advisor, spokesperson, or officer of the Corporation or any of its divisions, subsidiaries, or partnerships in the United States or abroad.

"All references to Mr. Ollonsun in the Summary Prospectus, Statutory Prospectus, and Statement of Additional Information are hereby removed."

Warren said, "October twelfth?"

"Yes," said Polter. "The current Prospectus was printed and delivered to the Postal Service three days ago so it arrives everywhere at the end of the third quarter on or around August first. If we get this one out anywhere near October 12, it will be an achievement. It will also nearly double the Prospectus section's expenditure for that month. Our printings are in the millions of copies, with proportional mailing costs."

Warren looked at Mr. Foshin. "And what does it accomplish?"

Foshin's hand rose from the table in a gesture that meant, "If you'll look, you'll see it," but there was nothing there. "It will let the clients, prospective clients, and any businesses know that he's not authorized to act on Great Oceana's behalf. It prevents any future Vesper Ellises."

Warren said, "It does nothing for the only Vesper Ellis who exists at present—the widow who has trusted Great Oceana for about ten years and has been robbed."

"Okay," Mr. Foshin said. "I understand you have a client and you have a duty to advocate for her and protect her interests. Everybody in this room has read the evidence you've provided, and our problem isn't that we disagree with you. We also know that besides being a lawyer you're a licensed CPA. But Great Oceana has hundreds of CPAs and many more lawyers than Warren & Associates, and we've already gone much farther and deeper on this than you have. Not only has Mr. Ollonsun been doing this for longer than the statute of limitations runs, but he has been doing it to people besides Mrs. Ellis. We don't know exactly how long, and we're not sure how many just yet. As of noon today, the number was twelve. They're working backward in time, and that means retrieving information from the company's archives in New York, London, Bangkok, Hong Kong, and elsewhere, some of it pertaining to clients who are deceased. It's a much worse problem than you know, and may be even worse than we know so far." He looked at his watch again.

"What is it you're asking for?" Warren said.

"Time," Foshin said.

"What for?"

"It takes time to collect the rest of the evidence, complete the full investigation of each account he might have been tapping, brief the police and the relevant federal agencies. We know he's guilty, but we also know he managed to do this without getting stopped by our system of audits, spot-checks, and safeguards. Is anyone else in the company doing this too? The truth is, we don't know. The day we drop the net on Mr. Ollonsun, of course he'll know he's caught. But so will anyone else who's doing it, or helped him do it or hide it. We can't take the chance of leaving some within our organization."

"Publicity."

"That too. There will be terrible press. The FBI will come for him. The SEC, the FTC, and the US Attorney will come for us. What weren't we doing to prevent it, what do we need to do now, who should have been doing what, how much will our fine be. I've been proud to work for this company for twenty-eight years. Now I have to fear that the rest of my time here will be spent defending it in court and trying to negotiate its penalties."

Warren said, "I'm sorry for your part of it."

"Does that mean that we can count on you to keep this out of the legal system and the public eye until we have time to prepare and get the answers we need? As officers of the court, you and I have a responsibility to act for the public good. I take that to heart, and I think you do too."

"I do. But as you pointed out, my main—as well as immediate—responsibility is to Vesper Ellis. And as you also pointed out, Great Oceana is an enormous corporation. You can pay what you're going to owe Mrs. Ellis today and have a signed settlement in hand within an hour. If you prefer to handle it online, we could probably do it faster than that."

"What do you see as an appropriate figure?"

Warren removed a couple inches of paper off the stack in front of him, retrieved the copy of his lawsuit, and set it in front of Foshin. He said, "Full repayment plus ten million dollars. The argument for it is in the lawsuit."

"Ten is far too steep. We could agree to full repayment plus one. That would still pay you adequately without penalizing Mrs. Ellis for being robbed. You'll take a full third, right?"

"Five million. We'd be giving you over a month and a half to clean house and prepare your case."

Foshin was leafing through the lawsuit, which he appeared to be scanning. "Three."

"Done."

Foshin held up the lawsuit and pointed at the hole. "What's this? It looks like a bullet hole."

"It does," said Warren.

Another man in a dark suit opened the door halfway and sidestepped inside, but made no attempt to move farther into the room or sit down. He simply stood waiting.

Foshin looked at him and said, "Hello, Phil." He said to the room, "We've got to leave for the airport now, I'm afraid." He stood. "Mr. Warren, will payment within seventy-two hours be acceptable to you?"

"Yes."

"Ms. Soames, will you please conclude our business with Mr. Warren?"

"Yes. Have a safe trip, Mr. Foshin."

Foshin shook Warren's hand. "You've done a fine job for your client, Mr. Warren. I'm sure we'll be in touch over the next year or so while this plays out."

"Yes," said Warren. "Thank you."

Phil the driver opened the door for Foshin and then moved ahead of him, probably to press the elevator buttons and open more doors.

Ms. Soames said to Warren, "I assume you'll have no objection to the nondisclosure clause in our standard liability settlement agreement?"

"I'm sorry. She can't agree to hush up felonies. At the moment I don't intend to go to the police before you've collected your evidence, and I don't have anything negative to say about your company or its management, but if she's interviewed by the authorities, she has an obligation to tell the truth."

"I understand," Ms. Soames said. "Anything else?"

"I assume this television system doesn't just function as a giant mirror," he said. "You should have an accurate record of what we agreed to."

"Yes, of course," she said. "We can have the agreement in your office by close of business today, and the settlement sent after it within seventy-two hours."

"Excellent," he said. "I'll call a ride service."

She looked at him. "You didn't drive?"

"No," he said. "Thank you all." He stood and walked out. At the seventh floor checkpoint he signed out, got into the elevator to the lobby, called for a Lyft ride, and then waited. In four minutes, the car was pulling up in front of the building, so he got into the back seat of the car quickly as possible. As the car pulled out, he searched for the white van.

It was gone, probably because the two men had assumed he would have called the police immediately. The ride to the parking lot to pick up his rental car was calm, almost pleasant. It occurred to him that it had been a beautiful afternoon. This was the first time he'd thought of it that way.

A half hour later he walked from the lot under his building to his condominium and unlocked the door. He turned the knob, but it wouldn't move. He was relieved, but only tentatively, because it was still possible that the two men who had been trying to kill him this afternoon could have gotten Vesper to open the door and then barged in past her and locked the deadbolt. He knocked. He heard her voice answer.

"Who is it?"

"Charles Warren." He heard her footsteps coming toward the door.

"Say something more. I want to hear your voice."

"I had my meeting, and decided to take the rest of the day off, so here I am."

She fiddled with the locks and he heard the clicks, and then the door opened. She only stepped back one step, so he had to slip in before she set the locks again. "How was it?"

"There were high points and low points."

"Highest point first."

"Great Oceana agreed to pay you back and give you an additional three million dollars for damages within seventy-two hours."

"Thank you, Charlie." She threw her arms around him and hugged him, but he stiffened and groaned in pain. She said, "I read the bar association rules. I won't bring charges, and you don't have to hug me back, so what's the moaning for?"

"That was the low point. I got shot in the back."

"You mean betrayed?"

"No, shot. Two guys in a white van were trying to keep me from getting to the meeting. One of them took a shot at me, but all the stuff in my backpack seems to have stopped the bullet."

"Let me look at your back." She pulled the shirt up and looked. "Oh, my God, Charlie. You have a huge bruise."

"It felt like I probably would. I should thank my laptop, which gave its life to save mine. This also taught me something."

"What?"

"Somebody at Great Oceana must have told them I was coming."

17

It was night. Patrick Ollonsun drove his BMW past his brother-in-law's house and kept going until he couldn't see the house's front windows, parked, and waited. After about five minutes Ronald Talbert came outside and walked down the dark street to Ollonsun's car. Talbert got in and clicked his seatbelt. He was prepared for Ollonsun to annoy him by roaring off up the road, but instead he drove off slowly.

Ollonsun said, "Did you bring the money?"

"Yes."

"Cash?"

"Yes," Talbert said. He held up a plastic pharmacy bag. Then he pushed it under his seat.

"Okay. I just wanted to be sure you understood. I didn't want to be too explicit. I knew nobody was close enough to hear me, but I couldn't tell what your situation was."

"What happened today, anyway?" Talbert said.

"The guys I hired to keep an eye on Vesper Ellis and her lawyer followed the lawyer along Olympic Boulevard to the Great Oceana Monetary administrative office. It wasn't the client financial services office

where I work. It was the building with the unseen stuff—the head offices
for the investment division, the staff for the overseas trading that goes
on all night, the legal division. He had to be meeting with them."

"You never saw him do anything, right? How do you know what—"

"The lawyer's name is Charles Warren. He had sent a letter to the
company about discrepancies in his client's accounts. Naturally the
inquiry was shunted over to my office. I figured that as long as my
office—meaning me personally—was handling the complaint, things
could be kept under control in the usual ways. Take a little money from
other accounts to 'correct the mistake' and the complaint fades away.
This time I played it safer. I started an account in her name with money
of my own, called it an investment subaccount, and pretended to move
it back into her main account. And I also took the precaution of hiring
these guys to keep an eye on the client and her lawyer."

"So what's the problem?'

"My guys saw Warren leave his office alone around noon today. They
called me and asked if I knew what he was doing, so I said, 'What I want
to do is make him more cautious—slow him down—so maybe it's time
to ask him. If that intimidates him, fine.' They tried, he resisted, knocked
one of these guys down, and drove off. The guy hit his head, lost his
temper, and took a shot at Warren. They saw where he went, and it was
the Great Oceana building I told you about—the legal division."

"That's why you dragged me out of my house on a weeknight, making
Fran wonder what the hell I'm doing, and probably my kids, and the
neighbors too?"

Ollonsun began to drive a little faster now that they were in the
dark and anonymity of Valley Vista. People drove too fast on this street
anyway because the mild curves and low hills along the north side made
it kind of fun. "Yes and no. What happened today is that we learned he

was going full-on into legal action. He's essentially moved our problem out of my office into the legal division. That means he's going to do the same at Founding Fathers Vested. I hope you've done what you can to make what you diverted from her accounts reappear—something like what I did, and then make all the levers and pulleys disappear."

"I've done that already."

"Good, good, good," Ollonsun said. "That's all you need for the moment."

Talbert said, "I've been waiting for a while now to hear what the cash is for."

"I'm sorry. Before we got into that, I wanted to be sure that you had taken the situation we're in seriously. The money is for a couple things. We have some help keeping a strong, steady hand on this thing right now. I owe them a few days' fees, which I plan to pay myself. One of the guys got hurt when Warren surprised him and hit his head on the concrete."

"Are you kidding? You're paying him extra because the guy he wanted to scare made him fall down and hurt himself?"

Ollonsun said, "Yes. And I'll tell you why that's a very smart move that only a guy who has been around would think to do. Guys like them, who have worn some uniform or other and seen some blood, have already been naive volunteers, and then fought their guts out and got nothing for it. The people in charge never hesitate to put guys like them in unnecessary danger. So now they work on contract. They don't have any illusions, and they don't hesitate to make it hurt if you don't live up to your agreement. The trick is to get them to see that you understand, that you're somebody who sees things the way they do. If you can do that, you own them. I figure that for an extra few thousand tonight, we'll get a hundred thousand in loyalty."

Talbert said, "How do you even know these guys?"

"I've had a client for years." He paused. "His friends call him Binky. He's somebody who makes a lot of money, and invests it mostly in municipal bonds to avert the tax liability. That helps keep one part of his life looking obvious and dull to make up for the secret, exciting parts. I asked him if he knew anybody who did this kind of work, and he did. I've hired them a couple times."

"And that's how you know all about their lives and their psychology and everything?"

Ollonsun looked at him, irritated. "Do you really think that question deserves an answer?"

"Look," Talbert said. "I'm out. I don't think it makes sense to get involved with people like that in the first place, and paying them money just to maintain good relations seems crazy. Whatever money we've got should be going to good lawyers."

They drove in silence for a hundred yards, each of them staring straight ahead. Then Ollonsun made a left turn onto Madelia Avenue, and Talbert assumed he was going to turn around and take him home. He didn't seem to find a wide enough part to turn around, and then he made a right onto Lacota Place.

As they passed a parked car, it pulled out and followed. "Too late," Ollonsun said. "That's them."

Talbert said, "I thought I was just bringing you some money because you were short. You didn't say we were meeting them here. I don't want to meet people like that. I don't want to know them, and I certainly don't want them to know me."

Ollonsun turned to him with his teeth clenched, then looked in the rearview mirror to be sure they were following. "Well, it seems you're going to. They had to know you were involved, because they had to know there was enough cash to pay them, and they had to know everyone who knew about them. You think they're going to be the muscle for an anonymous employer?"

"You hid this from me," Talbert said. "I would never have—"

"Look, Ron. Since you were married, I've been propping up your incompetence, teaching you things you should have known how to do, and trying to help you grow into the life you lucked into by marrying my wife's sister. At this moment I'm getting sick of the complaints. You've got about thirty seconds to pull yourself together. Do not let these guys see that you're weak. After that, you can make whatever decision you want."

He turned left onto Round Valley Drive and kept going until he reached a lot that had been cleared of a house that had been on it for an unknown number of decades. It was evident that someone had leveled the lot's surface with a bulldozer, and there was some chain-link fence in a cylindrical shape that hadn't yet been unrolled to define the construction site.

Ollonsun pulled off the road onto the remains of the narrow driveway and turned off the engine and lights. The car that had been following pulled in behind it and went dark. The doors opened and two men got out and walked up on opposite sides of Ollonsun's car.

They were both big, both in their late thirties or early forties, with dark hair and short facial hair of the sort that Talbert didn't quite think of as a beard. The one who leaned into Ollonsun's window had a mustache, and he was wearing a knitted cap. He said, "What's the matter? Get out of the car."

Ollonsun got out. There was a sharp rap on the window beside Talbert's head that made him jump. The man on that side beckoned impatiently, so Talbert got out too, but he was reluctant to let go of the door handle, as though he could pull himself back into the passenger seat—or maybe back through time—and be safe. He shut the door without slamming it, because he knew that there were houses in this neighborhood, even though he couldn't see any of them from here.

The man with the whiskers said, "You're Ron Talbert, huh? Got to check for surprises. Lift your arms up."

Hearing that the man knew his name made Talbert feel sick. He lifted his arms up so they were just below shoulder height, not sure what was necessary. The man grabbed his elbows and shoved them upward. He ran his hands along Talbert's sides to his ankles, spun him around and yanked his shirt up to his chest, spun him forward and then yanked the shirt back down. "He's clean."

The man with the mustache and knitted cap said, "Him too."

Talbert turned to see Ollonsun tucking his shirt back in.

The man with the mustache said, "Come on." They walked farther from the streetlights into deeper darkness across the center of the vacant lot. They were in two pairs with the brothers-in-law on one side and Ollonsun's two hired men facing them. The man with the mustache spent a few seconds staring back down the road they had traveled. Talbert saw that just visible under the rear edge of the knitted cap he had a patch of white gauze.

The man with the cap and mustache said, "Sorry about that, but once in a while if things get to this stage, other things start happening, and a client gets told that he'll get off if he cooperates and wears a recording device or a wire. So what have you decided?"

Ollonsun said, "We need to stop the clock. I think what Charles Warren did today was put our problem in the hands of the legal division. He was probably threatening a lawsuit. We need to get to him and his client and scare them enough get them to stop, at least for a few days. During that time, they'll realize that the missing money is already back in her accounts, so there's no point in causing themselves more trouble. Does that make sense?"

"Sure," the man with no mustache said. "Lots of people who've gotten their first beatdown learn a whole new way of looking at the world."

The man with the mustache said, "This isn't an exact science. What if they die? Are you prepared for that?"

Ollonsun said, "We just don't have the luxury of worrying about things like that. We stand to lose everything—life savings, jobs, careers, families—and going to federal prison. If we don't do what we can now, it'll be too late."

"I get that. So tonight is the time to decide. Do you have the money with you?"

"Yes."

"Wait, wait," said Talbert. "I don't think I'm ready to take the chance that somebody dies. This is too much, too fast. I need to think."

The man with the mustache said, "Fair enough. Good luck with your problem." He turned to his companion. "Let's stop for a drink on the way back." The two men turned and started back across the lot toward their car.

Ollonsun watched them for a couple seconds, then pivoted to glare at Talbert. "Are you crazy?"

"I didn't expect to have something like this sprung on me."

"I didn't spring it on you. Life sprung it on both of us." He suddenly pushed off and sprinted across the rough ground, paying no attention to the darkness, no concern that he might fall on something, no sign that he was even thinking. He caught up to the two men just as they were reaching the parked cars. He produced his keys, popped the passenger door of his car open, snatched the pharmacy bag out from under Talbert's seat, and pushed it into the hands of the man with the mustache.

Talbert stood still, not sure what to do. The man with the mustache pawed around inside the bag and then held his phone in it and pawed some more. Talbert watched from where he was. It was awkward and humiliating. He had done some stupid things, selfish things. He had robbed a widow who had trusted his company. He hadn't agreed to pay a couple thugs to beat her up and maybe kill her. At least he hadn't wanted to do that.

Another minute passed, and then the man with no mustache went and sat behind the wheel in their car. It would be over in another minute. Talbert looked at the summer sky, the stars like bright needle holes in a blanket. He looked back down at the cars, and his paralysis went away.

He began to walk toward the cars, then saw that the men's car was moving. The lights weren't on, but it was backing down the broken concrete surface of the old driveway.

Talbert's steps turned into a run. He could still stop them, if he was fast enough. He went faster, tripped on something and fell, scrambled up, and dashed down toward the driveway. As he did, the car swung around and headed away toward the end of the street. Its lights came on, it made the first turn, and disappeared.

Ollonsun opened the driver's door of his car as Talbert approached. He called, "I think it would be best if you called an Uber or something."

Talbert didn't answer, just kept running. Ollonsun stepped to the side to put the door between them, but Talbert got his arm over the top of the window and used his momentum to drag Ollonsun out onto the cracked and buckled concrete. They landed painfully side by side on the rock-hard, jagged surface, rose, and began furiously swinging punches at each other. It was too dark to see each blow coming, so many connected. They went for each other's eyes and noses—any place on the face or head. They fought to punish each other, until their arms were tired and carried so little force that the damage to their upper bodies had already been done. They pulled back from each other because they were out of breath. Ollonsun was bent over, leaning against the car as though he was about to collapse, but then he reached into the well in his still-open door and pulled out a gun.

"See this, you fucking idiot? Now stop it."

"A gun? You brought a gun?" Talbert said. "Why am I surprised?"

"We're just hurting each other and now we'll draw attention to ourselves. Stop fighting. There's nothing left to fight about. It's too late to change anything. We're both committed."

"I can't believe this."

"I'm going home. You can either get in the car and let me drop you off, or you can call for a ride looking like that." He got in the driver's seat and closed the door.

Talbert walked stiffly to the passenger door. As he sat in the seat, he wondered how he could possibly explain the bruises and swelling to Fran. He pulled the sun flap down and looked in the small lighted mirror. A black eye that was swelling shut, bloody nose, maybe broken, a split lip. He knew he wasn't going to sleep tonight even if he could get in without waking her.

His brother-in-law had just bullied him into bringing fifteen thousand dollars in cash to a meeting with criminals. No, it was worse than that. Pat had manipulated him into paying thugs to physically harm innocent people—to kill them, if that was the way it worked out.

18

At six o'clock Vesper said, "Let me take you out to dinner to celebrate your victory over Great Oceana this afternoon." Charlie said, "I'm afraid this isn't the time to be out in a public place. That guy today didn't threaten to shoot me. He shot me. If he had aimed anywhere but center mass, I could be dead right now. I've been thinking it might be time to hide you someplace where those people won't find you."

"They know where I live," she said. "I don't have a relative in this part of the country anymore who could put me up, and I wouldn't ask a friend to take that kind of risk. A hotel is a very public place full of strangers. I'd rather be here for another day. The parking lot has iron bars, the windows are too high to climb in, and I won't be alone."

"I'll call in a dinner order."

The food was delivered from Bernardine, and came in two large bags. He set the table with a set of plates that was formal and ornate, and heavy silverware. She looked at it and said, "What young, unmarried man has a set of dishes like this?"

"The answer is probably zero," he said. "They're the ones my mother and father got when they were married about forty years ago. Now she's living in a small rented place in Hawaii, so she made me store them. I've never used more than about a quarter of the set."

When he took the plastic containers of food from the bags, Vesper said, "This is shocking. I'm sure you don't eat this way, and I certainly don't."

"It's a special occasion. I read somewhere that you should stop to celebrate good things that happen. I forget why, since having good things happen ought to be enough. Anyway, this is the best we can do without taking risks. I also haven't done any grocery shopping since before you came to my office that day. If you need a third reason, I'll dream one up."

"Okay," she said. "I don't need to be coaxed any more than that, and just being near this food has made me really hungry."

He came around the table and pulled out her chair for her, and then sat down across from her. They ate some of the food and drank some wine and talked. The talk continued as they put away the rest and loaded the dishwasher, then drifted into the living room with their glasses and the rest of the bottle.

She told him about growing up with her mother, who based her system of values on being what she called "useful." "It always seemed to me to be a modernization of some leftover ancient worldview, but I never identified it exactly. A mother's ideas always seem to be the norm to children until they're proven either false or too constraining. My father was older. He was a doctor who worked at the UCLA hospital for nearly fifty years."

She said, "They were a good match, and good people. They raised me and my sister as though that was all they had to do, and nothing else mattered. It's kind of extra sad, because neither of us ever had kids, so we didn't get to pass any of that on."

"Is your sister older or younger?"

"She died of cancer a few years ago. She was older, but now I've passed her, so she's younger too, in a way. You're an only child, right?"

"Yes."

"You know how I could tell?"

"No."

"You can be funny, even say goofy things when you want to, but your first language is grown-up. That's what you're most comfortable speaking. Slang terms and bad grammar don't seem to occur to you except as afterthoughts. It's because in your earliest years there weren't other kids in the house, so most of the speakers you heard were adults."

"It's a good theory," he said. "I'll have to try it out on a few other subjects. But lawyers spend all day talking like people centuries older than their parents."

"I want to thank you for it," she said. "You've been wonderful."

"I'm pretty sure you did, right after I told you Great Oceana had agreed with us. You're welcome. But we still have to deal with Founding Fathers Vested. I haven't heard from them yet."

They said "good night" at eleven and were both asleep by eleven thirty.

The sounds were very faint and weren't continuous, so when Warren opened his eyes, it took a moment before he realized he had been hearing them for a while. They sounded familiar but out of place, like an electric toothbrush running, then stopping for a time, then starting again. His first thought was that maybe that was what it was. He reached to the side table and picked up his phone so the screen would glow.

He stood, found his pants and his shoes in the dim light of the phone screen, put them on, and went to the closet. He saw his golf bag, pulled out the nine iron because of the weight and pitch of its head, and stepped down the hall to listen. He followed the noise, kind of a buzz from a small, probably battery-operated, electric motor. There was a subtler background sound, like "err-err, err-err," as though something was moving back and forth. He moved toward the sound.

Warren stepped slowly around the living room in the direction of the door, trying to verify that was where the sound was coming from. He leaned close to the door and put his ear to the surface. The sound came again, and with his ear against the wood it sounded louder and higher pitched, like a dentist's drill. He put his hand on the doorknob. This time when the sound came, he could feel the vibration on the knob.

He needed to wake Vesper up, but how close were these people to having drilled the lock? He didn't want to leave the door if they were about to open it and charge inside. He used his phone to text her number the message GET UP. DANGER. BE SILENT. From his post at the front door, her phone's text sound in her bedroom was inaudible, but he hoped it would wake her. He pocketed his phone.

The drilling sound stopped. He put his back to the wall on the lock side of the door. If these were going to be the sort of experienced people he expected, they would look for trouble to come from the hinge side. He waited and listened for voices, or at least movements, but now he heard nothing. The window made the room slightly lighter than the bedroom had been with its blackout curtains, but he knew from experience that was still very dark for a person coming in from the lighted hallway. That might give him a few seconds of advantage.

He made final decisions. He was not going to let them get far enough into the condo to reach Vesper, and he would not stop fighting while he was alive.

He raised the golf club above his head and waited. He knew they must be listening too on the other side of the door, no more than a couple feet from him. He kept his breathing slow and deep, his eyes focused on the doorknob.

The doorknob turned, the door swung inward, and his arms were in motion, bringing the golf club straight down as soon as the space appeared. In the light from the hallway, he saw the head of the club land squarely on a man's forearm. The man let out a sound that conveyed shock and pain and dropped to his knees, trying to grip his injured arm. Warren was already raising the club for another swing, but when it was halfway up, he saw a second man step up behind the first. He recognized him as the one who had fired a shot through his backpack yesterday, and also recognized the movement he'd made to pull the gun out of his jacket.

Realizing that he didn't have the second he needed, Warren stopped raising his golf club, pushed off with his feet, and jabbed the club straight into the man's mustache, so it hit the lower part of his nose and his upper teeth at once. The man staggered backward, both hands coming up to clutch his face. Warren saw blood flowing between his fingers. Warren brought the club upward again and swung it down on the first man's back. The man let out a howl and began to crawl out of the doorway, but he was slow because his right arm was bent and held up to his chest.

Warren knew he couldn't afford to ignore the man he knew had a gun, so he charged out over the crawling man's back to reach the one he'd poked in the face. He swung hard at him in a diagonal, chopping arc, but the man saw it coming and dodged to the side, so the club's head came down in a glancing blow on the man's shoulder. Warren could tell it hurt, but it didn't seem to disable the man, because his right hand slid toward the inside of his coat again. The man was ignoring the damage he had sustained and moving faster now, and Warren saw the arm moving to withdraw the gun from the coat.

Warren took a two-handed swing that met the man's elbow as the gun hand emerged. In the instant when the impact pounded the man's arm back into his coat, the gun went off. The bullet didn't seem to hit anyone, and the gun slid down past the waist of his coat to the floor.

"Police! Nobody move!" The voice was loud and authoritative, but the man on the floor reached for the pistol on the carpet with his one uninjured arm. The same voice continued, "Go for it. Say hi to Jesus for me."

The assailant seemed to realize he had no chance, and he slumped down onto his belly with his arms out from his sides.

Another voice said, "I guess Jesus will have to wait."

The two men dressed in plainclothes stepped in, took the pistol, and put the second man belly-down on the floor. As they dragged the two intruders' wrists behind them for the handcuffs, both let out groans of pain. "I think it's broken," the one with no mustache said.

"Shut up," the other officer said. The two men on the floor didn't seem to notice that he and his partner were a bit older than the usual responders to emergency calls. Their rough, authoritative manner carried the kind of confidence that came with rank.

The Black officer tugged the arm of the man with a mustache. "Get up. You're under arrest."

"Call for an ambulance. This guy assaulted us."

The white officer said, "If you come easy, we'll get you fixed up. If not, you'll have to talk to the officers who come next."

The man with a mustache struggled to get up, so the two police officers tugged him up. His friend saw that, and tried to get up, so they pulled him to his feet too. The Black officer said to Warren, "Sir, you'll be contacted within a few minutes by officers who will take your statement. Please wait for them inside, and don't clean up anything out here."

"All right," Warren said. He watched Copes and Minkeagan pull the
two injured men down the stairs to the small lobby, out the front door
to the street. Warren stepped inside and nearly bumped into Vesper,
who was wearing the football shirt and pajama pants and gripping the
biggest butcher knife from the block.

She said, "Are you all right?"

"Yes, so far," he said. "How about you?"

"Nothing happened to me. I heard my kidnappers' voices. Did they
turn on you?"

"No, the opposite. I think Copes and Minkeagan must have been
keeping an eye on me so I wouldn't cut them out of the money I promised, and when they saw those guys had broken in, they followed them
and pretended to be cops. They're protecting their money, not us. And
they have guns again."

She said, "This is all so crazy." After a moment she said, "You're covered with sweat."

"It's been a while since I've been in a fight. I forgot how tired it makes
you, like you strained every muscle. And when the adrenaline stops
flowing, it leaves you feeling kind of hollow."

◆

Copes and Minkeagan pushed the two handcuffed men ahead of them
to the Ford sedan parked thirty feet past the edge of the condominium
building. Copes said, "Listen carefully. I'm going to ask you a few questions now. If you lie to us, I don't know what my partner will do, but I
know you'll wish you were back up there with that guy and his golf club.
First question. Is this your car?"

The man with the mustache nodded and the other said, "Yes."

Minkeagan patted that one down and took a wallet from his pocket, then did the same to the other one, who also had keys. He unlocked the car, opened the door, and used the dome light to search the wallets. He held up a plastic card. "This one is an ex-cop. It's an out-of-date ID from Missouri."

Copes said, "Check the other one."

After about five seconds Minkeagan held up another card, and said, "Him too." Almost immediately he added, "This one's older. He was a cop in Tennessee before that."

Copes said, "You guys were fired. Did you really think you'd get hired here? You can't just drive to a station in California and think your record hasn't chased you here. We probably already have it."

The one with the mustache said, "We weren't looking for law enforcement jobs." He had a hard time getting all of that said, and he'd started to bleed from his mouth again.

"I don't judge. It makes me feel a little sympathy for you." He looked at Minkeagan. "Do you think we could consider offering these two a break? A little professional courtesy?"

Minkeagan looked them up and down. "It depends on how bad they want out of this, and whether we can trust them not to be stupid. One chance."

"Thanks," Copes said. "What did you want with that guy with the golf club?"

The man with no mustache said, "We're registered bounty hunters. He's—"

The mustached man said, "Stop! Shut up!" Then he said, "Some people hired us to kick his ass. The woman's too."

"Good save. Your stupid friend almost got me to give up on you. Nothing personal, then?"

"It was a job."

"I'm sure you know how this works," Copes said. "What have you got to make us take the risk of letting you start your car and head east? One bid, and make it fast. We can't keep off the radio for much longer."

"The inside door panel on the back seat passenger side comes off. There's a white plastic bag stuck in the empty space."

"Have you lost your mind?" the man with no mustache said.

"You think they wouldn't find it when they searched the car at the station?"

Minkeagan opened the backseat door, took out a pocketknife, thumbed the spring assist so the blade flicked out, and pried the panel off. He reached in and pulled out the pharmacy bag that Ollonsun had given the mustached man hours ago. He looked inside, then pulled out his own pistol and held it on the two men and handed the bag to Copes. After a look, Copes closed it and said, "It's your lucky night."

Minkeagan straightened the row of ID cards and driver's licenses on the car seat and took a few pictures with his phone. Then he put his phone away and held his pistol on the two men while Copes took a handcuff key out of his pocket and unlocked the two men's handcuffs.

Minkeagan said, "I shouldn't have to say this, but since one of you is as sharp as a potato, I will. We'll be watching for you. If we see either of you anywhere in the City of Los Angeles again, or your car gets picked up on a license plate reader, you'll be charged with attempted murder of that guy upstairs. We have pictures of you, your ID, your car, the bullet hole in the wall, the gun that fired it, and your blood all over the carpet. If I were you, I'd be sure to drive at least until daylight before I stopped at an emergency room to get my golf injuries treated."

They watched and waited while the two men got into the car and the one with the blood-soaked mustache reached across his body with his left hand to start the engine and drove the vehicle down the street. Minkeagan said, "How much do you suppose is in that bag?"

"Too much for beating up a law-abiding couple, I think."

"Maybe they were supposed to kill them."

Copes and Minkeagan walked around the block to their car and got inside. Minkeagan bent down and flapped back the upper end of the rubber mat at his feet to retrieve the burner phone Warren had given him. He pressed number three and waited, then hung up. About a minute later his phone rang. He said, "Hi."

Warren said, "Tell me what you're doing."

"I just called to tell you those two are gone."

"You didn't—"

"We gave them an opportunity to escape prosecution. They're on the freeway by now."

Warren paused. "Thanks for coming by."

"Don't mention it."

The call ended. Warren put the burner phone back on the kitchen counter and plugged it in to charge. He looked at the clock on the screen. It was four sixteen A.M. He went to the door between the kitchen and the dining room and picked up the rubber doorstop that kept it open. He carried it to the entrance door the intruders had drilled open and jammed it under the door to keep it shut. Then he carried the coffee table over and propped it against the doorknob and said, "Let's try to get some sleep."

19

I t was after six when a garbage truck down on the street backed up, and its warning signal's repeated high-pitched beeps woke Charlie Warren. He got up, made coffee, and went to look at his door. It wasn't that he doubted his memory. He just needed to see it again while he decided what to do about it.

He went to his computer to find a locksmith. When he signed in he scanned the email messages, and found one that had been sent just after midnight. Then he heard the sound of Vesper's feet padding in from the hallway and looked up. "Good morning. Did the garbage truck wake you up too?"

"Yes," she said. "At first I thought last night was a dream."

"I can't blame you."

She nodded at the computer. "Anything interesting going on?"

He looked at the screen. "I think so. A message came in on the office email overnight. It's from Founding Fathers Vested. Want to hear it?"

"Sure."

He read. "Charles Warren & Associates and so on.

"Founding Fathers Vested Investments Fraud Division has investigated the claim you submitted on behalf of Mrs. Vesper Ellis. We have
found no evidence of any discrepancy in Mrs. Ellis's holdings with
Founding Fathers. The copies of monthly reports which you appended
to support her claim are partial and incomplete, and include only the
initial investments made by Mr. and Mrs. Ellis when the relationship was
established, and while they reflect a growth of value, recent quarterly
dividends, and interest, they don't include everything.

"There are two additional linked accounts, numbers FF 798423D and
FF 135834I, which were also established by the attachment to the agreement that Mr. and Mrs. Ellis signed at that time. These two accounts hold
the dividends and interest from quarters prior to the most recent two
quarters, as well as the proceeds from occasional sales of stocks, bonds,
or other securities, all of it held in cash equivalents for future purchases
or other uses as directed by Mr. and Mrs. Ellis.

"Attached please find the most recent reports for FF 798423D and FF
135834I, as well as this month's report for their principal investments. We
can see that Mrs. Ellis's claim is based on a misunderstanding, probably
caused by the unfortunate death of her husband, Mr. George Ellis. Had
his death been reported to Founding Fathers Vested Investments, her
advisor, Ronald Talbert, could have contacted her with useful information, as well as answered all of her questions. Please see Attachment 7,
Report of Change in Account Holder(s), which must be filled out and
returned as promptly as possible. Sincerely, Marissa Susquino Esquire,
Director, Fraud Department, Founding Fathers, etc., etc."

"I can't believe it," Vesper said.

"Look at these two attachments I've got on the screen. Have you ever
received one like them before?"

She leaned over his shoulder. "No."

"Then you're right not to believe it," he said. "Instead of telling you that one of their people has been robbing you, they've replaced your missing money in these two new accounts and they're time traveling to make the theft never have happened. They've probably got somebody creating monthly reports for the past few years right now."

"They would do all that?"

"It's a very risky strategy, but they obviously don't want to have anybody know the truth. My guess is that either Ronald Talbert has been doing this to other clients and they need to keep it quiet while they top off dozens of accounts, or they've already got some other problem, like maybe troubles with the federal regulators. It's got to be bigger than the damages they should have paid you, which they could have done after a half hour of investigating."

"What are we going to do?"

"If you do nothing, they'll replace your lost money. They're hoping you'll believe there's no point in pursuing a lawsuit or anything."

"But what do you recommend?"

"That we check to see if your money is really in the account. If it is, you close the account today and put the money in a bank. We can still come for them after that."

20

Most mornings, Patrick Ollonson came into the office at six fifteen, because that was nine fifteen Eastern time, and it made him seem to be a client advisor who wanted to be in his office and already reading the summaries and projections for the stock market session that would open fifteen minutes later. That had always been a pose, but it had seemed to work for many years to compensate for average performance. The bosses liked to see the troops at their posts early, prepared to detect the moment when all the indicators lined up to make a particular course of action a clear winner. It was true that sometimes the prize could be won by getting into a sure thing early, and sometimes it paid to be the first one out. But for Ollonsun, to be there early was an empty gesture. He had never sent a mass alert to his clients to buy or sell anything.

But this morning he had been in his office at 4:00 A.M. He had not wanted to see anyone coming in, not wanted to be in an elevator or a hallway with anyone. He didn't want anyone to see his face with its swelling, bruises, and cuts, or especially, to have to answer any questions about it.

Pat Ollonsun had married Christina Welbrower five years before Ron Talbert turned up and married Francesca, her younger sister. He'd had all that time to learn what marrying into the Welbrower family meant. The grandfather was Ted Welbrower, for Christ's sake. He'd been a B-17 bomber pilot in World War II, shot down over Germany and captured, and later decorated for organizing the escape of two dozen Allied prisoners. After the war he'd borrowed money to buy up cheap tracts of farmland ten miles out from various western cities. Then he had put up some land as collateral for more loans to start car dealerships so people could live ten miles out and commute to the city for work.

Land meant houses meant roads meant cars meant gas stations meant food sales meant warehouses. His son Daniel, the girls' father, was the educated version of the Welbrower girls' grandfather, and the education had been like adding a jet engine. He was one of the first to cater to the new suburbs with shopping malls. Every bit of family history was just as intimidating. The maternal grandmother came from an ancient aristocratic Scottish family with actual castles and miles of green rolling land and rocky coastline. The girls' mother seemed to have no ancestors who weren't professors, scientists, or something. The Welbrowers didn't think of themselves as snobs. They thought of themselves as superior. It was an opinion that everybody else seemed to share.

Being the first son-in-law had been a mixed experience for Pat Ollonsun. The good part was that Christina was beautiful enough to be an actress if that hadn't been too low-class for Welbrowers, and she had learned in college courses that frequent monogamous sex was one of the most wholesome and health-promoting activities humans could do. The bad part was his own status. From the first introduction, Christina's family and friends found Patrick Ollonsun to be an unsuitable match, so far beneath Christina that it had caused some of them to start introducing her to other young men to head off the marriage.

The truth about his marriage was more complex than he had understood at first. Christina had told him early on during a moment of tipsy honesty that his unending persistence in getting her to notice him, then date him, had made her think he could counterbalance the ferocious energy of the Welbrowers. The women, particularly as they were growing up, were prized and protected, but it was like being a treasure, not a person with agency. Christina had developed a resistance to being controlled by her family. She knew she was desirable, knew that most men in her social circle would want her. But an outsider like Ollonsun, who was about to take his first job in a California finance company three thousand miles from the nearest Welbrower, had been irresistible.

Five years later, when Christina's sister Francesca had brought Ronald Talbert around, Pat had understood. He had realized that what Francesca was doing was reacting to the rift Christina had created with the family and choosing Christina's side. For her it was rejecting the control of the old almost-medieval Welbrower patriarchy, being close to her beloved elder sister, and embracing the newness and freedom of California. She had even chosen a man who, from her flawed point of view, was like the one her sister had.

Pat had befriended Ron and taught him things that would help him survive in the world of the Welbrower sisters. To the extent that he could, he helped encourage and aid his wife's efforts to bring Ron and Fran into her own social circle to make up for being dropped from the one Christina knew would exclude them. He had been the wise older brother-in-law, and when the time came, the doting uncle. And he had helped Ron learn the ways to produce enough income to fund a marriage to a Welbrower sister.

And now here he was, hiding in his office with his phone connected in an endless call to his own cell phone so any incoming call would find the line busy. It wasn't really endless. He'd been in the office for over six hours. It was now a little after ten A.M., and he'd had to renew the call every two hours because that was when the phone company automatically cut it off. He looked as though he'd either been in a drunk driving accident and gone into the windshield or been runner-up in a bar fight. His brother-in-law, his protégé and supposed friend, had done this to him.

He had been sitting here for all these hours, trying to think his way out of this mess. He had made his best effort to hide his hand in Vesper Ellis's losses, but he had been skimming other clients' accounts for so long that the sums had gotten to be more than he could cover. He had longed to ask for help from his wife's family, but it was a solution he had tried before, and they had refused. Her father had actually referred to some warning he had given Chris when their engagement had been announced that when this day came, she shouldn't bother to ask.

When their grandfather had died, Christina and Francesca had inherited identical trust funds. Pat had gone to considerable effort to find a way into Chris's, but her grandfather's attorneys had anticipated that some future husband might do that and set the trusts up so that there were three trustees who had to approve any withdrawal. Ollonsun had been sure that Christina could get around that, but he also feared that asking her would start the avalanche of questions that would sweep him out of the marriage.

This morning he'd gotten out of the house early enough that she hadn't seen his face yet. She was used to not seeing him in the mornings, but by tonight he would need to find out from Ron what he was telling his wife, so their stories matched. He didn't look forward to that, and he would give Ron time to cool down first. Meanwhile he had bigger and more immediate problems. He had learned that his "get out of jail free card," the former mentor who had risen to be head of the European Division, had been quietly replaced during the past year; after he'd tried some inquiries of mutual acquaintances, he learned he had a fatal case of cancer.

Ollonsun had run through many possible ways of saving himself—framing someone else in the Great Oceana company—a brilliant young intern who had great computer skills; telling Vesper Ellis he'd borrowed some of her money to pay for his daughter Zelda's emergency surgery and would pay her back in installments; saying he had not known that her late husband George Ellis was dead, so he'd approved withdrawals requested in that name that had now been traced to North Korea or Russia or China. His ideas had become increasingly wild and unpromising. They had, as the morning went on, become scarcer, and their space in his mind was slowly being usurped by hopes that something he had already tried was going to work.

The hope his mind kept returning to was that the two men he had been paying to watch Vesper Ellis and her lawyer would save him. He had given them a lot of cash last night and they had agreed to hurt both client and lawyer badly—fifteen thousand, if Ron had counted right. It was entirely possible that they would do such a good job that Vesper Ellis and Charles Warren would back off, in physical pain and afraid for their lives. But Pat could still hear one of them ask if he and Ron were willing to accept the fact that the victims might die. He admitted to himself that this was actually a better outcome. Then there would be no victim anymore, and no lawyer to pursue the complaint. He started to pray for it, and then felt that somehow prayer didn't seem likely to help.

He was hearing the sounds of business going on outside his office door—footsteps as people walked up and down the open concourse where dozens of people worked in cubicles or in rows of computer screens arranged three to a desk in a fold-around arrangement. There was a woman's voice that had a melodious quality that carried and reminded him of Chris's voice as it came closer. Then he heard the "pock pock pock" of her high heels coming closer. They stopped, and he had a feeling of dread. She rapped on his door.

Ollonsun froze and listened, not daring to move in case his desk chair creaked to reveal that he was in. He and the woman listened for each other. He knew that if she gave up and left, he would hear her shoes. Instead, he heard her knock again, this time louder. After about ten seconds he heard her voice. "Mr. Ollonsun?" He waited for the shoes.

Instead, he heard a key in the door lock. His door swung open, and he saw her, the typical young Great Oceana executive—dark blue suit, silk blouse, straight dark hair cut at shoulder length. "Oh," she said. "Mr. Ollonsun, are you all right? We knocked, but since you didn't answer, we figured we'd better check on you."

"I'm all right," he said, then remembered he didn't look all right. "This was just a little bicycle accident. I slipped in a gravel patch last evening." He stood up. "I don't think we've met."

She stepped forward, smiling, and held out her hand to shake his. "Stacey Ramsdahl, admin." Her handshake was firm and energetic, and it reminded him that his right hand was in pain from a punch Ron had half ducked so Pat's fist had bounced off his hard forehead.

Stacey Ramsdahl was not here to waste time. "They need you right away in admin. Do you need a minute to freshen up or anything before we go?"

"Well, I was right in the middle of some things. Would it be possible to put this off until—"

"They need you there right away, I'm afraid." She turned and seemed to notice his sport coat hanging behind the door, "Oh, your coat's right here." The door of every office that people like him inhabited had a coat hook screwed into the back of it, but she greeted it as a great find. She lifted it off its hanger and held it up so he couldn't avoid slipping into it without physically resisting. "They said this won't take long."

She stepped to the door and pushed it open, and he saw the others. There was a man in navy blue coveralls with a tool pouch and a ring of keys on his tool belt. There was also a tall man about Stacey Ramsdahl's age who was built like a football player. "This is Dennis. He's going to give us a ride over to the admin offices."

Dennis was just as friendly. He smiled as he said, "Good to meet you, Mr. Ollonsun." Pat knew better than to let this one crush his hand, so he just raised it in a little wave, said, "Likewise, Dennis," and engaged his hands in adjusting the cuffs of his shirt and then the lapels as they began to walk. He was being dragged out of his office to some dreaded inquiry, as surely as though they handcuffed him or prodded him along with guns. He couldn't resist or escape or argue or, really, do anything except what this tall, attractive, cheerful young couple asked, or he would appear to be crazy or criminal on the building's surveillance cameras.

The three walked down the open concourse to the bank of elevators. Ollonsun felt as though people must be watching them, but nobody he knew appeared. He stood in front of the doors and stared at them so no strangers noticed his bruised and scratched face.

When they reached the ground floor, Stacey Ramsdahl led the way, and Dennis fell slightly behind. It was as though he was there to be sure Pat didn't change his mind and turn back. She pushed the door open and held it until all three were out on the sidewalk. A black car was parked in the five-minute loading zone, and she got in the back seat and patted the seat beside her, so Pat had to slide into it. Dennis slammed the door closed, got into the front, and drove.

Stacey Ramsdahl filled in the silence with small talk as the buildings floated by. "I'll never get used to Los Angeles. This part always seems like it's this plain, light-colored facade, so nobody knows that these dull, benign-looking buildings aren't just a bunch of dentists' and therapists' offices, but places where billions of dollars are changing hands twenty-four hours a day and deals for hundreds of movies and television shows and things are going on."

"I take it you weren't born here," Pat said.

"No. Rising Sun, Maryland. When I was growing up, I couldn't wait to get someplace where all the action was. I picked LA. Now when I tell people that, they say, 'Rising Sun. What a pretty name.' And I know it is, but it's funny that when I lived there, I didn't ever think of it that way. Where are you from?"

He said, "Evanston, Illinois. I went to college in Boston, and I met my wife there. The woman who was going to be my wife, I mean. The year I met her I waited to register for classes until she had registered and then signed up for every class she was in. Now they'd probably call me a stalker. Fortunately, she didn't take it that way."

"Oh, that's so sweet. And then you married and came here together."

"Yep."

He could see that the short ride was coming to an end. The building for Admin and the other parts of Great Oceana that didn't deal with the public was ahead. A few seconds later Dennis swung across the lane and up the driveway into the garage entrance. Then he got out and came around the car to Ollonsun's side to let him out so he would be aimed in the direction of the lobby entrance. The only other way out was over

Stacey Ramsdahl, who was already unbuckled and waiting for him to move.

The parking attendant got into the driver's seat and waited while Ollonsun and Stacey got out, then drove the car away. The three reassembled in their formation, with Stacey leading the way to the elevator, pressing the button, going in, then Ollonsun, and last, Dennis, moving in behind them and blocking the space until the doors closed and the elevator rose.

She had pressed the button marked 4. Ollonsun didn't know where they were going, but he was fairly sure that the floors with the bosses, the people to be feared, were at or near the top, which was the twentieth. He felt a moment of hope that maybe this really was a meeting about something routine. The doors parted and the three stepped out. In front of them was an arch, and above it, the words Human Resources. He felt even better. He had been here a few times over the years, always for some dull practical matter—hiring, getting a child added to his health insurance, signing things when the company improved the pension system. He just hadn't remembered which floor it had been on.

Stacey stepped out and led the way, and they proceeded inward. She stopped at the reception desk and said, "Gabrielle Nagata?" and the woman behind it pointed to the left and said, "Four eighteen." They made their way to the right number, and a small Asian American woman with short black hair was waiting for them at the open door.

"Hi," she said to Ollonsun, and reached out to shake his hand. He took a chance and shook it. "I'm Gaby Nagata, Mr. Ollonsun. Come on in." Ollonsun's two guides stepped aside so he could enter, and Stacey touched his upper arm and said, "We'll wait out here."

The room was large, with Gaby Nagata's desk and two others, but nobody was in them. Ms. Nagata dragged a chair up to the large desk, and said, "Have a seat," then went behind it and took a large folder from the left corner, slid it in front of him, and opened it. The printed forms inside were facing him. Still smiling, she leaned across the large desk and pointed to the first horizontal line at the midpoint of the first form marked with a red X. "Sign here," she pointed to the next, "here," the bottom, "and here."

"What am I signing?" he asked.

"This one is to claim your bonus package," she said. "You're welcome to take your time reading it. I can leave you alone here while you do it, but there are a lot of pages that need to be signed, so it may take a while, and I understand they're waiting for you upstairs."

"Let me just take a minute or two to scan through it." He looked at the top page and realized that the pages were separation papers. The bonus she'd mentioned was a severance package. He leafed through the papers quickly. He would get an extension of two years of his health insurance, including for his dependents. His pension accumulation would be removed from the Great Oceana account and made over to him in a lump payment, with a warning that it needed to be reinvested promptly in another retirement plan or be treated by the IRS as income. This added to his shock. They didn't even want him as a client.

He glanced at Gaby Nagata. She was staring into his eyes, and her smile had disappeared. He looked down again to check the last few pages. His last day of employment was filled in, and it was today. There was a page that tallied up the amount of his final paycheck, which would be mailed to him on payday. Then there was a long list of things he was responsible for returning: his company ID card, keys, parking pass, any company-owned electronic equipment, and other miscellaneous company property.

The final page, which was to be dated and witnessed, was a long paragraph stating that he understood that he was no longer an employee of Great Oceana Vested Corporation, and agreed never to present himself to any person as such in the future, or to state or imply that he was in possession of any company financial or investment information, all of which was to be considered proprietary, or that he was engaged in any official or unofficial relationship or connection with any employee of the company.

He looked at her again. "Two years' health insurance? That's nothing. It will go by in a flash."

She said, "It will go by in two years."

"You know what I mean. All of this is incredibly harsh."

Gaby Nagata studied him. "I don't really know anything about your individual situation. Those are the standard forms that everybody needs to sign on retirement. If you think you can negotiate better terms based on your particular circumstances, fine. I wish you luck."

"How often does that happen?"

"I've never seen it happen. If it does, they probably have Legal write a one-of-a-kind agreement, but I think they would send it here afterward so we could archive it."

"So I may as well sign this, I suppose?"

"If you get a different agreement, presumably they'll send it here to supersede this one. In the meantime, if you sign, you'll be sure to at least get this bonus, the pension money, and so on."

He took the pen she had used as a pointer and went from page to page signing his name or initialing various provisions. When he was finished, Ms. Nagata quickly used her fingertips to slide each page to the side until she had seen them all, then closed the folder over them. Then she stood and the smile returned. She said, "That's all I'll need. Good luck in your next position."

"Thank you." He walked to the door and went out to the waiting area, and saw Dennis and Stacey stand up from their chairs to join him.

They resumed their formation and the two men followed Stacey to another room, this one a small office inhabited by a man at a desk. He had a plastic tray on his desk, and he pushed it to the front so Ollonsun could reach it. He had a printed list. "Mr. Patrick Ollonsun. We'll need your company ID." When Ollonsun put it on the tray he checked it off his list and said, "Office keys." When Ollonsun had disconnected them from his keychain and put them on the tray, he went down the list. When he had gone through the list, he handed the paper to Ollonsun and said, "Please note the paragraph at the top. "The items you didn't have today must be returned by mail or messenger, or their cost will be deducted from your final paycheck."

Ollonsun took the list, folded it and pocketed it, then followed Stacey out the door to the elevator. This time she pressed 20. When the elevator stopped and opened again, Stacey led them to a waiting area. Ollonsun had never been up here before. He had always imagined it as an opulent, old-fashioned place that was mostly silent, with polished woodwork and antique furniture preserved from the original offices. It was not that way at all. There were dozens of men and women moving from one office or conference room to another, sometimes outsiders carrying briefcases, called in from other places for some meeting or proposal or report, but most of them twentieth-floor dwellers. He could see that the proximity to the centers of power gave them a kind of electric energy so they moved faster and kept their eyes ahead.

After a short time one of the women on the concourse veered to their waiting area. "Hello," she said, speaking only to Stacey Ramsdahl. "Is this Mr. Ollonsun?" Stacey said, "Yes." She said, "Okay. Follow me."

They followed her to one of the offices off the concourse, and all three of them followed her inside. The others sat and there was a free chair, so Ollonsun sat too. The woman said, "Mr. Ollonsun, I'm Hannah Soames, one of the senior attorneys in the Legal Division. Mr. Foshin, the head of Legal, assigned me to take this meeting with you. I assume you've been to Human Resources already, signed your exit papers, and so on."

"Yes," he said. "But I would like to discuss the terms on those papers."

Hannah Soames stared at him as though he were a strange substance that she'd just noticed on the bottom of her shoe. She said to Stacey Ramsdahl and Dennis, "Give us a few minutes, please." The two got up, glided out, and closed the door. When they were gone, she said, "What would you like to discuss?"

"In the first place, nobody came to let me know I was being let go, or talked to me about the size of my severance package, or how long I'd have health insurance for my family. All of these things are important. I don't want to have to turn this over to my attorneys. I would have assumed we had room to bargain a bit."

"Mr. Ollonsun," she said, "I get the impression that you sincerely don't understand what's happening. The company has investigated and verified the accusation that you've been stealing from one of our clients."

"Verified? That can't be," he said. "This isn't about the Ellis account, is it? I saw that she'd made an inquiry, I looked into it, and found that nothing was missing. I reported that to the head of client services."

"It's time for you to drop the pretense. Legal didn't just verify the Ellis complaint. Forensic accountants have looked into all your current clients' accounts, found several other looted accounts without even going into the archive of closed accounts, minors' trust accounts, etcetera, and realized that we had to come to an agreement with her attorney. We've paid her back and settled her lawsuit for three million dollars."

"But—"

"The company will have to reimburse and settle with an unknown number of other current clients, and the heirs of deceased clients, and do a great deal of reorganizing and restructuring to catch people like you in the future before they steal twice. The reason we're discussing any payment of any kind to you is that it's been decided it will be better for Great Oceana to let you retire, sever any connection the company has with you, and set the situation in order with as little publicity as possible."

"Okay, but there's still the question of the numbers. If I'm cooperating and helping with the cover-up, that should be worth something."

"Those are the numbers that would be appropriate for an employee at your level who is voluntarily retiring at your age." She added, "Let me make this as clear as I can. The other choice wasn't to negotiate what it would take to make you go away. It was to turn you over to federal law enforcement agencies along with the evidence of your crimes."

"You're threatening me?"

"On a personal note, I don't like you, but because you are a human being, I will give you the very best advice I can. Take the money and run. In fact, do it now, before the bosses have second thoughts."

Ollonsun stood up, turned around, and walked out the door.

Stacey Ramsdahl and her companion Dennis stood up from their seats in the waiting area and went with him. They ushered him to the elevator, to the parking level, to the car, and drove him to the building where he had worked for almost eighteen years. Dennis pulled up to the curb.

Stacey Ramsdahl said, "We'll walk you to your car."

Ollonsun said, "That won't be necessary. I've got to go back upstairs and pack up the personal belongings I have in my office."

She said, "Don't go back up. They've already cleared out the room for you. That man who let us into your office is a locksmith and he's changed the lock. Your personal things will be delivered to your home. You'll probably have them by tomorrow afternoon."

"I think I should check before I leave."

She reached out and placed her hand on his arm. "It's all meant to make things smooth and easy as possible for you. It's done. There's nothing up there anymore that belongs to you. Go home."

Dennis was already out of the car opening the door for him, and in another two minutes Ollonsun was sitting behind the wheel of his own car staring out the windshield at the bright, hot street.

21

At three P.M. Warren checked the Vesper Ellis account at Founding Fathers Vested on his computer, then looked up at her. "Take a look at this."

She came over to the kitchen table and looked at the screen.

"This is your current balance at Founding Fathers," Warren said. "It's the same as the latest monthly report you brought me, except that two lines have been added for the two imaginary accounts, and they are, for the first time, included in the balance. The total is a quarter million dollars higher. They gave you back what must be the amount Ronald Talbert siphoned off."

She hugged him. "Thank you. That's all because of what you did."

He said, "I think you should call them now and withdraw all your money. You don't need to tell the person on the phone anything other than that you're withdrawing it. Have it sent electronically to your checking account."

"Okay."

She went to the guest bedroom where she had left her phone charging, then came back. "Can you read the number from the monthly report for me?"

He did and she dialed the number and ordered the person who answered the call to complete the transactions necessary to liquidate the investments and send the proceeds to her bank. The process took around ten minutes, and when she was finished, Warren said, "Very good. Now I get to do my job."

"What's your job?"

"To put away all the suits we prepared against any company except Founding Fathers, and pursue getting that one to court. I'll compose a short letter to Founding Fathers now to bring them up to date, and ask Martha to have it messengered to them."

The letter didn't take long.

Dear Ms. Susquino:

We have received your letter in response to the claim Warren & Associates submitted on behalf of Vesper Ellis. We feel that, as a courtesy, you should be given notice that she is proceeding with her lawsuit against Founding Fathers Vested Investment Corporation.

Since Mrs. Ellis has brought our firm all the monthly reports ever sent by Founding Fathers to her or her late husband, it has been possible to verify that the two additional accounts you mentioned did not exist as recently as one month ago when she came to our firm about the discrepancies in her account. In the monthly reports, we retain permanent proof of those discrepancies, which vanished at the same time as the two new accounts appeared. Your own company's IT department can, I'm sure, confirm to you that the creation of the two new accounts and the erasure of the discrepancies can easily be detected, traced, and dated by law enforcement technicians.

Charles Warren, Attorney at Law

He sent the letter to Martha.

◆

Ronald Talbert had been in his office for hours dealing with clients when his cell phone rang. He looked at the screen to see who it was and had the urge to open the window beside him and hurl the phone out, letting it fall eight stories to the street. It was, like most urges of that sort, something he knew he would never do for a hundred different reasons, the first of them that windows in the Founding Fathers Vested office building couldn't be opened.

He touched the green circle and said, "What do you want?"

Pat Ollonsun said, "First, I want to apologize for pissing you off last night. I'm very sorry. I was in a desperate state and acted badly."

Talbert said, "Pat, frankly, no apology from you will ever fix what you did last night, and I don't want to waste another minute talking to you about it. I hope this is the last conversation I have with you about anything, but I know I'm not that lucky. What do you really want?"

"I came in after Chris was asleep last night, and I was at the office before she got up this morning. I'm on my way home, and I need to know what you told Fran about your face, so I can say the same thing."

"Home? Why are you going home so early? The New York markets haven't even closed yet."

"I got fired this morning, Ron. My career at Great Oceana is over, and I'm damned sure never going to get work in finance again. Please, just tell me, so I can at least make an attempt to salvage my marriage and family."

"Jesus," Talbert said. "I—" he paused. He had been about to say he was sorry, but it was automatic and not sincere, so he choked it off. "I told her we had stopped for a coffee at an outdoor stand on Fairfax and four young guys started making fun of us. You said something that gave them an excuse to attack us, and because it was two-to-one they got in quite a few punches before we chased them off."

"Okay, thanks, Ron." He paused. "Why didn't we call the police?"

"They were young and fast, so by the time we thought of it they were in their car and gone. Since it was a fight, there wasn't any actual crime we weren't also guilty of."

"Is that true?"

"None of it is true. Are you out of your mind?"

"No, I mean, if that really happened, they wouldn't be charged?"

"That's what I think, and that's all that matters to the story. When I told Fran she hugged and kissed me, but it could have been to check if I'd been drinking or smelled like another woman's perfume. So far, she's only talked as though she believes me."

"Okay," Ollonsun said. "It's worth a try. Thanks."

"You've got to use it. Just don't embellish it or change it. We both know the sisters are going to compare stories. Chris might even have heard it already." He saw a light flashing on his desk phone. "Look, I've got to go. Please don't screw this up."

"Bye."

He put away his cell phone and picked up the desk phone. "Ronald Talbert."

"Ron, it's Connie. Come see me in my office."

"I'll be right there." He stood up, but then he had to grab the desk to steady himself. He refused to think he was feeling faint. He had just stood up too fast and felt off balance for a moment. He had a mirror hanging from the inner side of his door so he didn't go out to greet a client with his collar inside out or his tie loose, and he looked at himself. He looked bad because of his battered and bruised face, made worse by his sour expression. He manufactured a smile, but that made it hurt, and the smile was too big. He modified it slightly, went out, and headed for Connie Pollock's office.

Connie had started at Founding Fathers at the same level as Talbert just months before he had eleven years ago. She'd had a pleasant-looking face, about average for a woman in her twenties, but she was smart and funny, and they had enjoyed each other's company. They had called each other Ronnie and Connie, and soon others picked it up. The work was hard and the hours were long. Sometimes after work a group of five or six of the newer employees had stopped in a nearby bar for a drink before splitting up to go back to their small, cheap apartments.

One night the others had dispersed quickly, and he and Connie had talked about staying for another drink, but she had suggested instead that they have it at her apartment. At the time they had both been single, and the idea had seemed to be a good one, and then so had spending the night. They had remained friends rather than a couple, but for a time they had gotten together occasionally to catch up with each other, always ending the night with sex. Within three years they had both gotten married, and the sexual part of the friendship ended. Over time the intelligence she'd shown had won her several promotions, and now she was the head of Talbert's section, his immediate supervisor.

They were still friends, but the situation was further complicated by the fact that a few times—most of them while they were out of town for a conference or training session—they'd gotten together again in one of their rooms at the hotel. He had never considered himself to be cheating. Connie was a special case. Most people had friendships with people of the opposite sex whom they hugged. In a way, their times together were like that—just a longer, deeper hug with a special friend.

He reached her door and knocked, and she swung the door open, let him inside, and shut the door. He said, "Hi, Connie." He noticed she seemed strange, but he maintained his smile and waited. She pointed at the chair in front of her desk. Instead of going to sit at her desk she pulled another chair up to face his. "What the hell happened to your face?"

"I fell."

She stared into his eyes. "Ronnie, you know that I love you. You've always been one of my very best work friends. I sometimes think having you around was the main reason I made it through my first year or two here."

"I feel the same way," he said. "You seem troubled. What can I do to help?"

She winced. "God, that's so like you, wanting to help me. For our whole time here, I've tried to look out for you, mostly by sharing any intel I got from on high that might help you avoid trouble or get a jump on something. Today I noticed you seem to be of special interest to the watchdogs."

"Watchdogs?"

"I think the Fraud division must be looking into one of your accounts. I was in a meeting with my boss when the fraud supervisor, Marissa Susquino, called his assistant and asked to come and see him right away. He said, 'Let me talk to her.' He got on and said, 'What's this about?' While he was listening to the answer, he said, "Hold on a minute.' He turned to me and said, 'We'll have to finish later. I've got to take this.' When I went past his assistant's desk, I saw she'd written 'Re: Ronald Talbert.'"

He could feel sweat on his forehead and under his arms. "Interesting." It was all he could manage.

She said, "Tell me what this is about."

"I don't know," he said. "Maybe one of my clients has been investing somebody else's money."

"Tell me what this is about," she repeated.

He ran his hand through his hair. "I'm in trouble, Connie. I never meant this to happen. It just did. As soon as I knew some ways to do it, the temptation was overwhelming. I've told you how Fran and her sister are. They grew up without ever having to think about money. It was just there when they wanted it. Fran hasn't ever even wasted money on crap. We have a normal house and two cars that are nice, but not crazy. It was just that their great grandfather, grandfather, and father each added to the family fortune, so they think of money as just something men take care of. I needed to live up to that." He looked down and away from her.

"You stole money. Is that it?"

"From a client."

"One client?"

He was silent.

She looked at him differently. All the confidence and charm and humor had been drained out of him. He was sitting a yard from her and she could see he was about to start crying. "Okay, more than one," she said. "I'll try to do what I can to help you, as I always have. But just let me ask you this. Did you ever think about what was likely to happen to me? I've been your boss for six years, the one who always gave you the very top evaluations, the one who was paid to know everything about your work."

"I know, I'm sorry," he said. "I'll make sure nobody thinks you were in on it or even knew."

"That isn't going to save my job. You couldn't have gotten away with it unless I was either not looking or stupid. I guess it was both. The truth is, we trusted each other, but one of us was wrong." She looked at her watch. "We may not have much time, so we'll stretch it. If you leave the building right now, I can use the injuries to your face to say you went to get them taken care of. You should go to your doctor or one of those urgent care places on the way home, so there's a record."

"Then what?"

"You'll have to decide for yourself. Stealing from a client is both a state and a federal crime. You could either get the best lawyer you can find, or fly tonight to a country that won't extradite you." She leaned forward and gave him a peck on the cheek. "If you do get on a plane, don't write. Now get going before they decide to stop you."

"Thank you, Connie." He got up and, instead of turning right to return to his office, turned left and took the elevator down to the parking level where his car was. He started it and drove out onto the street.

Upstairs, Constance Pollock ignored the fact that the telephone on her desk had a button lit up. She stood and put the two chairs back where they had been, then took her purse and went into the private bathroom next to her office. She looked closely at herself in the mirror. At some point very soon, she was going to have to meet with some of her superiors, and probably other people she knew only by name. She brushed her hair and repaired her makeup. She decided she should use this opportunity to pee. The bosses would agree that this matter had the same urgency as a house fire, and required that everyone put in continuous effort to tamp it down before it grew to take them all with it. Once this one got started it could last for hours.

She looked in the mirror again on the way out and set her face in a serene, confident expression. She found her assistant, Claire, standing by her desk. Claire said, "Mr. Herrod said to come back to his office, and this time bring the folder for Ronald Talbert."

22

During the early part of the day Warren spackled the bullet hole in the wall outside his door while he and Vesper waited for the workmen to come. The cleaning crew thoroughly removed the blood stains in the carpet of the hallway and stairs. The locksmith replaced the damaged lock with a new, heavier one with a steel plate that covered the space between the doorknob and the woodwork so it couldn't be jimmied or drilled.

After lunch Warren said to Vesper, "Do you think it's time to take a look at your house and see if those two guys that broke in here broke in there too?"

"I've got to find out sometime," she said. "It may as well be now. I can take an Uber or Lyft. I'll just pack my bag and go home."

"When I suggested taking a look, I meant both of us. I'll drive you," he said. "We've found some good guys for the repair if we need them. Their numbers are in my phone."

"Um," she said. "I wonder if you would mind packing a bag too. I feel pretty safe and confident right now in daylight, but I know that tonight if I'm alone in the house, every sound is probably going to terrify me."

He said, "Of course."

"I'm sorry," she said, "But the world looks like a different place to me lately."

Their packing took a short time, and then Warren went around his condominium checking window latches and door locks. They went out and he locked the door and pocketed his new key. They got into his rental car and drove toward Vesper's house in the Valley. He was extremely careful, taking the Lankershim Boulevard exit from the 101 freeway and driving to the Metro station across from Universal Studios and then down into the part of the parking lot that was at the bottom of the graded incline where they couldn't be seen from the street. They waited for five minutes, but nobody drove into the lot searching for them. He left the lot and went over the overpass above the 101 freeway, exited onto Laurel Canyon, and went the rest of the way to Encino on Ventura Boulevard.

They pulled into the Ellis house's driveway, and then walked to the kitchen door. Vesper unlocked the door and turned off the alarm, and they went in.

Warren said, "Try to arm it again."

She did and then the electronic voice said, "System armed," and the screen above the keypad began to tick off the minute they had if they'd wanted to leave.

Warren said, "That's reassuring. All the entry points are closed with no breaks in the circuit or it wouldn't do that." They still checked every door or window in the house for signs that they might have been tampered with, and didn't see any. They went from one room to another looking for any evidence that anyone had been inside the house while she had been gone.

When they reached the second floor of the house, which held the bedrooms, she said, "Nothing seems to be out of place."

Warren said, "Think back. I called you a couple days ago to say you needed to get out of here, and I was coming for you in fifteen minutes. Did you leave your house perfectly neat like this? Was there nothing out of place?"

She looked around her for a moment. "I remember checking the locks, and then going upstairs to look out the edge of the upper window's curtains to look at those two cars parked at the ends of the block, to try and see what the men in them looked like. I couldn't. I had wasted too much time trying to, I had to rush the packing and get downstairs. Then you called to say you were going to be fifteen minutes late, and I was feeling anxious, so I left my bag in the kitchen and came up here to look out again, but I ended up straightening the room to kill time."

He shrugged. "Okay, then. I guess I'll go down and bring our bags up here."

"I'll go down with you and check the mailbox. I've been having them hold my mail at the post office, but people are always sticking flyers and things in it, and I'm sure when they pile up, potential burglars must notice."

They started back down the stairs together and reached the first landing when his phone rang. He saw the caller's number. "It's Martha," he said. "Hi, Martha."

"Hi, Charlie. I've got a senior vice president at Founding Fathers named Ford Morham on the line saying it's urgent that he speak with you this afternoon. I can connect you, or make an excuse, or make an appointment. What's your pleasure?"

"Thanks, Martha. Put him on, please." He sat down on the carpeted stairs at the landing and Vesper went the rest of the way down.

He heard the clicks and the sound of moving air. "Mr. Morham? This is Charles Warren. I understand you'd like to speak with me."

"Yes, Mr. Warren," he said. "Thank you for taking my call. We'd like to arrange a meeting to discuss the issues raised by Mrs. Ellis's accounts with Founding Fathers Vested. If it's possible, we'd like to take care of this quickly. Is there a time today when we can get you together with our attorneys?"

"Do you have a time in mind?"

"How about four P.M. at our offices?"

"All right. I'll be there. Goodbye." He listened for clicks, then said, "Martha? Are you still listening in?"

"I'm here," she said.

"Then you know I'm going to be at that meeting at four, but I'll stop at the office ahead of time. If you've got anything I should be paying attention to, that would be a good time."

"All right. See you then."

He went the rest of the way down to join Vesper, who had made it to the mailbox and then back to the kitchen. He said, "That was the call we've been waiting for from Founding Fathers Vested. They want to meet with me at four."

"What does that mean?"

"I think it means that the people in charge of fending off claims got worried and talked with the people who actually know specifics about how their business is run and realized that they've got troubles."

"If something happens, great," Vesper said. "Just remember, you've already won. In trying to cover up, they restored what they took, and thanks to you, all the money I had invested with them is in my bank accounts. And you already got a ridiculous settlement from Great Oceana."

"It's not over quite yet."

"If this just ended here, I'd be perfectly happy."

"I get that," he said. "But I think we've got a chance to help another big company make it less likely for small investors to get robbed in the future."

"I understand," she said.

"I know this is going to sound like a waste of time, but I would like it if you would come with me and spend an hour or two in my office while I'm in the meeting."

"You don't think I'll be safe here alone?"

"Apparently nobody's broken in here. But those two guys who were watching this house and then broke into my place weren't random robbers, or they wouldn't have known to come to both places. They must have been working for somebody, and I don't know who. With the meeting, today just became one of those charged days when a thief might think it was his last chance to stop us from ruining his life. Maybe you should pack fresh clothes while you're at it."

She headed for the staircase. "I'll be right down."

When she came back downstairs, she was wearing a black pantsuit with black flats and carrying her overnight bag.

Warren said, "You look really nice."

"It's the default outfit that everybody owns. You can wear it whether you want to tap dance, deal blackjack, or bail out of a plane."

"Let's stick with the easy ones for now."

When they got to the office, he and Vesper sat in the conference room with Martha while she presented routine matters for his attention and gave him various papers to sign. After a few minutes Vesper got up and said to him, "Do you mind if I use your office to call Tiffany?"

"Feel free."

Martha gathered up the papers on the conference table. "I guess that's all the stuff you need to see and sign at the moment. I looked up Ford

Morham, so you can know who you're dealing with before you go at four. It's on the computers."

"Thanks, Martha."

He went to the computer in the spare office, signed on, and found the folder of entries she had compiled. Morham looked the way his name sounded. He was tall with a thin nose and bright blue eyes. He had been to a prep school in Pennsylvania that Warren hadn't heard of, then Duke, and then NYU for his MBA. The résumé was a steady rise over twenty-five years at three companies.

He closed the file and went into the outer office. It was getting to be time. He gathered copies of the past year's monthly reports for Vesper Ellis's account at Founding Fathers, copies of his lawsuit against the company, and copies of his letters to the company and their replies, and put them in a thick brown file envelope that tied with a string. He knocked and opened the door of his office and waved at Vesper, who was sitting behind his desk talking on the office phone. He said aloud, "I'm leaving now, Mrs. Ellis."

The Founding Fathers Vested office was too far to walk to, and his latest rental car was sure to be familiar to anyone who was hired to watch him, so he went down the elevator only as far as the second floor and stood at a window in the alcove that held the elevators, summoned a Lyft car, and stayed there to watch the street from above. Five minutes later he saw a car that matched the picture on his phone. He kept his eyes on the cars behind it and near it for a few seconds, stepped into the elevator for the one-story ride, and then made it out the door and into the car in about ten seconds. The driver was a man in his twenties who had a cheerful, friendly manner. Warren responded the same way and told him the address he had already supplied on his text message, so there was less chance of a misunderstanding.

The car slid into motion and took him toward Founding Fathers. He memorized the cars in the street behind the Lyft car, and occasionally checked to see if any new cars appeared. In twenty minutes the driver pulled up and let him out in front of the building where Founding Fathers Vested occupied the top five floors. Warren got out and headed inside. When he reached the lobby, a woman in her early forties wearing a gray suit cut across the lobby to intercept him. She held out her hand and said, "Mr. Warren? I'm Constance Pollock. We've been expecting you."

"Good afternoon," Warren said. "Thank you for meeting me."

She checked her watch. "You're early. It looks as though we have some time to kill before the meeting. Come on, we can wait in comfort upstairs." She pressed the elevator button and then hurried in and pressed the sixth-floor button. When the elevator opened again Warren saw that the floor had wide hallways lined with individual offices. She took him to a small conference room. She said, "Would you like coffee, tea, sparkling water, a soft drink?"

"Do you have just regular bottled water?"

"Sure," she said, and left him alone in the room. He sat down. It seemed to take a very long time for her to return. He wondered if she had gotten a call or been derailed by someone she'd met in the hall. Finally, he got up and went to the door, opened it, and spotted her about a hundred feet away heading in his direction with a water bottle.

He held the door open and accepted the bottle. "Thank you." He glanced at his watch. "Six minutes to four. Is the meeting on this floor, or should we get going?"

"It's a bit farther. Come with me," she said, and walked along the hall, turned a corner and then another.

He was impatient. He liked to be in a meeting room before the planned time. It gave him a chance to collect his thoughts and size up the other people as they entered the room. This Ms. Pollock had a relaxed manner that was becoming irksome.

She reached a door and swung it open. He could see the usual giant conference table, the large windows. This row overlooked the southern part of the city and ended in a blue stripe of ocean. He was relieved. She said, "Sit where you're comfortable. The rest of the group should be nearly ready to head over here."

"What do you mean?" he asked. "It's four o'clock now."

She looked at him, apparently puzzled. "Yes."

"Your Mr. Morham scheduled this for four o'clock."

"Oh, I'm sorry," she said. "Mr. Morham is a senior vice president. He's used to having other people scheduling meetings for him. He probably forgot that there are a lot of people who have to gather for this one, including someone who flew in this morning from the home office in New York. You could say that setting your meeting for four P.M. today was aspirational. At the moment you're set for four thirty."

"The only one they didn't tell was me?"

His phone rang and he reached for it. Constance Pollock said, "I wouldn't tie up your phone line if I were you."

"Why not?" He looked at the screen of his phone. It was Martha.

"If there's a change and they're ready early, they'll try to text you."

"Hello," he said into his phone. "What's up?"

Martha said, "I just got a call from Founding Fathers. They say you missed your meeting time, and they're getting ready to call it off."

"Call them back, tell them I'm in their building, and find out where the meeting is. I'll hold."

He kept his eyes on Constance Pollock while he waited. She was on her way out of the room.

He got up and kept his phone to his ear as he snatched up his file envelope and followed her out.

Martha said, "Room 901. It's a conference room."

"Thanks." He put his phone away.

He saw Constance Pollock disappear into one of the elevators and when he arrived he saw she had pressed the down buttons on all of them. He went into the stairwell and ran up the steps to the seventh, then the eighth, to the ninth, flung open the door and trotted only eight steps before he was at the door marked 901. He tried to open it, but it was locked. He knocked on the door firmly, waited, and then pounded on it.

The door opened and a man about thirty was standing there. "Mr. Warren?" the man said. He fiddled with the doorknob. "Sorry. This seems to have gotten locked."

"Right," Warren said. "Apparently there was a mix-up. Ms. Pollock was under the impression that this meeting was at four thirty." Constance Pollock was sitting near the far end of the table, and she pantomimed her surprise at what he was saying.

"We were about to give up on you," said the man at the center of the table. Warren recognized him as Morham from the information Martha had sent him. Warren realized Morham was almost certain to have realized that Constance Pollock had been trying to sabotage this meeting. He decided to say nothing further about her.

Warren's eyes left Constance Pollock. "Well, we seem to be here now."

Morham said, "Please have a seat."

"Thank you." He sat.

When Morham went through the polite ritual of introducing each of the sixteen people who were seated around the long table, he skipped Constance Pollock. Then he said to Warren, "I'm sure you must have guessed the reason I asked you to come. The director of our fraud division, Ms. Susquino, was struck by your response to her letter, and took a second look at your client's accounts. She decided to make the effort to investigate your assertions about them. She had our IT people look into when the computer files had been opened or closed, and what operations had occurred. It turns out that you were right. There was evidence that someone had made some changes to old information contained in Mrs. Ellis's file and tried to erase the times and dates of those changes. In addition, the files for the two cash accounts for investment were dated years ago, but were actually quite new."

Warren said, "I appreciate that Ms. Susquino was willing to do the extra work, and that you were willing to be open about what she found out."

"I understand that in the scramble to cover up the crimes, the perpetrator or perpetrators restored Mrs. Ellis's money, or came close to it, and that when she learned of this, she withdrew her investments and closed the accounts."

"That's correct," Warren said. "On my advice."

"Then I assume that means you and she are satisfied and we can put this unfortunate event behind us."

Warren stared into his eyes and said, "I advised it because I could see no reason to believe that she or any other client of your company could be confident that their money won't be siphoned out of their accounts tomorrow."

"There are many reasons, but I'll just mention three. The first reason is that we've already been accumulating evidence of who was responsible and how he went about it. We're also looking into the question of who else knew and might be part of the conspiracy. And three, we're looking very closely at anyone who should have noticed something wasn't right and pursued it."

"Personnel matters are up to your company, of course," Warren said. "Our lawsuit is only about my client's accounts."

"What does your lawsuit suggest she is entitled to?" Morham asked.

"I want to receive proof within thirty days that the federal authorities have been informed, and I want a suitable payment for expenses and damages to my client within ten days."

A man in the same side of the table as Warren leaned forward and said, "One million dollars."

Warren realized that the upper-level executive who had flown in from New York was not imaginary. He was here to make the settlement. Warren said to him, "Two million, in a cashier's check, within one week."

"Two it is, and you drop your lawsuit and do not do any press releases or public statements."

"It's fair to give the company time to revise its procedures and correct the problems before they're made public," Warren said. "If you live up to the agreement, we will drop the lawsuit and won't make public statements. We can't refuse to answer questions asked by the authorities."

"Founding Fathers will accept that," the man said. "We should have a contract ready for signature within a day or two."

Warren said, "I'd like the agreement typed up and signed before I leave the building. In fact, I have a version in my office computer right now. If you'd like, I can send it with my phone to any computer here that's connected to a printer."

The man down the table smiled. "I get that you anticipated the terms we would need. But did you actually anticipate the amount?"

"I knew what I would settle for."

The man said to the others, "You can all go, except for Mr. Morham, Mr. Caine, and Ms. Ostroff. We'll need you for the contract. Thank you all." As the others all filed out, he walked up to join Warren near the head of the table. "I'm David Stokes, in case you didn't remember from the long list of names." He shook hands with Warren. He said, "We'll wait while you send us the contract, and then Ms. Ostroff and Mr. Caine, who are attorneys, will read it, and then you, Mr. Morham, and I can sign it."

Mr. Morham said, "Send it to FMorham@Founding Fathers." Mr. Caine went out to a nearby office and returned with five copies. It was such a simple agreement that it fit on five sheets, including the signature lines. The two attorneys verified that it accurately reported the oral agreement. The two executives signed, Warren signed, and then the two company attorneys signed as witnesses. A few minutes later Warren was walking out of the conference room with a fully executed copy.

23

Ronald Talbert did some of his best thinking while he was driving. He had been driving for over four hours, but had not succeeded in working things out so there would be a satisfactory future. He had been struck by Connie Pollock's offhand remark that he could vanish into a country that didn't extradite American criminals. He had pulled his car into the parking lot at South Coast Plaza in Costa Mesa, plugged in his phone, and done some online research.

Out of 193 countries the United Nations recognized, the US had diplomatic relations and extradition treaties with most of them. Some that had treaties were capricious and couldn't be relied on to live up to the treaties—Ecuador and Switzerland, for instance. Others wouldn't turn over anybody who might be executed, but turned over everybody else. The ones who were left didn't appeal to him—places like China, Russia, North Korea, Iran, Syria, Afghanistan. The best exception seemed to be Bhutan, which was very high altitude and tiny, and didn't seem to have gotten around to making a policy on the topic. It might be possible for him to sneak into some foreign country, change his appearance, develop a false identity, and then sneak over a second border to avoid any searches, and live a miserable, solitary existence there. He started the car again and drove to the northbound freeway entrance toward home.

He knew Francesca couldn't run away with him, and it wasn't something he held against her. She had been heroic in fulfilling her part of the marriage, even though the marriage must have felt like he'd doomed her to a smaller life than she'd been raised to expect. She had never complained about that. When he'd heard her explaining to the kids why their family weren't going to Maui for Christmas or France for the summer like some of their friends, it had felt like he was being bled to death, but she said it with simplicity and good sense. "I promise you, it will be more important to you in a few years that you're able to go to a fine college because we didn't waste our savings on expensive vacations. Those are pretty, sunny places, but we live in a pretty, sunny place. People in those places pay to come here." When he remembered it, he could hear her voice. In order to cover up his thefts, he'd had to drain some personal savings in a hurry, assuming he could replenish them within a few weeks. It occurred to him that the transfers had included the kids' college funds, and that he wasn't ever going to be able to get near Founding Fathers Vested again.

He realized that he was an hour and a half from home, and Francesca would be expecting him in about an hour, so he drove faster. He knew that he should be using every second in some constructive way. He had to face one of the problems that he had been pushing out of his mind all day. He didn't want to go to prison. No, it was much worse than that. He would rather be dead. Lots of people thought that, but the ones who hadn't obtained the means for suicide and kept them where they could reach them quickly were trapped.

His cousin Tim had been a handgun enthusiast. He'd told Ron once a few years ago that his collection had reached a hundred. Ron had said, "I know there are two major kinds—revolvers and semiautos—but they're all tools that do exactly the same thing, aren't they? Isn't it like having a hundred hammers?" Tim was dead now. He'd been on this exact freeway when a big truck had swerved into his lane and knocked his car sideways into the concrete barrier.

Talbert checked his phone's directory. Tim's number was still in it. Before he could start thinking of reasons not to, he pressed the number. After a few seconds he heard Tim's wife answer, "This is Tina." He said, "Hi, Tina. This is Ron. Cousin Ron Talbert."

"Hi, Ron," she said. "I haven't heard from you in a while."

"Yeah, I'm sorry about that. Part of it is this business. I happened to need to drive to Irvine today, so I'll be going right past your house. I wondered if I could stop and see you and Ricky on my way home."

"Uh, sure. I guess so. Only he likes to be called Richard now, because he's older. How far off are you?"

"I guess about fifteen minutes. I just passed the exit for Route 133."

"Then it's eleven minutes. I'd better hang up and straighten out the living room. See you soon."

"Bye."

He thought about what he was doing and felt dread. Tina was not a stupid woman. She would already sense that he was after something. He hoped she wouldn't be unpleasant about it and humiliate him. When he reached Tim and Tina's house, it looked about the same as it always had, except that the yellow paint job was fresh. He pulled over in front of the house, walked to the front door, and rang the bell.

A moment later Tina opened the door. He had forgotten how pretty she was. She was wearing her black hair long and straight now, and she had more makeup on. She wore a skirt that was short and stylish, and high heels. "Hi, Ron," she said, and leaned out to give him a peck on the cheek. "Come on in. I just got home from work myself. Can I get you something to drink?"

"That sounds good," he said. "Just a glass of water for me."

She pivoted and headed for the kitchen and brought out a bottle of sparkling water and a glass. "Ice?"

"No, thanks," he said. She gave him the water.

"What made you think of us?" she asked.

"I think about you and Richard fairly often. We used to love having you three come for get-togethers around holidays, but as the kids grow older, they get to be hard to pin down. When they're little, you don't have to check their availability. When they're older, they'd rather be with their friends. And girls are the worst. They grow up faster. We finally got out of the habit of doing those dinners and things—gave up, really. We should start them up again."

"It might be fun. Holidays aren't only for kids. Nice to see you. But what happened to your face? You look like you've been in a fight."

"I wouldn't call it that. Some young guys saw me going into work before dawn, and I guess they thought they'd end their night out by taking my wallet to cover their expenses. Fortunately, they'd spent their money on drinks. You, on the other hand, look terrific," he said. "You said you just got home from work. Where do you work?"

"Thronebridge Fashions at Costa Mesa."

"Wonderful," he said. "Very high-end." He paused. "You remember, when I talked to you after the funeral, I asked you to get in touch with me if you or Richard needed anything. When you didn't get in touch, I didn't want to butt in, but I hoped it meant you were doing okay. I'm glad to see you've got a good job and you're thriving, but the invitation still holds. Things come up, and we all sometimes find hard things are easier if we face them as a family."

"We're fine, at least for the moment," she said. "How are Francesca and the kids?"

"Fine. For the moment, anyway." he said. "Knock on wood." He knocked on the coffee table. "The girls are lucky. They look like Fran."

"I'm sorry I didn't get to see them. Do you have pictures of them on your phone?"

"I know I should, but I'm not good about taking them. I'll send some recent ones when I get home." He sat staring at her sadly. "You know, I can't drive down here without thinking of you and Tim. I'm sure he told you how close he and I were growing up. In later years, we couldn't see each other as much as we liked, but when I look back on my life, he's still one of the most important people. I think about you both a lot. I found myself having to wipe tears out of my eyes today."

"I'd give a lot if Tim could hear that," she said.

"You know, I hesitate to even say this, but I wonder if you would do me a favor."

"What is it?" her voice was wary.

"I wondered if you could spare a keepsake, a token to remember him by."

"What sort of thing were you thinking?"

"He and I always used to kid each other, and we went back and forth all the time about his guns. I used to ask him questions about why he needed a hundred of them, and if he gave them all names, whether he picked them to go with different outfits, formal and casual, and so on. He would tell me what a bad citizen I was to not exercise my Second Amendment rights, and then switched to how I was so uncoordinated it was probably just as well."

"That's what you came for? You want one of Tim's guns?"

"It isn't what I came for," he said. "I came to see you and check how you and Richard were doing. If I was out of line asking, I'm really sorry. Please, just forget it."

"No," she said. "I'm actually relieved it was just that. Here, I've got them locked up in his gun safe where he left them. After he died and money got tight, I tried to sell them all at once to a dealer or another collector, but that didn't work, and selling one at a time was too complicated, with the laws and everything. Any one in particular?"

"No. Any one."

"Wait. I have to do the combination and all that." She went up the stairs, then came back down a few minutes later carrying a nickel-plated revolver and a box of ammunition. "I'm pretty sure these go together because he kept them on the same shelf." She set them on the coffee table.

He looked at them, and then looked up at her, and he could see she was gazing at him with something less than affection. "Good enough?"

"Of course," he said. "It's very kind of you. I'll think of both of you whenever I look at it."

"I'm actually doing it because I know that if you'd asked him, he would have given it to you. All I ask is that you remember you have kids in the house. If it's not locked up, they'll find it. Don't think they won't."

"I'll be sure to do that," he said. "And I know these things are expensive. Let me pay you for it."

"No. I told you, all I ask is that you store it safely." She paused. "You know, it's getting late." She hadn't looked at the time, and there was no clock visible from there. "You'd be smart to get on the road."

"I would, but I'd hate to miss seeing Richard."

"He's on the soccer team, so he won't be back from practice until it's nearly your bedtime. And any afternoon when you head for Los Angeles after around four thirty you're in rush hour traffic. Fran will be upset if you're not there in time for dinner. And I advise you to think about how you tell her about the gun. I remember she was not a fan of firearms."

Talbert had no choice but to pick up the gun and the box of bullets and put them in different pockets of his sport coat and walk to the door. When he came close, he leaned toward her intending to give her a hug and a kiss on the cheek, but she turned away. "Thank you again, Tina. Love to Richard." He stepped out past her. He went two steps and heard the door shut behind him.

He walked to his car quickly, eager to start it and get out of her sight. When he had turned the first corner and was making progress toward the freeway entrance, he tried to feel better, but he couldn't.

After a mile or two he thought about the way she might feel if he used the gun on himself. It was selfish to do it when he knew she would probably feel guilty and would certainly face some sort of official inquiry about the gun. But that would be in the future, and it would only happen if the future came and he wasn't in it.

24

Whon Warren walked in the door, he could hear Vesper and Martha in his office talking. He went to the printer on Martha's desk, scanned the signed settlement agreement, and sent it to Martha and himself, and then walked through the conference room to the back room and put the original into the safe. A moment later he heard Martha's voice say, "Holy crap, Charlie."

Vesper and Martha both came into the conference room. Martha said, "I knew it would be good. You had them tied up and boxed in. I just didn't think it would be that good or this quick."

"They were pretty eager to step on this before the word got published somewhere. They also didn't want to have the SEC, the FTC, the FBI, and the rest of the alphabet descend on them before they could clean up the mess and institute safeguards. The easiest part of this was to pay Vesper, so they're getting that out of the way."

"Congratulations, Charlie," Martha said. "I'm proud of you." She walked toward her desk in the outer office.

Vesper closed the door, turned to him, and said, "You not only got both companies to give the money back, but together you got them to give me five million bucks. I insist that you take the pay you earned. I looked it up online and the article said it was thirty-three to forty percent."

"I told you before we got started that I was doing it pro bono publico—for the public good. If nobody fights back when people are being robbed, it just keeps happening. The Bar Association recommends every lawyer do at least fifty hours of pro bono work every year, and I was behind this year anyway. I also think it's only the fair thing to do after Copes and Minkeagan snatched you to get to me."

She shrugged. "I'll have to strain my brain to come up with ways to thank you."

"After we're sure this case is really over, buy me dinner. Or tell your friends I'm a good lawyer."

"I'll think about it some more."

◈

Pat Ollonsun came home late for the second evening. He was exhausted. He usually arrived home in the late afternoon, when both Christina and Zelda were at home and unavoidable. They seemed to be in every room at once.

As soon as Christina came to know what he had been doing he would lose her. She would be making airline reservations with her phone on speaker to keep her hands free to pack two suitcases at the same time.

He didn't want to wake her up with the sound of the garage door opening, so he coasted onto the house's little parking lot behind the garage and turned off the engine. He listened to the road noise and closed the car door when he heard a motorcycle go by on Mulholland. He went in the back door into the dark kitchen. He could see the blue light above the dishwasher door, showing it was running, so Chris had cleaned up after dinner and moved on.

Maybe she was in Zelda's suite helping Zelda with her homework. That was another advantage to marrying a woman from a rich family. They were certain to have expensive educations, so they knew how to do just about anything the kids were learning, or could teach themselves to do it.

He went up the back stairs from the kitchen. The second set of stairs was an old-fashioned thing to have in a modern house, but the houses in this complex had been designed for people who were likely to have live-in servants. He climbed the stairs as quietly as he could, stepping slowly and shifting as much of his weight as he could to the railings. He made it to the second floor, looked down the hall, and saw that Zelda's suite at the far end of the house was dark, and so was the master suite at the near end. He was relieved. They both were asleep. It was still possible that they had been interpreting his absences as minor variations in the market-dictated hours of a financial advisor.

He took off his shoes and walked quietly to the master suite, opened the door, and stepped into his walk-in closet. He took off his coat and pants in the dark, and then heard, "Pat?" behind him. He turned. "You startled me," he said. "I hope I didn't wake you up."

She said, "Are you kidding? Do you think I've been sleeping peacefully when my husband has been missing?"

"I'm sorry," he said. "I haven't been missing. I slept beside you last night. I just had to get to work early today and stay late tonight. I've been dealing with some things that took a lot of time and attention."

"What the hell, Pat? Francesca called me before dawn to tell me all about how you and Ron had fought off robbers. You could have told me yourself, but you didn't. I don't know what I did to deserve to be humiliated in front of my sister, but I guess I'll find out in the fullness of time." She flipped the switch and they were bathed in searing light. She stopped a foot from him and stared at his face. "Jesus. You look terrible. Have you taken an hour from this oh-so-important business to go see a doctor?" She was wearing a gray silky nightgown that clung to her, and he could not ignore how beautiful she looked, and how angry.

"I haven't seen a doctor, but my face looks worse than it is. I've kept it clean, and I'm sure it's all superficial."

"Pat, you could have all kinds of things—a fracture of an eye socket, a concussion, even a brain bleed. You don't know."

"I guess you're right. I'll go to the doctor tomorrow."

"I hope you didn't wait long enough to get an infection." She pivoted and he watched her walk off toward the big bed. She sat down on the bed so hard she bounced, then pulled the covers up to her neck and turned to face away from him.

He said, "Do you want to talk?"

"No, Pat. I don't want to talk. I wanted to talk earlier. Now I want to sleep."

He turned off the light. He had been anticipating a big explosion that would obliterate the family. He had a sudden urge to tell her everything—or at least more—and end the dread hanging over him. This silent treatment was a one-night stay of execution.

He looked in her direction for a few seconds, wishing. Then he put his pants and coat back on, picked up his shoes, and walked out of the bedroom. He went back down the stairs and sat at the kitchen table to put on his shoes. He took out his phone and texted Ron Talbert the words, "Call me." Then he went outside and sat in his car.

His phone rang and he answered it. "Hi, Ron."

"What do you want, Pat?"

"I just talked to Christina for the first time since our little squabble. She went to bed not speaking to me, but she bought the story you told her sister, so we're not into a deeper discussion of this mess yet. All she seems to be mad about right now is that I dropped off her radar for a day and didn't call her to tell her the lie you made up before she heard it from Francesca."

"You're welcome," Ron said. "I guess you're okay, then. You seem to be living a charmed life."

"I got fired, Ron. They had me escorted off the premises. Their legal hatchet woman told me they know everything. They're paying off Vesper Ellis and her lawyer Warren to keep it all quiet until they've had time to clean up the mess and pay back the others."

"Are they turning you in to the authorities?"

"She told me they didn't plan to, but she reminded me that they're not doing it for me. It's only for the benefit of Great Oceana. They're trying to make things look like a chain of honest mistakes, no humans involved."

"I can't believe your luck."

"Not believing it is the point. It won't work. The time is going to come in a few days when they need to throw me in the fire."

"I'm already in the fire," Talbert said. "The only reason I'm free right now is that my boss tipped me off that the company was being sued and her bosses were freaked out and using my name a lot, so I should sneak out. She said she'd pretend I was at the doctor for my face." He sighed. "I'm really stuck, Pat. The life I've been living and working for is over. I've been looking at countries that won't extradite people to America. They're awful. Some are just giant prisons run by dictators and the others are backwaters. Fran would never go with me and take the kids to live in any of those places. I spent some time this afternoon thinking of killing myself."

"Come on," Ollonsun said. "That's crazy. And how do you even plan to do it?"

"I got a gun today."

"You did? Just like that, in one day?"

"Do you remember my cousin Tim, the one who died in an accident? He was a gun guy. He had at least a hundred of them when he died. I went and asked his wife, Tina, if I could have one of them to remember him by."

"Amazing."

"Why? You have a gun."

"Yes, I do," Ollonsun said. "I bought it the legal way."

There was a long silence.

"What?" said Talbert.

"I just had a thought."

"What's your thought?"

"That we're in terrible trouble, about to lose everything—our families, all the material things we have, our jobs, our pensions, our chances of ever getting a job in financial services again. No, of ever getting any decent job again. Our freedom. But right now, tonight, while we're sitting here feeling sorry for ourselves, we have one last chance to turn things around. It's only going to exist until some judge issues a warrant for our arrests. It's like sitting on a pile of explosives. In the instant when the spark comes, we're dead."

"It's our own fault."

"It's our own fault if we sit here waiting for it to happen. But what if we got rid of the spark? What provides the spark is Vesper Ellis and her very bright, greedy young lawyer. Do you think if they weren't threatening our two companies with exposure, Great Oceana and Founding Fathers would be about to get us arrested? No. They would quietly fire us, but they would never turn us over to the police. Doing that amounts to turning themselves over to the federal regulators, and ultimately get-ting fired themselves."

"Are you really—"

"Yes, I am," Ollonsun said. "I headed us for this a long, long time ago. It was my fault. I admit that. But now is a different situation. We have wives and children who depend on us, and need us. These people are endangering our lives and the futures of our families. It comes down to: Are we going to let our enemies kill us, or are we going to make our enemies die instead? Simple. We have guns. We have tonight. After that, we've got nothing."

"I don't know, Pat. This feels really drastic."

"Ron, you told me less than five minutes ago you had begged your cousin's widow for a gun to kill yourself. That's not drastic?"

"Yes, I guess it is."

"Pick me up in your car. I need to get some things together." He hung up and waited for a few seconds for Ron to call back and abandon him, and then went to the garage and picked up the unopened can of turpentine from the row of paint, brushes, rollers, and things leftover from the painters.

◆

Patrick Ollonsun and Ronald Talbert sat in Talbert's black SUV about two hundred feet from Charles Warren's condominium. Ollonson said, "The ones on the first floor have to be one, two, three, and four. Then it goes five and six in front, and seven and eight in back. Second floor, right front has to be his."

"His lights are still on," Ollonson continued. "He's probably working late up there, figuring out how to destroy somebody else's life. I read that he's big in the divorce business. He's even probably up there getting ready to sleep with the latest divorcée."

"I wish you hadn't said that," Talbert said.

"What? You hadn't thought of that yourself? Do you think after you lose Francesca she's just going to stop living or dissolve into thin air? She's young and pretty and healthy. She'll have about fifty years of life ahead of her. She's also going to be a woman with three kids and a mortgage, and she's nowhere near stupid."

"I just didn't need that right now."

"Maybe knowing it in advance will help. I factored it into my misery inventory as soon as I realized that I wasn't going to be able to get past this Vesper Ellis thing. I'll bet Christina has been thinking about a future without me even before this. She's been talking to me in a sort of snide way for months. And she keeps buying this incredible lingerie and wearing it—the low-cut, clingy kind you can sort of see through. I think she's reminding me what a prize she is, and at the same time, telling me what a disappointment I am. Wait until she knows everything."

"Fran hasn't been that way at all."

"I'm not losing sight of the fact that Warren is hurting Fran and Chris too, maybe more than us. Speaking of that, you did bring the keepsake you asked your cousin's widow for, right?"

"It's in the glove compartment," Talbert said.

"I hope you thought ahead to buy some ammunition."

"Tim had a box of it on the same shelf of the gun safe, so she gave it to me too."

"I hope you thanked her."

Talbert didn't want to relive the searing experience of asking her and then feeling her contempt, so he said simply, "I did."

Ollonsun opened the glove compartment and took out the pistol. "A Colt Python .357 Magnum. That ought to do it." He opened the box to reveal the bullets. They made Talbert think of hornets in their compartmented nest. Ollonsun said, "I'll load it for you." He opened the cylinder and pushed six bullets into it and then clicked it back into the frame. "There. All ready to go."

They watched and waited. At seventeen minutes after twelve the timer in the living room socket clicked over to the next minute and the light in the window went off. At twenty-three minutes after, the timer in the spare bedroom clicked and cut the power to the reading lamp there, and that window went dark. "It looks like he's going to bed," Ollonsun said. "Let's give him a little time to actually get to sleep before we make our move."

"That's one of the things I've been wondering about," Talbert said. "What, exactly, is our move?"

Ollonsun shrugged. "We've lost our jobs, we've lost the chance to work in finance again. But the worst thing is still on the table. Right now, the odds are that both Great Oceana and Founding Fathers are going to decide that their best hope is trying to pay off the clients and make it like nothing ever happened. The problem is that even though the bosses see it that way, this woman and her lawyer are refusing to let it go away. I did everything I could to avoid things getting to this point, but now the only way to make our problem go away is to make the people go away. You know that now, right?"

"I guess I do. But frankly, I started by shaving little slices off some accounts that the owners never even missed. And it seems like no time at all, and here I am with a loaded gun in my glove compartment waiting to murder a man I've never even seen. And then her too, right?"

Ollonsun sighed. "You may recall that I hired people to just scare them off, so we had a chance to avoid it coming to this."

"You gave them my money, and all they seem to have done was disappear with it."

"I'm just saying that my motive all along was to avoid getting ourselves directly involved. But sometimes you have to do what's necessary to survive."

"Yes," Talbert said. "I think that's true. And it's why I'm here. I think we should decide exactly what the plan is before we go get him."

"We have to be open-minded. I brought the turpentine and a lighter in case there's a chance to make it look like a household fire. Even having it look like arson would do, because arsons are usually done by the owner for insurance. Not only would Warren be a suspect, but so would the other seven condo owners."

"That's a problem, though. We might be killing eight people, or however many people live in the building."

"We have pistols. We can shoot him. A lawyer like him must have a hundred enemies. It's possible he has a gun too, so we can't hesitate. We find a way into his place, rush into his bedroom, and open fire right away. The .357 magnum you have has much more stopping power than a nine millimeter like I have, but that means it will have a kick, so be prepared for it. Hold it in both hands and put a round in his chest. Ideally the second round goes into his head, and we go out whatever way we came in. We can take a few seconds to steal whatever we can see—his wallet, watch, computer, that kind of thing."

"Wouldn't it be smarter and safer to use a rifle and fire through a window? No prints, no DNA."

"Have you got one with you?"

"I don't own one. My cousin's revolver is the only gun I've ever owned."

Ollonsun looked at his watch. "We've got tonight. I don't know if we'll have tomorrow to get this done. I think it's time to go do it." He

opened the glove compartment and held the revolver by the barrel so
the handgrip was in front of Talbert. He stared at it for a moment, then
reached out to accept it. They both put on the medical masks and baseball caps and got out.

They walked across the front of the building. There was a front
entrance that had a heavy conventional lock and a keypad that
might be an intercom or might be an electric second lock. Just past
that was the garage entrance, which had a big garage barrier made
of steel bars. They could see cars in most of the spaces, but they
had no idea which one was Warren's, and no idea what to do with
that information if they had it. They went past the door, turned at
the corner of the building, and found themselves in front of a steel
door set into a fence with spikes on top that made it around eight
feet high.

They kept going past the building and then the next one, and then
the next, which was older and had an open walkway. They followed it
to the back of the building, which had a pool and a patio. At the other
side of it there was a door in the cinder block wall separating it from
the next property. It was locked, but the wall was only five feet high,
so they scaled it and then crossed the next patio with a pool to another
wall. This one was more like seven feet, but they moved a metal table
beside it, climbed on the table, and made an even easier crossing to
the back of Warren's condominium building. They found a door at the
rear corner of the building near the enclosure that hid the dumpster.
Ollonsun tried the door and he was surprised when it opened into the
garage. He could see the street through the bars of the garage door
from there.

They went into the garage and found a door that led to a half-story
staircase. They climbed it and saw doors with the numbers 1, 2, 3, and

4 on them. They found the next flight of steps that led to the second floor. The first door on the left was 6. They moved close to it.

"The lock's not like the others," Ollonsun whispered. "Look at this. There's a steel guard so you can't jimmy it."

"It looks like the door's new, too," Talbert whispered. He leaned close and sniffed it. "Fresh paint."

"He's ready for this," Ollonsun whispered. "It's like he knew we were coming."

Talbert gestured to Ollonsun to come and began to descend the steps. They went all the way back down to the garage. They closed the door to the building, went to the corner of the garage, and crouched behind the last of the parked cars. Talbert said, "We could wait here until he comes out to get into his car and shoot him then."

"I don't know," Ollonsun said. As he came closer he stepped across an empty parking space, then stopped. "Look at the floor. The spaces are marked with condo numbers. The two that are empty have sixes painted on them. He's not even here. I'll bet they're at her place."

"You're probably right," Talbert said. "Let's head for her house."

Talbert drove up the block where Vesper Ellis's house was. "Which one is it?" he asked.

"The one with the big trees and the brick facade and the two chimneys. Number 43501."

"Okay, I see it." Talbert slowed his car down and crept along the pavement. They both craned their necks to see as much as they could.

"We should go around the block and park out of sight of any cameras on this street," Ollonsun said.

Talbert went around the block to pull up in front of a house on the street behind the Ellis house. He turned off the lights and the engine. "Okay. What now?"

"Just leave the lights and engine off while we figure this out," Ollonsun said. "Can you see the upper floor windows from here?"

"They all look dark to me," Talbert said. "If he's with her, they're asleep."

"That's perfect. Let's get out and take a look around."

They got out of the car and walked on the far side of the street so they could be an extra thirty feet away from the Ellis house and get a view of the whole property. They made a full circuit of the block, studying it. Then they extended the walk another half block and walked up the driveway beside the house. They looked closely at each window and through it at everything they could make out in the near-solid darkness. Ollonsun whispered, "The alarm's probably got a cover so you can't see if it's on or not."

"I think it's most likely to be on," Talbert whispered. "She's a woman living alone."

They came around the house to the upper end of the driveway and found a white hybrid Mercedes parked there. Ollonsun said, "There you go. We know she's home. And I don't see a car that could be his."

They both kept going and climbed the steps to the back door. The windows were dark, but there were glowing lights on the microwave, the two wall ovens, and the refrigerator. There was also a flat square plastic object on the wall that Talbert could see reflected in the glass front of one of the ovens. There was a closed cover, but it had a red light on the left side. "The alarm is armed," Ollonsun whispered.

"You have another idea?"

"I've got one that's so simple and straightforward that it's beautiful."

"What is it?"

"First, we cover your car's license plates. Then we drive it back, park it right in front of the house, and leave the motor running. It's good that we took your SUV tonight. It's closer to the kinds of car the LAPD uses than my sedan is. We go to the front door and ring the doorbell. We ring it and knock again and again. I'm pretty sure she'll come downstairs to the door. She'll look out a window or the peephole in the door. If one of us is standing on the front steps holding up an ID card she'll yell, 'Who are you and what do you want?' or the equivalent. We'll say, 'Police, Mrs. Ellis. We need to talk to you.' At that point most women will turn off the alarm and open the door. Bang-bang, we each shoot her, go to the car, and drive away. Mission accomplished. We throw the guns into a sewer, take the cover off the plates, and go home."

"We don't look much like plainclothes cops. We look like we've been in a fight."

"If she doesn't buy it, we shoot her through the door. If she just looks out a window at us, we shoot her through that. In fact, that's a better idea. We don't both have to be on the porch. One of us could be all ready by the nearest window, and shoot her as soon as she reaches the ground floor."

"It should work," Talbert said. "She knows she's involved in an investigation, so the police might need to get in touch and maybe protect her, right?"

"Right," Ollonsun said. "Just remember what's at stake. This is probably going to happen fast, so don't freeze up on me after it starts. Whatever thinking you have to do, get it out of the way now, before we ring the doorbell."

Talbert nodded his head, then stared at the ground for about ten seconds. Then he said, "Okay. Let's go get the car."

They set off walking around the block toward the car. As they walked, Talbert said, "What are you going to use for your police ID? Do you have anything with your picture on it?"

"Let's see. My driver's license, my Costco membership. She'd recognize those. My work ID would have been perfect, but they made me hand it in."

"I still have mine," Talbert said. "I sneaked out before they started looking for me."

"That'll do."

"It has my picture on it. I thought you would be the one on the porch. You know what to do and say. You're taller and older too. More like a ranking cop."

"Oh, I know," Ollonsun said. "My ID for getting into the front gate of our housing complex looks really official, and it has my picture on it."

They reached Talbert's car. He opened the hatch at the back, and took a roll of electrical tape out of his emergency toolbox, stretched it across the rear license plate, and cut off pieces. It took a few strips to change the numbers on the plate—3 to 8, 1 to 7, 5 to 6. Then he gave the little lightbulb above the plate a half-turn to remove it, and then gave the front plate the same treatment. When he got into the driver's seat of the car, Ollonsun was already sitting in the passenger seat looking at the plastic ID from his wallet with his small flashlight. He turned off the flashlight. "Ready to do this?"

"Yes," Talbert said. "Absolutely."

They pulled to the front of the house and parked the car but kept the motor running so she would be able to see the lighted dashboard. They stationed themselves at the front of the house so Ollonsun could ring the doorbell and Talbert would be at the front window looking in.

Ollonson rang the doorbell, then knocked on the door. He was cautious about keeping the volume of the knocking down, but he was confident that the doorbell would not be set at a decibel level that would wake the neighbors, so after a few minutes he kept pressing it over and over. He looked at Talbert standing near the side window with his revolver. He congratulated himself on the tactics, but why wasn't she running to the door?

He kept ringing for a long time, but heard nothing from inside. He said to Talbert, "Go around the house. Look for lights, shadows, anything. If you see her, shoot through the window." Talbert walked along the outer wall and peered inside each window. It took him another eight minutes to make the circuit.

When he reached the front steps again, he said, "I don't think she's here. Leaving her car here doesn't mean she's here. She wouldn't drive it if she was on a date. She might even have gone out of town."

Ollonsun took out a handkerchief and wiped his fingerprints off the doorbell button. They got into Talbert's car and Talbert pulled away. Talbert said, "Well, that's his place and her place. Maybe they're together."

"I'd bet on it," Ollonsun said. "You know, I got the impression from the research my guys did that he's sort of a specialist in finding and recovering money. He does a lot of divorce cases where the husband or wife is hiding assets, or there's some kind of a guardian who's skimming a trust fund. I'll bet he's really good at knowing when it's time to get out of sight. You know where I'll bet he is?"

"We looked at the houses. Where else?"

"His office. I'm not saying every one of his victims goes looking for him, but I'm sure some do, just like us."

"His office?"

"We know that he walked out of my company and your company within the past two days carrying written agreements of some kind. My company told me they agreed to pay his client three million. If you had a piece of paper worth three million—or maybe two worth six million, where would you put it?"

"A safe deposit box, I guess."

"Nope. These lawyers can't be running into the bank every day to unload papers from their briefcase. They have their own safes. They've got to. I know the address of his building. You want me to drive?"

"Just put it in your phone and it'll give us directions. And hand me that box of ammunition in the glove compartment."

◆

Vesper Ellis and Charlie Warren sat in the conference room in his law office. They had stopped at Art's on Ventura Boulevard to get chicken matzo ball soup, pastrami on rye, and Dr. Brown's cream soda. They had brought it into the conference room and served it on large sheets of wax paper on the conference table.

Warren had brought the original fully signed and witnessed agreements from Great Oceana Monetary and Founding Fathers Vested to put them in the safe. When he and Vesper arrived, they found that the payments from both companies had been wired to the office bank account after Martha had gone home.

Vesper said, "I'm really glad you thought of stopping at Art's. I didn't realize it at first, but I was starving. I hadn't been there in a long time."

"LA is full of amazing things to eat, drink, look at, and listen to," he said. He froze and his gaze went upward. "Do you hear that?"

"Sounds like an elevator."

"It is," he said. "Every office on this floor has been closed for at least three hours, and the cleaning company doesn't come again until Friday night." He got up and opened the conference room door, and Vesper stood with him in the doorway to the waiting room.

They could hear the sound of low voices outside the door in the hallway. Then they saw the doorknob wiggle back and forth a little, but it was locked and wouldn't turn. Warren took Vesper's arm and pulled her back a step, closed the conference room door and locked it, and then began gathering the papers they had been copying and collating. He took the papers in a single pile into the storeroom at the side of the conference room, where there was a copier, a wall of shelves to hold office supplies, and some filing cabinets. He bent over and worked the combination of the safe and opened the door. He put the documents in one of the safe's divisions, and then heard a loud thud and crack as a man threw his shoulder against the outer door of the office and the door swung inward.

On the shelf beside the papers Warren saw the two pistols he had taken from Copes and Minkeagan after they had kidnapped Vesper. He took them out of the safe, shut the door, spun the dial, pulled Vesper away from the door, and pushed the steel desk in the room up on its end in front of the door to provide a barrier.

He'd heard a voice, so there had to be at least one speaker and one listener. They could be Copes and Minkeagan turning on him, or the two men he had fought off with a golf club at his condominium coming back for revenge. They could be anybody. He found the magazine release on the first pistol, saw it was fully loaded, slid it back in, pulled back the slide and saw there was a round in the chamber, and slid it back. He had left the other pistol in the same condition.

He muttered, "I'm lucky I didn't kill us both."

"What?" she said.

"Nothing," he said.

They heard the men on the other side of the door throwing furniture in the conference room aside, and then the thud of a body against the door. The sound was repeated, but this door was different from the one in the outer office. It was steel, with a heavy-gauge lock and dead bolt.

There was gunfire. Warren could see the door vibrate three times, as bullets pounded the metal around the lock. He pulled Vesper down with him on the floor behind the upended desk while three more rounds pounded against the door.

There was silence, while Warren and Vesper waited. She whispered, "What do you think they're doing?"

"Trying to figure out if there's another way to hit us."

"Is there?"

Outside the building, Minkeagan and Copes were in their most recent car watching the office of Warren & Associates. Since Charlie Warren had been attacked by the two thugs at his apartment and Minkeagan and Copes had intervened, they had been observing him very closely. They had a certain expectation of the men who had attacked him. Charlie Warren had beaten them badly with his golf club, and they were sure those two hadn't forgotten it. The question was whether they would do anything about it.

Minkeagan said, "What did you hear? Was that three shots?"

"Let's go," Copes said.

They got out of the car and went across the street to the office building. They ran down the sloping driveway to the elevator, tried pressing the button, but the machine was dead. They tugged on the door to the stairway, but it wouldn't budge. Minkeagan said, "We'll have to bypass the switch lock."

Copes took out his knife, turned a screw, and popped the metal cover off the elevator controls. He and Minkeagan had taken an advanced class in Ely on rescue for firefighters, so they knew how to get power to an elevator if the problem didn't involve fire.

On the sixth floor, the gunfire resumed. This time the bullets weren't hitting the door to the back room. They were aimed at the wall to the right of the door, in three-round volleys. The door was steel, but the walls were plywood, two-by-fours, and plasterboard. The bullets that hit the spaces between two-by-fours pierced the wall. Most of them hit the upturned steel desk, punched through the steel bottom of the lowest drawer and expended their force ricocheting among the upper drawers and desktop. A couple pierced the wall and hit the opposite wall.

Warren saw a series of three that did this, and he realized he could sight from the hole in one wall to the hole in the other and know roughly where the shot had been fired from. He waited, saw three new holes appear in the wall, aimed at the wall and did his best to place five rapid shots on that line of bullet holes. He heard another volley beginning, stepped to the other side of the desk, and fired four more in that direction.

The gunfire through the wall stopped. Warren changed pistols so he had the one with a full magazine in his right hand. He listened, but heard nothing he could identify. He looked at his watch, stood with his back to the wall and facing the steel door and the entry holes.

Vesper said, "What's happening?"

"Not sure," he said. "I might have hit one of them, or scared them off. But I think they're reloading and waiting for me to open the door to see what's up so they can kill me."

They waited and listened, but a sound had to be loud to be audible through the wall.

They stayed where they were for five minutes, and then five more, and then Vesper said, "Do you smell something?"

"Yes. It's like smoke."

After a few more seconds she pointed at a bullet hole in the wall above Warren's head. "Look!"

There was a thin wisp of smoke seeping through the hole. Warren stepped close to the steel door, held his hand near to it, and then cautiously touched it and pulled his hand away, then let his hand stay on it for a second. "It's not very hot yet, but there's definitely a fire. We've got to get out," he said. "Here. This gun has about seven rounds left, ready to go. If you see a man, and he's not me, pull the trigger. We've got to stay as low as we can because the smoke will be filling the upper half of the room. We'll have to take the stairs. Okay?"

"Yes."

"Ready?"

"No choice."

He crawled to the edge of the door, very softly turned the knob for the dead bolt, then looked at her once more, held up three fingers, two, one, swung the door open, and lunged through it into the conference room with the pistol in a two-handed grip.

The men were gone. Warren moved to the door into the main office. He could see that the men must have poured an accelerant onto the furniture and wall of the waiting area. Bright flames wavered and sparked in that area and were moving across the space where the door was broken open and left hanging on one hinge. "Hurry," he whispered, and tugged Vesper into the open gap and over a foot of low flames into the hallway.

A door down the hallway opened a few inches, a hand holding a pistol emerged, and Warren yelled, "Drop the gun and get out of the building! It's on fire!"

The pistol roared, and Warren could see a spray of bright sparks. He fired three times into the dark, empty space where the gun was, the door opened farther and a man toppled outward onto the floor. A second man fired at Warren from the corner where another hallway met this one.

Suddenly, the elevator down the hall gave a "ding," Warren and the second man froze for a second, the elevator door rolled open, and two men dashed out into the hallway with guns drawn. One of them was Copes, who yelled, "Police! Drop your weapons!" Minkeagan shouted, "You're under arrest! Police! Show me your hands!"

The man lurched out from the corner where he'd been hiding, running toward them. He sprinted down the hallway, a pistol in his right hand. Warren had time to return fire one more time. He could tell that he had hit the man, who veered aside and dropped his pistol, which Warren could now see was a large revolver with a silvery finish. When the man reached his fallen companion, he went to the floor on his belly, so Minkeagan and Copes moved toward him. He picked up the semiautomatic pistol his companion had dropped, raised it to his head, and fired.

Minkeagan reached Charlie and Vesper. Minkeagan said, "What the hell? Why'd he kill himself? Who even are these guys, and why is the building on fire?"

Copes knelt by the other man who had been hit by Warren's shots. "This one's dead. Did he kill himself too?"

"Thank you for your concern," Warren said. "We've all got to get out of the building now, you first."

Minkeagan said, "Tell the cops you found those guns in the dumpster out back, and you were going to turn them in to the police in case they'd been used in a crime."

"Have they been?" Warren said.

"Not if the cops don't charge you for this."

Copes and Minkeagan stepped over the bodies and went to the stairwell.

Warren took out his phone and dialed. He heard, "Nine-one-one, what's the address of your emergency?"

Warren gripped Vesper Ellis's hand as he stepped into the stairwell and began to descend. "Fifty-six, nine eighty-nine Wilshire Boulevard. The building is on fire on the sixth floor, we have two men shot, and so we need ambulances, fire, and police. My name is Charles Warren, and I have a law office in the building."

Five hours later Charlie Warren and Vesper Ellis drove from the police station to Warren's condominium. The world outside had taken on a faint gray color that felt like a warning that dawn was going to come sometime soon. They mumbled goodnight and went to their respective rooms and went to sleep.

It was late afternoon when they were awake and met at the kitchen table. Warren was already making coffee, eggs, and toast. "Thank you, Charlie," she said. "I would have been happy to cook, but you beat me to it." He poured her a cup of coffee and set it in front of her.

He shrugged. "It's what I make most days. It's kind of automatic." He slid the eggs onto plates, the toast onto smaller plates.

She said, "Can I use that pad and pen on the counter?"

"Sure." He took a step to the side, picked them up, set them in front of her, and went to the refrigerator to get the strawberry jam.

She wrote a paragraph, dated it, and signed it with a flourish, and then pushed it across the table in front of him.

He read it silently. "To whom it may concern: I, Vesper Ellis, have retained the legal services of Charles Warren, attorney at law, from May 6 through June 12. He has successfully recovered all of the money that employees of Great Oceana Monetary Investment and Founding Fathers Vested had removed from my accounts, and obtained damage payments of five million dollars for me. Since he has insisted on taking my case pro bono, he has received no pay. I thank him profoundly and hereby, as of six P.M. today, discharge him and declare him no longer my attorney."

He walked out of the kitchen area to the living room, opened a desk drawer, put the letter inside, and closed it. Then he went back to the kitchen table and sat down to finish their food. After they had eaten, they loaded the dishwasher and started the wash cycle.

Warren went into his bedroom closet and selected some fresh clothes, set them on the closet island, and went into his bathroom to take a shower. He started the water, stepped into it, and closed the glass door. He had slept deeply, but endured several dreams that were variations on the gunfight and fire in his office and the long police interrogation afterward. He reviewed them as he soaped himself and let the warm water wash over his head and back and loosen his muscles. His eye caught something moving in the mirror above the sink, and turned. The door had opened and closed, and Vesper Ellis was standing there in a white bathrobe, staring at him.

She took off the bathrobe and hung it on the unused hook beside the glass door and stepped into the shower beside him. She said, "I hope you don't mind. It was the simplest solution and I'm already glad I did it."

"If I had any doubts, I would have locked the door." He put his arms around her and drew her body up against his, and they touched and kissed and stood there sharing the rush of warm water over them. They spent a long time getting accustomed to each other, and then he said, "Any plans for after this?"

"Before we fall asleep again, I'm going to be your girlfriend."

25

One week later, Charles Warren leaned back on the couch in his living room, and spoke into burner phone number three. He said, "Hi, Mom. This is your favorite son. Where have you been?"

"I was at the beach all morning, had lunch with a friend, and then I was outside gardening. I don't recognize this number. You're lucky I answered at all."

"It's part of a long story, but this is a temporary phone I had to buy because my regular one is involved in a case, and I don't want my personal calls to my mother recorded."

"Hard to blame you. So how have you been?"

"Busy. I just finished a complicated pro bono case, and I have a new girlfriend."

"Congratulations. I guess you found somebody who doesn't mind having a man with no time to pay attention to her."

"Not exactly, but she is an adult and acts like one."

"She must be right there or you wouldn't say such nonsense." She raised her voice. "Hello, new girlfriend. I hope my son is being nice to you."

"He's very nice," Vesper said. "And I'm pleased that you introduced yourself, Mrs. Warren."

"Linda."

"My name is Vesper Ellis."

"I'm eager to meet you. Charlie has very high standards."

Charlie said, "That just happens to be why I called, sort of. I wondered if you would mind letting Hawaii fend for itself and flying back to LA for a few days. I'm about to start working on something new, and it involves you."

"How can it involve me? Don't tell me I'm being sued."

"No," Charlie said. "I've been contacted by a pair of men who are in possession of the actual identification and the financial records of Mack Stone. I believe what they've got includes his birth certificate in the name he was born with, the documents issued by the companies where he reinvested your money, and enough other supporting stuff to find and claim it."

"After seventeen years? How can that not be a scam? Have you seen all these documents?"

"I haven't seen them yet. I expect to in a day or two."

"And why did they bring this to you?"

"The short answer is that they learned they couldn't claim it because it isn't theirs. It's yours. Not only did Mack steal it from you, but even if it had belonged to him, you were still legally married when he died, meaning it's now yours."

"You know what?" Linda said. "The time when we really needed the money was long ago. I think the final stage of my growing up was when I learned to do without it. I'm happy the way things are right now. I'd rather you keep it."

"We don't have it. Having you here in person would make it much easier to claim it."

"Well, all right. I've missed you since your last visit here, and I know I'm going to like Vesper, so I'll get on my computer and make a reservation. I'll email you my flight information."

An hour later she emailed her airline itinerary for a flight in three days. He emailed back, "Itinerary received. I'll pick you up by the baggage claim. Please bring the following documents, unless they're already here: your birth certificate, marriage licenses or certificates for both marriages, all documents you received after Mack Stone's death (death certificate, police reports, etc.), any official documents regarding his theft of money from your accounts. Also bring anything else that strikes you as relevant that's not mentioned here. It's all ammunition for the search and the court cases. Your Highly Skilled Attorney, etc."

◆

The next day, Warren used the number three burner phone to call Copes and Minkeagan. He started with Minkeagan. "I suppose you're wondering why you hadn't heard from me."

"No. You've been waiting for us to die of old age. Ain't going to happen."

"Mrs. Ellis's case has been settled. I'm ready to get started on the McKinley Stone case."

"Well, it's about time," Minkeagan said. "We were beginning to wonder if you'd found a way to screw us that we hadn't heard of."

"Does that mean you're ready?"

"Yes, it does. Do you want us to come to your office?"

"No. It might take months to fix up after that fire. I'll arrange a meeting somewhere else. The rest of the building is okay, so I'm trying to get them to move us to another floor."

"How do you want to do this, then?"

"I'll call you with the place, you bring the material you've got, and we can start going over it and making plans. Is that acceptable to you?"

"Let me talk to our mutual friend and I'll get back to you."

"Sure. Call me on this phone and let me know what you guys decide."

◈

The 11:50 A.M. Hawaiian Airlines flight from Kahului Airport landed at LAX on time and taxied toward the terminal. In a moment Linda Warren had her only bag on her lap and her seatbelt unfastened. She waited patiently for the crew of the plane and the ground crew to complete all the steps—the *Welcome to Los Angeles* announcement, the warning about bags in the overhead compartments shifting, making the accordion folds of the boarding tunnel outside stretch out to press against the plane's fuselage, the unsealing and opening of the door. When all that was done, the aggressive passengers who had to be first and had pushed their way ahead to the overhead compartments and were now occupying the aisle began their lockstep advance past her and out the doorway. She was now fifty-nine but had not yet let her hair go gray, so nobody stopped to let her into the aisle until another woman about her age came along, nodded, and smiled. She stood, said, "Thank you," slipped into the aisle, and headed for the door.

Linda Warren had moved away from Los Angeles before her fiftieth birthday. By then her only child had graduated from law school, passed the bar exam, and had started his own small law firm, seemed to be supporting himself, and didn't have time to accept much motherly attention. First, she had put her belongings in storage, rented out the house on the west side, and moved to a succession of different parts of the country.

She would stay in each place for a year or two until she felt restless again, and then move somewhere else.

She had lived in Hanover, New Hampshire, for long enough to explore New England, then wanted to be warm again, so she moved to Key West, Florida. She next tried New York City, but eventually found the crowds and tall buildings made her feel hemmed in. She then went to Hawaii, and after a time rented a house on Maui. The place suited her, and she made friends and felt happy until the fire, when four of the friends who lived in Lahaina died and the others were all displaced. She had put up twelve of them in her rented house on the north side of the island. They had all moved out and moved on now—the families first, then the singles, one at a time. She was now considering moving on herself, to put herself physically away from the memories. The fact that they were good memories didn't help, because they were memories of people and places lost. She liked being near the sea better than other places, and was considering either the northwest coast of Washington, or maybe a place in the east like Maine.

She walked with her head up and her spine straight, in her usual perfect posture. Her carry-on bag was strapped across her chest with her left arm resting on it. She kept her strides at the same pace from the landing gate, along the concourse, to the down escalators toward the baggage claim area where people were waiting for passengers. She saw her son before the escalator had taken her down five feet, and then looked for the girlfriend. There she was, just at his shoulder, looking up to study Linda as she came down the escalator. Of course, she thought, and used the time to study her. Very pretty face. Shoulder-length dark brown hair, done by a good hairdresser. A modest dress to keep the cute figure from being the only impression—either because she was meeting his mother or she simply felt it was tasteful—please make it be that. Vesper. It was odd, but she looked like somebody who was up to having a name like that.

She reached the shiny floor and walked toward them as they came to meet her. Charlie held his hand out to take the strap of her bag and then leaned in to give her a kiss on the cheek. "Aloha," he said. "Linda Warren, this is Vesper Ellis."

Linda held out her hand and Vesper shook it, and then Linda held on to her hand and said, "You look like a very nice person, Vesper. I knew you would be when we talked on the phone. I'm pleased to meet you."

"Thank you," Vesper said. "I'm very pleased to meet you."

Charlie said, "Is this your only bag?"

"Yes," she said. "I've become a very efficient packer since I moved away from here."

"It's great to see you again, Mom. I turned in my rental car for a nicer one in your honor."

"I'm flattered. Lead the way."

◆

They drove north on the 405 freeway past the exit for Charlie's office or his condominium. "Where are we going?" Linda asked.

Vesper said, "We talked and it seemed to us that it made the most sense if we all stayed at my house. It's bigger than Charlie's condo, and since your case could involve some pushback, the fact that neither of you are officially connected with my place might help keep things safer. There's plenty of room, so we won't feel crowded."

Linda said, "That's very thoughtful of you." She turned to Charlie. "Tell me about this 'pushback.'"

He said, "That's just it. I don't know what forms it might take. I've learned that one of the things that money does is attract predators, and sometimes it even turns people into predators who weren't before. I also know that Mack Stone was a criminal, and I assume he knew other criminals. We're about to start tracing things backward, asking questions that somebody may not want answered. Sometimes people will do desperate things to protect secrets. We need to use your name as our legal right to ask, and the attorney doing the asking will be me. Same surname."

Linda didn't take her eyes off him. He was keeping his eyes on the road ahead—or was he just avoiding looking at her? "I see," she said. "The real reason you wanted to drag me back to the mainland to Los Angles was that you didn't want to start this while I was living alone in Hawaii. You're trying to protect me."

"Well," he said, "your name is going to come up a lot."

The next morning Charlie drove his mother from Vesper's house to Warren & Associates. As soon as they were in the car and in motion she said, "I've waited a long time to see you with a woman like her."

He waited. Finally, he said, "And?"

"You're both adults. You'll figure it out."

They reached his office building and he parked in one of the spaces for visitors in the underground garage and they took the elevator up to the third floor, where his firm had been moved into a new office. When they entered the outer office Martha said, "Hello, Mrs. Warren. It's nice to see you again. Charlie, I put Mr. Copes and Mr. Minkeagan in the conference room."

"Thank you, Martha. Come on, Mom. Time to get started."

They walked into the big conference room. "Gentlemen, this is my mother, Linda Warren. And this is Alvin Copes and Andrew Minkeagan, the men I told you about."

She shook hands with them both, and then went to the chair that her son pulled out for her and sat.

"All right, gentlemen," Charlie said. "Are those the papers you referred to?"

Minkeagan said, "Yes. We put them in this filing envelope right away because the manila envelope was greasy and grimy. But this is everything, and all of it is just the way it was."

Copes said, "His name was Daniel Webster Rickenger. It's on his birth certificate, Social Security card, passport, and all the financial papers."

"I see," Linda Warren said. "Where is the birth certificate from?"

"Memphis, Tennessee." Copes peered into the thick brown expandable envelope and pulled out the birth certificate, then laid it carefully on the table in front of her so she could read it.

She looked down at it for a moment. "Daniel Webster. He wasn't much like the original."

"No, he wasn't," Charlie said. "What else have we got to work with?"

Minkeagan said, "The stack of regular-size papers are the receipts from his deposits and monthly reports on how his investments were doing. They have the names of the companies and the account numbers on them. I think those might be the big things. There are also the ownership papers for the BMW and a Los Angeles marriage license with your name and McKinley Stone on it."

"Ownership of things he wrecked, I guess." Linda said.

Charlie said, "Guys, do you agree that we should make copies of the papers to work with and keep the originals here in the safe?"

"We talked about that," Copes said. "And that's pretty much what we thought. There's no sense in bringing in people we don't know we can trust and paying them to guard our secrets."

"Right," Minkeagan said.

"Okay," Charlie said. "Let's all agree on where we start. A lot of the money Mack stole from my mother was in these accounts. There's a standard practice of all fifty state governments that requires that abandoned accounts be turned over to the state treasurer or similar official. An abandoned account is one that has seen no deposits or withdrawals or other activity for three to five years, depending on the state. That practice is called 'escheatment.'"

"Sounds like an excellent name for it," Linda said.

"Some states require the bank to publish the names of the account holders or do it themselves. Some states send a letter to the last known address," Charlie said.

"I never received anything of the sort," she said. "I guess Daniel Webster Rickenger didn't have the same address as Mack Stone."

"Which brings up our first problem. We have some bank accounts in this paperwork. Some, but only some, are located in the State of California. The US Office of the Comptroller of the Currency says the proper procedure in a case like this one is to start by sending an inquiry to the office of the treasurer of the relevant state. So we start by preparing to send these inquiries."

Minkeagan said, "Preparing to? What the hell?"

"First, we need to establish in court that the late McKinley Lawrence Stone and Daniel Webster Rickenger were the same person, and then prove that Linda Warren, formerly Linda Warren Stone, was his wife at the time of his death. That makes her his heir in the State of California," Warren said. "But there's no reason not to get the inquiries all ready to be mailed out while we're waiting to get this to court here in LA. Since the Mack Stone we knew was a very competent thief, I think we've got to ask all fifty states, Puerto Rico, and a few of the American protectorates. We should work out the procedures for Canadian and Mexican banks too. If there's anything hidden in foreign countries, we'll have to work through local attorneys in those places."

"What's next?" Copes said.

"We get started on the other assets. You said you've gotten in touch with some financial services companies that held stocks and bonds and things in Rickenger's name. As they told you, in seventeen years companies get bought out by bigger companies or merge or go broke or change their names, and so on. When an account is actively managed, some stocks get sold and replaced by other stocks or gold or bonds or real estate trusts or annuities or cyptocurrency or whatever. But every month the company will produce a report that says how many dollars the account's current holdings are worth on the market. Once we've established that Linda Warren is the owner of an account, we claim it. They will convert the account to cash and send the money. That's the rough description of the process. Any questions so far?"

"Jesus. How long does this take?" Minkeagan said.

"Months. Years if there's resistance and we have to sue," said Warren. "It won't take up all our time, but it won't all happen at once. We're starting by establishing that my mother is the heir because once that's done, we can do several accounts at once. Are you two broke?"

"Not yet," Copes said. "The wolf isn't at the door, but I can see him just peeking at us over the hill."

"I'll get some papers done to pay you a cash advance on your finder's fee. I'll call you when the money is here. Does anybody have any questions?"

"No," Minkeagan said. Copes shrugged and stayed silent.

Linda said, "Do you need me here anymore?"

"No. I'll have some papers for you to sign later in the day, but I can bring them to you."

"Good." She stood up and turned to the two old men. "Thank you for finding these papers. Meeting Mack Stone was the worst thing that ever happened to me. I hate remembering it, but it's been nice having some of my curiosity satisfied. Goodbye."

She walked to the door. "See you later, Charlie."

◆

A few days later Warren was in the Stanley Mosk Superior Courthouse on Hill Street filing the papers to have the former Linda Warren Stone declared the sole heiress of all money and property owned by the late McKinley Lawrence Stone, also known as Daniel Webster Rickenger, his original name. His claim included copies of many documents, some proving that she was married to him when he died, and others that showed that he had transferred most of her money to himself before his death. The explanation was complicated, but thoroughly detailed and proven.

It took six weeks for the court to approve the claim and declare her the widow and heir of the deceased under either of these names. Warren went back to his office that day and had the office's favorite messenger service pick up the box of letters of inquiry to mail to the treasurers of all fifty states, Puerto Rico, the District of Columbia, and several US protectorates in the Pacific, asking whether they had possession of any abandoned accounts of Daniel Webster Rickenger. There were also inquiries to the Canada Board of Treasury Secretariat and Mexico's *Comisión Nacional Bancaria y de Valores*.

Warren had already sent letters of inquiry to all the investment companies that had supplied Daniel Rickenger with proof of money entrusted to them. Warren had his mother sign papers allowing him to act as her attorney and spokesperson. Then he said, "Now that we've got that part done, it shouldn't take too long for the other states to answer. We can just sit tight."

"That's good to know," she said. "But I think I'm going to do some exploring on the mainland. I want to visit a few places and see if one of them might suit me for a while. Don't worry, I'll make sure you know where I am all the time."

26

"Daniel Rickenger," May said. "The letter is addressed to him. Not to McKinley Stone or Steven Wallace or some other name, and it doesn't say 'or current resident' or something."

"When did it come?" Peter said.

"Ten minutes ago. The mailman hasn't even driven his truck away yet. Do you think I'd sit here with this thing and not tell anybody?"

"It's weird," Peter said. "I've got to admit that. It must be fifteen years by now, isn't it?"

"Seventeen, actually," she said. It cost her no effort to put the subtle combination of false sorrow and forgiveness into her voice as she spoke into the phone, even when she was upset. Her brother Peter had to admire it. May was always the one that their parents had been proudest of for her seemingly natural presentation.

She walked back and forth across her living room for the eighth time, looked back toward the big mirror on the far wall and realized she'd lit two cigarettes at the same time, and set one in an ashtray at each end of the room. She saw that the one on the grand piano was the longer, so the picked that one up, took a long draw on it, and blew the smoke out through her nostrils as she walked back. "Says it's from the State of Arizona Department of Revenue, Peter. The state."

"That's actually good," Peter said. "Every time you register your car or they send your tax return, the paper says that stuff. This has got to be a computer thing. The name on his birth certificate found its way into their database the way everything does, is all. They probably want to make him vote so they can get reelected. He won't be the first dead man who voted."

"It says that the state took possession of money he had abandoned. That must mean he had it in a bank account. You know how you do—take something from your pigeon gradually, convert it to cash, and then deposit it in bank accounts in another state under another name the pigeon doesn't know. The state wants to know if he's forgotten about his money or he's disabled or no longer living or wants to claim it."

"Does it say how much money we're talking about?"

"No," May said. "I think it's like those lost and found offices. You have to say so they know it's really yours and you're not just trying to take it."

"I assume we are, though, right?"

"Why do you think I bothered to call you? I don't see how we can pass it up," May said. "All through that period, maybe the time when he was in his early thirties until he died, he was making piles of money, and I doubt that he got any worse at it."

"Are we going to bring everybody in on it?"

"Do you want to get killed by one of your own brothers or sisters? I don't. What if the state sent letters to everybody? Why don't you talk to Rose? We should probably all get together and decide before we do anything."

"I guess so."

May said, "Call her now," and poked the red circle to end the call.

Peter sat there for a minute on the big wooden porch of his lake house. He could never decide if it was the front porch or the back porch. The official front of the house didn't live up to the name. A gravel road through tall pine woods ran past a barnlike structure with a few stones leading to a block of concrete and three steps leading up to a door. This place on the opposite side of the house, where he sat, was fifty feet of platform outside of a majestic two-story arching window like a cathedral in the forest. Right now, while he was staring off at the shimmering surface of the lake, he saw a bass he estimated at five pounds leap out of the water a hundred feet offshore to snatch an insect out of the air and flop back in, leaving a splash of growing concentric circles on the glassy water. A tall heron stalking along in the shallows watched the ripples glide to his stilt legs, then dissipate on the sand behind him. How was this not the front of the house?

Peter was satisfied with his world as it was. If the news that May had told him on the phone had seemed to require anything risky or violent, he probably would have let it pass, but it didn't seem to. He also didn't want to provide May with an excuse to inject any poison about him into the rest of the family. She was a woman who had never had any reason to complain about anything, but just the fact that she wanted him to call their sister Rose was typical. She and Rose were volatile company. The Rickenger girls had both been born with genetic advantages that were amazing, the diamonds of the gene pool. He had gone to pay a visit to May only a few months ago when she was passing through Reno, and she still had all the attributes at forty—tiny waist, an ass like two bubbles, breasts like ripe fruit, luminescent wrinkle-free skin, and eyes that made men wish for things that they didn't know about a minute before. Rose was a different type, a couple years younger, an inch shorter, and dark-haired. She looked like a perfect little princess from another century.

He looked in his phone for the number. Mrs. Dale Stansfield these days. He tapped the number. A moment later he heard her voice. He had forgotten about their voices. They were soft and musical enough to put you into a fog when they could be heard by strangers. "Hey, Rose," he said. "It's Peter. If this is a bad time, just say wrong number and call when you're alone."

"No. Hi, Pete. We're in Chicago. Dale and his cronies are out now looking at real estate."

"They didn't hear Mother's rule about real estate, I guess."

"Don't take anything you can't carry when you leave?"

"That's the one," Peter said.

"It doesn't matter. Dale's too dumb and sweet to steal."

"Look, the reason I'm bothering you is that I got a call from May about five minutes ago."

"What does her majesty want from poor little us?" she said.

"I'm afraid it brings up a bad memory," he said, "but it's necessary. She got a letter today from the Treasurer of the State of Arizona. It says they're holding some money from an account that belonged to Daniel W. Rickenger. They want to give him a chance to claim his money."

"Oh, God," Rose said. "That woman has a talent. Those letters are nothing. Dale gets them all the time. He's always building something or putting money in accounts to prove he's got enough to buy something. Now and then he leaves it too long. It's never been twelve years, or whatever this is."

"May says it's seventeen."

"I defer to her exact figures. Since I never cared much about him any more than I care about her, she's more likely to be right than I am. You have to admit he was one cold, selfish bastard. And, speaking of Mother and Daddy's rules, how does May feel about him using her address and attaching his real name to it? I'll bet she likes that a lot."

"Believe it or not, it didn't come up. I'm sure it will at some point. What she wants right now is that all of the siblings know about it right away. She wants a meeting of everybody where we decide how to go after the money."

"Peter, look at yourself, and look at me. You spent at least twenty-five years shearing the sheep. You made enough money to go live in a fishing lodge or chalet or whatever it is, relax, and live the life you want. I'm the pampered wife of a very rich man who demands nothing more from me than to have sex with him once in a while. By the time I actually leave, taking a fortune with me won't even be stealing. By then the assets will be so mixed up even I won't know who owns them. Why the hell would either of us want to fool around and draw the attention of the State of Arizona?"

"I don't know if I do. I'm just being a good brother."

"To whom? Me, or her?"

"Both of you," Peter said. She heard him moving around, and then he said, "Hi, baby. I'll be off in a second." More movement.

"Got to go now," she said. "Bye." She cut the call, walked across the living room of the hotel suite, and into the bedroom she was sharing with Dale. There was a very comfortable reading chair that looked down on Michigan Avenue. She didn't want to use up any time on her brother Peter's regular appointment with one of his escorts, and particularly didn't want to hear anything. She only wondered whether she had succeeded in talking him out of going to the meeting about the late Daniel's money. The whole thing might be nothing, but she'd decided it wouldn't hurt to try and cut him out of his share.

She sat there and looked down at the pedestrians walking along both sides of the busy street. They looked hot. Some of the men had taken off their coats and a couple had even loosened their ties. Chicago could be so humid in the summer.

27

Warren opened the door of Vesper Ellis's house with the key she had given him on the day when the locks had been replaced. "Hello!" he called. "I'm back."

He saw her appear at the second-floor railing above the staircase wearing a white terry cloth robe. She waved. "Hi, Charlie." She turned and disappeared.

He climbed the stairs two at a time, and continued across the hall to the bedroom. "What have you been up to? Have you heard from my mother?"

"She hasn't called. You'd probably have better luck calling her a little later, when it's getting closer to dinner time in the Eastern time zone and she's back at her hotel."

"And to what do we owe this?" He gestured at the bathrobe.

"I did some yard work all morning, and then I was taking care of a bunch of business papers and things, and then I realized that what I wanted next was to take a bath. That was where you came in. How is your day going?"

"I was downtown in court most of this afternoon. The judge in my mother's case ruled that the marriage between Daniel Webster Rickenger and my mother was a real marriage that was binding on him even though he used a false name. I had submitted the license and a lot of photographs from the big wedding they had. I also submitted a lot of transfers as proof that the money they lived on came from her. I had interior and backyard photographs from different years, and papers showing that the house they lived in was the one she and my father had bought. I even had some business letters Rickenger sent referring to them as Mr. and Mrs. Stone."

"So you legally proved the late Mack Stone was the same man as this Rickenger guy?"

"Several times in different ways. The photographs of him were the same, as were the fingerprints from the old papers, the new papers, and the wrecked BMW. The medical examiner in Nevada and the police both had records of the prints taken from the body. He was also wearing the wedding ring when he died."

"Does this end it?"

"It essentially ends the part about the bank accounts in this state, and maybe any others we find that were turned over to other state governments. The evidence is so overwhelming we could do it all over again once a week. All that's left is going to be financial instruments like stocks and bonds. I don't know what that's going to be like. That's for another day."

"She'll be glad to hear it. She wants to have as little to do with this as possible. What's next on your schedule?"

"I have no plans."

"Then you can share the bathtub with me. It's nice and hot."

Peter couldn't help feeling a bit uncomfortable. The lake was in a forest of tall pines, and the road was narrow and thinly traveled. That was good, but there were other houses only a couple miles from this area, along the crestline of the Sierra Nevadas—not as many as there were around Lake Tahoe, but enough. He didn't want any of the people in those houses to take notice of his visiting relatives, so he had told them different times to arrive. One car on that road was just some tourist who took a wrong turn. Two at once was a parade.

He sat at the window where he could see the road starting at around ten A.M. The first one to arrive was May, of course. She had decided that it was necessary to transport her 125-pound body and a carry-on bag in a full-size SUV rental with oversize knobby tires designed for driving off-road. He was relieved when he saw Rose show up at quarter to four in a rented compact Mazda. He had Rose pull around the side of the house where her car would be obscured by the porch. He had gotten into May's SUV himself and parked it behind his boathouse where its fat-assed gaudiness couldn't be seen from the road.

He had already prepared the lake side of the house to host his sisters. He had restocked the bar on the side of the great room. He had group-ings of three chairs, each arranged in desirable places—the big porch overlooking the lake, inside in front of the two-story window, and on one end of the long dining room table. Wherever they felt like sitting to confer, he had it ready. He had been careful to discourage pairs of people sitting without the third, because opportunities like this seemed to enable secret deals and conspiracies. The history of the Rickenger family did not inspire trust.

Peter concentrated on showing each sister to the bedroom suite he had chosen for her and keeping the alcohol and snacks plentiful and in plain sight. He didn't give any signal to either that it was time to begin the meeting. Peter felt nothing but dread about it, and he knew that there were more demanding personalities present than his. Let them decide when they wanted to take up the business.

Beginning in late afternoon the siblings sat on the porch, looked at the lake and the peaks, made drinks, and lied to each other. He knew that everyone had, over the course of their careers, made money. Their parents had prepared all of them for a life of taking what they wanted. They were all quick to see vulnerabilities and quick to exploit them. He was sure they all had enough to be considered prosperous, but these rare meetings were reunions, a chance to give the other Rickengers the impression that you were richer, smarter, and better than they were.

As usual, he heard it all but didn't take it very seriously. If your whole life was dedicated to getting other people's money, you cared about money and thought about it and worried about it all the time. Peter had been just like them until one day something had happened to him. It was as though a circuit breaker clicked. It was right after the construction people had finished building this house and had driven away for good. He had suddenly realized he had enough money.

For a while he wondered if it meant he was dying. He waited, but didn't die, because the event wasn't medical. It was mathematical. He had paid for the house and had no more desire to go anywhere else. He realized that he could afford to live the way he did now until he was well over a hundred, a point he would almost certainly not reach. That day he stopped taking any risks to get more. He stopped caring about money, then stopped thinking about it. The way he thought about this transformation was that he had been cured of being Peter.

As he could have predicted, the one who began the money talk was May. She said, "Let's see if we've got all the facts about Daniel's money now. I brought with me my correspondence with the Arizona Department of Revenue."

"Correspondence?" Rose said, "Isn't it just one letter?"

"No," May said. "It's been nearly a month since they got in touch with me. I felt I had to begin finding out what the procedures are, and make their office aware that we're the heirs. I didn't want some deadline to pass before we even knew there was one."

Rose said, "Did you give them all our names as the heirs?"

"Well, no. I didn't feel I had the right to do that. They already had my name, probably because I live in their state, so I gave them nothing and got some information. Want to hear it?"

Rose said, "Uh-huh."

"They work out of a place on West Monroe Street in Phoenix called the State of Arizona Unclaimed Property Office. They have a website that tells you all about the process. If you're claiming property of someone who is deceased, just having the same name gets you nowhere. You've got to have evidence that you're now the owner. They also warn you that the process can take up to a hundred and twenty days before you get the money. If there are stocks, it takes an extra thirty days."

"What is there?" Rose asked.

"They won't tell you. You have to tell them."

"Anybody have any actual information?" Rose said.

Peter said, "I do."

May said, "What is it?"

"I got a notice from the California State Controller's Office about two weeks after the Arizona people contacted May. I was pretty angry to learn that our brother Dan had used my name for some purpose of his own all those years ago, and compromised my safety. I did what May did, and let them know I was planning to claim what Dan left behind."

"Interesting that you never mentioned it to me," May said. "I told both of you right away when I got my letter."

"You knew Dan was hanging around in California for years until he died," Rose said. "That's probably the place where most of his money is."

Peter said, "Well, I'm pretty sure none of this matters anyway."

"Why not?" May said.

"The only reason they got in touch in the first place was that somebody else had just filed papers to claim the money. That made them search the records for the first time in fourteen years, and they found that he had signed something with his real name once and offered my house as collateral, probably in some deal. Now that everything is computerized, it surfaced."

"What a disloyal bastard he was. What about the other claim?"

Peter went inside to the tall wooden desk on the far side of the great room, lowered the front to turn it into a writing surface, and then opened a drawer above the cubbyholes and pulled out a paper. His sisters sat on the porch and watched him through the big window. He emerged and read aloud from the paper. "On July 18, the Superior Court of the County of Los Angeles determined in conformity with the laws of the State of California that the late Daniel Rickenger, a resident of the state, was married at the time of his death to the former Linda Warren Stone, now Linda Warren. She is the sole heir to his estate."

May shot up from her chair so fast that it looked to Peter as though both her feet actually left the ground. "Shit!" she shouted. "Shit shit shit!" Her graceful hands were clenched into sharp little fists.

"It looks like this was a waste of time," Rose said.

"There's got to be a way around this," May said.

Rose said, "No, if there was a woman he was still married to when he died, and she didn't consent in writing to his leaving his money to somebody else, there's no contest in California. It's hers. I've used that one twice myself."

May said, "That explains something, anyway."

Peter appeared between them. "Another drink, May? How about you, Rose?"

The women ignored him. "Explains what, May?" Rose said.

"Why you slept with so many old men. I guess now we know what that was about."

Rose's smile was steely. "What was it about, May? It was about forty-six million dollars, give or take. And it wasn't a lot of work, either. When they're old, you're not expected to take part in threesomes or organize swaps or go jogging with them. You should have tried it while you still could."

Peter said, "Since we're together all at once, we should consider everything we now know and think of an alternative. It doesn't sound as though this woman Linda Warren has remarried in seventeen years, since she was called Linda Warren before she married Daniel and is now too."

Rose said, "Is her brush with Daniel long enough ago to make her lonely for male companionship again? Is she healthy? How old? What if she were to die, for instance? Would that mean the whole question of inheritance goes back to a clean slate, or are there a half dozen contingent heirs?"

May said, "Even if none of those avenues is a winner, I wonder if after she has the money in her possession, will she get careless with it? Lots of people who won some lottery a year ago are broke."

Rose said, "We could use Peter as front man. The strong, silent type who lives smack in the middle of nature. He's probably better bait at fifty-five than he was at twenty-five."

Peter said, "I'm not interested in telling lies to one of our brother's discarded women."

"Exactly," May said. "There's nobody a discarded woman will be drawn to like a handsome man who's not interested in talking to her."

"Forget it," Peter said. "I'm perfectly content where I am."

May said, "Let's stop wasting our time arguing about what the plan is until we know what the situation really is. We should sit down tomorrow morning in front of laptops and phones and find out everything about this woman—her finances, real estate, cars, living relatives, and anything else that comes up. Maybe, as Peter says, there's no way. If so, we will have wasted one day in his pleasant forest retreat together. We'll go home and sleep better than if we just let it go."

"Sounds good," Rose said. "I'll take that drink now, Peter."

"Me first," May said. "I need it for my headache."

◆

In the morning, Warren heard the familiar ring somewhere in the distance and felt his new smart watch vibrating. He looked at it. *Who the*—he was already on his feet and picking up the phone when he saw the number and tapped it with his finger. "Hi, Mom."

He heard her voice. "Hi, Charlie. Oh, I just noticed the time. It's three hours earlier there, but seven is not that early. Of course, with the number of times you woke me up when I was in Hawaii, it could be justice."

"Well, I am awake now." He went into the bathroom, closed the door, and said, "How are you? Is everything all right?"

"Sort of. I'm in Maine walking on the beach. I've got a room in a big old hotel full of ghosts, and I'm feeling like one of them. The water is frigid, the wind feels like it wants to pull the hair out of my head, and I'm getting ready to pack my bags. I got a call last night from Glen and Vivian Nostrand. You remember them?"

"Your tenants at the house."

"Well, they got word from their agents that the television show they've been working on the last few years is going to be canceled. They both miss England, so they began putting out feelers with friends at home in London, thinking maybe someone might be involved in a new project, and if not that, at least they'd put the word out that they were going to be free soon. It turns out they were 'at liberty' for about the first ten seconds of their first call. So they're moving out of the house at the end of the month when the show wraps and then they'll get on a plane."

"Do you want me to get a broker to advertise the house?"

"No, actually. I'm thinking about taking the house off the rental market and moving back in for a while. I'd rather spend next winter in LA than any of the other places I've been lately."

"It's not going to be claustrophobic?"

"You know, that's an odd thing. Since you managed to track down the late Mack Stone, a lot of those feelings have kind of faded. It's like old business has been settled. When Glen and Vivian made me think about the place last night, I realized that I was thinking about it as the place where your father and I, and then the three of us, lived, not the place where I got hurt and humiliated and robbed. The good old memories were still there, but the bad ones weren't anymore. Besides, since you and Vesper are there, I might get to see you once in a while."

"I think that's a good idea. You said something about packing. Have you made a reservation?"

"Yes. I'll be flying into LAX on Thursday at three twenty. American Airlines."

"I'll be there."

"That's very nice of you. I'll call you when I get there. Bye."

He looked at the phone and thought about his mother. He had just heard good news. She had spent the years since he'd gone to law school moving from one part of the country to another, like a person trying out each of the spots that other people said were the best. It was as though she thought happiness lived in a particular place, and she needed to find it. Now she was coming back to Los Angeles, returning to what he considered to be the real world. He should be thinking of this as a breakthrough, but maybe it was just another phase of the illusion. He stepped out of the bathroom back into the bedroom.

"Who was that?" Vesper was lying on the bed with her arm propping her head up.

"My mother. She says the tenants in the house here are going back to England, and she's coming on Thursday, apparently to go to the house and take a fresh look at it. She's thinking about moving in herself."

"You don't seem taken with the idea," she said. "She's great—friendly, cheerful, loving, and never bothers you, that I've seen."

"All true," he said. "But this feels a little bit off. She's refused to live in that place for at least ten years. I can't help thinking there could be something else."

"Do you think she's sick or something?"

"I don't know if this is anything, and if it is, then it would probably be my own tendency to see a silver lining and just think it arrived ahead of the cloud."

"Let's act on what we know," she said. "Which, by the way, is all good."

"You're right," he said.

She got up from the bed and went into the bathroom, and he walked to the closest suite, where he had taken to keeping some of his clothes.

He showered, shaved, dressed, and then went downstairs, where Vesper had begun to make their breakfast. She said, "Martha called. She said you weren't answering, and so she said she'd leave a message on your voicemail."

He found the message and tapped his finger on it. "Charlie, the last of the answers to our inquiries to the state abandoned assets offices came in. The ones who have Rickenger money are California, Arizona, Nevada, and New York. Arizona, Nevada, and New York are accepting California's determination that the marriage was valid and in effect the day he died. The weird thing is that there were other claimants, and they're named Rickenger."

Vesper said, "That is weird. I mean, the man was a thief, right? Aren't there legal implications to trying to claim money that's stolen?"

Charlie said, "I hope so. But it's possible that in practice the only punishment for making a false claim is not having the claim validated. It would be hard for the state to prove that any claimant except my mother knew the money had been stolen."

When they had finished their breakfast, Charlie went to the guest room upstairs, unplugged the number three burner cell phone, and pressed the number one icon. The phone rang and then Minkeagan's voice said, "Number One."

"Hi, it's me. Daniel Rickenger left money that was confiscated by the states of California, Arizona, Nevada, and New York. No other states. If I remember correctly, we didn't know about New York or Nevada, so he must have left the paperwork in safe deposit boxes in those places. That's good news. By now the states confiscated everything he had deposited. The money should come through. It's pretty much a sure thing now that they've accepted the marriage."

"Is this just a progress report or do you want something?"

"I want something."

"What is it?"

"We just found out that my mother is coming into town on a flight from Maine to LAX on Thursday. We also found out that there were some claims to the abandoned money made by people named Rickenger."

"You want us to watch your mother. Why should we?"

"Because on the day we made our deal, you agreed to help as needed. My mother is that jerk's heir. In other words, she's the beneficiary, but hasn't inherited yet. If something were to happen to her before she does, I'm not sure of the legal consequences, but it would at least add years to the payout process for you."

"What do you want us to do?"

"I don't need you to watch my mother all the time. Just be aware of roughly what she's doing. Check her surroundings to be sure nobody is stalking her. I'll be doing the same."

"All right. We'll do it."

On Thursday afternoon when he was at the airport picking up his mother, Charlie spotted Minkeagan and Copes in different places. Copes was in a car in the short-term parking structure across from the American Airlines terminal. Minkeagan was sitting in the coffee shop that arriving passengers passed on their way to the baggage claim.

Linda Warren didn't appear to notice either man. She was too interested in talking with Charlie and Vesper, who had come to pick her up at the airport and take her to Vesper's house to spend the first few nights while she waited for her tenants, Glen and Vivian, to clear out of the Warren family home.

The next night Linda invited Vivian and Glen out to dinner to congratulate them on their new job in England. Part of her motive was her extensive experience of moving from place to place. She knew that by the time a person was this close to moving, groceries were intentionally depleted to nearly nothing, and she wanted to be sure they were well fed.

Within the next few days Linda had begun to reconnect with friends she had seldom seen in recent years. Three of them got together almost immediately and nominated her for membership in their country club. Groups of this sort were something Linda had never joined during her years in Los Angeles, but in some of her other places she had found joining anything was an easy way to meet people, so she kept it in mind.

Part of her time she spent with Vesper. They went for daily walks and took each other to lunch. Vesper drove Linda to visit local places that Linda had missed, or that had changed so radically that they were largely new. Charlie and Vesper had been spending almost every night at Vesper's house, and after Linda arrived, it was every night.

The day came when the tenants had gone, the cleaning crew that Linda had hired were finished, and it was time to go to the Warren house. The house had been so vacuumed, waxed, polished, and dusted, its windows so thoroughly cleaned, that it seemed to admit more light than ever before. Charlie watched his mother's eyes and her mouth as she walked from room to room. She looked very alert and attentive, but not unhappy.

When they had been everywhere, she stopped in the middle of the living room. Charlie waited while she gazed at the ceiling.

He said, "Well?"

She said, "She wants a baby."

"Vesper?" he said. "Are you sure?"

"She told me she 'loves children.' But you have to start by loving one. You've never seemed to me to have any interest in that. You never seemed to me to want to hold on to any of the women you date very long either, but this time you seem more amenable to it. You're both in your midthirties. If you don't want a baby, you should tell her. If you do, it's beginning to be time."

"Thank you for telling me."

"It's part of the basic service package, and I haven't done much mothering for a long time."

"You've been fine."

"Thank you." She looked out on the back lawn, which was now shaded by trees that were ten years older and much bigger than they were when she had moved out. "I guess I will move in, at least for the fall and winter."

"Good," he said. "It will be nice to see you more often."

◆

Within a week she was settled again in Los Angeles and appeared to be occupied with friends most days and following routines of her own. Charlie had shifted his efforts back to operating his law firm's core business of estate planning, divorces, and civil suits. At the end of each week, he drove back to his condominium to pick up his mail from the locked mailbox and to check on the place. His refrigerator had nothing in it but drinks and mixers. The cupboards held a lot of condiments, spices, and canned staples. When he was satisfied, he went back out to his car and drove the rest of the way to Vesper Ellis's house.

One evening they were lying on the bed upstairs in Vesper's master suite, staring up at the ceiling, only the edges of their little fingers touching. He said, "So where do you think this is going?"

He expected her to say, "Where is what going?" but she didn't buy herself time to think, so he knew she had already thought. She said, "Life has taught me not to make assumptions about the future or make demands on it. Right now, I'm allowing myself to feel how great it is to be with you doing what I'm doing. I thought about relationships sometimes when I believed that was over for me—I learned more."

"Like what?"

"I was married for a pretty long time, and I knew that he would love it if I was wilder, freer, but I never tried. I would think, 'That isn't me,' or 'he'll think I'm stupid' or 'a woman shouldn't have to do that.' After he was gone, I wished I had been different, thrown myself into the relationship more. It could have been so much better. I promised myself that if I ever had another chance, I wouldn't live my life as though I was just a passenger. I would be shameless." She moved her hand. "I like to think that I am."

He laughed. "What about the future?"

"I don't want to talk about that. Right now, I'm feeling better than I remember ever feeling. I'm having fun. I don't expect it to last forever, or stay the same, or stay at all. I just told you I had learned not to demand that the future come up with some result."

"There's nothing wrong with talking about the way you want things to go."

"Okay. Where I want it to go right now is for you to put your hand on my waist and pull me over on top of you. The next part of the future will take care of itself."

28

Maureen Abbot looked through her oversize sunglasses across the giant swimming pool at the two women walking out from under the veranda roof of the main clubhouse carrying tall glasses with umbrellas in them. She stood up and waved, and both their sets of sunglasses turned toward her. Their steps took on momentum and purpose. They were making their way to the row of lounge chairs where Maureen and her old friend were taking refuge from the sun under a big umbrella.

Maureen stood when they arrived and said, "Hi, girls. Linda Warren, this is Mary and this is Wendy. Linda's an old friend, just moved back here from Maui."

Linda stood too and shook their hands. All the women smiled and said set formulas with "pleased," "pleasure," "nice," in them, and the two new women moved one long chair closer and sat.

Linda decided they were probably actresses who no longer worked, but had married men who didn't require much of their time. They appeared to both be in their late thirties or early forties, had enviable figures and pretty faces, and were expertly made-up, but they were inches too short to be models.

Wendy and Mary were immediately interested in Linda, wanted to hear about the tragedy at Lahaina, then about her life, friends, and family, her impressions of the places where she had lived. They told her things about themselves too, and gave the impression that they were pleasant companions who were always interested in social events or excursions. After about an hour Wendy and Mary said they had to move on. They had to catch a plane to Las Vegas because they had dinner reservations and tickets to a concert afterward.

When the two women left in a Mercedes, they drove for about a mile before they reverted to being May and Rose, née Rickenger. While Rose drove, May watched the street behind them to be sure that none of the cars back there were ones she had seen in the lot at the club, or anywhere. They had to be sure that nobody who knew them as Wendy and Mary would see them doing anything inconsistent with Mary and Wendy. Mary and Wendy had said they were going to be heading for the airport because Rose and May were going to catch flights home.

"What do you think of her?" Rose said.

"It's too early to tell," May said. "She's got some money, and I remember that when Dan died, the newspapers said he was traveling really fast, like he was in a big hurry."

"Meaning he believed he was on the verge of getting arrested," Rose said.

"Probably," May said. "The point is, when you have to make that quick an exit, it's almost impossible you've got everything. He may have left some of her money."

"He wasn't stupid enough to risk getting stopped for a speeding ticket for no reason, so you're probably right." Rose paused. "You don't think she's already been given the money from the banks, do you?"

"It's only been a couple months since the state sent the first letter. And say she did get a pile of money. It wouldn't retroactively change the way she lived. She's been drifting for, like, ten years, and most people can't do that. You also have to remember that he wouldn't have been with her at all if she didn't have anything to steal."

"Do you think there's a way to get what he had and hers too?"

May chuckled. "Remember what Mother always said when it was time to pack the car. 'It's the piggy who stays too long at the trough who gets butchered.' I think what the states are holding is likely to be plenty. It would be everything he had in any bank anywhere in the country, not just what he took from her. Getting that and then sticking around to pull a second scam would be pushing our luck."

"I suppose you're right," Rose said.

"I know I am," May said. She knew that Rose was certain to be thinking about how to pull the second scam by herself, because that was what she had been thinking about too.

"I'm tired, but I'd better get back tonight, or Dale will be pestering the women in his Chicago office. Do you think the next time should be in a week or two?"

"About then, but we might need to set aside a few days, because these early meetings should look like they're all just chance. I'll call you."

Rose drove to LAX, returned the car, and waited with May, whose flight to Phoenix left first. Then she caught her own flight to O'Hare.

❖

The next time they happened to be in the club at the same time as Linda Warren was in early morning a week and a half later. They found her in the women's gym, finishing a workout on an elliptical trainer. They greeted each other warmly but very briefly, and then she went to work exercising with kettle bells. Mary and Wendy were at first unsure about what to do next because they hadn't dressed or prepared for this, but then Mary stepped up on a treadmill and brought it up to a trot. That left Wendy to go into the locker room to get a massage. Afterward she happened to step into the shower when Linda went in, and they greeted each other again. Linda seemed to have formed a routine—aerobics, hand weights. After a quick shower she put on a bathing suit and went outside to swim lengths in the big pool.

All three met again afterward in the shaded patio area outside of the dining room and had lunch together. Wendy and Mary were both expert at giving impressions rather than information. Linda had become comfortable forming friendly relationships through years of talking with people she met in each of the cities where she had lived. She was clearly a person who didn't mind being alone, but she was also open to the right approach.

For the next few days Wendy and Mary showed up early at the club and performed variations on the ritual that Linda followed. This was not a strain for them. They had both made careers out of drawing the attention of men who were placed on the planet to be lured by women like them, and that had meant working to enhance and maintain their bodies with constant exercise and dieting.

After three more weeks, Mary and Wendy had become fixtures in Linda's second life in Los Angeles. The three went to the beach together, hiked in Griffith Park and on some of the trails in the hills, went to dinner at good restaurants. Linda learned from the two women that they had both divorced men who had been forced by California law to split the family assets evenly. Both husbands had immediately married the women they had been cheating with, and had subsequently become richer than they'd been at the time of the divorces. Mary said she was glad, because she hadn't wanted to feel sorry for that rat, and Wendy laughed and agreed. They were similarly philosophical and good-natured about nearly every topic. They had both married again, this time to men they considered improvements over the last ones.

Charlie Warren and Vesper Ellis were at Charlie's place. They had been out to dinner, and he was picking up some fresh clothes for the week's work and checking his mail on their way back to Vesper's house. When he heard the burner phone in his right coat pocket buzz, he was startled. He looked at the display expecting to see a wrong number, but the name was "2." He swept the green oval aside and said, "Hi."

The voice was Copes's. "Hi, Charlie. We've been keeping an eye on your mother. There's only one thing, but we think it's worth mentioning. She's been going to a country club in the morning with a gym bag kind of thing that has a shoulder strap. She stays about three hours, from around nine, goes inside to work out, then goes outside for a swim, eats lunch, and then drives home."

"Yep," Charlie said. "She told me pretty much the same thing."

"Did she tell you she's got some new friends?"

"Just that she's met a few people that she likes. Not much about who they are or anything. What's up? Has she met a man or something?"

"Not that we know of. What we've seen is women. There are a lot of people you see once in a while, only a few you see every day. There are two women in particular who come together most days, and they walk around looking in the main building first, and then outdoors by the pool, on the patios, at the putting green, and so on. Every time they come, they seem to get together with your mother."

"Is there something that I should worry about?"

"Not that I know of. We just wanted you to know we're living up to our agreement and keeping our eyes open."

"Thank you," Warren said. "I appreciate it."

"Just remember us on payday."

29

May and Rose arrived at Peter's lake house together in a Kia rental car that looked nothing like the Mercedes Rose had been driving in Los Angeles for a month and a half. The truck delivering the three kayaks was right behind them. The driver pulled it over to the side of the road far enough so that a skilled driver would have a hope of getting a normal automobile past it. He got out of the truck and opened the back doors, then pulled the first kayak out onto the hydraulic lift, then the other two, and lowered the lift to the ground. He used a two-wheel dolly to move the three to the side of the boathouse. He reloaded the dolly and handed Rose a clipboard with the order receipt uppermost of the papers. She took the pen, signed, and handed it back to him. He got into the truck and began to back it up toward the last wide area along the road so he could turn around.

Peter appeared at the door a minute later beside a younger woman wearing a creamsicle-orange tank top, tight white jeans, and short boots. She had both hands up behind her head sliding an elastic band over the ponytail she was using to confine her blond hair. She leaned close to Peter to kiss him, went down the steps, walked to the side of the house, lifted a helmet onto her head, started the motorcycle parked there, drove it slowly out onto the road, and off in the direction the truck had gone.

May got out of the Kia and went up to Peter. "Is it my imagination, or are they getting younger?"

"Probably just that I'm getting older." He kissed her cheek. "Thanks to them I'll have something to regret about dying."

Rose said, "Whichever one is on duty that day will pull your gold fillings and sell your organs."

"If she's any of the current ones she'll have earned them. You two must know by now that you're not going to shame me out of being a man and liking the things that men like. Give up."

"We will for now, but only because we need you for the Linda Warren thing. As your male-gaze-sharpened eyeballs must have told you already, we've brought the kayaks. We're probably going to be set a week from tomorrow, but we'll be in touch by phone up to the actual time. Can we put the kayaks inside the boathouse? They're plastic, so it won't hurt them to be out, but it would be best if nobody sees them."

"Sure. Let's do it now."

"By 'we' I meant 'you,'" May said. "We need to go into civilization and buy supplies, so they'll already be here."

"All right," he said. "Remember to pay cash."

"Yes, sir," Mary said. "You need any supplies for yourself and your lady friends? Breath mints? Birth control? Coloring books?"

"No, thanks," he said. "See you later."

◆

As Rose was driving the Kia back out toward the highway, she said, "Do you think he'll come through if we need him?"

"He'll be adequate for our needs. He's providing his lake house."

Rose said, "Do you know how many lakes there are in the Sierra Nevadas? Thirty-two hundred. We could have taken our pick. Still can."

"There's another thing he'll be helpful with. Remember, this woman fell for Danny and married him. Danny looked a bit like Peter, if you think about it. The same type—tall, with those eyes, and the earnest face. But he's better looking than Danny. Nothing against Danny, it's just true."

"I know," Rose said. "It's also true that he doesn't want any part of this. He's been trying to talk it down since he heard of it. He's got all the money he wants, and apparently, it's enough to keep him happy. He's out on his boat or hiking up here every day, and has a different little escort scheduled to show up every second day, and that's enough."

May said, "I don't give a crap if he wants this or not. He's a Rickenger. That means he's got to help us. It also means that in time he'll get over this and remember he likes money, as much as he can get. Now let's get into Reno, buy the groceries and supplies, get them stored in his house, and head for the airport."

◆

Three days later the women calling themselves Wendy and Mary were back in the club in Los Angeles. They were swimming lengths when Linda Warren came outside in a bathing suit, slipped into the water, and swam, as she had been doing every day for two months. Wendy and Mary knew that Linda would swim between ten and twenty lengths today because she had already done her elliptical, treadmill, and weights in the women's gym and was now mostly cooling off and relaxing her muscles.

When Linda got out of the pool and dried herself with a club towel, the two women knew, she would walk to the same space with the table under the umbrella. They knew there would be a psychological effect to her joining them that put her at a perfect level. She would come to them rather than having them come to her. That meant she hadn't been invited, but their greeting would reinforce the feeling that she didn't need to be invited because she was one of the gang. They got to it as soon as she had received a tall iced tea with a lemon slice and no sugar, her pulse seemed to be about sixty, and her breathing was around twenty. She was calm, relaxed, and feeling good after her workout.

Mary said, "We agreed weeks ago that Linda has proven herself, right?"

Wendy said, "Sure."

Linda said, "Proven myself to be what?"

Mary looked around them, craning her neck to see who else was nearby. Then she said, "This is not something we talk about out loud. There are people you can go places with and everybody has a good time, everybody relaxes, there's a lot of laughter, but not so much that it's exhausting and your face hurts. Then there are others who can be perfectly nice, but none of those things are true when they come along. I'm not talking about whiners or complainers or people who don't do their share or something."

"Come on, you know what she's talking about," Wendy said. "It's mostly mysterious. They just aren't any fun to have along."

Linda laughed. "Yes, I guess I do. I hope you're saying I'm not one of those people."

"You're the opposite," Wendy said "We don't want to sound like the mean girls in high school or something. That's why we spend time with people before we invite them on one of our trips. This way everybody fits and there are no hurt feelings. We're going up north soon, to this beautiful small lake in the Sierras for a few days. We hike on trails in these incredible tall pine woods that smell like nothing else on earth, and kayak on this glassy lake. There's a house. It looks like a ski lodge, and it's luxurious, but we cook on an outdoor grill—a stove, really. It's just a heavenly place to refresh and renew yourself, to think and talk about life and the things that matter. We'd like you to come with us."

"I feel as though I just got a very high security clearance."

Mary laughed. "It's nothing like that."

Wendy said, "Yes it is."

"When are you planning on going?" Linda said.

"If you're in, then it's negotiable and you get a say," Mary said. "We don't have jobs anymore, and our husbands are used to us going places when we feel like it, as long as we don't miss some big occasion that matters. On a trip like this one, we drive up, and leave on a Tuesday, Wednesday, or Thursday to stay out of weekend traffic."

Linda thought about it. She enjoyed their company and had not yet found much to occupy her time in Los Angeles except the club, and going back to Maui still felt depressing. She had lost friends there, but also several people who weren't even acquaintances, just nice people she saw around, or worked in businesses where she went. A short trip to a forest lake in the mountains sounded like a good way to spend a few days. "I could leave on any of those days next week."

"Wonderful!" Wendy said. "It'll be fun. Today is Friday. Want to make it Tuesday?"

Linda said, "Tuesday's fine. That will give me time to pick up some clothes. Most of my play clothes are in Hawaii."

Mary said, "Hiking boots and good socks, swimsuit, sun hat, water-resistant pants, rain jacket with a hood, and tops and fleeces as you like. Think about how you'll feel, not how you'll look. People are scarce, which is part of the point, really. It's hard to rest your brain when you think people are looking at you all the time."

That afternoon Linda looked online to find out where the best sporting goods stores were these days, picked three, and went shopping. She managed to make it to all three before she had what she wanted. She expanded the list to include some things that were merely sensible—a compact first aid kit, sunscreen, insect repellent, a pocketknife with six blades and tools, a flashlight, a compass, a pack of three disposable lighters, and a water bottle. As an afterthought she bought a day pack to carry them in.

That night after dinner she called Charlie. After the "How are you?" and the small talk she said, "I'm going up north for a few days next week to the Sierras."

"What's up there?"

"Tall, fragrant pine trees, mountains, a blue lake, a luxurious house that supposedly looks like a ski lodge. That sort of thing."

"Who are you going with?"

"You don't know them. Two women named Wendy and Mary. I met them right after I joined the club. They work out about the same time of day I do, so we got to know each other. They're at least ten years younger than I am."

"I'd be interested in meeting them."

"Probably not, but I appreciate your willingness. Sometime when it's in the natural course of things you and Vesper can come to the club for lunch. I don't think I'm ready to have a dinner party for you two and them and their husbands, but I may get around to it. We're leaving Tuesday, so there's not really time anyway."

"Can you give me a call after you get up there and let me know you made it?"

"Okay," she said. "I do have to ask, though. You know I went to all sorts of places while I was living in other parts of the country, right? Europe, Asia, Australia, and so on?"

"Yes. But since then, you can get signal bars almost anywhere, and it's easier to catch me when I can talk."

"Okay," she said. "I'll try to make up for all the calls I owe you."

"Thanks," he said.

"You can call me too, you know," she said.

"That's true," he said. "I just may."

The Mercedes arrived at Linda Warren's house at six A.M. on Tuesday, and Linda came out with her bag as Mary opened the trunk. Linda had looked up the distance and time from Los Angeles to Lake Tahoe, which seemed to her to be the general vicinity of their destination, and found it was 441 miles. That meant they would be on the road for eight hours and likely arrive around two P.M.

As she reached the car, she said, "Maybe I should take the first turn as driver. It's all freeway for the first few hours, right? You don't have to actually know the way until the end."

"You're a great addition to the crew," Mary said. "Take the wheel. If you can find your way to the Golden State Freeway—the Five—you will have us pointed in the right direction." She got into the passenger seat.

Wendy was in the back. As she lay down on the seat she said, "Thanks. That means I can get a couple more hours of sleep so I can wake up charming and companionable."

Linda hadn't spent much time driving in any of the places where she had lived in recent years, particularly on Maui, but she was still a good driver because of her years as a commuter in Los Angeles. She got them onto the northbound entrance and then onto the right strand of the tangled freeway as it passed through the narrow space between hills and gradually spread out and took several directions. She guided the Mercedes out on the right one and continued northward toward Santa Clarita and Castaic and Gorman, heading up the long state with the eighteen-wheeler trucks for Merced and Modesto and Sacramento. For four hours Mary dosed off beside her, so Linda's companions were both unconscious. She was comfortable with the silence. The Mercedes smothered the road sounds and the wind, and it left her time to think.

The solitude was preferable to the bright, mostly cynical chatter that the other two had learned in whatever their normal lives were. They seemed to have spent the past fifteen years in cocktail parties or the sort of dinners where the guests were expected to demonstrate whether they should be judged among the quick or the dead. She didn't blame them, but she wasn't surprised that they needed to rest in nature. The big thing that she had noticed about all the places out there in big nature—forests, oceans, mountains—was that they held long periods of deep silence. She had grown comfortable with that, partly because, once she had thought about it, she realized that it was a reassertion of the normal proportions. The world, at least in the vast spaces between cities, didn't need words, and simply swallowed them.

Linda had not transcended the human need to be accepted, liked, and admired, so she spent some of this free time thinking about ways to accomplish and preserve this effect. Often it was simply not talking too much or too little, appearing to like everything, and smiling frequently, so she reminded herself to do those things.

Wendy woke up first. "Hi, Linda. Where are we?"

"Just past Merced," Linda said.

"Wow. You've taken us so far."

"It's a start, anyway." Linda said.

"If you see a coffee shop or gas station, make a stop and I'll take the next shift."

The rest of the drive was harder for Linda, because the others were both wide awake and talkative. It occurred to her that she had probably made a mistake by taking the first driving shift, because it created a difference in their bodies' schedules. She had driven for four hours, about half the trip. When they reached their destination, it would only be midafternoon. They would be alert and she would be tired.

They stopped for lunch at a Denny's near Sacramento. In a way it made Linda feel more comfortable. They were two middle-aged women who didn't need to worry about money, but at least in this instance they weren't going to be pretentious and hold out for an expensive restaurant in the state capital, where politicians and lobbyists ate. They were more interested in the practical and efficient. They were well-fed and back on the road in forty minutes.

The rest of the trip was increasingly interesting to Linda, partly because as they were moving out of the long stretch of farmland in the middle of the state and into the zone of mountains and forests, there was more for her to see. It was also partly because her companions were talking about their lives. Wendy was a couple years older than Mary. They were both very attractive and vain, but they were in a lighter mood today, and willing to laugh at themselves. Wendy said she was having a hard time getting to know the controls on her new fitness watch. She couldn't make the watch give her credit for the exercise she got during sex with her husband. The watch seemed only to recognize footsteps and the motion on an elliptical trainer. Mary said maybe she should get her husband to chase her. Linda learned that she had been right about them. They had met in an acting class about twenty years ago, had gotten a few minor roles, most of them in commercials, and had stayed friends during the years when their careers didn't get better, when they'd married, divorced, and remarried, when they had been busy raising young children, and now, when they didn't seem to know what they should be doing, but knew whatever it was, it wasn't going to be work.

When they reached the turnoff onto the road to the lake, Mary was driving. Linda was attentive and curious, craning her neck to look out the windows on both sides and then leaning back to look up through the rear window to see the tops of the trees, and then, when they'd gone farther in, to see the first flashes of blue water through the spaces between the pines. The place was as beautiful as her two companions had promised.

The house was much as they had described. The part facing the road was a two-story rectangle, but the part that faced the lake rose into a tall A-frame. It was built on a grassy bank right above the lake, with a garage on one side and a boathouse on pilings over a dock jutting out above the water on the other.

The biggest surprise was the man who came out the front door to greet them as Mary glided to a stop. He was about six feet two with blond hair that was just beginning to shade off into silver at the temples. His straight posture made him seem taller, and his face had a sculpted look and a tan that made his blue eyes stand out.

Wendy got out of the car on that side and hugged the man, which was a profound shock to Linda until she saw it was quick and perfunctory, and said, "Linda, this is Paul, our landlord for the trip. Paul, Linda is a stray person we found at our club in LA and recognized as a kindred spirit, so here she is."

Paul nodded and smiled and said to Linda, "I hope your trip up here was pleasant."

"Yes, it was, thanks."

"Go ahead and hug her, Paul," Mary said. "Otherwise, she'll feel left out."

Paul leaned forward and gave Linda a brief, gentle hug, clearly only to play along, then endured a hug from Mary. Wendy said, "We've known Paul for years, and I'm astounded he'll still put up with us."

Paul said, "Let me give you a hand with your bags." Wendy pressed the key fob and the trunk opened. He slipped the strap of Linda's bag over his shoulder and lifted the other two bags and carried them inside. He carried them up the stairs and set them on the second floor in the hallway. "I'll let you sort out the bedrooms." He went back down the stairs as they were climbing up.

A few minutes later when the women came back down, he was standing in the big living room looking out the tall window past the deck at the water. He heard them come into the room and turned around. He said, "The keys are over there on the counter. I'm afraid there are only two sets, but I can get another made and drop it off tomorrow, if you think you'll need it."

Linda said, "I won't need a key. I'm sure they'll let me in."

Wendy reached into her purse and pulled out a leather checkbook. She opened it and took out a check that had already been filled out and detached and handed it to him. "And here's the rent."

He looked at it and put it into his shirt pocket. "Thank you. Paid in full. I'm going to go now and let you recover from the trip. If you need anything, you have my number."

"Thanks, Paul," Wendy and Mary said in unison. He reached the door and went out. The others were drawn in the other direction, toward the big window overlooking the lake.

Linda heard him lock the door from the outside, then heard the garage door roll up, and then a car engine. She heard his car pull out, then drive off down the road.

"What did you think of Paul?" Mary said. Her eyes were gleaming, as though she knew something.

The look struck Linda as presumptuous. "He seems nice." She said it with less enthusiasm than she might have if she hadn't been repelled by that look.

"He's more than nice," Wendy said. "She and I are both married, and I, for one, will never again get distracted by a man like that. That weakness was what obliterated my first marriage. But you're single, right?"

"Got me there," Linda said. "But I'm not looking for a relationship, just a few days outdoors with the girls."

"Okay," Mary said. "Who wants to go for a little hike? I feel like stretching my legs after sitting in a car all day."

Linda's mood crept up. "That sounds just perfect," she said. "We've got at least five hours of daylight left."

Wendy said, "I think I'll just unpack and get a shower for now."

The walk began on the road, which almost immediately began to lose its stretches of asphalt and was left with a layer of coarse gravel, and then lost even that and became two bare streaks the width of a pair of tires. After a couple hundred yards there was a path that veered off to the left through the trees while the road continued around the lake. Linda said, "Do you know where this goes?"

Mary said, "It's kind of interesting. I'll show you." They turned onto it and very soon it was too narrow for them to walk side by side. It wound a bit to avoid stands of particularly big trees, and it rose as it went on, forcing them to climb an incline that made their walk feel more virtuous to Linda. The air up here was cleaner but thinner, and so it took a bit more effort.

"Does this go to somebody's house? It seems to be pretty clear of small plants and things."

"That's sort of two questions. Yes, it originally led to somebody's house. We'll be there in a minute. But I think it is and always was a deer run. Or maybe elk. We've seen some on a meadow up there, so they've probably been here forever. My theory is that the people who built a house up there probably walked around the lake, saw the path, followed it, and picked a place where they could cut down some tall, straight trees to make a house."

"When was this?"

"I asked Paul, but he doesn't know. It would have to be a long time ago, before building codes and things like that. Maybe even in the days when you could go to a wild place and just decide to live there. You'll see."

They climbed another hundred yards and reached a space that was mostly flat. "There it is," Mary said.

They skirted the site. They could see an area about twenty by twenty feet marked out by large stones laid down as a foundation. Linda said, "They must have carried those stones up here from the lake. What do you suppose happened?"

"Paul doesn't have any real information. He said he's found old, rusted nails, and they're round, meaning mass-produced, not the square kind that were made by blacksmiths in the nineteenth century. There's a streambed over there that leads down to the lake, but I've never seen it except when it was dry in midsummer or later. Paul thinks it was probably either a fire—you'll notice there's no chimney—or maybe disease. If you got sick up here before there was a road, you'd have a hard time taking care of yourself."

"I suppose the winters up here are pretty brutal too."

"We've never been up here then, but I've heard they are."

They climbed up the trail for another fifteen minutes before they reached the meadow Mary had mentioned. It was about the size of a football field, and Linda imagined that the vanished people who had lived in the house had probably seen the large open place covered with weeds and wildflowers with tiny blooms and thought they could farm it. There were no animals visible at the moment, but she could hear a bird call from beyond the first row of trees on the far side.

"I suppose we should start back," Mary said.

Linda looked at their lengthened shadows and said, "You're right."

They walked back the way they'd come. At the top of the trail, just where the meadow ended, they could see the full length of the lake, like a blue shoe print pressed down into the mountains. "That's a beautiful sight," Linda said. "Nobody has said what the lake is called. What's its name?"

"Blucher Lake," Mary said. "It's kind of ugly, isn't it?"

"It doesn't do it justice, but maybe it's the name of that poor family who built the ruined house."

They walked the rest of the way down the path to the road, and then the house. The front door was locked, but Mary had her key, so they entered. Linda could see Wendy through the tall window on the lake side of the house. She was sitting on a long chair with a drink in one hand and the other hand holding a cell phone to her ear. As soon as she heard them come in, she quickly lowered her hand and the phone disappeared. She got up and set her drink down, then went to join them at the door from the living room onto the deck. "I was just having a little drink, now that the sun is sinking below the yardarm."

Mary said, "Houses don't have yardarms, but I think I'll make myself an ice-cold martini."

"I think I'll get a quick bath and come back for the drink," Linda said. She turned, went back inside, and climbed to her room on the second floor. Wendy had looked as though she felt guilty for making a phone call. Linda hadn't heard anything about an agreement not to use their phones, so she laid out some clean clothes on the bed, slipped her phone into her pocket, went into the bathroom, and dialed her son Charlie's number. The phone rang a couple times and then went to voicemail. She said, "This is your mother. We've arrived safely at a place called Blucher Lake and two of us took a hike. I don't see any other houses, and it's very pretty. There's one road that rings the lake. I'm going to send you a Google map, and it should show my exact location. I'm going to get a bath and a drink, and I suggest you do the same if you ever close your office. Love to Vesper. I'll talk to you in a day or two."

She sent the image to his phone and started the bath. In a few minutes she was feeling better than she had all day. She dressed in clean clothes and then looked at her phone. She had set it on the floor by the tub in case Charlie called her back right away. She had an odd feeling about it. She was almost sure the others must have an agreement that they wouldn't use cell phones on their trips to enjoy nature. She wasn't somebody who liked rules, but she could see the point of trying to keep a trip like this nonelectronic. She turned the sound of her ringer off, stopped the sound notifications, and then slid it behind two books in the bookcase at the head of her bed so she would hear it vibrate but nobody else would.

She went back downstairs and out to the deck. Mary held up her martini and then pointed to another stemmed glass on the bar across the deck. "I made one for you too."

Linda walked over to it and took a sip. "Perfect. Thank you very much." She sat on one of several empty chairs near the others. "And thank you both for inviting me to tag along. It's really a special spot. The walk we took was exactly the right thing."

"I agree," Mary said. She looked at Wendy. "You should have come."

"In a little while you'll be glad I didn't. The halibut is defrosting, the spinach and the baking potatoes are washed, and the peach cobbler dessert is already in the oven. I also unpacked, did an inventory of the meals for the next few days, got a bath, and locked the car in the garage."

"Thank you," Linda said. "That doesn't leave much for us. I'll clean up and do the dishes tonight, and cook tomorrow night."

Later, when they'd had the dinner that Wendy had prepared and Linda and Mary had cleared the table, done the dishes, and cleaned the kitchen, they turned on the gas fire in the center of the conversation area on the deck and talked while the flames coming up through the sand warmed them. The sky was as clear and cloudless as it had been during the day, and they could lean back in their chairs and see thousands of stars that were invisible in the city lights of Los Angeles. The other two women talked a lot about their children, but she noticed that they had little to say about their husbands. After an hour or two Wendy asked Linda about her husband. She said simply, "I don't have one. I'm a widow."

"I think I remember you saying you had children," Mary said.

"Just one. He's the reason I came back to LA for a while."

"What does he do?"

"He's a lawyer."

"What kind?"

"Civil. The boring kind. It's good, because I don't have to worry that he'll starve, but his job is to make sure nothing exciting happens to any of his clients, so he never has much to talk about."

They all seemed to Linda to be tired beginning around ten P.M., but the talk persisted for another two alcohol-fueled hours. She managed to avoid talking too long or specifically about herself or her past life by laughing when something one of them said was funny or particularly clever, and by reliable strategies she had picked up over a lifetime, such as mirroring the speaker's expressions. At midnight she gave herself permission for a sincere yawn. "I'm afraid it's past my bedtime," she said. "I can hardly keep my eyes open. I'll see you in the morning. Good night."

She climbed the stairs, went into her room, turned down the covers of the bed, and climbed in. She moved the two books hiding her phone and looked at the screen. Her message to Charlie was there, and the notation said, *Received*. She plugged the phone in to charge, and slipped it under her pillow.

30

Charlie Warren's life had been much better since he had finished Vesper Ellis's case. He slept later in the mornings. The final hour of sleep on most days was spent in dreams that were thinly disguised versions of reality in which he studied problems and tried to devise solutions to them. This morning a motorcycle roared past on the street behind the house and he sat up.

Vesper turned in his direction and squinted at him. "What's wrong?"

"I just had a dream about my mother."

"It might be worth taking an ambulance to the psychiatrist's office."

"A good idea, but I think not this time." He took his phone off the side table, looked at the screen, scrolled down, and read his way through it. "She sent me a Google map showing her GPS location. I think I'll fly up—I guess Reno is probably closest—rent a car, maybe check on her, just to be sure."

Vesper studied him. It was understandable that some deep-seated memory of the con man marrying his mother and taking her money might have been shaken loose by the unexpected appearance of the two old convicts with the rest of the story. He had just spent time tracking down and filing claims to the crook's bank deposits. There was also the fact that he was probably experiencing a natural reaction to the violence that they had just been through during her own case. She said, "Buy two tickets."

"You want to go too?"

"Yes," she said. "This is probably an unnecessary trip. If it is, then I promise that you will have a better time in a Reno hotel with me than without me. If it turns into an emergency, I will try to be helpful. I'm really good at things like calling the police."

He looked at her and shrugged. "Two tickets it is."

May and Rose were up early, sitting on the deck drinking coffee as dawn broke. May said, "I really had hopes that Peter would do the trick. I thought that she'd spend a few minutes near him and the rest would be like automatic pilot. He could string her along a little until she inherited Danny's bank accounts, with everything legal and simple, with her stupid son or one of his lawyer friends doing the work. Peter may not want to play the game anymore, but he still knows the moves. He's still got the charisma and he's in great shape, and he's so calm and reassuring everybody trusts him. I figured he could get her to invest in a joint project, maybe some land up here or anything else she likes, with him as managing partner."

"Well, she didn't go weak in the knees," Rose said. "She's been burned before."

"That's what gave me the most hope," May said. "The ones who have been taken are the easiest ones to take again. All you need is fresh bait."

"Well, it's not going to happen," Rose said. "Want to give up, or go with a second plan?"

"I don't give up. I think we have to go with the risky option. She hasn't got Danny's money yet. If she dies and the money shows up in her bank account, then we have a few days writing checks on it and using her cards until the last minute. I've got a few addresses where we can have merchandise sent, and a few contacts with companies that can accept payments and move the money through a chain of other companies in under one second, when it all dissolves into the air in another country. I'm sure you still have some too."

"Of course," Rose said. "They take a percentage, but losing a percentage is better than losing it all."

"Let's get some of these people notified today, before we start the clock running."

"I'll make some calls this morning to set up what I can. You'd better do it too. We have no idea how big Danny's stash is, and it's got to go fast."

May said, "I already started a few hours ago. Manaus is three hours ahead of us, and London is eight."

At noon, Charlie and Vesper's plane landed in Reno, and they walked through the long accordion tunnel into the airport. Charlie reached into his carry-on bag and turned on his two phones as they walked. The burner phone rang right away. He saw that the number of his caller was two. "Hello?"

"Hi, Charlie." Warren recognized the voice of Minkeagan.

"Hi. What's up?"

"We lost track of your mother."

"Don't worry. We know where she is. Where are you?"

"We're outside the club where she goes for her workouts. Usually about this time she comes out of the gym, swims a while, and then eats lunch with her best buddies. She's a no-show, and so are they."

"She sent me an email last night. She's with the two friends at a lake in the Sierras. Vesper and I flew up this morning, so you don't have to worry about her for a while. I'll call you if I need you again."

"Look, Charlie. I'm feeling a little uncomfortable about this. We're all waiting for some big money to arrive for her, and we know other people have applied for it too. Anybody who's trying to claim this particular guy's bank accounts knows that the front runner has got to be the guy's widow."

"What's wrong? Don't I seem worried enough about her?"

"I don't know," Minkeagan said. "Just don't lose our numbers."

"Thanks," Charlie said. "I'll keep this dedicated phone with me. I'll also call you when I know anything new about the decision on the money."

❖

Charlie and Vesper rented a car and checked in at the Peppermill, partly because it was near the airport and easy to find. He kept checking his phone while they were eating lunch in one of the hotel's restaurants. He saw the way Vesper was watching him and slipped it into his pocket. "I'm just checking for updates."

"I understand," she said. "You could tell her we're here and available if she needs us."

"She would be insulted."

"She would act insulted. She would be touched. And maybe pleasantly amused at us, and if she is, who cares? You're one of the toughest people I've ever met. You can take all the teasing she can come up with."

"I'll let her know we're here." He smiled. "Of course, I'll lie to her about why we came." He typed in her number on his phone and then typed in a text message. Then he put the phone in his pocket. "Thanks. I actually feel less anxious. She can laugh at me all she wants."

"That's the right attitude," Vesper said.

They finished their lunch and went up to their room. Charlie called Martha. "Hi. It's me," he said. "We're in Reno. Anything going on that I should know about?" He put the phone on speaker and set it down on the side table by the bed.

"Not you personally, but as Vesper's attorney, yes. The last of her money came in from Founding Fathers. It tops off the balance, so I believe that's the end of her case."

Vesper said, "Thanks, Martha."

"Thanks, Martha," Warren said. "If you don't have to be there, feel free to reroute the calls to the service and take the rest of the day."

"Thanks. Not sure if I will, but I might unless things get exciting around here."

❖

Linda Warren was third in the file as the three women walked along beside the road that circled the lake. They stayed on the shoulder of the road, because there were ruts in the surface that had been filled with gravel, where a hiker's feet would sink an inch or two and walking became difficult. The best places to walk were the flat stretches where the pine needles that had fallen from the tall trees were thick enough to prevent brush from growing up and presenting an obstacle to progress. She loved walking along the lake. She wondered about Wendy and Mary. They had both been up when Linda had come downstairs early in the morning, both staring at their phones in the predawn darkness.

It occurred to Linda that this might be the time of day set aside for communicating with their families. She also wondered if she had accidentally discovered that the two women's relationship was not what she had assumed. Had they both been up because they had been sleeping in the same place? She turned the idea over in her mind and came to no conclusion. It was none of her business and it didn't matter to her either way. She'd been enjoying the trip and felt gratitude that they had included her in it. She had traveled alone to a great many destinations, and stayed to live in several of them, but had never gone alone to a place where she was far from a good restaurant, a grocery store, and a hospital.

Wendy and Mary were talking about how the three should spend the afternoon.

Wendy said that taking Paul's powerboat out would give them a chance to show Linda the entire lake. Mary said that the boat's twin Mercury motors were loud and so fast that if they hit a floating log or something they could all be killed. Wendy laughed. "If I drive, then we won't have to worry."

"It's not funny," Mary said. "It's not some wild product of my imagination. If we hit something at fifty miles an hour it would be like doing it a car, only without seat belts or anything. It happens all the time, especially in lakes. They're the worst because they look the safest."

"What's your alternative?"

"Paul's got three or four kayaks in the boathouse. I saw them."

Wendy turned around and walked backward. "What do you think, Linda?"

Linda said, "I would say I'm more in the mood for the kayaks. As exercise, afternoon kayaking goes pretty well with this morning's hike.

It works your arms, your abdomen, and your back, but leaves your tired legs and feet pretty much at rest."

"All right," Wendy said. "I'm outvoted. We'll save the boat for a time when we're really tired or feel like exploring the far end of the lake."

They kept walking, and Linda felt happy. While she had been living in Hawaii, she had thought about how great the weather there was, how beautiful the tropical landscape. She had almost forgotten how close to perfect the thinly populated spaces of northern California, Nevada, and Arizona were. Here in the mountains, she kept moving her eyes and turning her head to try to take it all in.

◆

Charlie and Vesper were in the rental car driving toward the spot on the Google map where Linda Warren was staying with her two friends from the club. Vesper said, "I can understand why they chose to come up here for a few days. It's an ideal spot for three middle-aged women to go and relax. If you want nightlife, you're close enough to Reno to put on a nice dress and spend some extra time and effort with your hair and makeup and drive there for one evening. The rest of the time, you can wear baggy cargo pants and boots, and live the life of happy ten-year-olds trying to sneak up on the animals and take their picture or something."

"Yeah, I hope she's having a good time," Charlie said. "She kind of had the wind knocked out of her years ago when my father died. She was young. It seemed for a while when she was with Mack Stone—excuse me, Daniel Rickenger—she was happy again. After we found out that he had just been using her to get her money and disappear, a whole part of her personality was gone. It was as though she decided to let herself be old before she really was. Part of it, I think, was that she was so hurt and humiliated. A man she had married had just been leading her on, not feeling anything for her at all. She felt like that was the verdict on her, not him."

Charlie's phone buzzed, and he took it out of his pocket and held it out to Vesper. "Here, read this, will you? I'd better keep my eyes on the road, with these curves."

Vesper said, "It's a screenshot of a letter that Martha forwarded. It's got a big letterhead for the State of California. "Dear Mrs. Warren. The State of California has made an electronic transfer to your account at the Bank of America of $3,876,484.36. This sum represents the contents of the bank accounts held by the State Treasury for you, the widow of Daniel Webster Rickenger. It is up to you and your tax advisors to determine any liability that you may incur because of this transfer."

"Almost four million dollars," Charlie said. "And that's just California, and it doesn't count any money he may have converted from cash to other things, like stocks and bonds or land or whatever."

"That's very nice," Vesper said. "Should I forward it to her?"

"I'd appreciate it," Charlie said. "It might make her forget we came up here to violate her privacy."

"Done," she said.

"Still willing to do my job while I drive?"

"Of course."

"Then will you please forward the letter to Minkeagan or Copes too?"

"You mean to my kidnappers?"

"Yes," Charlie said. "Although I like to think of them as helpful older gentlemen rather than semiretired criminals these days. I want them to know that I'm not hiding anything from them."

"Because they'll kill you."

"Probably not, but I do like to keep things cordial and open."

She laughed and kissed his cheek, and then forwarded the email to their numbers.

◆

Linda shrugged off the straps of her backpack and said, "Can you wait for me a minute? I'm going to sneak off into that thicket up there and pee."

"Of course," Rose said. She watched Linda thread her way up the hill and disappear. She said to May, "Now. She's gone."

Rose kept watch from the side of the trail while May reached into the backpack that Linda had left there. She pulled Linda's phone out of the pocket and looked at the screen. "Oh crap," she whispered. "The clock just started."

"Tear a few checks from the back of the checkbook and take a phone shot of the credit cards before she comes back."

After a few seconds May said, "Got them." She stood up, sliding her flattened hand into her jeans to pocket her phone and the checks.

"Here she comes."

May glanced up the hill and whispered, "We can get started on the transfers tonight."

Linda reached them and bent over to pick up the backpack and put it on. "Thanks," she said.

"No trouble," said May. "It's life in the great outdoors."

They set off along the road to complete the loop around the lake. They walked a bit faster as they reached the part of the road that was fully paved again, and before long they were back at the house. Rose and Linda went inside and started preparing lunch. That gave May a chance to go into her room and hide the stolen checks and Linda's phone.

As she slipped them into her purse, she smiled about the fact that she knew she was using the most secure hiding place in the house. An honest woman whose purse was robbed would never think of looking in another woman's purse for her money. She also knew that the way the schedule was shaping up, it was possible that she did not have to do this. By evening, it was very likely there would be only two of them.

The women ate and washed the dishes, then went out to the boathouse to look at the kayaks, the double-bladed paddles that went with them, and the life vests that Paul the owner kept hanging on the inner wall of his boathouse. Then they went back into the house, changed into bathing suits, smeared sunscreen on themselves and one another, and then put on T-shirts and hats and went back out to the boathouse and put on the life vests. They pushed the kayaks from the dock into the water beneath the boathouse, then one by one, each climbed down the wooden ladder attached to the dock and stepped into a bright yellow kayak, holding tight to the ladder until her legs were inside the bow section and the paddle was in her hands.

Linda's first impression came from a few drops of water that fell from one blade of her paddle onto her shoulder. It was how cold the water was for the summer. Back in the Hawaiian Islands, the ocean water was eighty degrees. Here in this lake that she could see across, the water felt about fifty. She silently reminded herself that she was no longer in the tropics, and that the lakes in this part of the Sierras were very deep. She had read on her phone last night that Tahoe was 1,644 feet deep. Blucher Lake was much smaller, but she'd just learned it was deep enough to be cold. She would say nothing about it, because it wasn't a problem, but even more because she was determined not to utter anything that could possibly sound like a complaint.

She paddled a hundred feet onto the lake, looked back, and waited for the other two women to paddle and catch up with her. She found it interesting to see a house from the water side. They looked different, showing the eye hidden aspects of the house's nature. It was partly because of the distance. The house and its relationship to the land around it could all be seen at once. This one was better than most, because she'd had a day to get used to a different impression. Linda began to paddle along the shore.

The next time Linda looked back, Wendy and Mary were out from under the boathouse roof and gliding along at a good speed, taking long, rhythmic strokes. Linda was surprised at their course. She had assumed they would skirt their way along the shore, so that was the direction that she had chosen. The kayaks had a very small draught and could glide along in shallow water. She had been planning to stay close to the shore and get a view of the wading birds that might become visible, and the rock formations, and possibly even fish in the shallows. She had gone quite a distance along the shore, but they were paddling steadily toward the middle of the lake. It didn't take long before they were quite far from her.

She altered her course to intersect with theirs somewhere out there, but she made the angle small to give herself plenty of time to catch up. The way the two had operated so far, they often planned small surprises that would impress or amuse her, the new friend who had never been to this place and would appreciate it. She supposed that this time it might be a spot near the middle that was the best position to see some particular sight—maybe a break in the mountain range that allowed a view of a hidden valley beyond it, or another lake, or even a city. If it was Reno, there might even be lights. Which way was Reno from here? She had lost her sense of position during this period when directions beyond this circular forest road had stopped meaning much.

It took a while before the two other women stopped paddling. They didn't move toward her, they just sat bobbing peacefully in their yellow kayaks. From this distance the kayaks looked so small they could have been exotic yellow waterfowl. Linda didn't feel unhappy about any of this. Paddling around on a secluded lake was a pleasure, and the course didn't matter to her.

She began to pay more attention to her technique, taking strong strokes that sent the kayak forward and kept the bow pointed directly between the two becalmed yellow spots ahead of her, then half turning the paddle in her hands to bring the blade down on the other side while the kayak coasted, and make her left arm pull the kayak through another surge and glide, and then half turn the paddle again and pull the right blade. The motion became more and more comfortable and automatic. She could tell that as her form improved, her speed improved too. Before long she would be gliding right between Wendy and Mary.

31

Charlie and Vesper were in their rental car driving on the broad, open interstate highway. Charlie had engaged the voiced directions to Blucher Lake on his phone while they were still in the hotel parking lot. He had listened carefully and followed the instructions that the female computer voice gave him until he had pulled onto the main highway, and then it said, "Continue straight for twenty-eight miles." Since then, the voice had been silent. Every few minutes he would glance at his phone to see if anything new had appeared. The map showed a white arrow extending to the top of the screen and turning right. It looked the same, but the numbers changed, counting downward as the car approached the turn.

He said, "I'm sorry to drag you way out here into the middle of nowhere."

"This is hardly the middle of nowhere," she said. "We're moving along a wide, clean, well-maintained highway within fifty miles of a couple fair-sized cities. If you don't hit a bear or get a flat tire, we're fine. Besides, I did volunteer for this."

"Well, I'm feeling a little guilty."

"As your mother pointed out, the mountains are pretty, the forests are pretty, and unless she's lowered her standards, the lake will be pretty. I like pretty places."

They kept going, and eventually the female voice woke up. "In two miles, turn right onto Blucher Lake Road."

Vesper said, "There. See? We're right on track."

"I guess so."

In about a minute the voice said, "In one mile, turn right onto Blucher Lake Road." Soon they could see a street sign on a pole, and when they reached it, they turned. The voice said, "Stay on Blucher Lake Road for two point three miles."

The road was paved and began as a two-lane asphalt surface. After about a half mile the stretches of asphalt began to be interrupted by an occasional spot where a sinkhole had been filled with gravel. The next half mile included some longer graveled spaces where the asphalt was marred by long ruts. Charlie tried to keep the tires on the paved parts and out of the ruts, but as they proceeded, the gravel spaces became more common and larger. The next stage was when the asphalt had disappeared, and there were only gravel stretches and strips of dirt road. Charlie raised the windows to keep the dust from getting into the car. He said, "I think this might be the middle of nowhere."

"Don't exaggerate," Vesper said. "It's not the middle."

After another ten minutes the voice said, "In five hundred feet, your destination is on the right."

It turned out to be true. After about five hundred feet, there was a gap in the solid wall of trees and they could see a large stretch of blue lake. "It looks nice," she said.

"It does," Charlie said. He went on slowly. "This seems to be the road that leads around the lake."

She looked at the map on his phone. "I don't know if I'd call it a road."

He kept going. After a few hundred more feet they came to a two-car garage, then a house that at first seemed to be a large bungalow, but when they reached it they could see that the two-story plain part was only the front, and there was a tall A-frame roof behind it, and then after the house there was a structure farther from the road that had a dock leading out toward it. "I wonder if that's it," Charlie said. He kept going.

The road improved for a hundred yards or more before it began to get worse. He stopped. "What do you think?"

"I've been keeping my mouth shut, being a mere volunteer companion and all, but I don't think we should go any farther. Whenever there's a break in the trees, I look across the next part of the lake, and I don't see any other houses."

"Neither do I," he said. "There's some kind of a break up ahead. It looks like a trail goes up the hill to the left. It might make the road wide enough to turn around."

◆

Linda Warren's paddling was bringing her kayak up between the two other women's kayaks. She glided into the space and rested her paddle across her lap. "Well," she said. "Just catching up was a pretty decent workout in itself."

Wendy said, "I'll bet. I was getting tired just watching you."

"Is there something out here in this part of the lake that you wanted me to see?"

"No. But out here where it's sunny and there's a little breeze, there aren't any bugs, and you get the best view of everything," Mary said. She took a stroke with her paddle and glided closer to Linda.

"Well, it's certainly a great view. I'll give you that," Linda said. She was feeling a mild irritation with the others, but as she thought about why—that she had wanted to explore the shoreline instead of the middle of the lake, but that they had made the decision without speaking to her—it seemed so trivial that she dismissed it.

Wendy took two strokes with her paddle and drifted close to Linda on the other side. It made Linda feel even more silly because in moving close they were trying without words to reassure her. She looked at Mary, and then heard a swish behind her as the blade of Wendy's paddle swung and bashed the back of her head. She actually saw a flash, and the force of the blow propelled her forward so hard her face almost hit her kayak. She sensed that Wendy's paddle would be rising to take another swing, but instead it jabbed at her like a spear and hit her ribs on her left side. Linda brought her own paddle backward to slice at Wendy, but as she did, she saw Mary.

Mary had taken a hatchet out from under the foredeck of her kayak and raised it to swing downward at her. Linda reflexively lowered her paddle and changed the motion into a paddle stroke. She shot ahead just as Mary's hatchet chopped downward. The blade hit the hard plastic side of her kayak and bounced back, accomplishing nothing.

Linda's mind caught up with the past two seconds. She knew that Wendy had hit her in order to incapacitate and distract her while Mary swung the hatchet from the other side. It was inescapable that they were murdering her. She didn't understand how that could be, but she knew it and knew that she didn't have time to wonder about it. She had already taken a strong paddle stroke and her arms were in position to take the next, so she did, and she paddled fast and hard, alternating sides and heading for shore.

She heard the sound of splashing behind her and knew it was both women flailing to make their kayaks move forward from a standstill to catch her. She had to fight this regardless of what her chances were to hold on to life. She seemed to have nothing to preserve her but whatever her body could do at this moment of this day. It was going to have to be enough.

◆

Over a mile away, Charlie Warren drove up to the house and stopped. He turned off the engine and walked to the front door. He pressed the button beside it and heard the doorbell ringing. This was the only building that he and Vesper had seen since well before they'd left the interstate and driven to Blucher Lake. The doorbell seemed to be ringing from at least three places in the house. Whoever owned the place must be concerned that he never miss any visitors. Maybe nobody lived here all the time, and he was just a landlord who didn't like waiting for tenants to admit him to his property. Charlie was sure anyone inside must have heard the bell, but after he'd waited for about thirty seconds, he rang the bell again. He waited, then knocked.

His mother had told him she and her friends were here for the lake and the woods, and those weren't in the house. He walked back to Vesper and leaned close to her open window. "I don't think they're here. They're probably out enjoying nature."

"Of course," she said. "It's a long way to come to sit in a house."

"I'm starting to think this wasn't a good idea. I emailed her that we were up here and she didn't invite us to stop by, and we've never even met the other two women. I think we should just keep going the way we were headed and drive back to Reno. She knows she can call me."

"Maybe," Vesper said. "Sometime we can tell her we came all the way here, got embarrassed, and sneaked off. It'll make a good story."

He chuckled. "It is kind of funny."

"It will be, anyway," Vesper said. "After it's over and well behind us. Before I laugh, I'd at least like to be sure the two who've never seen us don't think we're criminals and call the police."

"Or shoot us," he said.

"Not funny," she said. "Too soon after that night in your office. Please, just call her."

He took out his phone and pressed his mother's number, then listened, but there was no answer. "Hi, he said. "It's just me, your favorite son. I'll try you again later. I hope you're having fun." He shrugged and put the phone away, then looked at the house.

"I'd at least like to look around for a minute to see if they're right nearby," he said, then started walking along the front of the house toward the boathouse. Vesper got out of the car, shut the door, and trotted to catch up. They turned the corner and walked toward the back of the house and the lakeshore.

The house reminded Charlie of an open treasure chest. The front of the place looked like a shoebox-shaped cottage. In the back was a section that rose up to form a glass-fronted living room with stylish furniture, polished wood floors, Persian rugs, and paintings on the walls. It opened onto a large wooden deck with stainless steel gas stove, wet bar, and the best view of the lake that he'd seen.

"Look!" Vesper said, and pointed.

Far off down the lake, there were bright yellow specks moving from about midway to the shore on his left. Two of them were close together, and another seemed to be leading them. He hadn't seen any other human beings or signs of them besides this house and the neglected road. "Are those boats, or what?" he said.

"They're too slow to be Jet Skis, but they seem about that size."

"I think you're right, but it's hard to judge size or speed from this distance. Whatever they are, there are three of them. It could be my mother and her friends."

"That's what I was thinking," she said. "If so, they'll end up here at some point."

"Unless this is the wrong house." He said, "I'd like to see if driving the road in that direction gets us close enough to see. What do you think?"

She said, "At least it's a plan, and I don't have one, so that's the plan."

They walked back around the house to the front and got into the car.

◆

Linda Warren was paddling at a rate that made her arms and hands strain to reach forward an extra inch and drag the blade backward another extra inch. Each stroke made her kayak roll from side to side a little bit, and she fretted because any lapse in form would take some of the speed away. Her ears were tuned only to the splashes of the other women's paddles, trying to judge how near the sounds were coming from and how rapid the repetitions were without stopping paddling to look behind her.

Everything else in her mind was like sights barely glimpsed from the seat of a speeding car. Nothing could be thought through or verified, because all of it was so horrible that if it was true, she had only seconds to live and had to paddle harder. Had Mary really tried to kill her with a hand ax? Instead of an answer her mind told her that enough wounds could look like the blade had been the propeller of a motorboat. The image was worse somehow than just dying, and it made her determination and her will to ignore the strain and discomfort stronger.

She heard one of the women—Mary, it sounded like—shout at her, "Wait, Linda! It was only a joke." She felt her chest swell with hope, because the voice had come from farther back than she would have feared, and Mary had just wasted a couple precious breaths shouting nonsense. She was beating them.

She was approaching the margin of reedy shallows near the shore now, and she looked for a clear place to land. She had to be on dry ground before either of the others, so they couldn't get ashore and ready themselves to attack her together as she arrived. She was taller and lankier than the others, and she sensed that she could outrun them if she could get a start on them. She suspected that they were thinking the same thing, so she aimed the bow of her kayak straight into the reeds and tried to go faster.

The kayak glided into the reeds and she heard the silky whisper of them sliding along the sides and bottom of it. She paddled against the weeds until her kayak stopped, then got out and splashed to the low, pebbly shore, up onto the level ground, already veering to the right, away from the house, and began to run.

◆

As Charlie drove beyond the house and the road began to curve gradually to the right, he noticed again that the pavement almost immediately seemed older and less cared for. It seemed likely that the contractors who had built the house had needed to improve and maintain the section from the intersection with the interstate highway as far as the house well enough and long enough so their trucks and earthmoving equipment wouldn't get mired in mud or tip over. That must have been expensive—maybe more expensive than constructing the buildings. The portion of the road beyond it that circled the lake was another matter, and it obviously dated from an earlier time.

The car bounced along over bumps that may have been caused by almost anything—buckled sheets of pavement, the old roots of vanished trees, or underground rocks that were slowly becoming outcroppings. There were potholes deep enough to jar a driver's jaw when a tire hit one. Before Charlie had driven a quarter mile, he had gotten out of the car twice to see whether a tire had gone flat or been knocked out of alignment. After the third time, he opened the driver's side door and leaned in.

He said, "You know what I'm thinking?"

Vesper said, "Is it what happens if the car stops working?"

"That's right," he said. He looked into the forest that began only feet from the road, then back in the direction they had come from, then back at her. "I don't relish the idea of backing up to where we started, but if we have to, I'd rather do it in daylight than after dark."

"Agreed," Vesper said. "If it will help, I can walk along behind the car and direct you away from the holes and ruts."

"That's very generous, but it's a last resort. I want to go forward for another few minutes and see if we can find a place to turn around. If we don't find one in, say, ten minutes, we'll start backing out."

"Okay," she said.

They moved ahead slowly, trying to find a good spot, but noted only that the road was beginning to disappear, replaced by a stretch of pebbly beach. Then, after about ten minutes, there it was. The road was now impossible to see, and the pebbles were replaced by a flat shelf of slate-gray stone. It looked slippery and slightly tilted, but it jutted several feet out from shore, widening the space by that much. Charlie stopped the car and walked to the shelf to examine it. Vesper came with him.

"This looks like it," she said.

"Let's try it. I'll turn to the left, back up and keep going as far as I can. You stand over there—not on the rock surface, but beyond it where the bank is pebbly, and stop me if I'm backing out too far."

"Just be sure you can see me in your mirrors and I'll keep you out of the lake."

Warren got into the car, moved it onto the rock, and turned it to the left as sharply as he could, inching along until the grille came within inches of a tree. He turned the wheel all the way to the right and backed up until he saw Vesper waving her arms and shaking her head, then went forward again. It took them three back-and-forth cycles, but they ended up with the car facing the end of the lake where the house was.

He got out of the car and joined Vesper. "Well, that's a relief," she said.

"It sure is," he said. He saw that Vesper had returned her attention to the lake. She was staring into the distance, and after a moment her face looked puzzled.

Warren stepped out a few paces on the stone shelf, trying to follow her gaze. "Do you see something?"

"No," she said. "That's the point. I mean, I see it, but it's different. I only see two of those yellow boats or canoes or whatever they are."

Warren said, "It looks like they're going the other way."

◆

The two yellow kayaks were close together, and the two sisters were paddling steadily, their eyes on the edge of the tall pine forest above the bank, trying to be sure they didn't miss the next glimpse of Linda Warren. She was a strong runner, and she moved faster than the two women could paddle a kayak. Every time May thought Linda must be exhausted by now and ready to collapse and rest, either she or Rose would catch a flash of white skin or the blue bathing suit between two trees above the shore, always lasting only long enough for the mind to verify what the eye had seen, and then gone again. Each time, the sight was farther away.

Rose said, "I think she's still building her lead on us."

"It can't go on much longer," May said. "We hiked all morning and then paddled, and now she's been running for at least a mile. She's got to stop."

"I know. And we're still just sitting and paddling and getting less tired. This time when we catch up, she's going to be too weak to fight."

"If you hadn't—"

"Stop! I'd advise you to shut up," Rose said. "If you want to play that, I can go on with it just as well as you can. If you had been so great it wouldn't matter what I did. You'd have killed her without me."

"Look!" May said. "Did you see her that time?"

"No."

"She's still running. I think we've got to head over that way and cut her off before she reaches the curve. If she keeps going straight from there, she could reach the interstate and flag somebody down. Then we'll be the ones who are in trouble."

Linda was keeping herself moving by walking twenty steps to catch her breath and then running forty, walking twenty, running forty. She had not formed a clear enough plan to stick to yet. Getting to shore and running had kept her alive so far. She was well ahead of the two women, but at some point, she was going to have to make a decision. Nothing in her life had prepared her for anything like this—except keeping fit, maybe—but now she had to choose. She began to climb higher up the hill to get deeper into the woods. And then she turned to cut back toward the house.

As she moved along under the trees, other parts of her plan began to form and add themselves to it. She had no key to the house, but there were rocks around it, some the size of a fist, and a few as big as a brick. She would break a window, get inside, find her phone, and call 911. Then she would do a quick search for weapons, checking now and then to see where the yellow kayaks were on the lake. If Paul didn't own a firearm or it was locked up, she could at least take a kitchen knife or two. She could stuff a few necessities into her bag and head into the woods again, this time along the road to the interstate highway. The police would have to come from that direction, and maybe she could meet them on the way.

◆

Charlie and Vesper walked along the lake quickly, always aware of the positions of the kayaks. They had still not thought of a satisfactory reason why they could only see two. Could one of the women have come ashore and walked back to the house? No. They would have met her on their way. And where was the kayak? Had it sunk? That didn't strike either of them as possible. Didn't they have buoyancy built in? Neither wanted to ask these questions aloud.

Then, as they reached a spot where the shore curved to reveal a large patch of reeds, they saw a straight line through it where the reeds had been pushed apart. At the end of the line was a yellow kayak. Charlie and Vesper ran to it. The kayak's bow was up against the bank, as though someone had plowed through the reeds until it hit the shore.

Charlie stopped and knelt to look at it closely, leaning forward to stare at the stern section without touching anything. It was what he thought he had seen. The discoloration was a smattering of drops, most of them extending down the sides into streaks. "Blood," he said. "Somebody is hurt." He looked down into the hollow where the occupant had been. "More blood inside it." There was also a deep mark just behind the seat on the outside, as though something had hit it.

"Oh my God," Vesper said. "Maybe the other two are taking the hurt one across the lake to get her help."

"I hope so. I'm going to call nine-one-one."

"I think we have to," she said.

He dialed his phone and heard about ten rings before he heard "Nine-one-one, what is your emergency?"

"I'm on the west shore of Blucher Lake, and we've just found a kayak left where the old road passes beside a patch of reeds. It's got what I'm pretty sure is blood on it and in it. Earlier we saw three identical yellow kayaks on the lake. The other two are still out there, paddling away from here. We need police and an ambulance."

"Your name, sir?"

"Charles Warren. I'm a lawyer from Los Angeles, and my girlfriend and I were going to surprise my mother, who is vacationing here with two other women."

"Please stay on the line for a moment while I dispatch the emergency people."

"I will."

A moment later the operator returned. "You said Blooker Lake, sir?"

"Yes. B, L, U, C, H, E, R. You head north from Reno along the interstate about twenty-eight miles and there's a Blucher Lake Road on the right. It leads only to Blucher Lake," Warren said. "If you have a cell phone number, I can send you a map showing the location of the house."

"Nope. I've got it. One more moment."

Warren waited. About thirty seconds later the operator returned. "Mr. Warren? Are you still there?"

"We're still here."

"The emergency crew are on their way. I'm afraid it will take at least half an hour for them to reach you. Can you stay and show them what you've found?"

"Yes."

"Then you can hang up. I'll give you a call when they reach the lake."

"Okay. Thank you." Warren hung up. He said to Vesper, "I think the thing to do now is probably go back toward the house, so we're sure the emergency people don't go the wrong way or something."

"Hello, Peter?"

"Hello, May." Peter's voice was distinctly weary and annoyed. "What is it now?"

"It's a mess, Peter. The State of California is wiring her Danny's money, probably today, but maybe yesterday. We needed to put her down so we could drain her bank accounts. We went out to the middle of the lake in the kayaks. When Rose went to split her head with a hatchet, she missed, believe it or not. I smacked her in the back of the head with my paddle so Rose would get another chance. This woman didn't react like normal people do, Peter. She doesn't get paralyzed and stupid. She starts paddling like she's the kayak champion of the world. She heads toward shore, and we can't keep up. She plows right through a bunch of weeds, gets out, and takes off like a goddamned gazelle."

Peter said, "Honey, this would be a really good time for you to go take that shower. I've got to finish this call."

"You have a woman with you right now?" May said. "Jesus, Peter, it's not even five o'clock."

"I'm living in a hotel in Nevada right now because you needed a favor. What am I supposed to do all day, gamble?"

"Rose and I need you, Peter. We're in kayaks on the lake. Linda Warren is out in the woods, and she's running. If she makes it to the highway, hell, if she runs into somebody with a phone, we're all cooked. I don't mean just us, either. She's met you, and she's slept in your house."

Peter took in a deep breath and blew it out slowly. "I'll be there as soon as I can." He ended the call. He spent a few seconds thinking about what he had just heard. His sisters had not only gotten him involved in this stupid attempt to get brother Danny's money after seventeen years. They had brought the woman they were going to rob to his house, ignoring his reluctance and stretching the bonds of blood relations beyond any reasonable limits. Now they had tried to murder her. He rubbed his eyes as he sat on the bed getting more and more furious at them.

Peter had never tried to murder anyone. At first it had been because of stories like this. Murdering somebody without getting caught was very complicated, and required incredible attention to detail. As he had gotten older and smarter it had been because he just didn't care enough about money to do it. Now he knew there was a strong chance he was going to be one of three people charged with attempted murder and convicted. He considered just not showing up. As he got angrier, he even considered going to the police and telling them what was going on. After a moment he abandoned that idea. May and Rose together could certainly get the police to believe that Peter was the guilty one. He heard the shower turn off and the hiss of water stop. He went to the closet and began to get dressed. As he was buttoning his shirt, he heard the door open behind him.

He turned and saw Trisha standing in the doorway of the bathroom with a big towel wrapped around her. She said, "You're getting dressed? Where are we going?"

"I'm afraid it's something I've got to do alone, honey. I should be back by morning. I can pay you now, if you want, and you can go, or if you'd rather just watch TV and get a good night's sleep, you can order dinner from room service. Just don't bring any other men to the room. That would piss me off and cost you a great deal of future income."

"I would never do that," she said. "That's so sleazy."

"I'm sorry I brought it up," he said. "I don't want to be offensive." He reached into the closet one more time and took a dark gray sport coat off the hanger.

Trisha stepped close to him and hugged him, at the same time letting go of the towel. As the towel slid to the floor at her feet she whispered in his ear, "Oops," and kissed him. As he pulled away, she didn't move or pick up the towel. "I'll be here."

"I hope so." He turned and went to the door. As he walked out the door and down the hallway, he thought about how much he resented the living members of his family. Then he thought about the nonliving members and noted that he hated them even more. He got to his car and pulled away from the hotel. He didn't stop until he could turn into a dark alley, open the trunk of his car, and retrieve his gun from inside the wheel well under the spare tire. Then he got back into the car and drove. He knew the best route and every curve or bump in the road. The place he was going was his own home.

◆

Rose and May were nearly to the eastern shore of the lake. They'd been paddling the kayaks for most of the afternoon, and their shoulders, backs, and even the muscles of their legs were sending pain messages to their brains each time they took another stroke.

Rose said, "It's getting to be a pretty long time since we last saw her."

"You don't have to tell me," May said. "I think she probably just ran as far as she could into the woods and then collapsed from exhaustion or hurt herself. I'll bet she's not more than a hundred yards from us right now, probably with a twisted ankle or a knee injury."

"I think so too," Rose said. "I think we should land at the last place we saw her, drag the kayaks up into the brush, and go in after her. Once you're in among the tall trees, the branches start higher up, and you can see between the trunks."

"Let's do it. We can take care of this, and then Peter can drive up the road along this side of the lake, put the body in the trunk of his car, and get rid of it."

They paddled along the shore to the spot where Rose had last seen Linda, beached the kayaks, and then dragged them up between the trees and left them uphill from a large rock. They walked to the east into the forest searching for any place where the deep layer of pine needles had been run through and displaced. They had only gone a few hundred feet before May said, "Today has been quite a workout. First the hike, then the paddling, and now this, whatever this is."

Rose said, "This is finishing her off. You gave her a pretty good whack with the paddle. You might have given her a concussion. By now, she could be unconscious. But let's be quiet so she doesn't hear us coming."

"Excuse me for mentioning it, but I'm very tired, and my whole body is beginning to hurt."

Rose said, "I guess you've just gotten too old for this. I hope Danny stashed so much money that your share will be enough to keep you from having to do things like this anymore."

May picked up the pace, stomping through the woods above the lake so she could get ahead of Rose and stay ahead.

They kept climbing the incline. They both knew that Linda's best bet was to make it out to the interstate and get picked up by a driver, and the most direct route was straight through the forest from the northern end of the lake, where they'd seen her running. But it was only a few minutes before Rose stopped on the hill, gazed back across the lake from their higher altitude and called, "Look!" May looked and saw what she was pointing at. They could see the distant figure of Linda Warren running south along the crest of the hill toward their brother Peter's house.

The two sisters moved quickly. They took a diagonal route down the hill to the trail that was the remnant of the road around the lake and raised their speed to a run. Rose gripped the hatchet handle just below the head, and May pressed her right hand against the sheath of the hunting knife so it wouldn't flap against her as she ran.

◆

Charlie Warren didn't see his mother running at first. He heard her. She passed a hundred feet above Charlie and Vesper in the deep silence of the late afternoon, straining to keep going. He heard her heavy breathing first, the gasps to bring in enough air, and the huffs to exhale it. Then he heard her steps, the running shoes landing flat on the rocky surface above the road.

He and Vesper stepped out to the edge of the lake so they could see the top of the hill, and there she was. "Mom!" he yelled. "Linda Warren!" He gave a loud whistle, and saw her turn her head, but at first she didn't stop. Her legs kept moving for four steps, as though they had acquired an independent will that had to be overcome. She stopped and looked down, then bent over for three seconds, trying to catch her breath, and then began to make her way down the hill toward Charlie and Vesper, who were climbing toward her.

When they met, she hugged them both at once. "They're chasing me," she rasped. "They're trying to kill me."

Charlie realized that the urgent thing was not to talk. "Come on," he said. "We've got a car."

He and Vesper each took one of Linda's arms over their shoulders and half carried her toward the spot on the road where they had left the car. As she recovered her breath she said, "I don't know why. They just changed instantly and went after me out on the lake."

"It's over now," Charlie said. "That's all that matters. We'll get you out of here."

Linda half turned her head and her eyes widened. "They're coming." The two women were on the road, running to catch up with them. Charlie handed Vesper the keys and said, "Keep going. Head for the car."

Vesper looked reluctant, but she took Linda's arm and tugged. "He's right. Come on." They began to trot to make it to the car, and Charlie turned to face the two sisters who were approaching at a run.

He stood where he was as they drew closer, but then he identified what the two women had in their hands. One was carrying a hatchet and the other a knife with a blade about six inches long. As they slowed their run to a trot, and finally, to a walk about thirty feet from him, they separated, so that they were advancing on both sides of him. The hatchet and the knife were no longer in sight. Their hands were now visible, so the weapons must have been tucked into their clothes. Was he imagining it, or were they both smiling?

No, he decided. They weren't smiles, exactly. They were expressions of eagerness. He called out, "Hello. I'd like it if you'd stop where you are, so we can talk. Why are you chasing this other lady?"

Neither of them spoke. They just kept coming, their eyes turning to exchange a look now and then. He realized the strategy was that one would sprint forward to force him to head her off. When he did, she would attack, or at least engage him, while the other would dash at him from behind and stab or hack him. He said, "You can choose to back away. I won't chase you if you do."

They kept walking. They had a flexible strategy, almost certain to keep him off-balance while both attacked him at once from different sides. If they wanted to kill his mother—and Vesper—they would have to kill him first, and they knew it. He wondered how long it would be before the police arrived, but he didn't dare take his eyes off them to look at his watch.

He squatted on the shore and picked up two water-smoothed oblong stones that fit the palms of his hands.

The two women reached positions on either side of him, each only about ten feet away. They both charged at once. He hurled the stone in his right hand first because he could simply pivot and throw. His target was the woman who ran at him holding the hatchet high.

The stone thudded against her just at the bottom of her rib cage. He extended his turn, passing the second stone from his left hand to his right and stepping to the side. The other woman was so close by then that he could hardly miss her. She slashed at him with her knife as he released the stone. It hit her shoulder and she cried out, clutching the spot.

He grabbed the arm and twisted it behind her so she dropped the knife. Then he pushed her away from him so he could pick it up, and kept moving to snatch up the hatchet that lay near the woman, who was lying with her arms hugging her ribs. He said, "Just stay where you are. There's nothing to gain by doing anything now."

He stayed close by, watching them. In another five minutes he heard his rental car's springs creaking as Vesper drove it along the rough road. When she reached the spot above the beach, she stopped. He could see his mother in the passenger seat, staring back at him. A moment later he thought he heard the same sound continuing, but the rental car hadn't moved. He looked across the lower end of the lake and saw that a police car and an ambulance were coming to a stop beside the house, and then a second police car pulled up behind the ambulance.

Warren felt his cell phone vibrate in his pocket. He took out the phone and heard the emergency operator say, "Mr. Warren? The police and ambulance should be arriving. Do you see them?"

"Yes I do," he said. "They're here. Tell them to come ahead."

◆

A few minutes later, Peter Rickenger was driving along Blucher Lake Road. He reached the spot where he got his first view of the lake, backed up about twenty feet, and got out of his car. He walked close to the edge of the woods, stopped behind the thick trunk of an old pine, and looked across the lake. There were two police cars, one of them parked in the road near his house and the other on the stretch of road on the west side of the lake. There was an ambulance on the road behind it, and the back door was wide open. There was also another car, smaller and white. He wasn't sure how to interpret that car. Usually white vehicles belonged to coroners, not the police, but this one was too small and it didn't seem likely that the coroner could be here so soon, even if his sisters had already killed Linda Warren and reported it. Either way, it didn't change what he had to do now.

Peter walked back to his car, got in and half closed his door very softly so the sound wouldn't carry, and then backed up to a spot that was wide enough for him to turn around. He drove out to the interstate and headed back toward Reno. Along the way he removed the battery and SIM card from his phone, and stopped to throw the phone out as far as he could into one of the lakes. Some of these lakes were so deep that he felt sure the phone would never be found. As he thought about it, he began to feel pleased. He could buy the newest iPhone tomorrow while he was in Reno. He wouldn't rush back to his home on the lake. He would wait a few days to get the call from May or Rose to let him know what had actually happened. Either his sisters had succeeded or they hadn't. At this point he didn't care very much which it was. They certainly hadn't cared much about him.

It was another half hour before he arrived at his hotel. When he had parked his car and taken the elevator upstairs, he was pleased that when he tried his key card on the lock of his room the green light went on but the door wouldn't open. After a few seconds he saw the little peephole in the door darken, and then Trisha disengaged the dead bolt and opened the door. She was wearing one of the two big fluffy white bathrobes.

She kissed him. "I'm glad you made it back so soon," she said.

"Me too."

32

Martha heard the outer office door open and looked up. She said, "Good morning, gentlemen. They're waiting for us in the conference room. We have refreshments in there—coffee, tea, soft drinks, water, Danish pastries, and so on." Then she closed the office door and locked it. "Follow me."

She walked ahead of them into the conference room. Seated around the table were Charles Warren, Linda Warren, and Vesper Ellis. Charles Warren stood up and shook hands with Copes, and then with Minkeagan. "Please take what you'd like to eat and drink, and then join us."

Minkeagan and Copes went to the counter along the wall and took bottled water and pastries, then sat down. Copes said, "I've never seen a law office that was open on Sunday before."

"You still haven't," Warren said. "This is a one-time private business meeting. It is now four months since the last of the claims we filed to get the money stolen by Daniel Rickenger, aka McKinley Stone. The final payment of the recovered funds arrived Friday."

He lifted a loose-leaf notebook that was thick with papers and handed it to Copes. "In that notebook are copies of the documents from the treasury departments of the six states showing the sums of abandoned accounts that they were transferring to my mother, Linda Warren. The second section is devoted to confirmations of the transfers of investment accounts from his name to hers by financial services companies. The last page is the executive summary that we compiled. As of the close of markets on Friday, the total amount recovered was sixteen million, four hundred eighty-two thousand, three hundred and sixty-one dollars and four cents. The investments have been converted to cash."

"So what do we get?" Minkeagan said. "And when?"

"Your share will be broken up into parts. You've each been paid electronically a million dollars. We checked this morning to see if it was posted in the holding account. The money is officially a fee for finding the Rickenger papers, researching them, and locating the rightful owner. That's in this set of papers over here on the counter. Fill in your full names, social security numbers, and addresses, and then sign. Do not use fake names or numbers. This is for your new bank accounts.

"You're also being retained as consultants to the firm of Warren and Associates. For that, you'll each get two hundred and forty thousand dollars a year deposited to the bank accounts in your names, twenty thousand a month beginning now and ending with your death. Your taxes will be figured and filled out here in this office, and deducted from your pay even if you move to another state. The taxes you owe will be paid on time. The reason for following these procedures is to keep you on the right side of the law and protect us all. Understood?"

"We can hear," said Minkeagan.

"Yes," Copes said.

"Is that agreeable?"

"It should be more," Minkeagan said. "We're old. We could die in a month."

"Then we won't miss it," Copes said. "You know it's more than we ever thought there even was, and it all got stolen from his mother."

"Okay, okay," Minkeagan said. "It's enough."

The next part of the meeting was devoted to having Linda Warren, Charles Warren, Minkeagan, and Copes sign legal documents and Vesper Ellis and Martha Wilkes sign as witness and notary. When this had all been accomplished, Minkeagan and Copes stood up. Copes said, "We appreciate that you lived up to our agreement. Thank you."

Minkeagan said, "Unless the reason you had this meeting on a Sunday was that the banks are closed so we can't check the accounts."

Copes shrugged. "Either way, we'll be nearby for a while." He walked toward the door. Mineagan said, "Easy to reach." He gave a nod to Charlie Warren, then turned and walked after Copes.

As Martha was collecting the papers, careful to be sure each page of each set was kept separate from the others, she picked up another set of papers with a cover on it. "What's this one? Were they supposed to sign it?"

"I don't remember what it is," Charlie said. "Take a look."

Martha opened the folder and read. "Bonus payment to Martha Wilkes. One million, four hundred thousand dollars? What the—"

"Oh, yeah," he said. "Now I remember."

Linda said, "I knew I wouldn't be able to sit here and give so much to them and nothing to you. It's to set the universe back in balance."

◆

One night six months after the meeting with Copes and Minkeagan, Charlie and Vesper were out to dinner at Paradis. As Charlie signed the bill and put away his credit card, Vesper said, just loudly enough so the older people at the next table heard, "I loved that dinner, but there must have been something in it. Now I can't keep my hands off you, so if I were you, I'd take me right home."

"Thank you. That's all I'm saying in public."

She whispered, "You're so fun to embarrass. I can't seem to resist."

"Maybe we can get out of here before you think of anything to add. Ready to go?"

"Yes."

They got up and walked out through the rounded arches of climbing roses and down the quiet street toward Charlie's parked car. When they reached the darkest part of the block, Charlie stopped, turned to face her, produced a small velvet box, and opened it. Then he got down on one knee.

"What a gorgeous ring, Charlie," Vesper said. "You have such good taste. And I'm flattered. But, um, no. Get up and come home with me."

He stood. "Why don't you want to get married?"

"I've been married. I mostly liked it, but nowhere near as much as I like being with you the way I am. And partly thanks to you, I have no practical reason to get married again. Give me a compelling reason to get married sometime and I will. Like one of us gets demented, or pregnant or something."

He stood up. "Do you want me to hold on to the ring?"

"I think it would be smart. Things change, and I love the ring."